Mid-City Errands

Mid-City Errands

Ronald Fisher

Firethorn Books
PENNSYLVANIA, U.S.A.

Firethorn Books
P.O. Box 144
Bryn Mawr, PA 19010
www.vonnyfoster.com

ISBN 13: 978-0-692-24537-8

Book design by Adam Robinson
Cover photo by Ione LeBlanc Fisher

First Edition September 2014
10 9 8 7 6 5 4 3 2 1

Contents

For my cousins

When one repeats a tale told by a man,
He must report, as nearly as he can,
Every least word, if he remember it,
However rude it be, or how unfit;
Or else he may be telling what's untrue,
Embellishing and fictionizing too.
He may not spare, although it were his brother;
He must as well say one word as another.
Christ spoke right broadly out, in holy writ,
And, you know well, there's nothing low in it.
And Plato says, to those able to read:
"The word should be the cousin to the deed."

~ Geoffrey Chaucer, Prologue
The Book of the Tales of Canterbury

One, or Bruno's

Jimmy Broom was hit by a car in front of Bruno's Tuesday afternoon. There's a bloodstain in the street where he got knocked down, about the size of a sewer cover. They say the broken broom handle went through his arm. Mister Bruno says he's at the Hotel Dieu. Even now, there is what's left of his white tee shirt in the street on top of the bloodstain. They say his leg is broken. Right below the knee. They also say that Jimmy might die. My Mother says that's why I was sleepwalking. I went over to my Uncle Roger's at three o'clock in the morning on Wednesday. Because Jimmy Broom was hit by a car in front of Bruno's.

I like to sit on the barstools at Bruno's. Of course, my feet dangle because my legs are too short. So, I can't reach the metal footrest on the stools like for most people whose legs are long enough. I can always get up on top of the black plastic stool seat by grabbing the bar and boosting myself up by using the footrest as a step up. I don't like the black plastic sticking to the back of my legs. Which it does if I have short pants on. So, if I get a little warning, I always try to have my dungarees on when I go over to Bruno's. But sometimes I don't get any warning at all. I just have to go.

I like the dark wood the bar is made of too. Mahogaknee, my Mother calls it. It took me a long time to learn how to spell that word. And I'm the best speller in second grade. Well, except for Sharon the Roach maybe. That one, I wish she would move to another school or maybe get her tonsils out and not come back. Which is what happened to that kid last year whose name no one can remember now. I don't know if that's a mean word or an impure thought. I can just add it to my list. But I know it's what I think just about every Friday when there's a spelling bee, when it's always me and her that last the longest, and when it's always her that wins the prize of the week. Which is usually a book only a boy would like, about sports, or soldiers, or bugs. I always win second prize. Which is always something like a free chocolate milk after Mass on First Friday.

Anyways, at Bruno's, I like the cool, dark wood the bar is made of. Sometimes, while I'm waiting there on that side of Bruno's by myself, I press my chin against the dark wood on the bar to feel how cool it is. If it's really cold and Mister Bruno is not looking my way, I'll drop my cheek down on the bar. I'm not sure why I like to do that. But I do!

I also like to go into Bruno's through the back door, the one on Columbus Street. I especially don't like the main door at the corner, the one near where Jimmy Broom got run over. First, it's too hard to open. It's made out of some kind of heavy, thick wood to begin with. Then, there is a heavy, thick piece of glass in the middle of it, up above my head. And finally, there is a huge grill made of heavy, thick, black metal over the top of the glass. Why even bother to have glass? You can't even see through it into the bar. If you were tall enough to see through it at all. Which I am not. Anyways, the door on the corner is not only heavy, but the doorknob is the kind that you have to press your thumb down on a kind of button and then push at the same time. I don't have the muscles in my thumb to even press the button down. Daddy says I have small hands for a kid my age but that I'll probably grow. Maybe I will. Sometimes, if there is another kid around, I can do the thumb part and the other kid can push the door open. But the other kids don't go anywheres near Bruno's. Lenny Mahoney told me his mother would brain him if she caught him pushing the door open for me. Brain him! Which I guess means she would beat him to a pulp.

So, I actually think Mister Bruno even put the back door where it is just for seven year old kids like me who are coming to buy cigarettes for their mothers. It's light, the back door that is. The wood is not very thick. About half as thick as the door on the corner. And it has a screen in it, top to bottom. To make it better, they always leave the heavy wood door behind it open. I don't think it's to let kids in. I think it's to let air in. Or maybe it's to let smoke out. There is always a lot of smoke in Bruno's. It's the one thing I really don't like about the place. That and the door on the corner. And maybe the old crocodiles. There's smoke coming from the kitchen where they make hamburgers and hot dogs and sandwhiches for people to eat at the bar and also to take home to eat. Remind me to tell you about when I learned how to spell sandwhich. Then, there's smoke coming from the old men and their pipes and their cigars. Which they smoke all day long. And there's cigarette smoke too. I pay attention when I'm in the barroom. And I notice that Mister Bruno, no matter what he's doing, Mister Bruno always has a cigarette burning away on the end of the bar while he's getting drinks for people, or sandwhiches, or in my case other cigarettes. There's always smoke there.

The other thing I don't like about going through the door on the corner is that there are always a few old men sitting near it. Mainly at the bar. They may not be that old. Maybe forty or something. But I say old because they look much, much older than Daddy. His skin is very smooth. Very, very smooth. Except when he forgets to shave or just doesn't want to. But these old men in the bar, their skin is bumpy, shaved or not. My Mother says they look like old crocodiles. She doesn't like the way they look at her if she goes to get cigarettes. She told Daddy she thinks they're all creepy. Which I agree. Daddy just laughs when she says that. "Well, maybe you shouldn't go down there dressed in nothing but your white shorts and a sleeveless blouse," is all Daddy says.

"It's too hot to put a dress on just to go down for cigarettes," is what my Mother says back. "Even a summer dress. And it takes too long anyways."

So, because it's too hot to put on a dress, even a summer one, and it takes too long to put one on anyways, I get to go on errands to Bruno's. Always through the back door. Because there's the problem that I can't actually get through the door on the corner. And there's the problem that I don't like to be on that side of the barroom where all the old men are. I don't know why. Maybe because my Mother thinks they're creepy. Or maybe because they all have crocodile skin. Or maybe because I'm just afraid of old men. Which I think is true. I'm also afraid one of the old men might be upset if I come in the corner door. They are always together at that part of the barroom. They whisper a lot. And even when I walk in the back door, after they notice me climb up on the barstool, they all look at me and start shushing each other. Like they're telling secrets or something. Or maybe I was afraid because they are all much bigger than me. Much, much bigger!

Anyways, the back door always seems to me to be the best for me. I can get through it. I can get into Bruno's, almost unseen. I can swing the back door open with one hand, scoot into the dark room over to a stool far away from the old men, climb up, settle into the stool, and lean over on the bar, sometimes feeling the cool wood with my face, waiting for Mister Bruno to notice me and say, "Kool Filter Menthols?" Which is what he always asks. I don't say anything. I don't want anybody to notice me. I just nod like I know what it means. The old men, once they notice me, sometimes one or two of them raise their little short beer glasses and nod their heads at me. I just wave at them, wondering what would happen if I ordered a beer to raise in a little short beer glass back at them. Mister Bruno would probably not let me buy cigarettes anymore. Not even if I use the back door. Then my Mother would be upset.

Even after my Mother sent me on an errand to buy cigarettes from Bruno's on the corner, I still didn't figure out what Monseigneur Deutsch meant when he talked in catechism class about impure thoughts. This was the class where he took over for Sister Marianna to help us all with our first confession. That was last week. They made it sound like the most serious thing ever. So, it made sense that Monseigneur would take over for Sister because, after all, it was his job to hear confessions in the first place. And it would be him or Father Roy who would actually hear our first confession. Probably, in fact, every confession we ever made after that. Besides, it would be odd, for most of us, for me too, to hear from Sister Marianna the list of all the bad things that we might have done, the mean words that we might have said, and the impure thoughts that we might have thought.

But Monseigneur Deutsch, he heard it all. That's what Daddy said. And he, Daddy that is, was for me at least the expert on just about everything that happened outside our house. Daddy said that Monseigneur could list out everything from bottom to top, small to large, venial to mortal sins. For example, Daddy said, it was one thing to stick your tongue out at your little sister. And when he said this at supper one afternoon, when all of a sudden everyone was interested in my first confession, Daddy winked at me. But it was another thing entirely, Daddy said, to stick an ice pick in her chest. My Mother hit Daddy in the arm with one of her little fists and Daddy pretended it hurt. I winked back at him. Or at least tried to. Monseigneur was from the old country, is how Daddy explained it. I do not know what country that is, or how old it is. But I did not want to go there after hearing Daddy's for example. Father Roy is from Holland, I know. What Sister Marianna calls the Netherlands. His nose was bit off by a horse. But I don't think that's the old country that Monseigneur Deutsch is from.

The next day in class, like Daddy wrote out his speech or something, Monseigneur Deutsch pulls a bunch of pages of paper out of his black coat pocket and drops them on the desk in front of him. He places his hands on his fat belly, like a shelf, a little resting place for his fat, red fists. He stares up into the ceiling and closes his eyes like he's waiting for the Holy Spirit to appear. And then, like a miracle, he reads out the same exact example to the class. Stick your tongue out or stick an ice pick in your little sister. Which was Daddy's story the day before! The girls in class all gasped at the same time and whispered to each other while the boys just sat there, mouths open, eyes wide, heads swiveling from one scared face to another. Except me. I had to smile. Daddy can do the same job as Monseigneur any time.

Anyways, between sticking your tongue out and sticking an ice pick in someone, there was a whole lot of bad things to do, mean words to say, and impure thoughts to think. Monseigneur's job was to take us through the whole list, once a week for six weeks, working his way up from the teeniest, tiniest sin to the worst of the worst. Teeny, tiny? Sticking your tongue out. Worst of the worst? Probably anything you do to another person with an ice pick. Somewheres in between? Impure thoughts probably.

Which was Monseigneur's way to prepare us to change from whatever we were to, what he called, a perpetual state of spiritual grace. Monseigneur said it was like a caterpillar turning into a butterfly. We were caterpillars now. Ugly, furry, squishy caterpillars. We were going to be butterflies. Beautiful, delicate, heavenly butterflies. Louie Canale, who was always goofing off, asked if we were going to be able to fly home from school when we were butterflies instead of walking or taking the bus. We all laughed. Louie is funny. But in a sad way. My Mother always says my Uncle Roger, who is really my cousin, is a disaster waiting to happen. That's the way I think about Louie. He is a disaster waiting to happen. Except with Louie, he happens about two or three times a week.

So, Monseigneur used Louie as an example. "The Lord forgives us," he said, "as I shall forgive Louis. The Lord forgives those who accept their penance." Which was Monseigneur's way of saying Louie will have to stay after school all week and clean the classroom for an hour while the rest of us fly home. "Children," Monseigneur said again, "the Lord knows that you are on the verge of the age of reason." Whatever verge means. "You are each going to become a responsible citizen in the kingdom of the Lord." This was news to all of us, not least Louie Canale. "Hence fourth," whatever that means too, "you will be accountable for your actions, for your words, for your thoughts, in the eyes of God." When he is talking to us, Monseigneur Deutsch always moves back and forth on his feet, back on his heels, then forward onto his toes, and then up on his tippy toes before moving back on his heels again. Somehow, whenever he says the word "Lord" or "God," he always winds up on his tippy toes. And whenever he is on his tippy toes, he stares straight up and into the ceiling like he's waiting for the Holy Spirit to appear.

Sister Marianna says I ask too many questions in class. But I was confused. Bad actions? Talking in class without raising your hand. I understand that. Mean words? I have a little sister. If you have a little sister, you understand mean words. Impure thoughts? Impure how exactly? So, I raised my hand.

"Yes?" Monseigneur asked. "Master." But he didn't know what to say after that because he didn't know my name. He looked at me. Then he said again, "Master?" Monseigneur rocked up on his tippy toes and stared at the ceiling like somehow maybe the Holy Spirit in the corner was going to tell him my name.

"Vonny," I said. The rule is, you don't speak until your name is called. Except if they don't know your name.

"Master Vonny?" Monseigneur asked. "A question perhaps? Please stand so that we can all hear you."

"Well, Monseigneur," I began, not really knowing what I wanted to ask or how to ask it. "Monseigneur?" I asked again as I stood up.

"Yes, my boy?" he asked again, rocking forward and staring up toward heaven.

"Well," I stuttered. "Monseigneur? What exactly is an impure thought?"

Monseigneur closed his eyes and scrunched his face up until it looked like his eyes, nose, and mouth might all wind up in the exact same place on the center of his head. "Well," he started to say back. "Master Vonny, did you say your name is?"

That worried me. He now knows who I am and what my name is. "Yes, Monseigneur." And he cared enough to ask. I figured right then that I would either be keeping Louie Canale company after school or, worse, bringing home a note to Daddy and my Mother.

"Well, Master Vonny," Monseigneur continued. "Why do you ask?"

"Monseigneur," I said back, without even wasting any time, "I want to make sure I have a good confession. I want to be forgiven. I want to." I stopped because a couple of the boys groaned. I was already marked as a goofball because I ended up being the last boy standing in the spelling bee every Friday, which for most boys was girls' work anyways. And in the arithmetic game every week too, which I almost always won since I can add in hundreds in my head. Except there are no prizes for arithmetic games. Except tickets for chocolate milk. Louie Canale cackled. But he already had to go to detention every day on account of the butterfly joke so it didn't matter to him.

"I see," Monseigneur said. "I see." He placed his fat, red fists behind his back, rocking all the while back and forth, back and forth. "So, tell me, Master Vonny. What do you think an impure thought is?"

If I knew, did it make sense for me to ask? That's what I wanted to say back to Monseigneur Deutsch. But I knew if I did, I was definitely going to be keeping Louie Canale company after school or, worse, bringing home a note to Daddy and my Mother. Just then, the heavy wooden door to the classroom creaked open and Sister Marianna walked in.

"Oh, Sister," Monseigneur said, walking toward her and waving at me. "Master Vonny here was just explaining to the class what an impure thought is."

Sister acted surprised. "Oh, my!" she said back.

"What?" I said out loud. Everyone in the class, all the boys and girls, all the goofballs and regular kids, everyone started laughing, Louie Canale loudest of all. Even the small girls who never looked anyone in the eye and never said anything to anyone were laughing with their hands over their mouths like maybe their teeth would fall out or something.

"Go ahead, Vonny," Sister Marianna said. I like Sister a lot, except she wears black glasses that make her look like an old lady. But she has smooth, very white skin like my Mother. Well, at least the skin we can see. Which was the little square of her face and her hands. Anyways, Sister is probably the same age as my Mother, except she married God instead of marrying Daddy. I asked my Mother once if she ever thought about marrying God instead of marrying Daddy, and she just laughed and laughed. At supper that night, my Mother told Daddy what I asked. He laughed and laughed too. And then Daddy said, "To you, Vonny, my boy, I am God!"

"Vonny?" I heard my name. It was Sister Marianna.

"Master Vonny?" It was Monseigneur now. I was cornered. "What do you think an impure thought is?"

My classmates fidgeted in their seats, watching me move back and forth by my desk. I was almost always the last kid standing, except for Sharon the Roach in the spelling bees, and now I was the last kid standing again. "I don't know!" I shouted. "I just don't know!" I quick sat down. I quick folded my arms. I felt the blood rushing into my ears and into my head. I knew my ears were red. That happened all the time. Almost every day.

Sister Marianna walked over to my desk and put her hand on my shoulder. "Now, now, Vonny. You're a brave boy to try. And the rest of you can stop fidgeting in your desks now." She walked back to the front of the class. "Well, thank you, Monseigneur," she said. "Boys and girls?"

"Thank you, Monseigneur," we all sang, followed by a cackle from Louie Canale. What a goofball!

I did not want to ask my Mother about impure thoughts. It didn't seem right somehow. Anyways, Daddy knows everything. So I asked one afternoon while we walked over to the horse race track. Which Daddy and I do almost every day sometimes. Except, other times, we never go at all. I never know why. When we go, we go over to the horse race track after Daddy gets back from work. My little sister asks to go too. But Daddy says she's too small. She's only five. Besides, he says, the horse race track is no place for girls. So, it's just him and me who go. And Daddy's right. I never see any girls at the horse race track.

After Daddy gets home, we walk down Columbus Street, past my Uncle Roger's house, past Bruno's on the corner, across the street to where the school is, past the school, across the next street, which is very wide and has a neutral ground and is where the laundry is. Which is the one where Mister Lee works, the man who has a hook where his hand should be. And we walk around the bend in the road, past the Bell movies, down past the Stallings Playground, and across the street to the horse race track. Which is called the Fair Grounds. We walk right up to the rail and Daddy boosts me up so I can sit on it. That's where we watch the races from. I asked Daddy once why we didn't watch the races from the big building where all the other people are and he just said we were better off standing where we were near the rail. He said the people down there in the big building all want to be on the rail where we were, but that they can't be because on the rail where we were is reserved just for people like him. For people with their kids. Daddy said he felt lucky because he had me with him so he can stand there on the rail. A boy in my class told me once that they don't let kids in down there in the big building and so that's why Daddy and I have to stay on the rail. I told him he doesn't know what he's talking about. Which he doesn't.

Anyways, the horses don't run as much as I want them to. We see them every now and then. But sometimes, not a lot. We don't even see them until the race is already over and they are not running fast at all. They are stopping in fact. They are running and they just stop and turn around right in front of us and head back in the other direction. Sometimes one of the jockeys, the men who ride the horses, will wave at us. Daddy will always ask a jockey what horse won the race because we're too far away from the finish line to know. Sometimes the jockey knows and sometimes not. Sometimes Daddy just says something like "Good ride" or "Tough luck" to a jockey. That's when they wave at us usually. One time a jockey made his horse come over by the rail. I thought he was going to knock me off. But he just leaned down and patted me on the head and called me "Buddy". I have a cousin named Buddy so maybe the jockey confused us. Although Buddy is much bigger than me. Daddy said that was the horse that won the race.

I like going to the horse race track with Daddy. Sometimes we even win money. Before each race a dark brown man, who is old like the men in Bruno's with crocodile skin, except in his case a dark brown crocodile, comes down and Daddy gives him money to bet. Daddy will tell him some numbers, like the horse number and some dollar number. Sometimes if Daddy wins, the man comes back and gives Daddy his money back and some extra money too. It depends. If Daddy gets extra money back, he always gives the dark brown man a dollar. He also gives me a dime or two while we're there. That's why Daddy says I always win at the horse race track, no matter what. Which I do.

Daddy always tells me what horse he bets on, so I can call out loud for him. I mainly say something like, "Come on, number eight!" over and over again during the race. Sometimes the race is not over when the horses come by. Which means the race is still going on. I like that the best because the horses go by fast. And I like that the jockeys lie down flat against the horses' backs, pressed down on them the way I press my face down on the cool bar at Bruno's. I asked Daddy once if I could be a jockey when I grow up and he says I'll be too big. I don't know why he thinks that. I'm much smaller than the jockeys now. I'm much smaller than almost everybody. Even Sharon the Roach is bigger than me. Much bigger! My cousin Pia, who is in my class, is bigger than me too. And she was born a month later.

Sometimes I get mixed up because Daddy's horse will be ahead when the horses come by and I think the horse won but he didn't because the race is still going on and the horses are still running. It's still a lot of fun. Daddy has these special glasses in a box that let him see far away, and he can look at the horses run around in the race even when I can't see them anymore. Which is most of the time. I tried to use the special glasses but Daddy says my head is too small and I mostly just wind up seeing out of one eye. Which is not a good way to see anything. Anyways, while the horses are running Daddy tells me what his number horse is doing. The horse is looking good or the horse is falling back or the horse is dying. Which does not mean the horse is dying like Jimmy Broom might die. It means the horse is running slower. If Daddy's horse is looking good, he gets more excited as the race goes on and he talks more and faster and more out loud. If Daddy's horse is falling back or dying, he just puts his special glasses on the rail and lifts his shoulders up and down. He just looks at me and says, "Can't win them all, Vonny, my boy. It's not fair to the other people."

So, one day, while Daddy and I were walking to the horse race track, after Monseigneur Deutsch had put me on the spot in class, I asked him what was an impure thought. Daddy, I mean. Not Monseigneur Deutsch.

"A what?" Daddy said back.

"You know," I said back, hoping he knew. "An impure thought. Like a bad thing you can do or a mean word you can say. It's for my first confession list."

Daddy laughed. "Vonny, my boy, you're too young to have any impure thoughts."

"That's not what Sister Marianna says," I said back again. We were crossing in front of Mister Lee's laundry and I was thinking about Mister Lee's missing hand and the hook that replaced it. And as I did, I was thinking that maybe that was an impure thought. Thinking about Mister Lee's hook.

"Sister Marianna doesn't know anything about impure thoughts," Daddy said back again. "She's a nun, for Christ sake."

Daddy used the Lord's name in vain! I pretended I didn't hear it.

"Well, she acts like she knows," I said back. "And what about Monseigneur Deutsch? You said it yourself. Monseigneur has heard it all."

Daddy smiled and put his hand on my shoulder as we crossed Gentilly Road by the Bell movies. "I said that?" he laughed. "Well, it's probably true. So, why don't you ask Monseigneur Deutsch what an impure thought is?"

"I did," I said back.

"Really?" Daddy was surprised. "You asked Monseigneur?"

"I did!" I said again.

"And what did he say?" Daddy said back. So, I told Daddy the story about how I asked Monseigneur in class, and how he put me on the spot, and how I was nervous, and how Sister walked in, and how I was cornered, and how everybody laughed, and how Louie Canale cackled. "That Canale kid is a little goofy," Daddy said. "I'm surprised they didn't send a note home."

"They just dropped the subject," I said back. "I dropped it too." Which is what I did.

We were coming up to the large gate at the entrance to the horse race track. Daddy stopped walking and then he kneeled down, one knee on the sidewalk, his face a few inches from mine. "Listen, Vonny, my boy" he smiled. "Take it from me. You did not have any impure thoughts. You have no impure thoughts to confess. You may have done bad acts, like talking back to your mother." Which I do. "And you may have said mean things. Especially to your sister." Which I never do unless she starts something first. "But, I promise you. I'm your father. I wouldn't lie to you. You never have any impure thoughts." Which, even as I listened to him, I wasn't sure. I just didn't know what or when.

I mean, I think the point of confession is so you don't do or say or think things that you will have to confess. It's kind of scary to admit that stuff. And I can stop myself from doing things. I just don't do them. And I can stop myself from saying things. I just don't say them. But I can't stop myself from thinking things! When I walk by Bruno's, I think about the men inside drinking their glasses of beer. When I walk by Mister Lee's laundry, I think about his hook. When I walk by the Bell movies, I think about popcorn. When I walk by Richard's, the five and dime store over by the bakery, I think about the time my Mother made me buy underwear there for my aunt. Who is a very large lady. Me! A seven year old kid! What was my Mother thinking? And maybe that's an impure thought. But I can't stop myself from thinking about the glasses of beer at Bruno's, or Mister Lee's hook, or the popcorn at the Bell, or my aunt's underwear over at Richard's. How am I suppose to do that? And how am I suppose to not think about the sales clerk at Richard's, who said to me when she saw the size of my aunt's underwear, "Oh, my! Your aunt must be a very large lady."

Anyways, Tuesday afternoon, after Jimmy Broom got run over by that black Pontiac, which is the kind of car that has the yellow indian head on it, my Mother called me inside and asked me to go on an errand to Bruno's for cigarettes. Which I did. In I went through the back door. Up the stool I went onto the black plastic seat. Down my chin went onto the cool dark wood of the bar, staring straight ahead into a mirror that was so dark you could only see the shape of your head in it but not anything else, like what color your eyes were or if you even had eyes. Mister Bruno was down at the other end of the bar talking to some old men about Jimmy Broom getting run over. I tried not to listen because I know I'm going to cry if anyone ever says to me, "Jimmy Broom is dead." I hate to cry. And I was especially going to hate to cry if I had to cry at Bruno's. Already, the old men there don't like me. The old crocodiles. I can tell that. They want my Mother to come down to buy cigarettes in her white shorts and sleeveless blouse. If Jimmy Broom died, some of them probably will be happy or something. One less kid buying cigarettes for their mother.

"I hear his leg was snapped in two," one man said.

"What were they doing in the street?" another man said back.

Mister Bruno said, "Playing baseball. Or maybe stickball."

It was stickball. That's how Jimmy Broom got his name. Because of the broom handle they use as a bat. Home base is always on the corner of Columbus and Dorgenois in front of Bruno's. I know how to spell Dorgenois because it's right on the street sign I pass under every day to go to school. But I don't know what it means. Everybody knows Columbus. Who was a sailor that found America one day when he was sailing the ocean blue. The other bases are always on the other corners where the streets meet. First base near the kindergarden school, second in front of the snowball stand catty corner from Bruno's, and third where the black and brown dog always barks at me from inside the fence when I walk on the sidewalk in front, the one I have to walk by when I go to the Triangle for my Mother. Jimmy Broom was going from third to home when he got run over by a car turning left onto Columbus. That's why the blood-stain is in on the ground in front of Bruno's. I can't help thinking about if Jimmy scored after he got run over. Which would be something. Your leg broken, a broom handle in your arm, run over by a Pontiac, blood everywhere. You reach over and touch home plate anyways. Which is just a piece of cardboard.

But Jimmy is a tough kid. He likes to fight. He's a very little kid who somehow really likes to fight. He's even smaller than me. And he is three months older. Jimmy will fight anybody. He was one time picking on a fifth grader. A fifth grader! I thought the kid was going to brain him. But Jimmy is a tough kid. And so the fifth grader just walked away. Jimmy had the kid scared and even yelled, "Chicken!" after the kid was walking away. Which almost made the kid come back and fight Jimmy. But he didn't. He just waved at Jimmy and kept walking. After that, nobody in the whole school messed with Jimmy. They didn't even try to punch him in the stomach for no good reason. Nobody did. Not even the eighth graders. Who were able to run over Jimmy even worse than the Pontiac did.

My Mother says Jimmy's parents don't give him enough attention. I don't know how she knows. She never goes to their house. I use to go over there and, if you ask me, his parents give Jimmy too much atten-tion. His father is always screaming at him about this or that. And his mother belts him on the head for nothing. For saying, "Mom, can me and Vonny have a cookie?" Then Jimmy gets a belt on the head. Even if he says "please" first.

"Dumb kids," the first man said.

"Somebody said the broom handle went through his arm and cut an artry. That's why there was blood everywhere." I asked my Mother later what that meant. She said artries are where your blood goes. It's a good thing I didn't know when I heard the old men in Bruno's. I might have cried right then and there.

Nobody even noticed me when I came in the back door. So, I closed my eyes and over went my head so I could press my cheek against the cool bar.

"So, is the kid going to live or what?" one of the men asked. I didn't want to hear the answer. I put a hand over my ear that wasn't pressed on top the bar and I opened my eyes. There, on the back wall at Bruno's, was when I saw the calendar.

Even with my hand over my ear, I heard Mister Bruno say, "He's at the Hotel Dieu." Which is a hospital. My baby brother was born there a few weeks ago. Which is how I know how to spell that word too. Dieu, I mean. Hotel, I see a thousand times up and down the highway when we go visit my Grandpa in the country.

"Well, somebody should clean up that mess out there," one of the men said. "That bloody tee shirt. It's disgusting."

"The police said not to," Mister Bruno said. "Something about an investigation. The guy in the Pontiac was drinking."

Seeing the calendar on the back wall at Bruno's for the first time, I slowly lifted my head from the bar, sat up, and swiveled the black plastic stool seat toward the back, away from Mister Bruno and the crocodiles. I saw right away that the calendar hanging on the back wall at Bruno's was just like a normal calendar. At first. A big red square with little red squares in it with blue numbers in the little red squares up to 31. In the little red square with a blue 17 in it, the calendar says "St. Patrick's Day". In the little red square with a blue 19 in it, the calendar says, "St. Joseph's Day". In the little red square with the blue 29 in it, the calendar says "Easter". In big red letters above the big red square, the calendar says "March 1959".

Easter! It hit me. Just looking at that word made me sweat. Because the week before Easter, two weeks from now, is my First Communion. And the week before that is my first confession. Me and Monseigneur Deutsch in a little dark box in the St. Rose de Lima Bean Church. Me telling him about my bad actions, mean words, and impure thoughts. Me telling him about how I wish Sharon the Roach will move to another school or maybe get her tonsils out and not come back. Me telling him about me sticking my tongue out at my little sister. Me telling him about me telling my little sister, and sometimes my cousin Pia when she gets on my nerves, to bug off. Both of us pretending we don't know who the other one is. Like I'm Jimmy Broom and Monseigneur is Father Roy. Him being the one who put me on the spot in class about impure thoughts.

On top of all that, there is the new calendar on the back wall at Bruno's with its big red square and little red squares and blue numbers and holidays. Which isn't the thing about the calendar that made me notice it when I had my cheek on the cool bar. The thing that made me notice the calendar, and that made me slowly lift my head from the bar, sit up, and swivel the black plastic stool seat toward the back wall was this. Which made it a not normal calendar. There, above the big red square on the calendar, was a picture of a lady sitting on a wooden box or something. She is holding what looks like some kind of hammer. She has long blonde hair. Just like Sharon the Roach. Only longer. She is smiling. Just like Sister Marianna does. With a lot of teeth. Except with Sister Marianna, all you can see is her face. So her teeth take up a lot of what you can see. But you can see more than the face of the lady on the calendar. Still, she has a lot of teeth too. And she is wearing white shorts. Just like my Mother does when it's too hot to put on a dress, even a summer one, and it takes too long to put one on anyways. Except with my Mother, she wears her white shorts with a sleeveless blouse. But you can see more of the lady on the calendar because she is not wearing a sleeveless blouse. The lady on the calendar is not wearing any kind of blouse. Or any kind of shirt even!

I grabbed the bar and slowly stepped down onto the metal footrest and from there onto the floor. Mister Bruno and the old men were still talking about Jimmy Broom, and how he is in a bad way, and how his parents must be worried stiff, and how kids are goofy, and how the poor guy driving the Pontiac probably only had one beer, and how now he's in jail because he ran over Jimmy Broom, who probably should have held at third base anyways. None of them noticed me when I came into Bruno's through the back door. And none of them noticed me standing right below the calendar where I could reach to about the middle of the month of March 1959, right about St. Patrick's Day, but no higher. Which was high enough. Because then I was able to pull the calendar page up, the one with the squares and numbers, and then I was able to do what I wanted to do. Which was look at April 1959. I never saw a calendar like the new one on the back wall at Bruno's, but I was not surprised by what I saw on the next page. Which was another smiling lady, standing up this time, only with long brown hair, the same big smile, the same big teeth, another kind of hammer, blue shorts, and no shirt. I knew what was coming when I lifted up the next page and the next page and then July 1959, my birthday month, where the smiling lady, who was undressed like all the others, had long red hair.

I know how many months there are in a year, and right about September 1959, who also had red hair, I remembered something that happened at the end of last school year. At the end of first grade. The last spelling bee of the year.

On Monday of the last week of last school year, Sister Marianna said there was a special prize for the spelling bee that week. It was a book about a girl who becomes a novice, which is on the way to being a nun, and what her life is like, and where she lives, and what she does during the day, and how she gets dressed in the morning, and what she wears, and what she eats, and how she prays, and how she gets ready for bed at night. All the boys in class groaned. Which I did too. Who wants a book about a girl? Especially a girl who is going to be a nun. What about the books about sports, or soldiers, or bugs? At first, I didn't think much of it. Those boys were groaning for nothing. They had no reason to be upset. Which they were anyways. But, if they thought about it, which they didn't, it was going to be either me or Sharon the Roach who would win that book. Which is what happened. I knew it was probably going to be Sharon the Roach. It was always Sharon the Roach. Which was because she could always spell just one more word than me every week. Every time! Just like I could add faster in my head than her. Every single time! In fact, after a while, Sister Marianna would just tell me to sit down and let the other kids have a chance. Which I did, wondering why she never asked Sharon the Roach to sit down and give me a chance.

That night last year at supper, when I told Daddy and my Mother about the special prize, my Mother said, "That's interesting." Except she said it like she was not even a little interested.

And Daddy said, "What's so great about a book about a nun?"

"Not really a nun," I said back. "A novice." I had to look that word up after Sister Marianna said it because I didn't want to ask my Mother or anybody else how to spell it. Which I did. Look it up, that is.

"A what?" Daddy said back. I explained the whole thing to him, the dressing in the morning, the eating, the praying, the getting ready for bed at night. "Doesn't sound so interesting to me." For a while, I felt the exact same way. I was going to win a book about a girl nun, and what would that get me? But every morning that week Sister Marianna announced about the last spelling bee of the year and the special prize, which was the book, and what a big deal it was and the boys groaned and the girls smiled and Sharon the Roach gave me a look and I knew what it meant. And then, the more Sister Marianna brought it up, the more I began to think about it. The girl dressing in the morning, getting ready for bed at night. That's what Sister Marianna said every morning. And my Mother says I'm very curious. Which I am!

So, from out of nowhere, all of a sudden, I wanted to win that book. I wanted to beat Sharon the Roach in that spelling bee. Because of the special prize. I was going to study the vocabulerry words in the Reader's Digest every month going back to the beginning of time. I know that's not how to spell it, but I'm in a hurry and don't have time to look it up. So, look it up yourself if you care enough.

Anyways, I studied and studied. All Wednesday night and Thursday night of that week last year, after school, I made my Mother ask me the words and I spelled them back and I never missed one. I even told Daddy one day I wasn't able to go to the horse race track because I had to work on my spelling words. He looked at me a little funny and said, "It's your funeral." Whatever that's suppose to mean. But I wanted that book. I really wanted it!

On that Friday of the last week of last school year, I got to school and I was tired. Dog tired, is what my Uncle Roger calls it. I could barely keep my eyes open. Because I didn't sleep. I didn't sleep because I was nervous about the spelling bee. When I got into class, I looked over at Sharon the Roach and was hoping she was as tired as me. But she was just sitting at her desk reading a book, not paying attention to the kids talking around her. I figured the book was called something like "The Hardest Words to Spell in the Whole Wide World."

I don't know why I was so worried. It was always just one teeny word more every week that she won by. It wasn't like she ever slaughtered me. I beat every other kid in the class every week. Except Sharon the Roach. I was a long shot. That's what Daddy called me at supper the night before. "And long shots win too," Daddy said. "That's why they run the race instead of just giving a ribbon to the best looking horse."

And on that Friday last year, after about only thirty minutes, it was down to us two again. Just me and you know who.

"Furlong," Sister Marianna said. "The definition is." I didn't have to hear anything else. My heart almost popped out of my mouth. I know what the definition is! One-eighth of a mile. Furlong? I know it! Furlong! I know it! Sister finished, "An eighth of a mile."

But it wasn't my word. It was for Sharon the Roach. I was probably going to get something like vocabulerry. "Furlong," Sister Marianna said again. I looked at Sharon the Roach and thought about if she ever went to the horse race track. It's not that far away. Just across the street where Mister Lee's laundry is. She probably did maybe. Except she's a girl. But I hoped. And I hoped.

"Furlong," Sharon the Roach finally said back. "F-I-R-L-O-N-G. Fur-long." Sharon the Roach smiled at Sister Marianna. Who did not move or say anything back. Then Sharon the Roach looked over and smiled a little cold smile at me. And this time, just this once, I smiled back.

"Vonny?"

"Yes, Sister?" I asked, smiling an even bigger smile at her, me being the only kid in the class who knew what she was going to say next.

"Can you spell the word furlong?" The little cold smile on Sharon the Roach's face melted into a tiny frown. I just kept on smiling. Can I spell the word furlong? Can I spell the word furlong! You bet I can, Sister! Which I did. "That is correct, Vonny," Sister Marianna said, and every boy in the class clapped their hands as hard as they could, like when the witch melted into a puddle of water in that wizard movie. Two boys jumped up and clapped me on the back and another one shook my hand.

Even Louie Canale made a scene by sticking his tongue out at Sharon the Roach. Which he will have to put on his confession list, I guess. "Okay, boys," Sister said. "Let's quiet down now. Let's quiet down." Which everyone did. Except that goofball, Louie Canale, who got himself sent to the principal's office again for throwing a balled up piece of paper at Sharon the Roach. But once things calmed down, Sister Marianna said to me, "Vonny, would you please use the word furlong in a sentence for the class?"

A sentence? Why not, "Vonny, would you please come and get your special prize?" A sentence? Everyone was staring at me. Sharon the Roach was still standing. Like she wasn't already the loser. Use the word in a sentence? That was never part of the rules!

But I just said back, "The eighth race today will be run at a distance of six furlongs." Which is what I heard at the horse race track with Daddy all the time.

Every head in the class turned to the front of the room, where Sister Marianna looked down and placed the paper with the spelling bee words back on her desk. I started to smile again. The boys were on the edge of their desk seats, waiting to jump again. But Sister Marianna said, "Don't make me send any of you to join Louis downstairs." And then she turned to me. "Congratulations, Vonny." Only a couple of boys clapped and I fell back into my desk. Sharon the Roach sat down too and covered her face with her hands. She was crying. "Come up here and get your prize, Vonny." Which I did. When Sister handed me the book, I quickly flipped it over and saw that it was a book about Jimmy Doolittle and some raid on Tokyo in the war. Jimmy Doolittle? "Sharon," Sister Marianna said. "Come up here and get the second place prize," which she held in her hand and which I saw was the special prize, the book I wanted to win. I was just standing there like a dope looking at the special prize that now Sharon the Roach was getting because Sister then said, "You can sit now, Vonny."

And that's the story I was thinking about as I turned the calendar from September 1959, not paying attention to anyone else at Bruno's.

"Find one you like?" I was scared and tried to run out the back door, which is right there by the calendar, but he caught my arm. "Where are you going?" It was Mister Bruno. I twisted a little, but he had me good.

He leaned over. "I like October, myself," he said. "Go take a peek at her while I get those Kool Filter Menthols. One pack or two?"

"One," I said back, reaching into the pocket of my shorts to find the two dimes my Mother gave me to buy them. "Please," I said again.

"I'll get that later," Mister Bruno said back. "When you're finished finding out what day Christmas is on this year, just jump back up on the stool there."

Which I did. And while I was waiting there on the stool, the plastic sticking to my legs, now and then looking over at the blonde lady from March 1959, I also saw the old crocodiles down at the other end of the bar, three of them now. All of them looked at me, pointing at me and raising their glasses of beer at me.

"You got good taste, kid," one of the men called over to me, his beer glass even higher in the air than the others.

Mister Bruno shushed him. "That's enough of that!" he said out loud. "The kid's just here to get his mom some Kools." It was just about then that I think I figured out about impure thoughts. And I wondered if I had to tell Monseigneur about the crocodiles and the ladies with no shirts on.

At supper Tuesday night, after I came back to our house from Bruno's, Daddy was pretty funny, telling a story about a guy at his work who went fishing and got another guy's fishhook caught in his nose. And how they just kept fishing anyways. I told about Jimmy Broom and about what the crocodiles at Bruno's said. Daddy said he heard that Jimmy Broom might die. And then I started to tell my Mother about the new calendar on the back wall at Bruno's, but before I was able to Daddy just looked at me and said, "Not in front of your sister, Vonny, my boy." Whatever that means.

Anyways, I went to sleep Tuesday night thinking about Jimmy Broom and if he will die and about the kid who went to have his tonsils out last year and never came back to school and about my confession in a couple of weeks and where Bruno's will fit into all that.

Wednesday morning at breakfast, Daddy was still talking about the guy with the fishhook in his nose, making just me and my Mother laugh more and more, because my little sister is too little to laugh at any stories you say. While we were still eating breakfast and listening to Daddy tell stories, my Aunt Anna, who is my Uncle Roger's wife who lives in the house next door which is the same house where Jimmy Broom lives on the other side, came over and asked if our bathroom was broken because I woke up her and my Uncle Roger, who is really my cousin, by knocking on their door at three o'clock in the morning to ask if I could use their bathroom. And then I used it and I just said thank you and left.

My Mother fell down on her knees, right there in the kitchen where we were eating breakfast, and she grabbed at me. My Mother hugged me so hard I thought my heart was going to pop out of my chest. "Oh, Vonny!" she said out loud. "You're worried about that little boy, aren't you? I knew you were. That's why you went sleepwalking. Oh, Vonny!"

I didn't remember going to my Aunt Anna's at three o'clock in the morning to use the bathroom. But every now and then, Daddy says he finds me sleeping in the bathtub at night and I don't remember how I got in there either. I don't even know it happens. It just does. So, I guess maybe I do walk in my sleep. Which is scary. Because, what if I stick an ice pick in my little sister's chest while I'm sleepwalking one night? Or get run over by a black Pontiac?

Two, or Picou's

You're probably thinking about how is Jimmy Broom doing. Me too! Because, so far, I don't have any news. And my Uncle Roger even lives exactly next door to him. Which was why I sleepwalked over there and made my Mother hysterical. Which I know how to spell because it was in the Reader's Digest last month. But I still don't know how Jimmy Broom is doing. I can't find out yet.

So, here's what happened instead.

This coming weekend, which is the one while Jimmy Broom is still dying at the Hotel Dieu and my Mother is trying to figure out how to stop me from sleepwalking and I am trying to figure out when I can go back to Bruno's again and, if I do, what more actions, words, and thoughts will have to go on my confession list, Daddy and my Mother are going to the movies with a bunch of other people, like my aunts and uncles and some cousins who are a lot older than me. The movies is not at the Rivoli or the Bell but is downtown at a place where you have to dress up to go just like it was a Sunday Mass, and a High Mass too, because they even have ushers. Which are people that wear uniforms there at the movies and show you where to sit instead of the lady wearing glasses and a flowery dress like the ones who work at the Rivoli and the Bell and just sell tickets so you have to find your own place to sit. I know about Daddy and my Mother having to dress up because I had to run an errand to pick up Daddy's sports coat from Mister Lee at the laundry and my Mother made me pick up his tie too. Which I don't really like to do, meaning go to the laundry. Because of Mister Lee's hook.

Anyways, the movie Daddy and my Mother are going to is about some guy named Ben. Who races around in a chariot. Which is another way of racing horses. It's not like the kind that I go to with Daddy where the jockey rides on the horse. This guy Ben, who lived back when men were wearing what look like the dresses that little girls in kindergarden wear now, only a white dress, was not a jockey. He is too big for that. He looks more like Hercules or like Samson, like a guy who might knock a building over if you looked at him crooked or cut his hair off. Mister Muscles is what Daddy would call him. Plus, he had to ride four horses. Which is not really easy or even possible if you have only two legs. Which he does. You might be able to ride two horses by standing on their backs if they were real close together, like the one time I saw that at the circus. But not four horses at one time. So, instead of riding on top of the horses, Ben and the other guys in the race are behind them in this kind of wagon that doesn't have a top. Which is called a chariot.

When I first heard about the chariot races and the movies about this Ben, which I think was from my Mother talking to my aunt on the telephone, the first thing I did was ask Daddy if I could go to it. Just like I go to the races at the horse race track with Daddy. "You're too young," is what he said back. Daddy was reading the newspapers and didn't even look at me. This was last Sunday just before we went to Mass. Which was even before Jimmy Broom got run over and before I saw the new calendar on the back wall at Bruno's.

I thought about saying to Daddy, "Sure, that makes sense." Which it didn't. "I'm old enough to go to the races at the horse race track with you, but not old enough to go to the chariot race movies?" But I decided not to say it. Because Daddy might get it in his head that I'm too young for the horse race track too. So, I didn't bring it up.

"Besides," Daddy said again, "you need to stay here on Friday night and keep your sister and brother company." I didn't say anything back. Already, I was having thoughts that might have to go on my confession list. Not the ice pick or anything, but I really am not keen about the idea of keeping my little sister and baby brother company on Friday night.

First of all, my baby brother is not very interesting. Because he was just born in January. So, he is very small and very wrinkled. He moves his head around when he looks at you like he doesn't exactly know where you are. My Mother says he's not blind but that he can't see so good. He mainly cries a lot or messes his diaper. That's a part I don't like. Who likes to smell dirty diapers? He's pretty cute most of the time though.

That much everybody says. But he's only a couple of months old and he just makes a lot of noise. Sometimes, my Mother will ask me to hold him. Which I do. But my baby brother just scares me. I mean, what if I drop him by accident? My Mother says my Aunt Junie dropped my Uncle Roger, who is really my cousin, on his head when he was a baby. And now, she says he's a disaster waiting to happen. I really don't want my baby brother to become a disaster waiting to happen just because I dropped him.

And then, there's my little sister. I don't know where to start with that one. She's like Sharon the Roach, only worse. More annoying. A lot more annoying! And, the only best thing about Sharon the Roach is, she doesn't live at our house. Worst of all for me, my little sister does live at our house. It's like a spelling bee every single day. She follows me around all the time. She even tried to follow me into Bruno's one day. I had to tell my Mother about that. Which my little sister cried about for almost a week. One solid week! She likes to cry, my little sister does. She sees my baby brother crying and so then she cries and then they both cry all day. And about nothing! Why would I want to keep those two company on Friday night?

So, I just said back to Daddy after he said I'm too young to go to the chariot race movies, "What do you say we stop at Picou's on the way back from Mass?" Because it was last Sunday.

Which finally made Daddy look up from the newspapers, fold it up, put it on the table, and then stand up. He rubbed my head and messed up the back of my hair. "Vonny, my boy, you are a very smart little guy," Daddy said back, and he kept rubbing my head like I was the pet poodle dog the Garamel sisters have down the block on Columbus Street.

"I'm not little!" I said back.

"Don't do that," my Mother said when she walked into the kitchen holding my baby brother. "You'll mess up Vonny's hair."

Which only made Daddy put both his hands on my head and completely mess up every hair on my head. Then, he pulled a black comb out of the back pocket of his pants. "So, now we'll make it all right again," he smiled. Which he did, combing every single hair back where it was before I talked about going to Picou's Bakery, and even the wave that he combs up in the front to make me look like a movie star.

The good thing about Picou's Bakery is the smell. Which is the most amazing smell ever. They never stop baking things at Picou's. Bread, cakes, cookies, rolls. And doughnuts! It never closes and so you can smell them baking all the time. It's only a block away from our house. Maybe a block and a half. Just down the street from Bruno's on Dorgenois Street. Sometimes, we're right in the middle of supper, eating something my Mother cooked, which could be good or could be not, and then the smell from Picou's will come in through the open windows and all I want to do is eat a piece of cake or a cookie or a doughnut. Whatever they are baking at the time. Even Daddy says so. He sometimes says, "I think I'm going over to Picou's for some doughnuts." Right in the middle of supper, he says this. "Anybody want to go with me?"

Like the dope I am, I raise my hand, like I'm in class or something. Right there in the kitchen.

My Mother says back to him, "Albert! You're going to get them excited, Albert!" And my little sister is excited. She's giggling and hopping around the kitchen table like a Mexican jumping bean and waving her little arms in the air. If I did that, my Mother would probably smack me. No, she would absolutely smack me. But they just think my little sister is cute. Both of them. "You see what you did now, Albert?" my Mother says again. "Calm down, sweetheart," she says to my little sister. "Daddy's just teasing."

Which he is. He teases a lot. And Daddy only smiles. "We'll go on Sunday," he says back. Which makes my little sister stop hopping around and start crying. I already put my hand down because I kind of knew it anyways. And I also felt like a dope. But, now who's the dope? It's in the middle of supper on a school night. We're not going out for doughnuts in the middle of supper. Not on a school night!

But Sunday comes along and, after Mass, we always stop at Picou's on the way home and we always get to pick out something special, me and my little sister. I like jelly doughnuts. In fact, I love jelly doughnuts! My little sister usually gets something sticky and gooey, usually a cupcake shaped like some goofy animal that she winds up getting all over her good dress. My baby brother doesn't get anything because he doesn't even know what a bakery is yet and, even if he did, he can't see good enough to pick something out of the shop window and, even if he was able to see good enough, he can't talk yet to say what he likes or what he wants. He's like that Helen Keller girl my Mother is always talking about and made me read about. She and Daddy always get cinnamon rolls. My Mother. Not that Helen Keller girl. Always! Daddy says Picou's has the best cinnamon rolls anywheres. Which they do. "Always have and always will," Daddy says. Except I like jelly doughnuts better.

So, one day while we were having breakfast after Mass, Daddy says, "So, what do you think they do with all the doughnut holes?" I didn't think he was talking to me so I didn't say anything at first. I was busy reading the funny pages, Prince Valiant especially. I can never figure out what the Prince and his friends are talking about, but I like the pictures a lot because they have horses in them and remind me of King Arthur, which I have a book about, and the guy who saves Sleeping Beauty at the end. "Vonny, my boy?" Daddy says. "I'm talking to you."

"Me?" I said back. "What, Daddy?"

"What do you think they do with all the doughnut holes?" Daddy says again.

"I don't know," I said back. I just lifted my shoulders up and down. "I never even thought about it." I went back to reading about the Prince.

"I know! I know! I know!" my little sister says, hopping up and down like she's on a pogo stick.

"So?" Daddy asks her, winking at me. "What do you think they do with all the doughnut holes, sweetheart?" I can't believe it! There is no way my little sister knows what they do with doughnut holes. Because a doughnut hole isn't even anything! She doesn't even know what a doughnut hole is. Because she eats cupcakes. And she's not even in kindergarden yet. So, how could she know? My dopey little sister. "So?" Daddy asks again. "What's the answer, sweetheart? Tell Vonny."

"I know! I know! I know!" My little sister is still hopping around. Daddy and my Mother think it's cute when she hops around. They probably would think it was cute if she stuck an ice pick in someone's chest.

Tell Vonny? Why tell Vonny? I don't care about doughnut holes. Besides, the Prince is talking to this guy about jousting. Which is what I am interested in because there are horses and knights and racing. And besides, there is no way my little sister knows anything about doughnut holes. Which don't even exist anyways! She is hopping around like a jumping bean again, her little arms waving in the air above her head. How could she know?

But then, my little sister giggles again and says out loud, "They eat them!"

I drop the newspapers and the Prince and then crack up laughing. What a dope! I can't stop laughing. "How can they eat something that's not even there?" I say. I try to wink back at Daddy, but both of my eyes close and I blink instead. Which happens to me sometimes.

Daddy hands my little sister a piece of cinnamon roll with peanut butter on it. "That's right, sweetheart," he says. Right? How can that be right? How can you eat something that isn't even there? I don't believe it. It can't be! But Daddy says again, "She's right, Vonny, my boy." I still didn't believe it. How can you make doughnuts out of doughnut holes? Something out of nothing? I figured Daddy was just teasing us. He teases us all the time.

"But how can you make something out of nothing?" I said back. "It's a hole. There's nothing there. How can you make doughnuts out of holes?"

Daddy just went back to reading his newspapers. "I know it's hard to believe," he says. "But she's right. In fact, that doughnut you're eating right now, that doughnut there," he points at mine, "is probably made out of doughnut holes. One hundred percent doughnut holes." Daddy smiles at my little sister. He thinks she's cute. It's like living in the same house with Sharon the Roach. Plus, jelly doughnuts don't even have holes!

Anyways, the good thing about Daddy and my Mother going to the movies with a bunch of other people, like my aunts and uncles and some cousins who are a lot older than me, to see some guys race chariots, including Mister Ben Muscles, is my cousin Charlene is going to babysit me and my little sister and my baby brother. And, even better, I read in the newspapers that there is a movie on about Notre Dame. Which is a college somewheres where they do nothing but play football.

I saw this in the newspapers a couple of days after Jimmy Broom got run over. A lot of kids in my school can't read the newspapers because they're still on the red reader or the blue reader or, like goofy Louie Canale, even just the green reader. Which even a goofball like him should be able to read by the second grade. My Mother says I should not be kritikal of other kids. But I can't help myself. Like I already told, you can't stop yourself from thinking things. I can stop myself from saying Louie is a goofball. But I can't stop myself from thinking it.

And so I read the newspapers almost every day, especially when it rains after school and I have to stay inside anyways. Which it was doing a couple of days after Jimmy Broom got run over. In fact, Jimmy Broom getting run over was the reason why I was reading the newspapers when I saw about Notre Dame. I figured that if a black Pontiac ran over a kid in our neighborhood, that the kid being run over would be news for everybody in town. Everybody would want to know about a kid who got run over by a car. It doesn't happen every day. It's news. So, since a couple of days before, as soon as I got home I would open the newspapers thinking there would be a story in there about how this poor, little kid got run over by a black Pontiac in front of Bruno's at the corner of Columbus Street and Dorgenois. Maybe there would even be a picture of Jimmy Broom in the newspapers. Jimmy stretched out in a pool of blood after he got run over. Or in the ambulance. Or at the hospital. Which was the Hotel Dieu. He was famous already in our neighborhood. The blood, even a couple of days later, was still in the middle of the street. Only it was dried up now and looked brown. Almost like dirt. Poor Jimmy!

Anyways, there wasn't one word about Jimmy Broom in the newspapers. It made me think that black Pontiacs were running over kids every day in town. It made me think that maybe Jimmy Broom was still alive. If a kid got run over and died, they would have to put his picture in the newspapers. They would have to warn other kids about playing stickball in the middle of the street. Or else it could happen again. Every single day. Kids dying from playing stickball in the street. Every single day!

Usually when I read the newspapers, I go straight to the comics. They're black and white, except on Sunday. Which is okay because I don't have a lot of time to stare at the pictures anyways. I just look at Prince Valiant to see what he is doing and then look at the word puzzles. Which I can't even figure out what the rules are, so I never get them right. Who is doing those puzzles in the comics anyways? They're too hard for kids. And grown ups would have to be goofy to even read the comics. But after Jimmy Broom got run over, I looked at the newspapers from front to back, top to bottom, left to right. Every picture and every word. Over a half hour trying to see if there is anything about Jimmy. Which there isn't.

First, I checked all the pictures on every page. Then, I had to go back to the front and read everything on every page. Not really read it, but look quick to see if I saw Jimmy's name. I could skip pretty fast through the sports section because a kid getting run over is not a game. But then, I was thinking, Jimmy did get run over while he was playing stickball. So, I looked harder anyways. Even at the sports section. Also, I didn't have to read the pages about the dead people. Except I did look for his name in the list of dead people. Sometimes I wonder what it will say in the newspapers about Jimmy if he dies. A seven year old kid run over by a black Pontiac. Will they say that his parents gave him too much attention? Which I think. Or not enough attention? Like my Mother thinks.

Anyways, like I already told, there wasn't one word about Jimmy Broom in the newspapers. But, in the TV section, I saw two things when I was looking in the newspapers about Jimmy. First, I saw that Johnny Horton, that battle of New Orleans singer, was having a show here where we live. Which is in New Orleans too, the same place as where the battle was. I wanted to go, but Daddy would just say I'm too young. Why bother asking? I saw that because I was looking quick for the word Jimmy and then I saw the word Johnny. Then, there he was! A picture of this Johnny Horton wearing a funny looking, white cowboy hat was right in the middle of the top of the first page in the TV section. He didn't sound like a cowboy. Then, I saw about this movie about Notre Dame that is going to be on TV on Friday night. I was thinking that maybe my cousin Charly likes football. I think she does. Anyways, I know all about Notre Dame because I saw that movie about the best football coach ever. Whose name I can never remember. It's not like Jim or Bill or Joe. Or even Vonny. It's the kind of name that's easy to forget. I'll ask Daddy at supper. He'll know for sure.

So then Friday comes a few days after Jimmy Broom got run over by the black Pontiac, and we had another spelling bee in class. And guess what? Sharon the Roach was sick. Something called pink eyes, Sister Marianna says. Louie Canale has to laugh at that one. "Pink eye!" he shouts, and then cackles. He can't help himself. So, I win the spelling bee for the first time this school year, the first time since I won it last school year by spelling furlong right.

It was a crazy week! Jimmy Broom run over. Johnny Horton in town. Sharon the Roach with pink eyes. Me winning the spelling bee. Sister

Marianna giving me a ticket that gets me free chocolate milk after Mass on First Friday. Which is the exact same thing I get when I lose and come in second place every week. And now I have to wait another whole month almost to use my prize. Because we already just had First Friday Mass this morning. I put the ticket in my right hand pocket of my khaki pants. Which is where I put anything I don't want to lose. But, why am I getting the same ticket for free chocolate milk when I win as I get when I lose to Sharon the Roach when she gets a book a boy would like whenever she wins? Which is every week!

When Sister Marianna handed me the ticket for free chocolate milk, she said, "Just take this, Vonny. I forgot the first place book back in the convent." Which is where Sister lives with the other Sisters. "You'll get that book the next time you win." The next time I win? When's that going to be? Next year? Maybe not until eighth grade! I wondered if pink eyes will make you go blind and then I will be able to beat Sharon the Roach every week. Then I was thinking whether that was an impure thought. I didn't want her to go blind. I didn't wish for her to go blind. I just wondered if she might. The thought just popped into my head. I don't want Jimmy Broom to die. I just wondered if he might. It's just a thought. So, I figure out it's not an impure thought to wonder if Sharon the Roach might go blind because of having pink eyes. Even if it could happen. And then I was thinking about what my life will be like after that. With lots of tickets for free chocolate milk.

So, after school on Friday, I rushed home, past first base by the little wooden building on the corner where the kindergarden is, across Dorgenois to home plate in front of Bruno's where the brown stain of Jimmy's blood in the street makes you look at it even when you don't want to, past my Uncle Roger's house where Jimmy Broom lives on the other side, through the gate in front of our house, into the alley along the side of our house that leads to the back yard, and then into the kitchen through the back door where my Mother made chocolate chip cookies for us to eat on Friday night when Charly is coming over to watch us. Cookies! I can smell them when I walk into the kitchen through the back door. I can smell something baking.

"Vonny, baby," my Mother says when I come in.

"Vonny! Vonny! Vonny!" my little sister is hopping around and talking out loud. Which makes me nervous. My little sister likes to say things in a very excited way and to say them over and over and over again. At least three times. I think it's annoying. Daddy and my Mother thinks she's cute.

"Isn't it cute how much she loves you, Vonny?" my Mother says. Which is when, without me wanting it to happen, I think about an ice pick. I reach down and hug my little sister very quickly because, if I don't, she will start crying and then I won't get any cookies.

"I won the spelling bee," I say.

"Congratulations, Vonny. That's wonderful!" my Mother says back.

"Sharon the Roach has pink eyes."

"She has pink eye?" my Mother says back.

"No, Ma'am," I say back. "Both of them."

"Let me see your eyes." My Mother grabs my head, puts her hands over both my ears, and then stretches my neck in all directions while she stares into my eyes like some kid punched me or something.

"I'm okay, Mama. Really," I said back. "I'm okay!"

"Here, give me your book bag."

"Anyways, I got another ticket for chocolate milk."

"That's wonderful, Vonny." My Mother doesn't realize that it's what I always get. She thinks it's a big deal. "Look what's in the newspapers today." She hands me a folded up section of the newspapers where there is, finally, a picture of Jimmy Broom. Only it's his school picture. Before he got run over.

"Did he die?" I said back.

"Just read it," my Mother said back. "I have to change your brother and then get ready to go out with Daddy. He'll be home soon."

"Vonny! Vonny! Vonny!" my little sister says again, and she starts hopping around the room and waving her little arms in the air and then slapping at the newspapers section in my hand. With all of that, I completely forgot about the cookies.

New Orleans – March 6, 1959 – A boy was struck by a moving vehicle on the afternoon of Tuesday, March 3rd, at the corner of North Dorgenois and Columbus Streets in Mid-City.

Columbus is my street. And Mid-City is what Daddy calls our neighborhood.

The boy, James A. Brown, 7, a resident of Columbus Street, was struck by a black 1956 Pontiac operated by an unidentified male driver. The boy is a student at St. Rose de Lima School.

Which Jimmy is.

The driver was questioned by police at the scene following the incident. Police are investigating.

Police are investigating? That's it? Police are investigating! I thought the old crocodiles at Bruno's said the driver was in jail. Drunk or something. And what about Jimmy? Is he alive? Dead? Unidentified male driver? Is that it? Incident? It wasn't a incident. It was an accident. Maybe I don't really know the difference between a incident and an accident. Maybe a incident is on purpose. Maybe the unidentified male drive ran over Jimmy Broom on purpose. I looked at Jimmy's picture in the newspapers again. His face was made up of all these little dots, a lot of little dots. I put the paper up to my nose and tried to make out how many dots were in Jimmy's eyeball.

Just then, Daddy walked in from work. It was only four o'clock, but he was home already. "Hey, Vonny, my boy!" he smiled. "How's my boy today?"

"I won the spelling bee!" I said back.

"You did?" Daddy said back. "Was Sharon Roach sick or something?"

Like I said. Daddy knows everything. "Pink eyes," I said back.

"Pink eye?" Daddy said back again.

"No, Sir," I said back. "Both of them."

"That's very contagious," Daddy said back. Then he smiled. "Maybe she looks like a rabbit now," he said and laughed. I laughed too. It was something Louie Canale might say in class and then be sent to the principal's office for. Sharon the Roach with pink eyes like a rabbit. I never noticed before that rabbits have pink eyes. "How's my sweetheart?" Daddy said to my little sister who was hanging on one of his legs like it was some kind of pole and giggling all the time. My little sister is laughing all the time. I don't know what she's got to be so happy about. But sometimes I think she may be as goofy as Louie Canale. Except he's three years older. My Mother sometimes says that Louie isn't goofy. He just needs to grow up. Maybe my little sister just needs to grow up. Anyways, Daddy just reaches down and grabs her off his leg and gives her a big hug and shakes her around a little before putting her back down. "Mmmmm!" Daddy says. "What smells so good?" He finds a plate of cookies in the corner of the counter, back where I wasn't able to see it before, and then puts it on the kitchen table right near me.

My little sister says, "I want one! I want one! I want one!" And so Daddy gives her one of the cookies. But she drops it on the floor right away before she can even bite into it. Which makes her start crying. My little sister is crying all the time. With my little sister, she's either laughing all the time or she's crying all time. One or the other.

Daddy picks up what's left of the cookie, a few big pieces and a lot of crumbs, and puts it on the table. He kneels down and hugs my little sister. "You want another cookie, sweetheart?" he says. But she doesn't say anything back. She just nods her head and holds out her hand. "Here" he says. "Hold onto this one."

"May I have a cookie, Daddy?" I said.

He looks at me, still kneeling down with his arms around my little sister, and says, "Just one, Vonny. You don't want to spoil your appetite," as if I just asked to eat the whole plate of cookies. "Okay. Now, you two behave," Daddy said too. "I have to go and get ready with your Mother." Which he did.

My Mother's cookies are not like the cookies at Picou's. Which are better. My Mother's cookies are smaller and not as round and most of the time they are either dark brown or sometimes even black on the bottom. But they taste good anyways. My Mother always makes chocolate chip cookies and I like the chocolate a lot. At Picou's, it's mainly oatmeal cookies with raisins and sometimes sugar cookies. They are big, about the size of Daddy's hand, and very round and the bottoms are light brown. Very crispy. The first thing I do with a Picou's cookie is break it in half. Because it makes me think I have two cookies. And it's easy to do. The cookies just snap right in two. Snap! They are delicious! I sometimes take Picou's cookies with me to the movies at the Rivoli. Which is only a block away, closer than the Bell. But it makes so much noise when I break them that I wait until there is something loud happening in the movies, like a cowboy shooting a gun or a car crashing or a rocket ship blasting off. And then nobody notices. Except me.

Anyways, while Daddy and my Mother are getting ready for the movies, I sit at the kitchen table with my little sister, eating our cookies, me thinking about Jimmy Broom. My little sister takes another cookie after she finishes one. And then another one after she finishes that one. "You're going to spoil your appetite," I say to her. But she doesn't care. Maybe she is goofy like Louie Canale. Anyways, I just eat one cookie. Like Daddy said. And I can't even break it in half because it's too small and too hard to break with your fingers. At least my fingers. Daddy could probably do it.

"Hello. Hello!" That's Charly! She's at the back door, the one to the kitchen. Charly is my cousin too.

I jump up from the chair. "Charly!" I say back.

"How's my Vonny?" she says back. "I was going to say my little Vonny," she says again, "but you're not that little anymore. Come give me a hug." Charly always says something nice to me. Really, she's always saying something nice about everyone. She's my favorite babysitter. My little sister just sits there at the table stuffing her face with cookies. She's up to five by now. Charly reaches over, picks up the cookie plate, and puts it up on the counter. My little sister stands up and follows her, throws her two little arms up reaching for the plate and following it with her hands and eyes as it travels from the table through the air and back onto the counter. I can see in her eyes that she wants to shout and cry but her little mouth is so stuffed with chocolate chip cookies that she can't do either. Which is good.

"You don't want to spoil your appetite, now, do you?" Charly says. But my little sister, who can't talk and who can't cry to get her way because her mouth is stuffed with hard, little chocolate chip cookies, just nods her head up and down like a dope. Of course, she wants to spoil her appetite! She wants to eat every cookie on the plate! I start laughing. My little sister makes me laugh sometimes. I think she's cute too. Especially with her little face stuffed with hard, little chocolate chip cookies, her head bobbing up and down, her little arms waving in the air, her not being able to shout or cry. For once! Charly just says, "Don't you want to eat some of the doughnuts we're going to make tonight?" And just like Louie Canale might do, my little sister just starts nodding her head faster and faster. Sometimes my Mother calls her a little monkey. Just now, that's what my little sister looks like, because she is running faster and faster around the kitchen, the cookies jammed in her mouth, and she wants to say back "Yes! Yes! Yes!" to Charly's question about the doughnuts. But she can't.

Finally, my little sister swallows enough cookies to be able to say back out loud "Yes! Yes! Yes! I want some! I want some! I want some!" at the top of her little lungs. But instead, she sounds like someone just stuck an ice pick in her chest.

"Calm down, sweetie," is all Charly says back, and she kneels down next to my little sister to hug her and to calm her down. But I know what's coming next, so I start moving toward the back door of the kitchen.

Then I hear my Mother call from the front of the house, "Vonny! Vonny! You get in here right now!" Which is the last thing I am going to do. I know better. "Vonny!" I can hear the shower running in the bathroom. Which is in the middle of our house. That's a good thing too. Daddy's in there and probably can't hear anything. "Vonny! Don't make me come back there." Which she does anyways. Which my Mother always does anyways. She's getting closer. From the next room, my Mother shouts, "Vonny! Did you hit your little sister? Didn't we tell you not to hit girls?" I start edging the screen door at the back of the kitchen open. Just in case. Charly is between me and my Mother, kneeling down with my little sister, when my Mother rushes into the kitchen. Before she sees Charly, because she's got a towel on her head to dry her hair and isn't wearing her glasses yet and can't see anything, my Mother says again, "Did you hit your sister again, Vonny?"

This is something my Mother thinks I do all the time. Which is hit my little sister. But it's not even on my confession list. Because I never hit my little sister. Never! I never even raise my hand or act like I'm going to hit her when she comes over and jumps on my stomach with both feet while I'm reading the newspapers on my back on the floor. Which she does! But, to hear my Mother, it's like I hit my little sister ten times every day. If I hit my little sister as much as my Mother thinks I do, she would be in the hospital bed at the Hotel Dieu next to Jimmy Broom. But for some reason my Mother thinks that anytime my little sister gets hurt, no matter how or where, I had something to do with it.

For instance, back when we lived in California, my little sister, who was my baby sister then, walked into a swing that two kids were on and got a bad cut right by her eye. What a goofball! She walks right up to the swing because she wants to get on it and the other kids won't let her because they are on it first and don't want to get off. So, my baby sister walks right into the swing like it's not there! "Why didn't you stop her from walking into the swing, Vonny?" Which I was a thousand yards away from! With my back turned because I was playing catch with a kid from across the way.

Also for instance, another time, my baby sister walked up to a kid right at the time he swung a baseball bat in a game we were playing. The boys, that is. Because she wanted to play baseball too. But nobody wanted her to play. None of my friends in California. Or even the kids that we didn't know. Not me either. And so she got another cut over the same eye then too. "Didn't you see her walking into that bat, Vonny? Why didn't you stop her?" Which I was in centerfield and tried to. I saw what was coming. But I could only get to second base by the time there was blood everywhere and my baby sister was screaming like she was going to die. I didn't like it either, my baby sister being hurt. Who would? It made me sick to think that my baby sister was hurt and she might die or something. Blood all over the ground and on the bat and all over her face. I was sick. I ran to get my Mother as soon as I saw what happened. "Why didn't you stop her?" is all my Mother kept saying out loud to me as we ran together to home plate where my baby sister was lying down and howling like a monkey. "Oh, my precious baby girl," my Mother said to my baby sister, holding her while we hurried back to the house together. "Why didn't you stop her, Vonny?"

"Vonny hit me," my little sister said when my Mother rushed into the kitchen with the towel over her head and not wearing her glasses yet.

"Vonny!" my Mother said out loud. "What did I tell you about hitting girls?" By this time, I was already outside the door in back of the kitchen staring in through the screen from the back steps.

Charly stood up just about the time my Mother was able to see, now with the towel in her hand. "Vonny didn't hit her, Nanny," Charly said. "She just wants more cookies."

"Charly!" my Mother said back. "I didn't hear you come in."

"I just came in the back, Nanny. I figured you were getting ready and didn't want to disturb you by knocking up front."

"Oh, sweetheart. Thanks for sitting for us," my Mother said back. Then she saw me standing outside. "What are you doing out there, Vonny? Get in here and say hello to Charly."

"Mommy! Mommy! Mommy!" My little sister was hopping around again.

"What, sweetheart? What does my precious little girl want?"

"Can I have a cookie, Mommy?" She already ate five!

"Of course, you can, sweetheart." But my Mother wasn't able to find the cookie plate at the same place on the counter where she left it. Because Daddy moved it. "Vonny!" my Mother said to me. "Where did you move the cookies?"

"They're here on the counter, Nanny," Charly said back.

"Oh, here they are, sweetheart," my Mother said. "Here's a cookie for you."

I came back into the kitchen and stood by Charly. Who had her hand on my shoulder and hugged me against her leg. "May I have one, Mama?" I said.

"You'll spoil your appetite."

I could see that my Mother was calmed down now. So, I said back, "Charly said she's going to make us doughnuts tonight."

"Doughnuts! Doughnuts! Doughnuts!" my little sister said out loud, hopping around again with her cookie and waving her little arms in the air.

"No, I didn't," Charly said back. "I didn't say I'm going to make doughnuts. I said we're going to make doughnuts tonight. You and you and me!" She pointed at me and my little sister. "We're going to make them together." She patted me on the head. And my little sister ran over and threw her arms around Charly's other leg.

"That's sweet of you, Charly," my Mother said. "But you don't have to do that. I'll have Albert run over to Picou's before we leave." But Charly said back that it was okay, that she had this recipe from her grandmother, her other one, not the one we have together that is dead. And that the doughnuts from the recipe were delicious and that she knew how to make them and that she would teach us how. So, Daddy didn't have to run over to Picou's before they leave. "Well, that's very sweet of you, Charly," my Mother said back. "You're such an angel." Which Charly is.

"You go get ready, Nanny. I'll take care of Sharon," Charly said back. That's right. Sharon! My little sister has the same name as Sharon the Roach. Plus, she lives at our house.

Charly and my little sister and I sat down at the table to play a game that Charly got out of the toy box in the next room. It's the one where there are ladders and these slides, the one where you want to go up but sometimes you have to go down depending on where you land. I don't

like the game much because it doesn't matter what you think or what you know. It's a dumb game that anybody can win. Even my little sister who doesn't even know how to read! So, we played that and it was fun because I could talk to Charly.

Then, after we played a couple of times, which my little sister won one and Charly won one, Daddy and my Mother came into the kitchen from their bedroom in the front of the house where they were getting ready to go to the chariot race movie. They were all dressed up.

My Mother has very big blue eyes and she was wearing a blue dress. She calls it her powder blue dress. I don't know why it's called powder blue because powder is white. But that's what my Mother calls it. Daddy calls my Mother beautiful all the time. Which she is! She looks like the women in the movies. The movie stars. Except my Mother has very big blue eyes. Which look even better than the movie stars. She doesn't get dressed up like this all the time. But when she does, I feel like my Mother is the prettiest mother in the world. And she's my Mother! When she has to come to my school for something, to meet with Sister Marianna or to help with breakfast after First Friday Mass or for the spring festival, my Mother gets dressed up too. And when she walks into a room, everybody stops talking and just stares at her. The kids in my class. Their parents. All the teachers. It makes me proud how pretty my Mother is when she's dressed up.

And Daddy is handsome too. At least, that's what Charly says. She says he looks like some guy named Rock. That's a funny name. Rock! I think that's the name of that Notre Dame guy, now that I think about it. Anyways, when Daddy and my Mother walked into the kitchen, Charly said, "Uncle Albert, you look just like Rock" and then she says some name I can't remember. "You're so handsome. With that wavy black hair."

Daddy laughs. "Hi, Charly," is all he says, and he kisses her on the forehead. Daddy is wearing a brown suit, like the one I have for my First Communion, and he has a white handkerchief in his coat pocket. His black hair is combed back like the way he combs mine on Sunday morning before we go to Mass. Very shiny and black. Like the movie stars. With a wave in front! Daddy is wearing his tie. Which he never does unless he is going out with my Mother. Except his khaki uniform tie. Which he wears to work when has to go to drill every month. His tie he has on to go to the movies is narrow and shiny black with a little blue swirl on it. That looks like a fish. He always wears a little clip on his tie, to hold it to his shirt so it doesn't fly around in the wind. I have one too. For my First Communion suit. Which is brown too. My suit and my tie. "So, you guys are going to make doughnuts tonight?" Daddy says, smiling a big smile. Just then, like a miracle, we could all smell doughnuts baking at Picou's. It was like a cloud of doughnut smell just floated into the house right when Daddy talked about us making doughnuts. We all just looked at each other. Then Daddy laughed. "I can run over there quick, if you want," he said. "It will only take me a minute. Then you can just eat doughnuts instead of having to make them."

"Doughnuts! Doughnuts! Doughnuts!" Guess who that is? Again, she was hopping around the kitchen like a goofball.

"That's okay, Uncle Albert," Charly said back. "Our doughnuts are going to be better." Charly winked at me. I tried to wink back but both of my eyes closed and I blinked instead. There was a knock on the front door. Which only me and my little sister heard. She ran off into the next room. Which is the one where she and I sleep. And I followed her there and through the hallway by the bathroom, then through the room where Daddy and my Mother and now my baby brother sleep and then into the front room where the door was open to the front porch and the street. The sun was starting to go down, but I could see through the screen door that it was my Aunt Gwendolyn. Who is Charly's mother. Who is also my Mother's sister and is almost as pretty as my Mother when she is dressed up.

My little sister was still saying out loud, "Doughnuts! Doughnuts! Doughnuts!"

"Don't those smell good?" Aunt Gwendolyn said. She thinks my little sister is cute too. Even more than my Mother does. I flipped the hook off the latch and she opened the screen door. "Are your parents ready?"

I told her they were in the kitchen with Charly. "We're making doughnuts with Charly tonight!" I said back again while we were walking through all the rooms to the kitchen.

"Is that what I'm smelling?" Aunt Gwendolyn said back. "That smells so good."

I told her that the smell was from Picou's. And then I said back, "But Charly says our doughnuts are going to be better."

"Well, if you're cooking with Charlene," Aunt Gwendolyn said back, "it will be a venture for all of you." Whatever that means.

"Doughnuts! Doughnuts! Doughnuts!" my little sister said while she was running to the back of the house again.

When we got back to the kitchen, Daddy and my Mother were already giving Charly good-bye kisses. "Make sure you put them to bed no later than nine," my Mother said to Charly.

"I don't want to go to bed," my little sister said back, and I thought she was going to cry. She does that a lot. Laughing like crazy, then crying like crazy. My Mother would always say something to my little sister in French when that happened. Something that her mother, who is my Grandma that is dead, told her that means if you laugh too much you're going to cry. It never made sense to me. Why would you cry just because you laugh too much? Except for my little sister, it doesn't make sense.

But Charly just bended over and picked my little sister up, tickling her ribs and kissing her on the head. My little sister started squirming and laughing. "You're going to be so sleepy after you eat all of those doughnuts," Charly said to my little sister, "you won't even be able to keep your eyes open." And then, when Daddy and my Mother had their backs turned saying hello to Aunt Gwendolyn, Charly winked at me. I didn't even try to wink back. But I knew what she meant. I would be able to watch the Notre Dame movie on TV after all!

"Charles is waiting in the car outside," Aunt Gwendolyn said, meaning Uncle Charles. Which is Charly's daddy. "We'd better get going if we're going to be there at six for our supper reservation." All three of them were all dressed up. Movie stars going to the movies! They kissed us all and hugged us all and then they all went through all of the rooms in our house, one after the other, and then out the front door. We followed them out onto the porch and waved at Uncle Charles. Who was dressed up too. Aunt Audra and Uncle Martin were already in the back seat of the car. They live two houses away from us, the other side from where my Uncle Roger lives. Which is the side where Bruno's is. We waved at them and they waved back too.

The smell from Picou's was all over the neighborhood now. I wasn't able to tell if it was cookies or cakes or bread or doughnuts. But it sure smelled delicious. Lenny Mahoney was sitting by himself on his porch next door. He is my age and lives in the house between us and Aunt Audra and Uncle Martin. I waved. But Lenny didn't see me. He was alone on a chair reading a book. I don't know how he could see. It wasn't completely dark yet, but it would be in no time. I thought maybe to shout hello but didn't. Lenny seemed happy all by himself.

"Let's get inside," Charly said to us. Which we did. After she put the latch on the screen door, she closed the wood door behind us too and then locked it too. "Don't want the boogie man to get us, do we?" she laughed.

"Boogie man! Boogie man! Boogie man!"

My Mother left some cans of soup and some sandwhiches for us to eat for supper. Which we did. Except that my little sister, who does not eat anything that's good for her, only ate a spoon of soup and about half of a half of a half of her sandwhich. Which didn't bother Charly. My Mother might send my little sister to stand in the corner until she ate more of the sandwhich. But Charly just laughed after a while and patted my little sister on the head. Finally she said, "So, let's make some doughnuts."

Which we did. Except I kept watching the clock because the Notre Dame movie started at eight o'clock on TV and I didn't want to miss a minute of it. Charly started mixing up the batter for the doughnuts at about six thirty. Then she put a pan on the stove and filled it with oil. "Okay," she said, "we'll get this to heat up while we're cutting out the doughnuts." When Charly was finished, she came back to the table. "Now, you sit there," she said to my little sister, and "you stand here," she said to me, "and you'll see how this is done," she said to both of us. "Vonny, I need a large glass and a small glass." Which I got for her out of the cabinet. I had to stand on one of the kitchen chairs to reach. But I got one of the ones we drink water from and then a little one that we drink juice from.

"Charly," I said, "is it true that you can make doughnuts out of doughnut holes?"

My little sister stuck her tongue out at me. Which she will have to put on her confession list whenever she makes her First Communion. If she remembers. "Watch this," Charly said and then she rolled out the dough on the table on top of a lot of flour. Which my little sister kept putting her hands in and then putting in her hair. What a goofball! When my little sister was done, she looked like a little ghost from all the flour on her face and in her hair. "See, the dough is rolled out," Charly said. "Now, watch what we do." And then she pressed the large glass down and into the flat dough a bunch of times. "See there," she said. Then, Charly held the flat dough sheet by two corners and pulled all of it off of the table. Except six circles of dough stayed on the table where she had pushed down with the large glass. "Vonny, hand me that little glass." Which I did. "Oh, no," Charly said. "That's too big. Isn't there a smaller glass?"

"That's the smallest one," I started to say. But then I remembered the even littler glass that Daddy uses to pour whiskey when he makes himself a high ball. Which I got down for Charly.

"Perfect!" she said back to me, and then she pressed the little glass into the middle of the six dough circles that were still on the table. "Okay," she said. "We're ready to fry the doughnuts now."

"Fried doughnuts! Fried doughnuts! Fried doughnuts!"

One by one, Charly pulled up the dough circles on the table and put them into the hot oil in the pan. Which right away started spitting oil all over the place until she put a cover on the pan. I went over to look into it, but Charly held me back. "Stand over on that chair, Vonny, so you can see." I got onto the chair that I used to get the glasses. Which was not right by the stove. And then Charly pulled the cover off of the frying pan where I could see six doughnuts, little holes in the middle, cooking in the oil. After a minute, Charly flipped them over so the other side could cook. I could see that the tops were now very brown. Browner than the doughnuts at Picou's.

My little sister wasn't paying attention at all. When I got down from the chair, I saw her playing with the flour and with the pile of dough that Charly had pulled off of the table. And there on the table in front of her were the six little circles that were left when Charly pulled up the doughnuts to put in the frying pan. The doughnut holes! Six of them right on the table. One for each doughnut that was cooking.

"Charly," I said, already knowing what she was going to say back, "what do you do with the doughnut holes?" Charly scooped them up in her hand and plopped them into the pile of dough in front of my little sister. "We make more doughnuts out of them," Charly said back.

"Oh!" I said back. "Now, I get it."

"Now, I get it! Now, I get it! Now, I get it!" my little sister said. She had dough in her hair and on her face too and all over her clothes. She was licking her fingers and putting them in the dough. Which Charly then took away from her and started rolling out for another batch of doughnuts.

By eight o'clock, we had cooked about two dozen doughnuts. Which Charly sprinkled with powdery sugar and put on a plate that I got her from on top of the cabinet in the kitchen. I had to get all the way up and stand on the counter to reach it. But she was busy with my baby brother and didn't see me. She might have fainted.

So, a little after that, Charly came back into the kitchen where my little sister was still eating too many doughnuts, holes and all. Charly didn't make her eat any supper. No soup for her. No sandwhich either. Just cookies before supper and doughnuts after. I knew she was going to be sick. So, I knew she was going to cry. Which she does a lot anyways. At least she was going to have a belly ache to blame this time.

As for me, I ate everything. Except just a little of everything. One cookie, one bowl of soup, one peanut butter sandwhich, and one doughnut. Which was not nearly as good as Picou's doughnuts. Not nearly! Even if I didn't tell Charly.

Then two things happened to ruin what was a great Friday night.

First, Charly said she looked in the newspapers and the Notre Dame movie was not about a football team at a school somewheres but instead was about a church someplace called Paris. Which is in France. I learned about that a few months ago in geography when we were studying other countries where people dress different from us and don't speak English as good as we do. Goofy Louie Canale started to sing, "I see England, I see France, I see." But Sister Marianna grabbed him by the collar and snatched it up around his ears so he was almost hanging over his seat from his khaki shirt and wasn't able to say anything else. We didn't see Louie the rest of that day after he was sent to the principal's office and so we never found out whose underpants he saw.

Anyways, that Friday, I didn't believe Charly because I saw with my own eyes in the newspapers about the football movie so I wanted to see on television to make sure that the newspapers or Charly or any of them was wrong. But Charly said the movie was not for little kids.

"I'm not a little kid," I said back. "I'm making my First Communion in a few weeks." Which was true. Even Monseigneur Deutsch said I was about to become a responsible citizen in the kingdom of the Lord. I could see for myself and make up my own mind. As a responsible citizen.

"Maybe she's still a little kid," I whispered to Charly, pointing at my little sister who had her head down on the table and was starting to moan a little, like she was tired or maybe even sick. "But not me!"

"I just don't want you having any nightmares," Charly said back.

"I never have nightmares," I said back. "I just walk in my sleep when I'm disturbed about something. At least, that's what Mama says about me."

Charly just laughed and laughed when I said that back. I didn't think it was funny though. I could get run over by a Pontiac like Jimmy Broom while I'm sleepwalking. I even sleepwalked outside to my Uncle Roger's house!

Anyways, Charly said to my little sister, "Are you ready to put on your pajamas, little monkey?"

My little sister didn't say anything back. She just kept her head down on the table and moaned louder. Then she said, real slowly, "My belly hurts. My belly hurts. My belly hurts."

"What's the matter, little monkey? Didn't you like our doughnuts?" Charly asked. But the little monkey didn't say anything back again. She just kept her head down on the table again and moaned even louder and louder and louder. She was so loud that my baby brother started crying in the other room.

And that's when the second thing happened to ruin what was a great Friday night. My little sister threw up all over the table!

It was everywhere. All the cookies and all the doughnuts she ate. Even all the doughnut holes she ate! My little sister definitely spoiled her appetite. And that wasn't all! The entire table was covered with that goop, and the throw up was even dripping on the floor now. I jumped up and ran through the room where my little sister and I sleep and to the bathroom, kneeled down in front of the toilet, and just waited. I knew what was coming. I can't stand even the sight of throw up. It makes me gag right away.

Poor Charly! I heard her in the other room. She had to get my baby brother first and try to hold him and calm him down and then calm down my little sister who was crying now that she had emptied her little hurting belly. I was the only one who wasn't causing a problem and I was about to vomit myself. Alone!

But, after a few minutes, it was a miracle. I didn't even spit. I just closed my eyes for about five minutes and told myself to make the sight of the vomit go away. It was like the opposite of an impure thought. With my eyes closed, I made myself see the display case at Picou's and I remembered how good the jelly doughnuts are there and how good they smell and how good they look. And then, all of a sudden, after a while, when I didn't hear my baby brother or my little sister crying anymore, I felt like a dope, kneeling there in front of the toilet. After all, I ate my supper. Which was my soup and my sandwhich that Charly gave me. And, I only had one cookie and only one of Charly's doughnuts. I didn't spoil my appetite. Why should I be sick?

I didn't even eat any doughnut holes because the doughnut I ate was from the first batch. I closed the toilet seat and lid, jumped up again, washed my hands, even though I didn't do anything, and then ran out to see Charly who somehow cleaned up all of the vomit in the kitchen plus cleaned up my little sister with a dish towel plus put her in her pajamas plus got my baby brother and my little sister to both stop crying at the same time. I don't know how she did it. That was a miracle too!

Anyways, when I got back to the kitchen, I said to Charly, "Maybe she's allergic to doughnut holes."

Charly looked at me and crinkled her eyes. Which she does a lot. "Who?" she said back.

"Her," I said back, pointing at my little sister. Who was lying on the floor in the corner.

Charly crinkled her eyes again. "What makes you think that?" she said back again.

"Well," I said back again, "I only ate one doughnut and it came from the first batch. Which was the one with no doughnut holes."

"So?" Charly said.

"And I didn't get sick," I said back, smiling. It was a smile like Daddy smiles when he says something smart. Which he does a lot.

Charly crinkled her eyes again, this time even more than the times before, and then she started to laugh and then she laughed louder and louder and louder. She put her hands on her stomach and bended over. "Vonny," Charly said, barely able to get a word out she was laughing so hard, "you crack me up, boy." She reached out for me and rubbed my head. "You really do. Where do you come up with those ideas of yours?"

I just lifted my shoulders and said, "I don't know, Charly." Which I don't. I don't know where I get any of my thoughts. I just get them.

"Run and turn the TV on while I get your little sister and baby brother to bed," Charly said.

Which I did. But Charly was right about the Notre Dame movie. It was not about football. It was more like a monster movie about a really ugly guy who is in love with a pretty girl who is not in love with him but feels sorry for him anyways. I had to put my hands over my face whenever they showed the guy. Just like I use to do when they showed the flying monkeys in that wizard show. Because I didn't know they were just pretend. I couldn't look.

After a while, I went to get my pillow from my bed and I watched the movie lying down. Then, whenever they showed the ugly guy, I just put my face into the pillow. One time when I had my face in the pillow, I probably just fell asleep. Because the next thing that happened was that somebody turned on the light in the front room and Daddy and my Mother were home and Daddy was talking very loud and even my Mother seemed a lot happier than when they left. She is pretty happy, my Mother, but she was very happy after they came back from the Ben Muscles chariot races movie.

"Vonny," my Mother said, rubbing my head, "what are you doing up so late?" I tried to say I was sleeping on the couch. But I didn't. "You have to get up very early tomorrow to go golfing with your Uncle Martin," my Mother said again. "Did you forget about your golfing date with Uncle Martin?" Which I did. "You're going to be his caddy again."

"Was the movie good?" Charly asked.

Daddy laughed and said, "What can you say about a movie where all the guys are dressed in skirts without shirts and the women are all dressed in sacks?" Everybody laughed very loud. Even my Mother. I even did too. Even if I didn't know what Daddy was talking about. "What are you laughing about, Vonny, my boy?" Daddy said.

I don't know why, but when Daddy said skirts without shirts I thought about the ladies at Bruno's. I wasn't even able to help it. I wish I never saw that calendar. My confession is going to last an hour! But I didn't say anything back to Daddy. I just lifted my shoulders.

"He was a big help tonight, Nanny," Charly said. "But the little monkey may have a bug. She got an upset stomach." I liked the way Charly said that. Even the word vomit makes me sick. So, from now on, if I throw up, I'll just say I got an upset stomach. "Or maybe just too many cookies and doughnuts."

I just said, "It was probably eating too many doughnut holes that made her sick."

Charly laughed. And so did Daddy.

But my Mother looked at me and folded her arms. "Vonny! Did you make your little sister eat too many cookies and doughnuts tonight?"

Where does my Mother come up with these ideas of hers? "Oh, Nanny," Charly said back. "Vonny was a perfect little gentleman. And a big help to me too." Which I was! Except I'm not little.

On the coffee table in the front room I saw a book about the Ben Muscles movie with a picture of a guy in a chariot. Sure enough, he was wearing a skirt without a shirt. Just like Daddy said. Another guy just like him was next to him in a chariot just like his. Everybody looked angry. Even the horses!

"Off to bed with you now, Vonny," my Mother said. "Give Charly a kiss." Which I did. "And me and Daddy too." My Mother bended over and wrapped her arms all the way around me. "We missed you, Vonny." Then she kissed me in the middle of the forehead and held me tight. "Now, hug your daddy and off you go. You have to be at Uncle Martin's at six in the morning."

"What time is it?" I said back.

"It's almost midnight," Daddy said back. He picked me up and rubbed his beard on my cheeks. It wasn't too bad because he shaved again before they went to the movies. "Have fun with Uncle Martin tomorrow," Daddy said again. "I'll see you when I get back from fishing. Here, take your pillow with you."

I rubbed my eyes, took the pillow from Daddy, and headed out of the front room through the room where Daddy and my Mother and now my baby brother sleep through the hallway by the bathroom and into the room where my little sister and I sleep. Just as I was pulling the covers up, I heard everyone laughing again in the front room. And then I heard my Mother say to Daddy, "Albert, don't forget to tie Vonny's foot to the bed post. Like the doctor said."

Three, or City Park

Just like my Mother said, I had to get up early the next day. This was Saturday, the day after Charly made us doughnuts and my little sister got an upset stomach and we watched the wrong movie about a monster at Notre Dame. And, especially, it was the Saturday after Jimmy Broom got run over by a black Pontiac in front of Bruno's and wound up at the Hotel Dieu. And now the police are investigating. Right on Columbus Street. Right on our block!

About six o'clock on Saturday morning, my Mother came into our bedroom, the one where me and my little sister sleep across from each other, me nearest the front room, her nearest the kitchen in the back, and shook me a little until finally I woke up. She untied the rope she told Daddy to put on my foot. Which was tied on the other end to my bed post. I did not like that idea when I first heard it. But I was so worn out and tired Friday night when they got back from the Ben Muscles movie that I didn't even know he really did it.

I thought it was a joke when the doctor told my Mother to tie my foot to the bed post. She took me there the day after Jimmy Broom was hit by a car in front of Bruno's. Which was the day after the night I sleepwalked. "We have to hurry, Vonny," she said when I got home from school that day.

"But why do I have to go to the doctor's?" I said back before she even finished. My Mother doesn't agree, but going to the doctor's is not always a good idea. Especially if you feel good and don't feel sick. Which I did and I didn't. "I feel good, Mama," I said back again. "I don't feel sick!"

I don't like going to the doctor's. They always talk to me like I am stupid, in a voice they don't use with my Mother. They say I should be a good boy and don't be afraid and where does it hurt and then, even if I say it doesn't hurt anywheres, before I know it, my pants are down or my shirt sleeve is rolled up and they are giving me a shot and asking me if I want a hard candy. My Mother calls these booster shots. Which I don't like. Especially if I feel good and I don't even feel sick!

"Because I said so, Vonny!" my Mother said back. "We can't have you walking all over the neighborhood in the middle of the night. Or falling asleep in the bathtub in the middle of the night. You could get run over by a car. Or drown. In the middle of the night!" My Mother wasn't hysterical yet. Like she was that morning when my Uncle Roger's wife, who talks in a funny way, came by and said did our toilet break because I was at their house at three o'clock in the morning to go to the bathroom. "Now, let's go," my Mother said. "We have to drop your little sister and baby brother off at Aunt Audra's on the way." Which was only two houses down the block.

Believe me, when I heard the doctor say it, I did not like my foot being tied to the bed post. What if the house caught on fire? My Mother said the house would not catch on fire and even if it did they would come and get me first. I was glad my little sister didn't hear that. "What about me!" is what my little sister would probably say back and then cry for about an hour. "What about me! What about me!" Like my Mother will forget her or my baby brother or something.

But, I said back, "What if I trip and fall because I don't know the rope is on my foot and I fall on my face and break one of my new teeth?" Which my cousin Pia almost did last year with the gate fence.

"Don't be so dramatick, Vonny," my Mother said back while we were walking back from the doctor's office on Esplanade Avenue, past the baby cows' head shop on Bayou Road and then the Triangle and then the house where the black and brown dog always barks at us on the corner where Jimmy Broom got run over and then past Bruno's and then past Uncle Roger's house and then to our house. This was my Mother saying that I am too dramatick. My Mother who was hysterical just because I sleepwalked!

Anyways, my Mother came into our bedroom about six o'clock on Saturday morning and shook me a little until finally I woke up. It was then that I remembered about going with Uncle Martin for his golf game. It was then that I also remembered about the night before and the hunchback and my little sister getting an upset stomach and me almost getting an upset stomach too. But then I realized that all that happened yesterday and today was Saturday. Which meant no school!

When my Mother woke me up, I was very, very hungry. I felt like I didn't eat Friday night. But my Mother said I would have to wait to eat because I was late. I was suppose to be at Uncle Martin's house right then at six o'clock in the morning. After I got dressed, I walked up to the front room to look out to see if the sun was even up yet. Which it was. Just barely. But I noticed Daddy was gone when I walked through the room where he and my Mother and now my baby brother sleep. "Where's Daddy?" I said to my Mother.

"He went fishing with Uncle Charles," my Mother said back. "That's what too much alcohol will do for you." Whatever that means. Daddy always left very early when he went fishing. Even if he didn't sleep a lot the night before. Which he didn't.

The first thing Uncle Martin said to me after I walked down the block to his house, which was only two houses over, was, "You want to stop at Picou's for doughnuts before we go to City Park?" I really like Uncle Martin. Who is my Mother's brother. He's older than Daddy and not as big. But his hands are very big. Very big! And his skin is dark. Very dark! I think that's because he works out in the sun all day. And when my Uncle Martin smiles, he has a lot of teeth. My Mother smiles the same way. A lot of teeth. Except my Mother will bite you if you don't pay attention. And sometimes even if you do.

So, we got in Uncle Martin's car, and he drove to the corner where Jimmy Broom got run over, and then turned down the block to Picou's where we parked right out front because it was very early and there were no other cars like there always are on Sunday mornings after Mass at St. Rose de Lima Bean Church. "What do you want?" Uncle Martin said.

"Jelly doughnut!" I said back, of course. "Please." And then I said, "Sir."

"Can you eat two of them?" he said back.

No one ever asked me that before, so I didn't know. "I can try!" I said back. I was very, very hungry. So, my Uncle Martin got four jelly doughnuts and a coffee for him and a chocolate milk for me. The kind I always get for free after Mass on First Friday because I always lose to Sharon the Roach in the spelling bee. There is a brown cow on the carton that is smiling. Until I saw that carton, I didn't even know that cows are able to smile.

"Okay, Vonny," Uncle Martin said while we got back into the car. "Here's your two doughnuts. Eat them slowly so you don't get sick." Which I did eat slowly. My Uncle Martin started the car back up and headed over Bayou Road, past the Triangle and the baby cows' head shop, and then to Esplanade Avenue, the street where my doctor is. But instead of going left to the doctor's, we went right. "So, what do you think about that little boy getting run over?" Uncle Martin said. He only had one hand on the car wheel because he had his coffee cup in the other one. Which sometimes he handed me to hold while he grabbed one of his doughnuts to eat. If my Mother sees me with only one hand on my handlebars on my bicycle, I get punished. My Uncle Martin's mother, who was my Grandma, is dead. I never got to meet her. So, he does whatever he wants.

"I don't know," I said back. I was worried about Jimmy Broom. But I felt bad. I forgot all about Jimmy last night because of Charly's doughnuts and the movie and my little sister getting sick.

"You think he's gonna make it?" Uncle Martin said. He didn't say going to. He said gonna like the way guys do in the Dick Tracy cartoons in the newspapers.

"I don't know," I said back again. "The stick went right through his arm! And he broke his leg too."

"I know," Uncle Martin said back. "I saw it happen just as I was coming home from work."

"You did?" I said back. No one told me that. I was thinking if even my Mother knew. Then I remembered about the police investigating. "Did the police talk to you to ask you questions?" I said again. "About what you saw?" I thought about Uncle Martin being one of those guys on the TV programs my Mother always watches and sometimes Daddy.

All the rooms in our house are in a line, one behind the other, from the street to the back yard. The kitchen is all the way back just in front of the back yard. Then the room where my little sister and I sleep is next and right behind a little hallway where the bathroom is which is right behind the room where Daddy and my Mother and now my baby brother sleep which is right behind the front room, which my Mother calls the parlor, where Daddy and my Mother watch TV at night after they make us go to bed and which leads out to the front porch and then to our street. Which is Columbus Street. Sometimes I get out of bed when I'm not sleepy, even on school nights, and I sneak into the room where Daddy and my Mother and now my baby brother sleep and I hide behind the door to the parlor and I watch the TV programs from where they can't see me but where I can see the TV. All the lights in the house are off like at the movies. Which is why they can't see me. I don't know why they don't just leave the lights on. But they don't. Which makes it easier for me to sneak up front!

One time I even sneaked all the way into the front room and hid behind the sofa that my Mother was sitting on watching TV. I don't know where Daddy was that night. But I was able to peek around the edge of the sofa and watch a whole TV program lying down on the floor sideways on my belly. It was a TV program about some guy who got shot by a gun and some guy who did it. My Mother didn't even hear me the whole time I was back there. She was sitting on the sofa and I think she was eating popcorn like at the movies. Which, after a while, made me want to eat popcorn too. All during the TV program, which was a little scary because the guy who was the killer had a big, ugly scar on his head, even if it was pretend like Daddy says, all I could smell was my Mother's popcorn and all I could think about was that I wanted some. So, to show you what a dope I am, after the TV program ended and before the next one started, I sneaked back out of the front room and then all the way back into the room where my little sister was sleeping. And then I waited for a while and then I walked back up the whole house to my Mother, like I just woke up, and said "Mama, I just had a bad dream. Could I have some popcorn, please?" Pretending I was asleep the whole time like a good kid would be. I should maybe put that on my confession list. Except maybe not. Because pretending is not the same as telling a lie. It's just pretending. At least that's what Daddy says.

Anyways, my Mother looked at me in the dark room and smiled with all her teeth. Which is like what Uncle Martin does. "You know, Vonny," she said, "would you mind looking behind the sofa to see if there is a mouse back there?"

"A mouse?" I said back.

My Mother was just smiling at me with all her teeth. "Yes," she said back. "I think there must be something back there because all during Perry Mason I could hear something squirming behind the sofa."

What a dope I am! "It was me, Mama," I said back before I could stop myself. I couldn't help it. For one, I did not want to look behind the sofa for a mouse. Not in the dark! And two, I felt bad about sneaking up behind the sofa where my Mother didn't even know I was. I couldn't let her think it was a mouse.

My Mother just smiled at me. "It was?" she said back and then started to laugh. "Did you like Perry Mason?" I just nodded. "Were you able to guess who shot that man?"

"I don't know," I said back. I had no idea who was the killer until the very end when the police put him in hand cuffs.

"Well, here," my Mother said back. And she handed me a little popcorn. "Now, get off to bed or you'll be too tired for school in the morning." Which I did and which I wasn't.

After that, I didn't sneak all the way into the parlor anymore but just hid behind the door between it and the room where Daddy and my Mother and now my baby brother sleep. Although I did wonder if there were any mouses there after that. And the one thing about the TV programs my Mother liked to watch is that some guy was always killing some other guy. Sometimes a lady got killed by some guy. And sometimes a guy got killed by some lady. But usually only with poison or by accident. I don't think I ever saw one where a lady killed another lady. And I know I never saw a TV program where anybody killed a kid. Not on purpose at least. An accident maybe, but not a incident.

Anyways, in those TV programs, the police were always investigating. And they didn't wear uniforms either. Just suits. With a tie. Like the kind Daddy use to wear when he worked for that other company before he went back to work for the government. And I figured that was the kind of police that were investigating Jimmy Broom getting run over and that they will want to talk to my Uncle Martin because he saw it happen just as he was coming home from work. But I was wrong.

"Nobody asked me anything," my Uncle Martin said back after I asked him if the police talked to him to ask him questions. About what he saw. "Nope," he said. "I just ran into Bruno's and called the police on the pay phone and they sent an ambulance to pick up the little boy.

Who was bleeding. And then they bundled him up and took him away. No questions. They just took him away. And then they took the driver away too."

"Bundled him up?" I said back.

"Yes," my Uncle Martin said back again. "Wrapped his arm and his leg in bandages to try to stop the bleeding. And then they wrapped him up in blankets so he wouldn't die of shock and put him in the ambulance to go to the hospital."

"The Hotel Dieu, right?"

"That's right," Uncle Martin said back. "And then they talked to the driver and finally took him away too and towed his car away."

"The black Pontiac?"

Uncle Martin turned and smiled at me with all his teeth. "You sure know a lot about all of this, don't you?"

"I saw it in the newspapers," I said back. Which I did. "It said the police are investigating."

"I forgot about you and your newspapers," Uncle Martin said back. "Well, I'm sure they are investigating." He turned the car into this parking lot in the middle of City Park. Which we already got to. "Okay, then. Finish up that doughnut and your milk," he said. "Then you can help me get my clubs out of the trunk."

City Park is not so far from our house. So, it was a short drive. We can walk to it from our house, it's so close. But we almost never do now because it's a long way to push my baby brother in the baby carriage. Which mainly my Mother does, but sometimes I do too. Also, where we live, you never know when it's going to rain. One minute, it's a sunny day. The next minute, you're drowneded by rain. Or maybe it's drowned. Either way, we almost always drive now to City Park when we go. Which is a lot. Especially during the summer.

It is a very nice park, very big. Daddy always talks about how he use to play football there when he was at high school. I never played football there though. I did go there one time for the fishing rodeo. We didn't win, me and Daddy. We didn't even catch a fish. Even if we had the best ever worms that Daddy trapped underneath the house.

And too, my Mother and my little sister went a lot of times with me to the playground in the park where they also have rides. I like the carousel the best because I can pretend I'm on a horse at the races. Even if later

I may be too big to be a jockey. Which Daddy says I will be. My little sister always climbs up things and then falls down off of them. Then, she gets to cry. I don't cry anymore myself. My Mother told me once when I was crying, "If you don't stop right now, Vonny, I'm going to give you a reason to cry." My little sister doesn't need a reason. She just climbs up things and then falls down off of them.

Anyways, in the parking lot at City Park with Uncle Martin, after I finished my second jelly doughnut and my brown cow milk, there were a lot of men walking around with these shoes on that had metal points on the bottom of them like baseball cleats except much tinier. If a man dragged his feet on the blacktop in the parking lot, the back of my neck felt like it does when Sister Marianna runs the chalk sideways on the blackboard. Screech!

"Why are they wearing cleats?" I said to Uncle Martin. He was sitting on the back of the car with the trunk open already by the time I got out.

"Those are spikes, not cleats," he said back. "It's so they don't slip. You know. When the grass is wet. Same reason you wear cleats when you play baseball." Which I do with Daddy. "But they're called spikes instead."

"Do I need spikes?" I said back.

Uncle Martin laughed and rubbed my head. "You're just the caddy today. But when you start playing, we'll have to see about getting you spikes too."

A couple of years ago for my birthday, I think when I turned six, my Uncle Martin got me some plastic golf clubs to hit around the back yard. No, that's not right. We lived in California when I turned six. It was last summer that he gave me the golf clubs. When I turned seven.

Anyways, so I set up a little golf course in our back yard. But just two holes. Which now I know is very small. One hole near the back door to the kitchen and one hole near the wood fence at the very back of our back yard. I liked to play by myself because I could get some peace and quiet out there. So, it didn't seem small.

Also, I got pretty good at it. I was never perfect. I wanted to be perfect. Like a three hundred in bowling. Or a pitcher throwing to just twenty-seven batters. I always wanted to be perfect. But I never had a perfect golf game on my little golf course in our back yard. I never had a score of two. Which is just one shot for each hole. One shot to the back fence, then one shot to the back door. But I did get pretty good, and my best score was five. Two out and three back. The hole at the back fence was easier because the hole near the door was on the brick sidewalk that was not flat, with bricks sticking up all over. So back there I never knew where the ball would go. I came close to getting four a lot of times. But something always happened and I never did. And I never once got a hole in one shot. Not one time. Never. So, a total of two was impossible. For me, at least. It was perfect, but impossible.

Still, I liked to play golf on my little course in the back yard until one day I hit the ball at the hole that was near the back door to the kitchen and just then my little sister ran out of the door because, of course, she wanted to play golf too and before I could even say no, which I was going to, she started crying, fell down the back stairs all by herself, opened her lip, and then started screaming blue murder. Then, when my Mother heard her and then rushed into the back yard where she saw me with the golf club, saw my little sister lying on the brick pavement on the patio, saw my little plastic golf ball near my little sister's lip, saw my little sister's lip opened up, and then heard my little sister screaming blue murder, she became hysterical and she screamed blue murder too. My Mother, that is. And that was the last I saw of my little plastic golf clubs and my little plastic golf ball for a while. It made me angry. But I knew that it was just a toy for a little kid anyways, so I didn't mind that much. It just didn't seem fair.

"When do you think I'll be big enough to play golf?" I said to Uncle Martin while he put his spikes on at City Park. He was sitting on the back bumper of the car, almost in the trunk.

"Not that long," he said back. "Maybe a year. But being a caddy is a good way to learn to play golf. Even if you don't swing a club, just watching is a good way to learn. It's how I learned. It's how all my brothers learned. All your uncles. We were caddies right here, right in City Park when we were kids. It was a great way to make some pocket change and every now and then some rich guy would get tired of one of his clubs and give it to you. That's how I got my first set of clubs. Not really a set. But some good ones anyways." He brushed my head again. My hair wasn't greased up like it is on Sunday, so it didn't matter. "And it's a good way to learn golf etiket too."

"What's ekitet?" I said back. I didn't even say it right the first time I tried.

"Etiket?" Uncle Martin said back. "It's like manners. It's how you behave yourself on the golf course. When you can talk and when you can't, when you can move around and when you can't. You'll see. You're a smart boy. You'll learn quick enough."

When I got home I asked my Mother how to spell etiket and she said to go look it up in the dictionary. Which I did. But I never found it. Maybe it's a word from Australia. Uncle Martin married a lady from Australia, my Aunt Audra, who lives a couple of houses away too. She talks in English like we do but not exactly like we do. I understand her mostly but sometimes I don't. My Mother laughs whenever Aunt Audra says anything. Anything!

Anyways, once Uncle Martin got his spikes on and loaded his golf bag, with the clubs and balls in it, on this metal cart with two wheels, he asked me to push it behind him. Which I did. It was easier to pull it, so I did that later. Instead of going into the green building that was near the parking lot, we went around it to the other side of it where there were a lot of tables and chairs and a lot of men standing around talking to each other. All of them had golf bags, some on carts like Uncle Martin's, some on the ground. I saw some men nearby who looked like they were getting ready to play golf, swinging their clubs but without using a ball, and then one man who was further away who actually hit a golf ball and then said a bad word that I cannot write here unless I want to add it to my confession list too. I did not see any other kids my age or even any age.

"There's your Uncle Stephen," Uncle Martin said to me. "Your parain."

Uncle Stephen is my godfather and I call him parain, which my Mother says is a French word. Which means the same thing as godfather. He is a very big man, my parain, tall and wide. But not fat. Just big. He is older than Daddy and even older than Uncle Martin. Whenever I see him, he always kisses me on my cheeks and then rubs his whiskers on them and then gives me whatever change he has in his pockets. Nobody else does any of those things to me. Not even one of them. But my parain does all three all the time!

"Vonny! My boy!" my parain said to me. And all of the men back there stared at him. He has a loud voice.

One of the men nearby said, "Quiet, please," and pointed to a man getting ready to hit a golf ball a little ways away.

"Come and give us a kiss, Vonny," my parain said, this time not so out loud. "You know you'll never be too old to kiss your parain. We're French. We kiss each other. Even us men. It's what we do. We're not like these Americans. Don't ever tell me you're too old to give your parain a kiss." Which is what he said every single time I saw him. While he was rubbing his whiskers on my cheek. "You're lucky I shaved this morning, Vonny. So, how's your mother?"

"She's okay," I said back.

"I'm her parain too, you know," he said back. Which is true. I have the same godfather as my Mother. Which is her brother and my uncle. He has big hands too, my parain. He reached into his pockets and said, "So, let's see what we have here for Vonny today. Oh, no! Not so good for you, Vonny. I'm broke. Not even a penny. Oh, well. Shake my hand anyways so I can see how you're going to say hello to everyone else but your parain." Which I did. "Give me the firm grip, Vonny." And then he tugged me in again and gave me more kisses and squeezed me until I thought my eyes were going to pop out of my head.

"Hey, Stephen," Uncle Martin said. "How are you doing?"

My parain kissed Uncle Martin too and hugged him. "Hey, Black!" he said. Why he calls Uncle Martin that I don't know. Then he looked at me and said, "It's what we do. He's my brother. You see?" I just nodded.

Then my Uncle Charles walked up. My other Uncle Charles. Which is not the one who went to the movies with Daddy and my Mother on the night before and was fishing with Daddy just then. This Uncle Charles is my Mother's brother. He is the smallest of my uncles. He's not too tall. About the same size as Uncle Martin, but he's very skinny. Very, very skinny. But, like my parain, and like Uncle Martin, his hands are big. And his eyes are very blue. Very, very blue. Almost as blue as my Mother's eyes. Sometimes when I look at my Uncle Charles, if I just look at his eyes, I think he has the same ones as her. "Hey, Charlie," Uncle Martin said. "How are you doing?"

My Uncle Charles rubbed my head. "So what's Vonny doing along today? You ready to play?" he laughed.

"I'm going to caddy for Uncle Martin," I said back.

"Caddy? Is that right? And what about me? Why aren't you my caddy today?" Uncle Charles said back.

"Because Uncle Martin asked me first," I said back, and I smiled when I said it back. Which made all three of them laugh at me.

"Smart kid," Uncle Martin said.

"How's your mother?" Uncle Charles asked.

"Good," I said.

"Still the prettiest girl in the neighborhood?" he said back.

I didn't know what to say. I just nodded. I think my Mother is very pretty. But I don't ever say it. The other kids would brain me!

"So where's the other one?" Uncle Stephen said.

"He'll be along," Uncle Martin said back. "He moved again. Out to Gentilly now. Left the neighborhood. And I think Maggy is pregnant again. Or maybe not." Pregnant is when you're going to have a baby. Or at least a lady is. My Mother was pregnant last year until my baby brother was born in January. Which was a few weeks ago.

"Well, we're up at seven ten," Uncle Stephen said, "so he'd better get a move on."

Just then, my Uncle Gauthier walked out of the green building that we walked around. Uncle Stephen, my parain, noticed him first. "Hey, Black!" he called out to him. Uncle Stephen calls Uncle Gauthier that too. And then someone told him to be quiet again. He's got a big voice, my parain. "You're not suppose to walk through there with your spikes on, you know," he said in a lower voice, like before. Uncle Gauthier just lifted his shoulders up and smiled. Except the way he does. My Uncle Gauthier is half like Uncle Charles and half like Uncle Martin. The half like Uncle Charles is that he is very skinny and he has a lot of very black hair that he combs with a lot of grease in it. The half like Uncle Martin is that he has these marks on his face from the chicken pox, my Mother says, or something she calls acme, which I don't even know what it is, and also he smiles a lot when he talks. Except Uncle Gauthier doesn't show his teeth the way Uncle Martin does. His mouth just curves up at the ends and his eyes twinkle. That's how I know Uncle Gauthier is smiling. And he's like Uncle Martin because he has dark skin, brown in the summer, just like me and Daddy. Also, Uncle Gauthier is younger than my other uncles, and he wears very baggy pants that flop around when he walks. He always looks relaxed. And he hardly talks.

"Don't worry," Uncle Gauthier said to my parain, "I don't think the wax on the floor in there did my spikes any harm." Then he smiled the way he smiles, with his mouth curving up and his eyes twinkly.

A man with a paper in his hand walked over to us and said in a low voice, "You gentlemen ready to go?"

"Oh, yes," my parain said back in his usual loud voice.

The man put a finger over his mouth and pushed his other hand up and down to say not so loud. "This ain't a baseball game, pal," he said back.

My Mother says ain't is not a word. "Ain't ain't a word, Vonny," she says sometimes. But people say it anyways and sometimes when I forget I say it too. I hope she doesn't see I wrote it.

Anyways, all of my uncles started to push their golf carts over toward where the other men hit their golf balls a little while ago when, all of a sudden, I had to go. I told Uncle Martin and he pointed at the green building that we walked around and Uncle Gauthier walked through. "In there, Vonny," he said back. "Hurry though. We tee off in a minute." From where we were standing I could see a big open, green field stretching down from the place where the other men hit their golf balls, down through some trees on one side and the road on the other, almost like an alley. The field went up to what looked like a little hill behind a pit where there was some sand that was white like a beach, not like the brown river sand on the baseball field at the park. While my uncles walked over there, I turned around and ran back to the green building. I had to go!

But it was scary. First, there were no other kids. No kids at all! I didn't see any other kids my age or even eighth-grade kids anywheres. It made me think about the horse race track where we had to sit out on the rail with Daddy instead of going up to the building where all the other people were. I wondered whether somebody might tell me I wasn't suppose to be in there and that I had to go somewheres else. Which nobody did. A man wearing a hat like the kind Daddy use to wear when he worked for the insurance company for a little while looked at me and said, "You lost, son?"

I didn't know if that meant I shouldn't be there or if it just meant was I lost. I just lifted my shoulders. The man smiled and pointed up a hallway. Even he knew I had to go and by then I really did need to go. Plus my stomach was hurting from the jelly doughnuts. Which was on top of the doughnut Charly made. So, I went down the hall where a man was walking, his spikes clicking on the tile floor.

When I went in the bathroom, it was really creepy. Very dark with only one little light in the corner. But there was nobody else in there. The floor was made up of these little white tiles that had six sides on them. I counted them. The sides, not the tiles. There were too many tiles to count. It was probably really hard to put down all of those little tiles and glue them in place. Especially in the dark. Water was dripping from somewheres. But I couldn't tell where from.

I never really liked to go anywheres else except at my own house. One time I went to a football game with Daddy. Which we went to at Sugar Bowl stadium, which is called that not because it looks like a sugar bowl, which it doesn't, but because that's where a football game is played on New Years Day. Daddy and I went to the football game with my cousin Earl. Who goes to college. While we were driving to the football game, I kept asking Daddy to look at the tickets because I always like the way football game tickets look with a picture of some guy throwing a football or running with one of his legs up high like he was going to jump over somebody and the names of the teams, which one of them was always Tulane, and the date and the time. But Daddy just said back that Earl was taking care of everything. Which I figured meant that Earl had the tickets.

So, when we met my cousin Earl, who is shorter than Daddy, out in the parking lot by Sugar Bowl stadium, I said, "Can I see the tickets?" My cousin Earl just smiled at me and then just smiled at Daddy. "Please, could I?" I remembered to say.

But all my cousin Earl said back was, "I got a friend."

"A friend?" I said back. My cousin Earl didn't say anything else and just smiled at me again. He smiles a lot anyways. A friend? Which I still don't understand. I have a friend too. Like Jimmy Broom. And Lenny Mahoney. But what does that have to do with looking at football tickets?

So, we started walking toward the stadium where as we got closer there were more and more people and then a lot more people and then even, if you ask me, too many people. Like it is on Mardi Gras day when it seems like the whole world is on Canal Street. And we were all bunched up with everybody else and not moving very fast and just shuffling along and all I was able to see was people's belts in front of me and the white stadium lights in the black sky above us. Daddy was holding my hand so I didn't get lost and even maybe kidnapped like some kid I watched about on a TV program. I don't want to be kidnapped because I like being home with Daddy and my Mother. Except when my little sister is crying.

Anyways, we were taking little tiny steps in the crowd and my cousin Earl was in front of us and Daddy was holding my hand. When we got closer and hardly moving at all, there was a man taking tickets from people and tearing them in half and handing back a half ticket to everybody before they walked into the stadium. I kept waiting for my cousin Earl to pull the tickets out of his pocket. But when we got up to the man, my cousin Earl just shook his hand and the man pretended to hand Earl back half a ticket. But really, the man just gave him back nothing!

"These two are with me," my cousin Earl told the man and the man then pretended to hand us back half a ticket too. Daddy even pretended to put the half a ticket in his pocket. I still don't know even if Earl gave him any tickets.

At halftime of the football game, I had to go. Which I told Daddy. I didn't like that bathroom at all. There were a thousand men in there all making a lot of noise, standing in line to go, some of them drinking beer, and everybody laughing and loud. I asked Daddy if there was some other bathroom where I could go by myself but he said back, "This is all there is, Vonny, my boy. It's all we have." But when I got up to the front of the line and was standing there with my zipper open and all these guys standing behind me and making noise and standing in line and drinking beer and laughing and loud, I started thinking that they were all looking at me while I was trying to go and it made me nervous and finally I realized I couldn't even go!

So, I zipped up my pants and turned around and went back to Daddy. Who made me wash my hands. When we were walking back to where my cousin Earl was sitting, I told Daddy that I wasn't able to go because there were too many people. "You know what that means, Vonny, my boy?" Daddy said back. I just shook my head. "It means you really didn't have to go." But which I did! Daddy took me back later in the middle of the game when there weren't so many people there and I was about to go on myself.

But that's what I was thinking about in the bathroom at the golf course in City Park while I was going and I could hear somebody's spikes behind me clicking on the little white tiles. So, I hurried up, like Uncle Martin said, and washed my hands, and then ran out the green building to where I saw all of my uncles standing around. There was another man there who said to me when I got back, "Hey, kid. No running."

My parain and Uncle Martin were standing over in front of the green field and each of them was holding a golf club and getting ready to hit a golf ball toward the little hill. They didn't see me because I was standing behind my Uncle Charles and Uncle Gauthier. Who were talking to the man who said "Hey, kid," about was it busy and what a nice day it was. Which my Mother calls small talk because it doesn't really matter whether it was busy or if it was a nice day.

But I could hear my parain and my Uncle Martin talking where they were too and they didn't know I was there. Which I was. And they were not talking about small talk.

"The cop told me the guy was drinking before he hit the kid," Uncle Martin said.

"Drinking a lot?" my parain said back.

"Enough. They arrested him right away and then had his car towed later in the afternoon."

"How bad off is the kid?" my parain asked.

"I couldn't tell," Uncle Martin said back. "There was blood everywhere and the kid was screaming blue murder." Which I would do too if I had a broken stick in my arm and a broken leg. "I wanted to go over there, but instead I ran into Bruno's to call the cops and by the time I got back he was surrounded by a crowd of people."

"What was he doing in the street anyways?"

"Stickball," Uncle Martin said back. "What else? Which is how he got a broom handle stuck in his forearm. Poor kid. And a broken leg to boot."

"He's lucky he's not dead," my parain said.

"Well," my Uncle Martin said back, and he lowered his voice but not enough where I didn't hear him, "I'll tell you, Brother, the car didn't even try to slow down while the kid was crossing over and it almost looked like the guy went out of his way to try to hit the kid."

"No!" My parain looked shocked. "Really?"

"It did. I saw it with my own two eyes." Which is the only way to see anything anyways. "The car turned closer to the curb where Bruno's is than he had to. He could have been out wider to miss the kid when he was turning left off Dorgenois. But he didn't. I tell you. It looked to me like, I felt like he tried to hit the kid."

"Did you tell the cop?"

"What could I tell him?" my Uncle Martin said back. "That it wasn't an accident?"

"You know the guy?"

"What guy?"

"The driver?" my parain said back.

"Of course not! Where would I know that guy from?"

"He's not from the neighborhood?"

"I don't know where he's from," my Uncle Martin said back. "Never seen him."

"Maybe you should call the cops and tell them," my parain said back.

"But it was only a feeling," Uncle Martin said back. "When I saw the guy didn't swerve. Why didn't he swerve? And the guy is already in a lot of trouble. He's in jail."

"But what if the kid dies?" my parain asked.

My Uncle Martin just shook his head. "He's at the Hotel Dieu," is all he said back. "I'll wait and see what happens."

"Okay, fellows," the man standing by my other two uncles said. "It's your turn. Let's get up to the first tee, please." It sounded like it was the first time the man ever used the word please. And it did not sound like he meant please either. It sounded like he just meant get up to the first tee.

Golf at City Park was not at all like golf in my back yard on Columbus Street. In the back yard, I only had two holes, like I said, one by the fence and one by the back door to the kitchen. I just hit the ball back to the fence, then hit it back to the door over and over again until it was boring or maybe my little sister came out and ended my peace and quiet. Golf at City Park never went to the same place more than once. Every hole is different and there are eighteen of them. That's right. Eighteen holes! So, it didn't take just a little while to play. In fact, it took all morning long and my uncles didn't even let me swing a club. I asked to play just one hole. But my uncles, every single one of them, said that wouldn't be a good idea because there were people in back of us. I didn't mind if there were people in back of us. It's not like in the bathroom. But I minded a lot that I was just the caddy and couldn't even play golf. Which they didn't let me.

After a while, Uncle Martin saw I was a tired and tried to pep me up. "Let's go, Vonny," he said. "If you keep up, I promise I'll take you to the driving range after work one day this week." I don't even know what that means. I'm too little to drive. I couldn't even see over the wheel without a booster seat. But by the way my Uncle Martin smiled at me when he said it, with all of his teeth showing like the way he always smiles, that made me know whatever taking me to the driving range was, he thought it was good. So, it must be.

Anyways, all my uncles are pretty good at golf. They hit the ball a long ways and it goes straight in the green grass in front of us. At least all of them except my Uncle Gauthier. His ball was under some trees some of the time. In fact, his ball was under a lot of trees a lot of the time. He would swing his club, the ball would head straight for the trees, my Uncle Gauthier would say a bad word or two, and then everybody would laugh. Except for my Uncle Gauthier. And, guess who got to go and look for the missing golf ball?

In a way, and maybe only because I did it a lot, it's fun to look for golf balls in the trees. Except my Uncle Martin always says to be sure to take a golf club and shake it around on the ground in front of me just in case there is a snake there. The idea is to warn the snake so it goes away. Because if it doesn't go away, then guess who got to be bit by a snake? And I don't really like snakes or even the idea that there are snakes under the trees where the golf ball is. But except for the snakes and except for golf balls being made out of some rubber stuff, looking for a golf ball in the trees is a little like an Easter egg hunt. Which I like a lot. Except when I find a golf ball, I don't want to eat it.

One other time I went to City Park with my Uncle Martin because he had a golf match. Which is when there are two golfers and they play to see who's better. Like a boxing match, except no punches. Anyways, the other man hit his ball into the same trees where my Uncle Gauthier was hitting his ball all day. And just like Saturday, guess who got to go and look for that ball? It was my first time being a golf caddy for my Uncle Martin and I knew some of the etiket rules. But I didn't know about the rule that you're not suppose to pick up anybody's golf ball. So, when I found the other man's golf ball and picked it up and said, "Here it is," instead of everybody saying, "Hey, thanks a lot!" my Uncle Martin and the other man just stared at me, then at each other, then at me again, and then at each other again. For about a minute. Back and forth.

"You lose the hole," the other man finally said to my Uncle Martin. "Your caddy touched your opponent's golf ball. In fact, he's holding my golf ball." I dropped the ball right then and there. I thought my Uncle Martin was going to be upset. But he wasn't. He just explained I wasn't suppose to touch any of the golf balls when I find them. Just let everybody know where they are. Which I did. All that afternoon. And my Uncle Martin won anyways and after only fifteen holes too.

So, when I was looking for my Uncle Gauthier's golf ball under the trees, I knew better than to pick it up and I just called out to everybody where it was. This went on all morning. Then after the ninth hole, my Uncle Stephen, my parain, said, "Fifty-two for Black, forty-five Charlie, forty-three Black, and forty-two for me," and he pointed at my Uncle Gauthier the first time he said black and at my Uncle Martin the second time he said black.

"I thought I had a forty-two," my Uncle Martin said.

"Nope," my parain said back, "I got you down here with five, five, six, three, four, five, six, four, four. Forty-three."

My Uncle Martin asked to see the scorecard. "Uncle Martin," I said. I tapped his arm. Which is skinny and dark like mine. Not with a lot of muscles like Daddy.

"Just a minute, Vonny," he said back, "I want to look at this scorecard." Which he did. And then he said, "Bogey, par, double bogey, birdie, bogey, bogey, bogey, par, bogey." Whatever that means. "That's what I had."

"But that makes forty-two," I said to my parain. All of my uncles stared at me when I said that. So, I said, "Two sixes and a three make fifteen, three fives make fifteen, which is thirty, and then three fours make twelve, which makes forty-two total." Then they all stared at me even harder.

"Where did he come from?" my Uncle Gauthier said after a while. "I mean, boy, where did you come from?" he said again. His eyes were twinkly.

"Give me that card, Black," my parain said to my Uncle Martin. Which he did. Then he counted up the numbers again and said, "That little rat is right!" My uncles all laughed.

"How did you come up with that, Vonny?" my Uncle Charles said.

I just moved my shoulders up and down and then said back, "I don't know." Which I don't. It's like when I think something. I just think it. It's the same way with numbers. I just add them up when I hear them. I can't help it. Except I don't ever have to put adding up numbers on my confession list.

Then my Uncle Martin rubbed my head and said, "You're a great caddy, Vonny. Keeping my score in your head."

"And Parain has a forty-three," I said again. "Not forty-two like he said."

"You little rat!" my parain yelled, and he came up to me and started to tickle my ribs. I couldn't get away. "How do you figure I had a forty-three?" And then, while I was laughing because he was tickling me, I told him how I figured it out, calling out his score on each hole and then multiplying the number of fours and the fives and then adding them and then adding the threes and the sixes to them for the total. Which was forty-three.

"He's right again!" my Uncle Martin said. Because he was looking at the scores again and checking the numbers.

"What did I have?" my Uncle Charles said.

"Same as Parain already said," I said back. "Forty-five." And I called out his scores too. And how I added them. And then I did the same for Uncle Gauthier. Whose score was fifty-two, like my parain said to begin with. Everything was in my head. Every single shot.

"How much are you paying this boy?" my parain said to my Uncle Martin.

"To tell the truth," my Uncle Martin said back, "I wasn't planning to pay him anything. Except for the two doughnuts he ate this morning. But I guess I'll have to pay him at least a quarter now that's he caught you trying to cheat us."

All of my uncles laughed. My Uncle Gauthier said, "Where did Irene find this kid?" Who is my Mother.

Then my Uncle Charles walked over to me and put his hand on my shoulder. "Next time we're in town, Vonny, you're going to be my caddy. I'll pay you fifty cents."

All of my uncles laughed again. "Well, gentlemen," my parain said back. "We have nine more holes of work to do." He tossed the scorecard into the trash can on the next hole. "We won't need this though. Vonny here is going to keep all of our scores in his head." Which I did.

Some of the golf holes were very long and others were not so long. While we were walking, my Uncle Martin explained to me that some were par threes and others were par fours and still others were par fives. Which means that you want to get the ball in the hole after that many number of hits. So, for a par three, you get three hits. Par four, four hits. Like that. It doesn't matter whether it's a long hit or a short hit. They all count the same. Even little ones. It's the same in my back yard. If I hit my little plastic ball all the way to the back of the fence, that counts as one. If I just hit it a few inches to get it in the little cup I used, that counts as one too. It's not like baseball where it's better if you hit it far. But that made me wonder. So, I said to my Uncle Martin, "What's a perfect score in golf?"

"What do you mean by perfect?" my Uncle Martin said back. "For me, eighty is pretty good."

"No!" I said back. "Not a good score. I mean perfect. Like in bowling. If you get all strikes, it's three hundred." I saw that on a TV program one time. "And in baseball, if a pitcher gets all three batters out in all nine innings, that's a perfect game. Like that guy did in the World Series. Twenty-seven outs in a row. So, what's a perfect score in golf?"

Just then we got to my Uncle Martin's ball. Which was right in the middle of a pile of sand that was near the green. Which is what he called the place where the hole was with a little red flag on a pole in the middle of it. I never had flags on my golf course in our back yard. This hole was one of the shorter ones. A three par. "Oh, boy," my Uncle Martin said when he saw his ball. "A fried egg." Which I knew then he wasn't going to tell me yet what's a perfect score in golf.

"A what?" I said back.

"See how the ball is settled right down in the middle of that ring of sand?" my Uncle Martin said back. "It looks like a fried egg." It didn't to me. But I eat scrambled eggs anyways. Egg juice gives me an upset stomach. "Well, Caddy," he said. "Let me have that sand wedge." Which almost sounds like sandwhich to me. So I smile whenever my Uncle Martin says it.

"Here's your sandwhich," I said back while I was handing him the club. I can tell the sand wedge from the other clubs because it is the fattest one that is made of metal. Uncle Martin didn't laugh at my joke. He just smiled at me. He knew I know the difference.

When my parain is playing golf, my Uncle Stephen, he talks almost the whole time. He hardly ever stops talking except when other people are hitting or getting ready to hit. But when he's hitting, my parain is talking to everyone around him like he wasn't even doing anything. If he's telling a story when he gets to his golf ball, he just keeps telling the story while he stands by it and hits it. He doesn't even stop while he's hitting it. Same if he's telling a joke. He just keeps telling the joke while he's hitting the ball and sometimes is laughing right when he is hitting. But my Uncle Martin is very quiet. And he wants me to be very quiet too. And he also wants me to stand in a particular place. Which is behind him. But not too close behind him where I could get clobbered by the club when he hits. But not too far away that he can't turn around and just hand me the club without walking too far. This is part of golf etiket, is what Uncle Martin says.

So, after I handed him the sand wedge, Uncle Martin walked into the little pile of sand and was very quiet. And then he stood over the ball for a little bit. He looked at the fried egg, he looked at the red flag, then the egg again, then the flag again, the egg again, the flag again, and then finally the egg one last time. And then he raised up the club and dropped it down just behind the egg. Which was the golf ball. Which made sand blow up in the air and back at him and back at me too. I closed my eyes and never saw the ball or my Uncle Martin either. But then after a while, I heard my parain shout out in his very loud voice, "Great shot, Black!" I could hear my other uncles clapping.

Just when I got my eyes open again, my Uncle Martin was stepping out of the sand and handing me the club. We were both brushing sand off of us. "Now, Vonny," he said as I took the sand wedge from him, "that is as close to perfect as you get in golf." Which I didn't understand what he meant. "Now, do me a favor, would you? Please run and get that ball out of the hole." Which I did. Out of the hole? My Uncle Martin got a two! I hardly ever get twos, even on my little golf course in our back yard.

After my parain and my other uncles finished that hole and everybody made their first hit on the next one, my Uncle Martin first because he had the best score on the hole before, which is also part of etiket, I said to him, "So, would a two on every hole be perfect score in golf?" The next hole was a long one, so we had a lot of time to talk. My other uncles were walking in front of us, the three of them pushing their carts on the green grass with the blue sky in front of them and us just a little behind.

My Uncle Martin laughed. "Well, I guess one way to look at it, Vonny, would be to say that, in golf, par is a perfect score," he said back.

That didn't make sense though. Right away, it didn't make sense to me. I didn't want to contradict my Uncle Martin. But I couldn't help myself. "You just had better than par on the last hole," I said back. "You had two hits on a three par. One less than par. So, par can't be perfect. If it was, then you made one better than perfect. And you can't do better than perfect. That's what perfect means."

"Who says you can't do better than perfect?" my Uncle Martin said back.

"But that's what perfect means!" I said back. "It means the best. You can't be better than the best."

"But I can be better than my best," my Uncle Martin said back. "Better than your best is something, isn't it? To have your best score? What's your best score on your two holes in your back yard?" Which my Uncle Martin knows about.

"Five," I said back.

"Never scored a four?" he said back. I shook my head. "Well, what if you scored a three one day? Just three shots for your two holes. Wouldn't that be perfect enough for you?"

"Perfect enough?" I said back. "That doesn't make sense! Perfect would be just two shots. Just one shot on each hole. Straight into the cup. Both holes!"

"One shot a hole?" My Uncle Martin whistled and his eyes looked up into the blue sky. He pushed his hat back on his head and then straightened it back where it was. "Is that what I need to be perfect? You're tough, Vonny. You're saying a guy has to shoot a score of eighteen to have a perfect round of golf?"

I just lifted my shoulders. "Eighteen is the least hits you have to make, right?" I said back.

"But that's impossible, Vonny," Uncle Martin said back.

"Don't you try to get the lowest score in golf?" I said back.

"But it's impossible even to just take two shots for every hole. Or just three. Nobody ever does that."

"Just because nobody ever does it doesn't mean it's not perfect," I said back. "Before anyone pitched to just twenty-seven batters in a baseball game, that was still a perfect game."

"Only if none of them reached base," my Uncle Martin said.

"Okay," I said back. He was right about that. "But before anyone bowled twelve strikes in a row, that was still the perfect score, wasn't it?"

"How many of these examples do you have?" Uncle Martin said back. We reached my other uncles who were all standing near his ball. He got to hit first again because he didn't hit his ball as far as the other ones. That's part of etiket too. "So," he said to my other uncles, "Vonny and I were talking about what a perfect score in golf would be?"

"Par, of course" my Uncle Charles said back. "That's what you're suppose to get."

"Wrong," my Uncle Martin said back. "According to Vonny here."

"One better than you ever did before," my Uncle Gauthier said back. "What's more perfect than the best you ever did?"

"Wrong again!" my Uncle Martin said back.

"Eighteen," my parain said back. "A hole in one on every hole. That's as perfect as it gets."

I started smiling. My Uncle Martin laughed. "Well, Stephen, you're not his godfather for nothing." Then I started laughing a little bit. But then Uncle Martin turned to me and said, "Six iron, Vonny." Meaning I should hand it to him. Which I did.

Everyone got very quiet. All of my uncles. And I stood behind my Uncle Martin. But not too close behind him where I could get clobbered by the club when he hit the ball. And not too far away that he can't turn around and just hand me the club without walking too far. Then my Uncle Martin stood over the ball for a little bit. He looked at the golf ball at his feet, he looked at the red flag flapping in the wind a ways away in front of the blue sky, then the ball again, then the flag again, the ball again, the flag again, and then finally the ball one last time before pulling the club back and hitting it down at the ground just where the ball was. A big slice of green grass flew up in the air and landed on the ground a few feet in front of us. But the golf ball went out and up into the blue sky and flew right at the flag like it was a bird heading south for the winter. Except south was on the green about a foot away from the bottom of the pole that the flag was hanging on.

"Another great shot, Black!" my parain said. "Must be your caddy." He smiled at me and bended over and kissed the top of my head.

"Vonny," my Uncle Martin said, "was that perfect?"

I lifted my shoulders. "Did it go in the hole?" I said back.

My uncles didn't stop laughing for about ten minutes.

Four, or The Triangle

I don't know what other neighborhoods are like. But ours has everything in it. When I watch these families on TV programs, I don't know where they live because all they have around their house is a lot of grass and some trees. Like a park. And then there are some other houses on the other side of the grass. It looks a little like where my cousin Charly lives. I mean where my Aunt Gwendolyn lives. Who is Charly's mother. Which is who Charly lives with. We don't have a lot of grass in our neighborhood. Or trees. Except for at City Park or Stallings Playground. Which is where we go if we think about wanting to be on grass or around trees. Which we do sometimes.

But in our neighborhood we have everything. A lot more than just houses. I already told about Bruno's on the corner. Which is where home plate is and where I buy cigarettes for my Mother when it's too hot for her to put on a dress, even a summer one, and it takes too long for her to put one on anyways. And the kindergarden building is across Dorgenois Street from Bruno's. Which is where first base is and where my little sister is going to school next year. And the snowball stand is back across our street again, across Columbus Street, catty corner from Bruno's. Which is where second base is and where if we're lucky we get to go on really hot days in the summer after Daddy comes home from work. My Mother says catty corner is not a word. But I looked it up in the dictionary. So, it must be. And there is the house back across Dorgenois again where the black and brown dog is always barking at us through the fence. Which is where third base is and which is where Jimmy Broom was suppose to hold instead of heading for home and getting run over by a black Pontiac that the police are investigating.

And there is a lot more even than that in our neighborhood. Which is why I can't even think about living anywhere else. We have everything we could possibly want right around us. For instance, the school is just next to the kindergarden in the next block. Which is where I go. The school, not the kindergarden. Which is called St. Rose de Lima. Like the bean. Which is where almost all of my cousins go to school too. The school, not the kindergarden. At least a lot of them. Then the back of the church is just across Columbus Street from that. Daddy and my Mother got married in the church. Which is also called St. Rose de Lima. Also like the bean. My Mother says her parents got married in the same church. And it was where my Mother was baptized. And where I was baptized too. And my little sister and my baby brother too. We all got baptized there. Except Daddy.

Around the corner on Broad Street, which is the big, wide one that Daddy and I have to cross to go to the horse race track, there is the laundry where Mister Lee with the hook on his hand gives you a ticket that has a number on it. Down the block from that is the new hamburger shop that I went to with my cousin Floyd last summer. Which is where I first found out about machines making cold air in a building and about birch beer. The hamburger shop is just past Burdine's on the corner of Bayou Road. Which is the hobby shop where I buy model airplanes and navy boats to put together whenever somebody gives me money. Like when my Grandma, Daddy's mother, not my dead one, gives me two dollars for my birthday. Or when my Uncle Charles, not my Mother's brother Charles who plays golf, but the one that is married to Aunt Gwendolyn, gives me money when he loses his bet on my report card. Or the tooth fairy leaves me a quarter under my pillow. Which is a lot lately. Or when Daddy gives me change at the horse race track that he gets from the dark brown man when his horse wins.

And there is Picou's Bakery. Which I already said is the best bakery in the world and which is on Bayou Road just down from the front of the church. And in between the church and the bakery, there is the Richard's Five and Dime where my Mother made me buy underwear for my aunt, who is a very large lady, and the music store that sells instruments to the kids at school when their parents have enough money to buy instruments. Which I am not one of them. And there is the Buster Brown shoe store where my Aunt Tallulah bought red shoes for my cousin Dottie that were too big for her and that my Mother tried to make me wear to school one day. Which I didn't because they were girl's shoes. Red ones!

I don't even really know why I like all the stores on Bayou Road. But, I do!

Anyways, across Bayou Road from the front of the church where everybody got married and baptized, there is the grocery store that sells eggs and fresh chickens. Which are always making a racket when you pass by. Probably because they know somebody is about to chop their neck. I would probably make a racket too if I was going to have my neck chopped. I bet you would too! Except Daddy says I'm too young to bet. And down the street from that is the butcher shop where sometimes I have to close my eyes when I go there, especially if they have pieces of cows that look disgusting in the meat case. Which is what liver and kidneys and brains are. And tongue! My Mother calls them organ meats. But an organ is what they play music on at St. Rose de Lima Bean Church. Even sometimes they have a whole cow's head. A baby cow's head! A little baby cow! Right in the window with all the organ meats! It almost makes me get an upset stomach when I go there, even with my Mother. So, I have to look the other way. And across the street from the butcher, back on the side of Bayou Road that is a block away from the church, catty corner across Dorgenois Street from Picou's, is the Triangle. Which is one of my favorite places because they make the best roast beef poor boys I ever ate. The best in the whole wide world! And then across the street from that is the Rivoli movies. Which is where sometimes Lenny Mahoney and I go and watch these guys go out into outer space in rockets and is where the lady who sells you tickets and pickles wears glasses and a flowery dress and treats you like a pain in the neck even if you are polite and just say, "May I have a pickle, please?" instead of running up and down the aisle like a maniac. Which is what my little sister does.

We have everything in our neighborhood! Our school, church, laundry, hamburger shop, five and dime, music store, shoe store, cookie, doughnut, and cake bakery, grocery, egg, and dead chicken store, regular meat shop, disgusting meat shop, which is the baby cows' head shop, the best roast beef sandwhich shop in the world, movies, and a snowball stand. And a place to buy cigarettes for my Mother. Which is Bruno's. All in our neighborhood. All right where I can walk to them from our house on Columbus Street without even having to get into a car or take a bus or ride my bicycle or anything.

Those families on the TV programs have a lot of grass all around their house. And trees too. But I don't know where they even buy their groceries. Or anything else. They never buy anything on TV programs. They just already have everything. But we don't have anything unless we go and buy it somewheres. And in my family, I'm usually the one who has to go on errands and get it.

Anyways, after my uncles finished up golf at City Park, they all wanted to stop in the little green house that we all walked around it except my Uncle Gauthier who walked right through it with his golf spikes on. They all had some peanuts and bottles of beer. Which I only had some peanuts and a coke. Sometimes Daddy lets me take a sip of his beer. But not my uncles. So, I had a coke to drink. Which I had to buy with a nickel from the quarter that Uncle Martin gave me for being his caddy.

"There's nothing like drinking a cold drink that you buy with your own money," my Uncle Martin said right after I gave the man at the counter my quarter and he gave me back two dimes and my green bottle of coke. "Isn't that right, Vonny?" he said, and he rubbed my head.

But I didn't say anything back. I'm sure my coke would taste just as good if one of my uncles bought it for me. Maybe even better. But I didn't want to contradict my Uncle Martin. My Mother says I contradict people too much anyways. Which is how I know how to spell contradict. And which is why sometimes I get a G in conduct at school instead of a E. Which costs me a dime. If I did it as much in school as I do at home, my Mother says, I would get a U in conduct. Which is the worst grade you can get. It's what Louie Canale gets just about all the time. But I don't always know when I'm contradicting somebody. It's just like when I think something. I don't even know when I'm doing it most of the time. It just happens.

So, my Uncle Martin and I got back to Columbus Street a little bit after lunch time and I was real hungry. Very, very hungry! Because I only had two doughnuts this morning and my appetite was definitely not spoiled after all of the walking around we did on the golf course. Which was a lot! Even after two doughnuts, my appetite was still working.

When we came back home in his car, my Uncle Martin went the back way. Which is the way that goes down Dorgenois Street and then you have to turn left on Columbus Street right in front of Bruno's. Which is exactly where Jimmy Broom got run over by the black Pontiac and which is exactly what I was thinking about when we rolled over where his dried out blood was in the street between third base and home plate. Some kids were playing stickball, as usual. It wasn't a school day. My Uncle Martin was driving very slowly, even before he got to the corner. So, the kids stood on the side of the road while he turned in front of Bruno's. There was an open parking spot right across the street from his house, which is two houses away from ours, and he pulled in. When he did, for no reason, I just said, "Do you think that man in the black Pontiac really tried to hit Jimmy on purpose?"

My Uncle Martin turned the car off, turned toward me, and then smiled with all of his teeth, the way he usually does. "Now, what put that into your head, boy?" he said back. He laughed the way he laughs. A little laugh.

I just lifted my shoulders. I didn't want my Uncle Martin to know that I heard what he said to my parain at City Park before they started playing golf. "I just heard it," I said back. I don't know if that was a lie or not. Sister Marianna sometimes talks about sins of commission, which is when you do something you're not suppose to do, and sins of omission, which is when you don't do something you're suppose to do. I can explain the difference. But I can never tell them apart when I do them. And all I said to Uncle Martin was that I just heard it. Which was true. But I didn't say where I heard it. Which maybe I should have. But it's not a lie. Because I did just hear it. On the golf course. From him.

My Uncle Martin stared at me, smiling at me with all of his teeth still. Sometimes my Mother smiles at me with all of her teeth, but it turns out she isn't really smiling. I never know when it's going to happen with my Mother. She smiles just like she normally smiles, with all of her teeth, and I walk over to her thinking she is going to pat me on the head or kiss my forehead or give me a big hug. And then, out of nowhere, a slap. Not a slap that hurts, but a slap anyways. Sometimes on my bottom, but sometimes right on my mouth. It's always because I forget to say Ma'am or Sir to somebody or when I contradict my Mother without even knowing it.

I don't know if my Uncle Martin does that too when he's smiling. I mean, not really smiling. "Well, there's no reason to believe it's true," my

Uncle Martin said back. "That the driver did it on purpose, I mean. The police will get to the bottom of it," he said again. "You can bet on that."

My Uncle Martin never goes to the horse race track though. If he did, he would know that I can't bet on anything. That's what Daddy says when we go to the horse race track. They don't let kids bet there. Even with the dark brown man with the crocodile skin who comes around between the races to take money from people standing by the rail knows that kids can't bet. He says hello to me all the time, but he knows that Daddy is the only one who can bet.

"Why would a guy want to run over Jimmy?" I said back.

"Boy," my Uncle Martin said, "sometimes it makes sense not to ask too many questions."

"But we get extra points in class for asking questions!" I said back. Which we do. Or at least those kids like me who ask questions in class, kids who like to ask questions in class. And then I realized that I just contradicted my Uncle Martin.

But he didn't get upset the way my Mother sometimes does when I contradict her. "Well, the world is not like your classroom, boy," my Uncle Martin said back. I'm not his boy, but it doesn't bother me for him to say so. "In fact, it's just about the opposite," he said again. Which is why I am a dope at the house when I raise my hand to answer a question that Daddy or my Mother asks at supper. "Your little friend is being cared for at the Hotel Dieu, and the police are investigating the whys and the wherefores." I liked the way Uncle Martin said that. The whys and the wherefores. "We should just leave well enough alone." I liked well enough alone too.

But what Uncle Martin said made me think about the article about Jimmy in the newspapers. "Is that the difference between an accident and a incident?" I said back. "One is not on purpose, but the other one is on purpose?"

"What?" my Uncle Martin said back. And then he laughed. "Boy, where do you come up with these ideas?"

"The newspapers," I said back. "They said that the police questioned the man following the incident. But, I thought it was an accident. I don't know the difference between an accident and a incident. I thought it was an accident, Jimmy getting run over."

My Uncle Martin got out of the car. He was laughing. He waved at me to follow him. Which I tried to do. But it took me a long time to close the door because the car was leaning toward the curb and the door was heavy and I had to push it uphill. He came around to help me. "An incident is something that happens," he said to me. "An accident is something that happens, but nobody expects it to."

"So a incident happens on purpose?" I said back.

"That's one way of looking at it," my Uncle Martin said back. And then we crossed Columbus Street together. He had his hand on my shoulder. "I guess that's right. But an accident never happens on purpose."

"That's what I thought," I said.

"Well, you thought right," my Uncle Martin said back. "Except it's not a incident. It's an incident. An incident. They teach you about vowels at that school of yours, don't they?"

"Oh, sure," I said back. We were crossed over Columbus Street and on the brick sidewalk in front of his house. "I know all about vowels."

"I'm sure you do, boy," he laughed. "I'm sure you do." But he didn't let me tell him any of it. "Well, say hello to your mother for me," he said and held his hand out for me to shake. My Uncle Martin is French too just like my parain. But he doesn't kiss me.

"Did you see what happened?" I asked. I already knew the answer. My Uncle Martin looked at me again, this time not smiling any kind of a smile. Maybe now he knew that I heard him talking at the golf course to my parain about Jimmy and how he saw that it almost looked like the guy went out of his way to try to hit the kid and didn't even try to slow down while Jimmy was rounding third base for home. Maybe now he knew that I knew that he did not tell the police everything he saw when he was coming back from work.

"What makes you ask?" he said back.

I just lifted my shoulders again. "I don't know," I said back. But I knew that it was a lie. That had to go on my confession list for sure.

"Well, you know, boy, sometimes you see things and are not sure about what you saw. And even if you are sure about what you saw, it's not always clear what the meaning is of what you saw." I don't understand what that means. But then Uncle Martin said again, "My car was moving too, you know. And I was paying attention to those kids too, making sure I didn't hit any of them. So, I wasn't really paying attention to the black car in front of me. You understand that, don't you?" I said I did. "Now, you get on home and say hello to your mother for me."

"I just hope Jimmy is okay," I said back. And then I ran down the block two houses to where mine is. Daddy wasn't back from fishing yet. His car was missing from in front of the house. The front door was locked, so I ran into the alley and went around the back. Besides being very, very hungry, I was very tired too. Very, very hungry and very tired.

"Vonny, Vonny, Vonny!" is what I heard when I walked through the back screen door into the kitchen. My little sister hugged me around the waist.

"How's my boy?" my Mother said. I am her boy. Daddy's too. She gave me a hug and kissed me right in the middle of my forehead. "How was golf with Uncle Martin?"

"He says hello, Mama. I'm very, very hungry," I said back. "And very tired too."

"You want to take a nap before you eat?" my Mother said back.

But I didn't. My Mother always wants me to take naps. Even now that I am big. She acts just like I'm not even in second grade. Like I'm a little kid. "No," I said back.

My Mother smiled at me with all of her teeth and lifted her right hand a little. I knew that was one of the smiles that are not really smiles. "No, what?" she said back.

"No, Ma'am," I said back again. When I'm very tired, I forget to say Ma'am. "I think I just want to eat something now."

"Well," my Mother lifted her shoulders. "Daddy has the car and we don't have anything in the house. You ate the last can of soup last night. You want to run an errand for us and go over to the Triangle for a roast beef poor boy to split?"

Like I already told, I'm usually the one who has to go on errands and get everything in our house. Especially when Daddy has the car and is not home. And even if I was tired, the Triangle has the best roast beef poor boys in the whole wide world! "Sure!" I said back. "How many should I get?"

"Your little sister already ate. So just get a large one. Dressed all the way," my Mother said. Dressed means with lettuce and tomatoes and pickles. "Mayonnaise and creole mustard," she said again.

"What about chips?" I asked. I already knew she was going to say yes because she always did.

"Of course," my Mother said back. "Here's a ten dollar bill. Make sure you have at least five dollars of change. Six or seven maybe. It won't be more than three or four dollars."

"What about root beer?"

If I asked my Mother questions fast enough, she always says yes. She wanted chips. She wanted root beer. "Oh, of course," she laughed. "One for you and one for me. I can never say no to you, Vonny. You're a trickster." Which I don't think I am. I just talk fast. "And a pack of Kool Filter Menthols too," she said again. "So you should get at least four dollars change back. Maybe five. Hurry now." Which I did.

"Can I go? Can I go? Can I go?" My little sister was hopping around on both feet again. Like she never got an upset stomach last night.

I didn't want to take her, so I just lifted my shoulders, looked at my Mother, and said, "What about poor Jimmy, Mama? I would hate for anything to happen to our little monkey too."

"You're right, Vonny. You're a very thoughtful big brother." Which I am. Just maybe not always the way my Mother thinks I am. She leaned down to my little sister. "Sweetheart, it's just too dangerous for you to cross the street."

"And there's the blood in the street too," I said. Which was what I was thinking about.

"Get along with you, Vonny," my Mother said. Which made my little sister start crying.

I walked up through the house and out the front door. Which I unlocked first. I had the ten dollar bill in my pocket. Also, I still had two dimes left over from what Uncle Martin gave me. I could hear them jingling against each other in my other pocket. I walked down the steps onto the brick sidewalk. It is not very smooth, and if you don't look down at the ground while you're walking it's very easy to trip and fall over one of the bricks that is sticking up. Which there are a lot of and which I have done a lot. Especially when I try to roller skate on the bricks. Once I got to Bruno's, the sidewalk was smooth, gray concrete with a line every few feet, all the way around the corner. That was the best place to roller skate on all of Columbus Street.

As I walked by, I thought about going in the back door at Bruno's and buying my Mother's cigarettes there instead of at the Triangle. But then I also thought about the calendar with the ladies with no shirts and about impure thoughts. So instead, I just walked to the corner where the same kids who were playing stickball when I drove by with Uncle Martin were still playing stickball right in the street, running between third base and home right over the spot where Jimmy's blood was all dried out with dirt on top of it. What if the police came out to investigate now? They might not even see the blood!

"You want to play?" one of the kids asked me when I got to the corner. This was a kid who did not go to my school. I think his name is Bobby or Robby. He is bigger than me but not by much. He had a sawed off broomstick in his hands. I shook my head. "You hear what happened to Jimmy Broom?" he said.

"I know," I said back. "He might die. They arrested a guy."

"That guy tried to kill him!" the kid said back.

Another kid who was in the exact middle of where the two streets crossed screamed out, "Hey! Batter up! We got a game here." He was a little kid. A little kid with a very big mouth.

Bobby Robby ignored him. "He never even slowed up." He pointed at the spot where the little screaming kid was standing. "See there! Not even a skid mark in the street. He never even touched his brakes until right when he hit him. Just kept on going."

"Were you here?" I said back.

He nodded. "Right there!" He pointed across the way. "I was over at second by the snowball stand just before the car showed up. Or else it was me underneath it!"

"Black Pontiac, right?"

The kid shook his head. "Pontiac, I don't know. But it was black. There was like this yellow indian head on the front of it."

"That's a Pontiac," I said. My Aunt Tallulah has one like that with this little yellow indian on it. I don't know what indians have to do with cars since they are always on horses when I see them on the TV programs.

"Hey! Let's go," the other kid screamed from the middle of the street. "You gonna play or not?" Dick Tracy again!

Bobby Robby threw the broomstick down. "When I'm good and ready," he shouted back. "So just shut up for now!" All the other kids groaned. There were two other kids playing the field, not counting the big mouth, screaming pitcher, and there were two kids on base. Six total.

"Well, whatever kind of car it was, that guy was aiming right at Jimmy. Right at him! And he got him!"

"He's in the hospital is what I heard," I said again.

"The Hotel Dieu," Bobby Robby said back. Only he pronounced it like d-you. "Hotel D-you," he said again. "That's a funny name."

"My uncle saw it happen," I said and right away wished I didn't say it.

"Did he talk to the police?"

"I don't know," I said back. And I lifted my shoulders. Which I always do when I don't know something. But I did know. So, again, the confession list.

"Well, I hope they put that guy in the electric chair," Bobby Robby said.

"Jimmy?" I said back.

"No, dope! The guy in the car. He really tried to kill Jimmy Broom. You want to play or not?"

"I can't," I said back. "I'm going to the Triangle."

"Where's that?"

"It's over on Bayou Road," I said. "Across from the movies."

"Why?"

"I need to get lunch for my Mother and me."

"You got any extra money? Get us some bubble gum, would you?"

I hardly know this kid. I just nodded. "Sure," I said. But I knew I wouldn't.

Bobby Robby turned to the kid in the street. "Hey, Skippy. You gonna throw that ball over here today?"

I walked across Columbus Street and didn't even get to third base before the black and brown dog on the corner rushed up to the fence snapping his jaws at me, his teeth biting on the metal like he was going to chew through it. Whenever he does that I get a chill on my neck. Like when I watch a monster movie. I get the shivers. That's what Charly calls it. Which I try not to do. But sometimes I have to watch monster movies when Charly comes over to babysit. And I get the shivers. If the other kids weren't there playing stickball, I would probably just walk all the way around and go down the other side of Dorgenois to Bayou Road before crossing back over to the Triangle. I do that most of the time when I'm alone anyways. But I didn't want anybody to think I'm afraid of a dumb dog. Which I really am. If the dog got to me, got through the fence, there would be blood everywhere. It's a very big dog. Even bigger than me. Sometimes I want to just kick that dog in the mouth. I think he's the devil or at least he's like what the devil would be like if the devil lived on Columbus Street. It makes me angry just to think about that dog. It makes me angry to be afraid of it, and it makes me angry that I even think about being afraid of a dumb dog. Which I do anyways.

So, I just tried to ignore the black and brown dog when I walked by. Which I could hardly do. And then I heard the kids screaming behind me because Bobby Robby had smacked the ball down my way on Dorgenois half way to Bayou Road. A kid was running as fast as he could after the ball. Which was a waste of time because Bobby Robby was already rounding third by the time the kid even got to it. And the dog was barking like crazy too because of all the noise.

After he scored, Bobby Robby walked back across Columbus Street and the dog rushed up against the fence, snapping his jaws like he did to me. Bobby Robby kicked the fence and hit the dog right in its black and brown mouth. I could hear the dog squealing half a block away. It was a bad thing to do, but I hoped that Bobby Robby got him good.

The Triangle is called that because it is on three streets. Bayou Road is on one side and the street where the Rivoli movies is on the other side. Which I don't know how to spell the name of, but it starts with a K. And then Dorgenois Street is in the front. Which is where Bayou Road and the K street cross and where the door to the Triangle is. The building is painted all white on the outside. Even the windows on the side are painted all white. Which you cannot see into. Or out of. You can only see through the windows in the front. On top of the door there is a fancy light that is green and it spells Triangle in script letters. Below it is another light that is red that spells out BAR and RESTAURANT in block letters that are smaller. Just like the way I just wrote it. At school, we do mostly block letters, and some kids are learning to do script. Mainly the girls. Who are the kind of kids who like to spend a lot of time looking at how everybody else writes their letters. Like it matters. Sister Marianna makes me write script too because I can read everything she gives me to read that is printed. I think she thinks it's harder to read script. Which I don't. Anyways, the signs at the Triangle are always lighted up, green and red. They never turn them off. Because they probably don't even have a switch.

Inside the Triangle, it's not like Bruno's because there is a lot of light and because there are ladies there. Ladies who work there and ladies who go there to get sandwhiches or to eat other things. I am the only person in my family who almost always goes there though. I was almost never there with Daddy or my Mother or my little sister or of course my baby brother. Who can't even eat sandwhiches. And I always get the same thing. Every single time!

"Large roast beef poor boy, dressed all the way, with mayonnaise and creole mustard," I said to the lady who was sitting behind the counter right inside the screen door at the front. There was a square sign in front of the counter in black, block letters again that said ORDER HERE. Which I did.

"Anything with that?" the lady said back. Only it sounded like she said, "Anyting widdat?" Like she didn't know how to talk. She was also a very large lady. Like my aunt. And I couldn't help it, but I wondered whether she bought her underwear at the Richard's Five and Dime too or whether she made her sister send her little kid to do it for her. It was just something I thought about.

"Two Barq's and two bags of chips," I said back.

"What kind?"

I said back, "Barbecue." Which is a hard word to spell. But which my Mother made me look up because it says on the bag only BBQ. Which is some kind of code. "Oh, and a pack of Kool Filter Menthols," I said back again.

The lady was writing everything down without even looking at me and then all of a sudden stopped and then looked at me like something was wrong. "Who are they for?"

"The chips?" I said back. And then I didn't even wait for her to answer. "Mainly me, but some for my Mother."

"The cigarettes, kid," the lady said. "The cigarettes." She acted like I was a pain in the neck. Which I was not.

"My Mother," I said back.

"She outside in the car or something?" the lady said back.

"At home. Over on Columbus Street," I said back again. "I get them all the time for her." Which I do. Except I get them at Bruno's.

The lady came out from behind the counter, and I could see that she was even more very large than my aunt is very large. "Hey, Larry," she screamed. "Larry! Come out here, will you? I need to talk to you about this kid."

I could have bought the cigarettes at Bruno's is what I was thinking while the more very large lady was screaming at Larry. Which I could have. "That's okay," I said. "Just the sandwhich and the soft drinks and the chips."

But, the lady just looked back at me, and then a man came out of a room in the back of the Triangle and yelled across the room over the top of everybody's heads, "What?"

Now everybody in the Triangle was staring at me like I had a gun in my hand and was robbing the place. Which was a lady in the corner who was with her baby in a baby stroller by the table and who was reading a magazine while she was eating a sandwhich. And also two men in the middle of the room who were talking to each other and drinking beer out of the same beer glasses that the crocodiles use at Bruno's. And also a girl who looked like Charly with a boy her age who were eating a banana split together in another corner. All of them were now staring at me while the more very large lady and the man named Larry screamed at each other from opposite ends of the Triangle.

"This kid wants to buy cigarettes," she said back.

I said again, "No, that's alright. That's okay."

"Do we sell cigarettes to kids, Larry? Is that okay?"

The man screamed across the room at me. "Those for you, kid?"

"No, Sir," I said back. "They're for my Mother." I lifted my shoulders. "Over on Columbus Street."

"Columbus Street? You know the kid who got hit by the car?" he shouted.

"Yes, Sir," I said back. "He goes to my school."

"Is he okay?"

"He's at the Hotel Dieu," I said back. Only I think maybe I said D-you. Like Bobby Robby does. "Broke his leg. Arm too."

"How come you don't buy the cigarettes for your mother at Bruno's?" the man said back. Which was Larry. "It's closer, isn't it?" Except he said ain't. Which my Mother punishes me if I say it, and I hope she doesn't even see I had to write it.

Larry was right. I even thought about going to Bruno's myself before I was talking to Bobby Robby. So, I said back, "But they don't have the best roast beef poor boys in the whole wide world." And after I said that, then everybody at the Triangle started laughing like I told a joke. The two men in the middle of the room laughed. And the girl and the boy too. The girl who looked like Charly put her hand over her mouth like her teeth might fall out like the little girls do in my class. Even the lady with the baby. Except not the baby. And the more very large lady and the guy named Larry were laughing like crazy.

"Sell this kid some cigarettes, would you, Marge?" Larry said. "He's our best customer!" Except there was another word he said between best and customer that I can't even write and can't ever say unless I want to spend the rest of my life punished. Because it was taking the Lord's name in vain. Larry went back into the room. Which is where I think he makes the food.

"You're a funny boy," the more very large lady said to me, and then she walked back behind the counter and got back up on the stool she was sitting on. She looked at her notes. Which she couldn't even read. Probably because she used script. Anyways, she said, "Did you say large roast beef?" So, I told her everything all over again, and then she screamed again, "Larry! Large roast beef, all the way, mayo and creole."

In the back, Larry screamed back, "Check!" But he didn't come out again.

"You can stand over there," the more very large lady said. Which was by a pinball machine that was against the front wall between the door and where the lady with the baby was sitting reading and eating her sandwhich at the table in the corner. The baby was probably sleeping. Because it wasn't crying. Which is what my baby brother does a lot when he's not sleeping.

After a while, one of the men sitting in the middle of the room drinking beer walked to the back, to the side of the room that was away from Dorgenois Street. He went into a door all the way in the back where there was a sign over it sticking out that said, in block letters, GENTLEMEN. Just like the way I just wrote it. Across from the room where Larry was.

Then the other man who was drinking beer with him stood up and walked over to the pinball machine by where I was standing. He looked at the pinball machine like he was reading something on it. And then the man looked at me. "You want to play, kid?" he said.

I just lifted my shoulders. I never played pinball because I was too small. I could barely see over the top of the glass. "No, thank you," I said back. "Sir."

"You're a polite kid," the man said. "You live over on Columbus Street?"

"Yes, Sir," I said back.

"You have a dime on you?" I nodded my head right away. Like a dope. My Mother always said it was not a good idea to talk to strangers. And now I was talking to a stranger about my money. Which was probably a worse idea than talking to strangers about something stupid that doesn't even matter. Like the weather, for instance. What my Mother calls small talk. "You want to go cow with me?" the man said again.

"Go what?" I said back. "Sir."

"Go cow?" he said again. "You don't know what that means?" The man stepped to the front of the pinball machine like he was getting ready to play. "Here's how it works." He reached into his pocket and pulled out a dime. "Here's a dime. You give me a dime. If you have one. I play the machine with your dime and mine. We go in halfsies. We go cow. And then, if I win, you and me, we split what I win. Fifty fifty. You and me." I looked around the room. Nobody else heard him say this to me. Not the girl or the boy, not the lady with the baby, not the baby, and not even the more very large lady. Who was right by us but was too busy writing something.

I just lifted my shoulders. "Well," I said back, "what if I don't have a dime?" Which I did.

"Well, then we can't go cow, can we?" I shook my head. Then, like a dope, I put my hand in my pocket to make sure I still had the two dimes that were left over from the quarter my Uncle Martin gave me for being his caddy. I heard them jingling in my pocket. The man heard them too. He looked at me and put his dime on the glass on top of the pinball machine. "So, what's it going to be?" he said again.

I looked around the room and then at the more very large lady. I thought about my baby brother because the baby in the corner made a little noise right then. And then I looked up at the man. Who had twinkly eyes like my Uncle Gauthier. And then I pulled the two dimes out of my pocket, and I put them on the glass next to his. "Here," I said. I might not be able to bet with Daddy. I might not be able to bet at the horse race track. But I could bet at the Triangle.

"Okay!" the man said back, rubbing his hands together. "We're in business. And I see you're a big spender too." He pulled another dime out of his pocket and put it next to the other three. "Here's another dime," he said again. "So we can be equal partners. Now, let's shake!" And he held his hand out for me to shake. Which I did. He put the four dimes in the machine and started to play, the whole time talking to me. "So, what's your name, kid? I like to know who my business partners are."

"Vonny," I said back. "Sir. Vonny Foster."

"Vonny Foster, glad to know you," he said back. "I'm John Smith."

I knew that name from Thanksgiving last year. "Like the guy who was saved by Pocahontas?" I said back. Sometimes I can't help myself.

"Who?" the man said back.

"John Smith," I said again.

"Oh, right. That's me," the man said. "Who's Poca whatever?"

"Pocahontas," I said back. "Didn't you learn about that in school? At Thanksgiving?"

The man was busy playing the pinball machine. Which was making a racket. With bells clanging and lights flashing. "Oh!" the man shouted. The baby woke up and started to cry a little bit. "Almost there, kid." Then he said, "Me? School? I quit when I was fourteen. The nuns made me crazy."

"I like Sister Marianna," I said back. "I had her in first grade too."

"Well, that's great, kid," John Smith said back to me. He never once looked at me. The whole time he just looked at the pinball machine. Which he was playing. "So, tell me something, Vonny Foster. What do you know about the kid who had the accident the other day? The one who got hit by the car over on Columbus Street."

"You mean the incident?" I said back.

"Incident, accident, whatever," he said back. "The one who got his leg broke in front of Bruno's."

"And a broomstick in his arm too!"

"That too," John Smith said back. By now, the baby was screaming its lungs out the way my baby brother does when he is too dirty or too hungry or too tired or too something my Mother can't even figure out. "So, you know his name?"

"It's Jimmy," I said back. "We call him Jimmy Broom because he always has a broomstick with him to play stickball with."

"Jimmy Broom? You know his family?" Then he shouted, "There!" For the first time he turned in my direction and looked at me. "Vonny Foster, you are about to become a very rich boy. I just need to get one of the next two balls in the twenty slot, which will make five hundred points, and then we'll split twenty five dollars. What do you think of that, Vonny Foster?"

"Twenty five dollars?" I said back. The baby was still screaming. But I wasn't paying any attention to him. Which John Smith was not either. Or maybe the baby was a girl. I couldn't tell.

"You know what half of twenty five dollars is?" he said. "It's over ten dollars."

Which I already knew. "It's twelve dollars and fifty cents," I said back.

"Okay!" John Smith said back. "How did you figure that out so fast?"

"Well," I said back, "half of twenty is ten, and five is four plus one, and half of four is two, and half of one dollar is fifty cents, and ten plus two plus fifty cents is twelve dollars and fifty cents."

John Smith looked at me with a funny face. "I'm sorry I asked!" he said back. "You're something else, Vonny Foster. You're quite a character." He turned back to the machine. "But, that's not a bad deal, right? Two dimes for twelve fifty? Now, hold on a second. I need to concentrate." He pulled on the plunger and let it go. But then he kept on talking. "So, you know the kid's family? The one who got run over?"

"Sure," I said. "Sir."

"Good family?" he said back.

I thought about what my Mother said, about her thinking Jimmy didn't get enough attention from his parents, and about me thinking maybe he got too much attention because his parents were always screaming at him the way the more very large lady was screaming at Larry. Which she did. "I guess so," I said. "I just know Jimmy from school and from playing in the neighborhood. I hardly ever see his parents."

"They live over on Columbus Street too?"

"Right by my Uncle Roger," I said back. "In the same house. Other side. Just next door to where I live. Next to Bruno's."

"The bar down the block? At the corner down there?" John Smith waved down Dorgenois toward Columbus Street. And then he said a bad word. He said a word I can't even write down without getting into trouble. And I would have to put it on my confession list too! "I'm sorry, kid," John Smith said. "I should watch the way I talk. It's just I lost that ball. So, now we're down to our last one. I hope that wasn't your mother's money or you're going to have some explaining to do."

"It's mine," I said back.

"Really?" he said back. Like he was surprised. Which he was. "So, what about this Jimmy Broom? You know what his dad does for a living?"

That was a good question. "What does that mean?" I said back.

"It means where does he work?"

That was an even better question. I don't even know where Daddy works. I know he fixes airplanes for the government. Daddy does. But, I don't know where exactly he fixes airplanes. Jimmy's dad has this big red truck out in front of the house, and it always has tires in the back of it. And there were always these long strips of rubber from the tires in the back of the truck and sometimes on the ground. Which we tried to use to make a sling shot or something to shoot birds with. Or even mosquito hawks. "I think he fixes tires," I said. "In a truck in front of our house. He has a big red truck."

Just then, I saw Larry the cook bring up a brown paper bag to the more very large lady behind the counter. I also was able to see the white paper they use for wrapping sandwhiches sticking out of the end of the bag. The more very large lady said, "Hey! You there!" I turned around, and she was pointing at me. "Your order is ready. You owe me six even."

And then, before I could even move, the pinball machine starting making a lot of noise and flashing. "Holy smoke!" John Smith shouted. And he grabbed my hand and started shaking it and said, "Vonny Foster, you are a good luck charm. A lucky charm!" He walked over to the counter to the more very large lady. "He don't owe you nothing," he said. I was surprised because, until then, John Smith was a good talker. "You owe him, lady. And you owe me too. That's five hundred points on that machine."

"Larry!" she screamed again. "Larry, I need you for the pinball machine."

He was already on his way back to the kitchen. "What's that, Marge?" Larry said back. The lady in the corner was trying to rock her baby, but he was still crying. Or she was. The girl and boy quick finished the banana split and quick walked past us and out the front door.

"Why don't you just pay me the six dollars," the more very large lady said to me, "and then you fellows can settle up together with Larry?"

I walked over and did what the more very large lady asked me to, making sure she gave me back four dollar bills. Which she did. The other man who was drinking beer with John Smith came out of the bathroom just about the time that Larry turned around, and the two of them walked across the room side by side. Except they ignored each other.

When Larry got to the counter, he said, "So, what about the pinball machine, Marge?"

"This guy has five hundred points there," the more very large lady said. And then she whispered, "And he wants to get paid."

Larry the cook stuck his hand out. "Larry Robichaux," he said to John Smith. There's a girl in my class with the same name. Robichaux. Which is how I know how to spell it. But her name is not Larry. "And who are you?" Larry said again.

"Smith," the man said back. "John Smith." And he shook Larry's hand.

Just then, the other man who was drinking beer with him before walked over by John Smith. Who gave him an elbow in the ribs. "Hey!" the other man said out loud. "What was that for?"

"Glad to meet you, Larry," John Smith said. "I hope this is not going to be a problem."

"Not at all," Larry said. "Not at all. I just like to know who I'm doing business with. You come here often?"

"First time," John Smith said back. "We were just passing through, and we heard you have the best roast beef poor boys in the whole wide world." He looked down at me and smiled with twinkly eyes.

Larry folded his arms and said back, "But you didn't order one."

John Smith said back, "We were just having a beer before ordering. We'll take two large poor boys dressed. To go." He smiled at me again. "But first, I owe my business partner his half of the winnings. So, how about paying us what we got coming?"

Larry walked over to the pinball machine, looked at the numbers on it, which said five hundred, which even I could see because they were high up on the board against the wall, then pressed a button on the back of the machine, which made the numbers go back to zero, then walked back behind the counter where the more very large lady was, pressed a button on the machine on the counter, which made a drawer pop open, and then counted out two ten dollar bills and a five into John Smith's hand, who put the five back on the counter.

"Could I get change for the five?" John Smith asked. "With a dollar of quarters too." Larry the cook counted out four ones and four quarters. "Thanks, buddy."

"Holy smoke, Jake!" the other man who was drinking beer with John Smith said. "Pretty good deal."

Larry said, "I thought you said your name was John Smith."

"Nickname," he said. "Jake is what my friend's call me." And then he pointed at the other man who was drinking beer with him. "And they call him Pocahontas."

I laughed when he said it. It was funny. A guy named Pocahontas. Who was an indian girl.

"What's so funny, kid?" Pocahontas asked me.

I was still laughing. I still laugh about it now. I tried to stop laughing, but I just moved my shoulders up and down. "I don't know," I finally said back.

"Here you go, partner," John Smith said, handing me a ten dollar bill, two ones, and two quarters. "Here are your dimes back. Which ain't really dimes." Which isn't really a word. "But they're a lot better than dimes. I bet your maw is going to be proud of you today."

I never call my Mother maw, and I knew she was not going to be proud of me. I put the money in my pocket, and when I did it made me think about putting the ticket for chocolate milk in my khaki pants at school. The one I got because I won the spelling bee because Sharon the Roach had pink eyes like a rabbit yesterday. And I thought about the quarter I got for pushing around my Uncle Martin's golf cart all morning after getting up at six o'clock in the morning. I couldn't even use the ticket for another month, and I had to use five cents to buy my own coke, and now I had twelve dollars and fifty cents of my own money just for talking to a stranger and going cow with him on a pinball machine game in a sandwhich shop. Which is the same thing as betting! Which Daddy says I'm not suppose to. And as a reward for all those bad things I did, I was going to have the best roast beef poor boy in the whole wide world for lunch. With a root beer and chips! "Well," I said back, "I have to go home now."

"You take it easy, kid," John Smith said back. And he reached up and gave me a salute like the soldiers do in the movies. Kids at school do the same thing. I sometimes salute Daddy when he's wearing his uniform.

"You too," I said back. "Sir." And I gave him a salute too.

On the walk back to my house, with the brown paper bag under my arm, I could smell the hot roast beef coming out of the white sandwhich wrapping paper. I held the bag up to my nose. The smell made me want to walk faster. Which I did. I was still very, very hungry.

I crossed over the K Street, and I could see down Dorgenois that Bobby Robby and the other kids were gone already. Which I was happy about for two reasons. First, I did not get Bobby Robby any gum, and I couldn't tell him it was because I didn't have enough money. Because I had a lot! And also, I could cross over Dorgenois and walk on the other side from third base and the house where the black and brown dog was. Which I did right away.

As I crossed the street, I saw a boy on a bicycle riding a ways up the street on Dorgenois, coming at me like he might be going to the Triangle for his mother too. He was a brown boy. Negro is what my Mother calls brown people. Daddy says another word sometimes, but my Mother says I'll be punished forever if I ever do. I hope she sees I didn't write it.

In the dark shadows under the trees that are on both sides of Dorgenois Street I could see the boy's white eyeballs and white teeth getting closer and closer. While he was riding up, he was smiling at me. Like he was my friend at school. Which he wasn't. Or like we play stickball together. Which we don't. Because I'm not allowed to play stickball with anybody. Also, he was whistling a song while he was riding his bicycle.

While I was walking up the street, and the negro boy was smiling at me while he was riding his bicycle, I was afraid he was going to say hello or stop to talk because everybody says you have to be careful about talking to negro kids. There are a few families who live on the street behind us. The street behind our back yard, the one behind our house on Columbus. Sometimes I ride my bicycle around the block, up and around Dorgenois, and I see those kids playing on their street. But there are no brown people on Columbus Street. Or at St. Rose de Lima Bean school either. Or even at the church. And now that I think of it, the only time I ever see the negro kids is when I ride my bicycle around the block or they ride by on their bicycles sometimes. Like the negro boy I saw while I was walking back from the Triangle.

Anyways, I just put my head down so he wasn't able to say hello even if he wanted to. And out of the corner of my eye I saw him still smiling as he rode by me, still whistling. He even waved at me. For a second, I almost waved back. Then I realized what a dope I am. I already did a lot of things I could get in trouble for. Mainly going cow with John Smith. Which was betting. Which I was not suppose to do. And now I had more money than I would be able to explain to my Mother how I got it. Which was going to be a problem.

So, I just kept walking. When I got to the corner in front of the snowball stand, second base, the black and brown dog started barking at me from across the street by third base. I looked both ways on both Columbus and Dorgenois. I thought about going over and kicking that dog right in its black and brown mouth just like Bobby Robby did. But which I didn't do. Instead, because there were no cars coming from any direction, I just ran catty corner across from second base to home, from the snowball stand to Bruno's. When I did, I wasn't able to stop myself from looking at the spot where Jimmy's blood use to be. Except now it was just completely covered over with dirt. It was almost like Jimmy Broom was never run over by a car. All of a sudden, staring at the street, I got the shivers and wondered how he was. If he was still alive even. Over at the Hotel Dieu.

When I got the shivers, I decided to run home. I felt like, if I ran home instead of walking, I could run away from Jimmy Broom's blood in the street, run away from the black and brown dog snapping at me, run away from the negro boy waving at me and whistling, and run away from going cow with John Smith at the Triangle. If I ran fast enough, I could run away from all of the bad things I ever did, and the mean things I ever said, and the impure thoughts I ever thought.

So, I ran past Bruno's, past Jimmy Broom's house, and past my Uncle Roger's. I picked my feet up high when I ran, so I wouldn't trip over any bricks sticking out and wouldn't skin my knees. Which if I do, my knees sometimes bleed. I opened the black iron gate to our house and ran up the four steps. Which are painted gray. I walked across the wood porch. Which is also painted gray. And then I heard a car behind me and turned around before going into the parlor through the front screen door. Which was opened. When I was turned around, I saw it was a black Pontiac. With a little yellow indian on the front.

And who do you think was driving it? Pocahontas. That's who!

And who do you think waved at me from the side of the car that I could see best? John Smith! Or Jake. Who waved at me. Just like the negro kid. And he even smiled at me too!

I got the shivers again. But before I went into the parlor, I looked at the license plate on the car. Which was like all the ones on all the other cars on our street. Blue with white letters. Three numbers, then a pelican bird, and then three more numbers. Three. Six. Seven. Pelican bird. Four. Seven. Four. It reminded me of the golf scores on my parain's scorecard at City Park. Except for the pelican bird. I turned back and closed my eyes just before opening the screen door and walking into the parlor. And in my head, I saw a sign that said 3 6 7 4 7 4.

And then I even got the shivers again. Because I thought about the black Pontiac with the little yellow indian on the front rolling over the dirt covering up the blood on Columbus Street right where it had run over Jimmy Broom while he was trying to make it home instead of holding at third base like he was suppose to.

Five, or Burdine's

Last summer I was sitting on the porch next door talking to Lenny Mahoney. Next door is where the Mahoney family lives. Not the side where my Uncle Roger lives next to Jimmy Broom. But the other side.

Lenny and me, we were talking about the world war and what our fathers did in it and where they went and how long they stayed there and whether they fought against the Germans or what Lenny calls the Japs and what kind of guns they had and whether they killed anybody and whether they got shot up and how brave they were.

This was something a lot of kids at my school like to talk about. One kid's father was a cook on a navy boat in the ocean and the boat was hit by a torpedo and it caught on fire and the kid's father had to jump into the ocean with a bunch of other guys and some of them were eaten by sharks at night. Which is scary! And another kid's father sat in a tent in the middle of the desert in Africa and decided what tanks to bomb and what airplanes to bomb them with and it was very hot for a long time because it was the desert. Kids liked to talk about what their fathers did in the world war.

But Lenny is a quiet kid. Which I am sometimes too. Except Lenny is a very quiet kid. Which I am not. I am just quiet. Except in school. I am not quiet in school. I am not even a little quiet in school. And Lenny goes to my same school, and he is quiet even there. Which all the kids in my neighborhood do. Go to my school. At least, almost all of them. There are some kids that don't. Like Bobby Robby I already told about, the kid who was playing stickball on the corner when Jimmy Broom got run over by the black Pontiac. He goes to some public school. Which I don't even know where it is. One time, I called the kids who go to public school publicans and my Mother had a laughing fit. And too, none of the negro kids who live on the next street go to my school either. Not one of them. But except for the publicans and those negro kids, everyone goes to my school, including Lenny Mahoney. Who lives next door.

Lenny is not in my class. He's in the second grade like me. Except he's in another teacher's class. Another teacher who is not Sister Marianna or even any other Sister at all. Lenny's teacher is a regular lady who is bigger than Sister Marianna and older. My Mother says it's not polite to call people fat. So I just call Lenny's teacher bigger. Which she is. I think they study the same things in that other class that we do with Sister Marianna. But I'm not for certain. For example, I asked Lenny one time if he could tell me his eight times tables, and he looked at me like I was talking Australian like my Aunt Audra does or some other language from some other country.

Anyways, we were sitting on the porch next door one day last summer talking, Lenny Mahoney and me, and we were with Lenny's cousin from Florida. Whose name is Red, like the color. Like a red nose reindeer. It's a funny name. Except Red is not a funny kid. He's not funny at all.

"My pop was in the army and killed a thousand Germans," Red said on the porch. Which is where he was with us while he was visiting Lenny for a couple of weeks last summer. Red's parents weren't married anymore. So his daddy sent him every summer to live with Lenny's mother. Who was his sister. Red's daddy's sister, I mean. "Maybe more!" Red yelled. "Maybe two thousand Germans! Cut their throats right in two. With a dagger. Blood everywhere." Which is scary! Even cutting only one German's throat with a dagger is scary.

Red is older than us. Two years older. But he is still only in third grade. He should be in fourth grade, Lenny says. But Red had some problems in school. He didn't get held back. He just had some problems, so he stayed in third grade. Lenny said that too. When I asked Lenny what kind of problems, Lenny just lifted his shoulders up.

Both of us are afraid of Red because he's the kind of kid who will punch you in the stomach for no good reason. Which I don't understand how he can do that. Even if you are his cousin. Which Lenny is. And Red is bigger than us and taller than us. So he can get away with it. At school, if a fourth grade kid picks on me, my cousin William just comes over and stands by me until the kid leaves me alone. Just about everyone at school knows that William is my cousin. He's in the fourth grade, and he's even bigger than Red. But William doesn't live close enough to us to help with Red or to stand by me until Red leaves me alone. William lives over on Broad Street. Way past Mister Lee at the laundry on the corner of Columbus Street and even way, way past the school.

So, I have to be careful around Red. Who always talks about people killing people too. Like when he was talking to me and Kenny on the porch last summer about dead Germans and blood being everywhere. When he was telling about his daddy, Red reached into his dungarees and pulled out a pocket knife. A third grader with a pocket knife! Even if he should be in the fourth grade. "My pop says he used this knife here," Red said again, and he pressed a little silver button on the handle and a blade popped out. "It's called a switch blade." The only other kid I know who calls his daddy pop is Jimmy Broom. Who he also calls old man.

"Your pop gave you that?" I said back. I said pop so Red would know who I was talking about. I didn't like that Red had a pocket knife. Or that he will punch you in the stomach for no good reason.

"What did I just say, you dope!" Red said back. He always called me a dope because he could get away with it when Lenny's mother wasn't around. Which she wasn't. Around Lenny's mother and around my Mother too, Red always acted like a good kid, smiling at them, opening the door for them, saying ma'am to them. And then when they weren't around, all he did was call me and Lenny dopes and pretend like he was going to punch us in the stomach and sometimes he didn't even pretend and he just punched us in the stomach. One time, I told my Mother that Red punched me in the stomach and he got in trouble with Lenny's mother and couldn't come out to play for a whole day. And the next day, when nobody was around, he punched me in the stomach again and said, "If you tell your maw, I'll punch you in the mouth the next time." Like I said, Red is not funny at all. And I'm a very skinny kid. I don't have much of a stomach. Not like Louie Canale at least.

So, Red started back up. "My pop got hit by shrapnel ten times. One time right by his heart. It's still there! They never got it out." Red kept poking the knife at Lenny like he was going to stab him. Lenny didn't even move. "So," Red said again, "what did your pop do during the war?" I made sure not to look at Red unless I had to. So I thought he was talking to Lenny. Then Red nudged my arm. "I mean you, dope."

Red makes me angry. He's like the black and brown dog across the street at third base. Which is always barking at me. I feel like punching him in the stomach. Which is Red. I feel like kicking him in the teeth. Which is the dog. Like Bobby Robby did. That may be a bad thought. But the commandment only says you can't kill somebody. And I don't want to kill Red. I just want to punch him in the stomach the way he does me. Except without him punching me back. Which I don't do. Because I don't understand why you would punch somebody for no good reason. And I don't want to be punched back either.

Anyways, when Red asked me about Daddy and the war, I just lifted my shoulders up. Like I didn't know. Red just stared at me with the pocket knife in his hand, and I tried hard to think of something to say. Then I had an idea. "Hey, Lenny. Why don't you go first? What did your daddy do in the world war?"

"Daddy!" Red screamed. And then he started laughing. "Daddy! Daddy? You mean like daddy-o. Hey, daddy-o," he said again. And then he snapped his fingers. Which I can't even do. This was the part where I didn't know what to say next because Red is not the kind of kid you know what to say next to without thinking if he isn't going to punch you in the stomach for no good reason. Or even stab you. Especially with a pocket knife in his hand. "You mean his pop?"

I lifted up my shoulders up again. That's all Lenny and me can do with Red. "Right," I said back. "His pop." I said it like I was Jimmy Broom.

"That's boring!" Red yelled. "His old man was in the navy on some island in the middle of the ocean doing nothing. Typing up reports like some girl. No Japs. No battles. No blood. No shooting." For Red, you had to punch someone. Or stab them.

"He was a spy," Lenny said. Except in a very low voice. He was afraid that Red might punch him too. Even if they were cousins.

"He wasn't no spy!" That's the way Red talks all the time. "And besides, your pop was an officer." Red grabbed his belly and laughed out loud. "An officer in the navy! He didn't shoot nobody. All he did was sit at a desk. That's what my pop says. He was like a boy scout at a camp out. That's what my pop says. My pop was in the trenches slitting German throats. Blood everywhere. And besides all the shrapnel that hit him, he got shot three times too." Red kept pressing the little silver button on the switch knife, popping out the blade, and then folding it back into the handle. "Or at least, wounded."

"I think that's the same thing," I said back. I tried to smile.

But before I could, Red was screaming again. "Who cares, you dope?" Red said back.

"But shot and wounded is the same thing," I said again. "Unless you die. And then you're just dead."

"His pop was sitting at a desk somewheres and my pop was killing Germans. So, what about your old man, Vonny? What did your daddy do in the war, daddy-o? And what kind of name is Vonny anyways? It sounds like a girl's name to me." Which sometimes I think it does sound like too. But at least it's not a color. Which I was thinking, but I did not say. "What did your daddy-o do during the war, Vonny?" And he said Vonny like it was Betty or Patricia or Suzette. Red was singing my name like sometimes the girls sing their names at school when they are jumping rope.

Red had me. He didn't know it. But he had me good. I either had to leave or talk. And if I talked, I either had to make something up or tell the truth. I wasn't even in second grade yet last summer, and I didn't even know about making something up. So, I finally just told the truth.

"He was a newspaper boy," I said back. Red starting howling like a monkey. "But he was only thirteen when the war ended," I said again. "Only in eighth grade."

"A newspaper boy?" Red laughed, and he put the pocket knife back in his dungarees. "Did he kill any Japs with his newspapers? Did he get shot with any rubber bands?"

I just lifted my shoulders up and down. "He was just a kid," I said back. "What do you expect? They don't let kids join the army." Which they don't!

"My pop was a kid too!" Red said back. "He dropped out of school and faked his birth certificate so he could get in the navy."

"I thought you said he was in the army," Lenny said.

"You shut your trap!" Red shouted at Lenny. Who stood up. "And don't even think about going to get your mother." Red stood up too and balled his hand up into a fist. Like he was going to punch Lenny in the stomach for no good reason. Like a dope, I was still sitting down. "It don't matter whether my old man was in the army or the navy." If he didn't call his father pop, he called him old man. Like Jimmy Broom does. "He killed a thousand Germans. Two thousand! And he didn't spend the war sitting behind a desk like some boy scout." I finally stood up because Red could also kick you for no good reason too. "Or throwing newspapers," he said. The he looked at me. "Like some baby."

Just then, Lenny's mother walked out on the porch and Red just smiled at her, as usual just acting like a good kid. Which he wasn't. And then that was the end of him talking about his pop. Lenny and I could only just stay away from Red as much as possible and wait until school started and then Red would have to go back to Florida. Back to his pop, the German killer.

But that was last summer. And next summer, when Red is suppose to come back again, hasn't even started yet. It was still only March. But it was Saturday. So, no school! And I went with my Uncle Martin early in the morning to caddy for him playing golf at City Park. Where he did not get a perfect score. And then I went to the Triangle to get a sandwhich for me and my Mother. Where I went cow with a man named John Smith, who is also called Jake, and I won more than ten dollars. Which meant I had to figure out what I was going to tell my Mother when she found out I had more than ten dollars and wanted to know where did I get it and how.

So, even before I left the Triangle, the first thing I did was I put my Mother's change in one of my pockets of my dungarees and put the twelve dollars and fifty cents I won from John Smith playing pinball in my other pocket, the one where I use to have the two dimes I had left over from the quarter Uncle Martin gave me for being his caddy and then made me pay for my own coke. That way I didn't make a mistake and give my Mother back more money than she gave me to go get the sandwhich. Which was ten dollars.

After that, I walked home, where from the porch I saw John Smith and his friend Pocahontas driving by in front of my house on Columbus Street. Like I already told. In a black Pontiac. Just like the one that ran over Jimmy Broom in the incident that the police are investigating. I saw too Daddy's car parked on the street in front of our house. Which is yellow with a green roof. Our car, not our house. Our house is white with a black roof like every other house.

"Hey, Vonny, my boy!" It was Daddy talking when I went in the front screen door. He was sitting in a chair in the parlor with his shirt off. There was a baseball game on the TV. "Come and give me a hug." Daddy was all red from being out in the sun. I pressed my finger on his arm and at first it turned very white and then when I moved it his skin got red again.

"You have a sun burn," I said back.

"I know," Daddy said. "Maybe I should leave my shirt on next time. I look like a boiled crab, don't I?"

I started laughing. But I don't like boiled crabs. Especially the eyes that look at you. "You do, Daddy," I said back. Those little black eyes on the crabs scare me. What do crabs see with those little black eyes? "You look just like a boiled crab," I said again. Which he did! Except Daddy's black eyes were moving around.

My Mother came in the front room holding my baby brother. Who was quiet for once. Where was my little sister, I was thinking. "What took you so long, Vonny?" my Mother said. "Did you stop at Burdine's on your way back?"

Burdine's? What a great idea! I never thought of that. My Mother always has great ideas. Burdine's! My Mother always saves me. Even from herself. What a great idea! I said back. Except not out loud. I just said it to myself. In my head. It was a thought. Inside my head, I said, "Great idea!" But outside my head, where my Mother can hear, I just said "No, Ma'am. I went straight to the Triangle and came straight home." Which I did. Except for talking to Bobby Robby about Jimmy Broom. And going cow with John Smith on the pinball machine.

"Well," my Mother said, "sit on the sofa right there and hold your baby brother while Daddy and I have lunch in the kitchen." I was surprised and I frowned. "That roast beef poor boy should be big enough for him and me."

"What?" I said back.

My Mother said back, "What what?"

That confused me. "What?" I said back again. I was upset and didn't know what else to say. "What, Ma'am?" I said again.

"That's right!" my Mother said back. "What, Ma'am! What's the matter with you, Vonny? You're not making any sense. Are you going to contradict me again?"

"Mama," I said. I realized I was whining. I hate to whine. I try not to. But, by now, my little sister would be doing more than whine if someone gave away her sandwhich that she just went to get. She would be crying all over the place. And I was thinking it wasn't fair to send me to get the sandwhich and then not let me eat it. Also, I was very, very hungry. "What am I going to eat for lunch?" I said again.

"I know I said we could split the poor boy, Vonny. But I didn't know Daddy would be home already. Maybe if you didn't take so long to get there and back. You can have a peanut butter and jelly sandwhich after Daddy and I finish our lunch. Mean time, you have to hold your baby brother on the sofa. Hold him on your lap and put your hand under his head because he's not strong enough to hold it up himself. And don't drop him on his head like what happened to your Uncle Roger when he was a baby." Because then my baby brother would be a disaster waiting to happen.

But it made me angry. Angry and hungry at the same time. Now, after everything I did, talking to Bobby Robby, and two times walking by the black and brown dog which I don't like, and listening to the more very large lady scream, "Larry! Larry! Can I sell this kid cigarettes?" and going cow with John Smith, and making sure I had the right change and in the right pocket, after all that, my Mother was going to make me eat a peanut butter and jelly sandwhich. Which I do not like!

For some reason, my Mother thinks my little sister and I like peanut butter and jelly sandwhiches. My little sister just puts hers behind the frigidaire when my Mother is in the other room. She doesn't even eat them. Not even one bite! She just pretends like she eats them. Which Daddy says pretending is not the same as a lie. And then my Mother says to her, "Oh, you're such a good little monkey." But me, like a dope, I eat them. The whole thing. And then the top of my mouth sticks to my tongue and little pieces of peanuts get in my teeth and I feel like I'm going to choke and when I ask for some more milk so I don't choke my Mother says we don't have that much and she has to save it for my baby brother and the milkman doesn't come again until some other day. And in the mean time, I have a ticket in my pocket where I can get free choco-late milk after Mass on First Friday. Which is not for another month! So, I just feel like I'm going to choke. Which I also do not like. Which is why I don't like peanut butter and jelly sandwhiches. Which I don't!

"I'm not hungry," Daddy said. "I'm too tired. Just give me the baby, and go and eat with Vonny in the back. I'm going to take a nap when you're finished."

"You want me to save you half?" my Mother said.

But Daddy just shook his head. "Let Vonny have it. He's needs it more than I do." Which maybe I do. "He's nothing but skin and bones, this boy." Which I am skinny.

So, Daddy took my baby brother from my Mother and held him and his head up on the sofa while he was watching the baseball game on the TV in the front room, what my Mother calls the parlor, and my Mother and I went in the back of the house, in the kitchen.

"Was it crowded at the Triangle?" my Mother said.

"Eight people," I said back.

My Mother laughed. "Are you sure?" she said back. "Did you count them all?"

"One, the lady behind the counter. Two, Larry, the cook. Three, a girl who was like Charly and, four, her boyfriend, eating a banana split together. Five, a lady with, six, her little baby that was sleeping mostly. Seven, a guy named John Smith." I stopped right there. "I mean, seven, a man drinking glasses of beer at a table with, eight, another man."

My Mother laughed. "Where in the world did you come from, Vonny? You are so observant."

"I am?" I said back.

"Do you know how to spell that word?"

My Mother is always asking me if I know how to spell words. I nodded my head. "Observant," I said back. "O-B-S-E-R-V-A-N-T. Observant. It was in the Reader's Digest last month," I said back again.

"Do you know what it means?"

I nodded my head again. "It means I look at things. I notice things. I pay attention to things."

"So, are you sure you didn't miss anyone?" my Mother said back. She was smiling with all her teeth.

"Oh, right," I said back, and I smiled too. "There were nine people, not eight. I forgot me."

My Mother laughed again. I like it when I make my Mother laugh. She kissed me on my forehead. "Okay, let's eat this sandwhich," she said back. "You have my change?" I pulled it out of my pocket and put it on the table while my Mother was opening up the white wrapping paper around the roast beef poor boy. I like the wrapping paper because it's almost like it's a birthday present. Which it isn't. The sandwhich smelled delicious and when the paper was all opened up a little smoke came up out of the bread. Or steam maybe. I don't know the difference. The roast beef was hot with a lot of gravy. Just like I like it. "You want to open the Barq's for us?" my Mother said. Which I did. I got the church key, which is always on the counter in the kitchen in case Daddy wants to open a beer or my Mother needs to open vaporated milk, and snapped the cap off one root beer bottle at a time. "Here's a few paper napkins," my Mother said. "They never put enough in the bag like they should." She took a big bite of her half of the sandwhich. And I did too, except my half of it. My Mother smiled at me, and I smiled back. "Oh, that's so good, isn't it, Vonny?"

I just nodded my head. I opened one of the bags of chips and ate a few. Everything was delicious. And it didn't make the top of your mouth stick to your tongue. While I was chewing my sandwhich, I was thinking about Burdine's and the money in my other pocket. Burdine's was how I was going to spend the money I got from John Smith after we went cow. Twelve fifty. Burdine's is a place on Bayou Road where they have lots of model kits. It's the one on the corner of Broad Street. Whenever I get money for my birthday or whenever else, a lot of times I go to Burdine's to get a model airplane or sometimes a model ship or sometimes other kinds of model kits to put together. One time I got the U.S.S. Arizona that got sunk at Pearl Harbor and that started the world war when a lot of sailors drowneded. Or maybe it's drowned. I put that one together last year. It took a long time to make, and Daddy had to help me. But just a little. It was easier for me than for him because my fingers are smaller. There are a lot of little parts and sometimes the glue gets everywhere. I needed Daddy to put the decals on when I was finished because I didn't know how to do it then. Which I do now. I could go to Burdine's and spend the money I got from going cow with John Smith on a model and pretend the money was from my piggy bank from my birthday or whenever. And Daddy says that pretending is not the same thing as telling a lie.

"So, who's John Smith?" my Mother asked me when she was wiping some roast beef gravy off of her chin with a paper napkin.

I almost choked on the piece of roast beef I was chewing. How did my Mother know John Smith? She wasn't at the Triangle. And then I remembered, and it even made me laugh. "Oh," I said back, "you mean the man who discovered Pocahontas, right?" My Mother went to the same school I did a long time ago, so I thought maybe she probably heard about John Smith back then too.

My Mother laughed too. "No, silly," she said back. "Not that one. The John Smith at the Triangle." I looked at her and was trying to remember. How did my Mother know about John Smith? "You said that one of the men drinking beer together at the Triangle was named John Smith," my Mother said back. What a dope I am! I did tell her! I told my Mother John Smith's name! And I did it by accident. Not on purpose. "I think he was number seven," my Mother said. "You didn't talk to him, did you, Vonny? You know I don't like you talking to strangers."

"Oh, no, Ma'am," I said back. Another lie for my confession list. I couldn't even pretend that I was just pretending. I couldn't even pretend that it wasn't a lie. "I heard him tell the lady behind the counter when he ordered a sandwhich before he was leaving." I took another bite of my poor boy.

"Was he there with Pocahontas?" my Mother said back. She was laughing when she said it.

And like the dope I am, I almost said yes he was. Which he was because that's what he called the other guy. But instead, I said back, "Just another man, Mama. But he didn't say his name." I just kept chewing. "The other man."

"Oh!" my Mother said. "That reminds me." And then she stood up and reached to pick up something on the counter. "I have a surprise for you." All the talk about John Smith was enough of a surprise for me. I wasn't ready for another one. And not this one! But then my Mother said again, "Uncle Martin came by when you were out running your errand at the Triangle and brought something over for you." She held out her hand and right in the middle of it was a nickel. "He said your Aunt Audra told him he was suppose to buy you a coke instead of making you pay for your own. So, here's your nickel back. You still have your two dimes change from the quarter Uncle Martin gave you, don't you?"

"Of course," I said. And I cleaned the gravy off my hands on a paper napkin, and then I put my hand down in my pocket. And then I almost choked again.

"So, let's see them, Vonny," my Mother said. "I want you to put those dimes in your piggy bank with this nickel. You've got to save your money so you can buy school supplies next summer." School supplies? That's what my Mother thinks kids need to spend their money on. Pencils and erasers and notebooks and rulers. I pushed aside the paper money in my pocket with the back of my hand and reached down to get the dimes. "I can hear them jingling in there," my Mother said.

But then I felt them, and I remembered that it wasn't dimes in my pocket anymore. The dimes were gone! The dimes my Mother asked me for were gone! What was jingling in my pocket were the two quarters that were part of the fifty cents that were part of my half of the twenty five dollars I got for going cow with John Smith. The dimes were gone! It's what I put on the pinball machine to go cow with him. I gave them to John Smith. What a dope! And now all the change I had in my pocket was two quarters. And my Mother was sitting there with her big blue eyes and smiling with all her teeth and waiting for me to hand her two dimes. What could I tell her?

I pulled the two quarters out of my pocket and put them on the table. "Here they are," I said, and I pretended they were dimes. I didn't even look at my Mother. I just kept my head down and chewed another bite of my poor boy.

Then, my Mother said, "What's this, Vonny? Those aren't dimes."

I pretended I didn't already know. "Oh, you're right," I said back. I was thinking, thinking, thinking. And then I said, "I must have switched them around by accident."

"Switched what around?" my Mother said back.

"You know," I said back. "Your change and my money. I must have mixed them up, Mama. Your money and the two dimes Uncle Martin gave me." I felt really bad. Just about every word coming out of my mouth was another lie and would have to go on my confession list. "I thought I put your change in one pocket and the dimes in the other pocket. So I could tell them apart."

"So, where are your dimes then, Vonny?"

"I must have put them in my other pocket by accident, Mama. The one with your change." I call my Mother mama, and when I said it, for no reason, I was thinking about Red and how he calls his father pop and I was thinking maybe he calls his mother mop. But I said again to my Mother, "You must have the dimes now, Mama. I already gave you back your change."

"Vonny!" My Mother put her sandwhich down on the table and wiped gravy on a paper napkin. "Are you sure it was an accident, Vonny? All you gave me was four dollar bills." Which is what I gave her.

"Sure, it was an accident, Mama! Don't you believe me?"

But why would she believe me? Me! Nothing I was saying was true. If my Mother believed me, it was only because I was very good at lying to her. And I couldn't tell her about going cow with John Smith and winning twelve dollars and fifty cents. It was talking to strangers. It was betting. It was lying. It was everything a seven year old kid should probably not even think about. And I did it already!

"Come here, Vonny," my Mother said. "Sit here on my lap for a minute." I'm too big to sit on my Mother's lap now. I'm a skinny kid. But my Mother is skinny too. So, I just leaned back on her knee, halfway standing and halfway sitting, and she put her arms around me and gave me a hug. "So, Vonny. You know you can tell me what happened to those dimes. You don't have anything to hide." Oh, yes, I did! I had a lot to hide. "So, tell your Mother, Vonny. Tell me what happened to the dimes. Did you swap out your dimes for my quarters before you gave me back my change?"

"No!" I shouted back.

"Vonny!" My Mother squeezed me with her arms. "That's no way to speak to somebody who loves you as much as I do, Vonny. No, what?"

"No, Ma'am!" I said back.

But my Mother said back, "No, Ma'am, what?"

No, Ma'am, what? I thought. No, Ma'am, what? No, Ma'am, was always the end of it. What was I suppose to say after that? No, Ma'am, Ma'am? What am I suppose to say? If I say what really happened, I am a kid that talks to strangers and bets and lies. If I say I swapped out my dimes for my Mother's quarters, then I am just a kid that steals. Which might be better than a kid that talks to strangers and bets and lies. But I am not a kid that steals. I never steal! And I especially never steal from my

Mother. I like to run errands at all the stores. My Mother is never going to let me run errands if I am a stealer. Which I am not!

"Vonny! Vonny! Vonny!" Suddenly, my little Mexican jumping bean sister came hopping into the kitchen, waving her little arms in the air. She was at my Aunt Audra's all that time playing with my cousin Suzette. Who is a little kid too.

"How's my little monkey?" my Mother said. And then she picked up the little monkey.

After lunch, I went over to Burdine's with Lenny Mahoney. It didn't take long to walk there and we looked both ways when we crossed over Dorgenois and then Columbus Street and walked down the alley by the church to Bayou Road and then over to Broad Street. When we got to Burdine's the door was open and they had a fan running above. It wasn't hot, but the store always had a odd smell. There was a lot of plastic in there. And glue. And paint. Most of the stores don't like having kids in them. Until all the people in the shops knew who I was because I went there with my Mother, they always just said, "No kids, kid!" and pointed at the door. Like the man at City Park who said, "No running, kid!" The people just said, "No kids, kid!" and pointed at the door. I sometimes said back, "But." And before I said anything else, around the counter they come with a hand in the air like they might swat us. Didn't they know we were good kids? Me and Lenny Mahoney.

But at Burdine's, they like kids like us. In fact, they had a sign on the door that said, "Children 7 and Over Welcomed." Not welcome. But welcomed. I guess it means the same thing. It was on yellow paper with big red letters. And we were seven, me and Lenny. So, when we walked into Burdine's the man behind the counter said to us, "Good afternoon, boys. How are you doing today?" And he meant it. "What can I help you with?"

"We're just looking," I said back. Which we were.

"Well, then, boys, be my guest and look away," the man said back. "Look away."

And then some man in the back of the store sang, "Look away, Dixieland." And the man behind the counter laughed. But not me and Lenny.

"What is that guy talking about?" Lenny said to me. I just moved my shoulders up and down. "So, what are you looking for?" Lenny said again.

"Something big," I said back. "I have a lot of money saved up and I want to spend it all." I didn't tell Lenny about me talking to John Smith or his friend Pocahontas or Larry the cook or the more very large lady behind the counter at the Triangle. He didn't have to know about me going cow with John Smith or what happened to the two dimes and did I swap out quarters from my Mother's change. He didn't have to know about John Smith asking questions about where Jimmy Broom lives or about what Bobby Robby saw or about what my Uncle Martin saw. Lenny doesn't even know Jimmy Broom because his mother told him he can't even talk to Jimmy Broom. Which I can. And Lenny can't play stickball in the street. Which I can't either. So, I couldn't tell Lenny why I had twelve dollars and fifty cents or why I needed to spend it on something big.

"How about this?" Lenny said back.

"Not big enough," I said back. It was some kind of airplane kit. "Plus it has double wings." One wing above the other one. "I can never get the two wings to line up right and connect together."

"My dad says they don't make the wing struts big enough and you have to make your own," Lenny said. I just lifted my shoulders up. This time, it was Lenny who was talking Australian. "What about this one?" he said again.

"It's not even a fighter or bomber," I said back. Which it wasn't. It had Boing 707 on the box. Or maybe Boeing. But that makes no sense. "What does Boing mean anyways?" I said to Lenny. The plane was for flying people to places, not for shooting things or dropping bombs. Like the time I flew to Florida with my Mother to see Daddy after he came back from the war. But not the same war where Red's pop killed two thousand Germans. And not the same part of Florida where Red lived.

Lenny started saying, "Boing! Boing! Boing!" Just like the sound that a pogo stick makes in the cartoons at the Rivoli movies.

"Don't be a dope, Lenny! And it's only four dollars," I said back again.

"Three ninety five," Lenny said.

"I need something that costs at least ten dollars."

"What about this?" Lenny said. It was a big aircraft carrier. I already did one of those last year. I was just about almost done putting it together when my little sister stepped on it. By accident, my Mother said. But I say it was an incident.

"How much is it?"

"Six ninety five," Lenny said back.

"You're getting warmer, Lenny," I said back. "Hey, what's this?" It was a large box with a picture of a man on it. Except you could look right through his skin and see all of his insides, all of his bones. Nothing but skin and bones! And you could see his guts and all these blue and red lines. Usually models were ships or airplanes or sometimes cars. I never saw a model of a guy. And all the guts made me think of all the organs at the disgusting meat shop. It said "VISIBLE MAN" on the box in block letters.

Lenny looked over my shoulder. "Hey, it's the invisible man!" he said.

"I think it says visible man," I said back. Which it did. "Not invisible."

Lenny was thinking about the movie we saw last summer at the Rivoli across from the Triangle where it was always just him and me watching the movies on Saturday afternoon. For some reason, all they show at the Rivoli is movies that scare the daylights out of kids. "But he looks invisible," Lenny said back. "You can see right through him." Which Lenny was right about, in a way.

"But the box says visible," I said back. And I thought about what Lenny said anyways. Then, there it was. The price. Five ninety five. "It's too cheap." I said again. I thought it would cost at least ten dollars. There were tons of tiny bones to put together.

"There's another one!" Lenny said. "The invisible woman." And he was right. Just next to the visible man was another box with a visible woman in it. Same bones and same guts and same blue and red lines. Except not exactly the same.

And seeing all the bones on the boxes made me think about Jimmy Broom's broken leg and the broomstick that went through his arm. Maybe with the visible man I could figure out what bones were broken and how to put them back together again the right way.

"I could get them both," I said back. "Two times five ninety five would be almost twelve dollars."

"But five and five is ten," Lenny said back.

"The two visible people cost eleven ninety, Lenny."

"How do you figure?" he said back.

I said back. "What's two times six?"

"Twelve."

"Okay. How much less than six is five dollars and ninety five cents?" Lenny blinked at me, so I said it again a different way. "So, six dollars less how many cents is five ninety five?"

"Less a nickel?" Lenny said back.

"Right!" I said back. "Less a nickel. So, how much less than two times six is two times five ninety five?"

Lenny blinked again. "Less a nickel?" he said back.

"A nickel?" I said back. "Less a dime, Lenny! If one time is less a nickel, then two times is less a dime, right?"

"If you say so," Lenny said back.

"It's not just me who says so, Lenny. Two times five is ten. And two times a nickel is a dime. And what's a dime less than twelve dollars?" I said.

Lenny just moved his shoulders up and down. "Eleven dollars and ninety cents?"

"That's right, Lenny. Eleven ninety!" I said. Except too out loud. Which I did because sometimes I don't get Lenny. He was too quiet. He didn't always know his eight times tables. And he thinks visible means the same thing as invisible just because you can see part way through something. The two visible people cost eleven ninety. "It's perfect!" I said again.

"Hey, what's going on back there?" It was the man at the counter. He heard me shouting at Lenny.

"Oh, nothing," I said back. There was nobody else in the store now. Except me and Lenny and him. But the man at the counter could not see us because we were half way to the back of Burdine's.

"Well, keep it down back there, young man!" he shouted.

"Children are welcomed," I said to Lenny in a low voice. "But kids are not." Anyways, I started to walk to the front of the store with the two visible people models, one on top the other. And because the boxes were big, my eyes were barely sticking out over the top of them. When I came around the corner of a shelf where they had all these wooden airplane kits with little engines that could really fly if you didn't live in a crowded neighborhood like we do, which is what Daddy said when he told me they weren't for kids like me, and who do I see just outside the glass door about to come into Burdine's? You would never believe it. And I didn't either. It was Pocahontas! Right away, I spinned around to head to the back of the store and then bumped into Lenny, who was right behind me and made me drop the visible woman box. Which was on top of the visible man box.

"If you break it, you own it!" the man up front shouted again.

I was going to say something back, but then I heard the bells on the front door jingle, which means that Pocahontas was coming into Burdine's right then. Right when I wanted to go up front and pay for the visible people models. So, instead of going up front, I said again to Lenny in a low voice. "We have to get out of here."

"But the door's that way," Lenny said back, pointing to the front of the store.

"Shhhh!" I said back. I was still talking in a low voice, and I picked up the visible woman box from the floor where I dropped it and started walking on my tippy toes to the back of the store. "I know," I said back. Then I heard the bells jingle again.

The man in the front, the one who was shouting at me before, said, "Good afternoon, gentlemen. How are you doing today? What can I help you with?"

And then I heard another man ask, "You got anything here I could bring a kid in the hospital?" I knew right away it was John Smith. Who I went cow with. Which is why I was at Burdine's with Lenny. Who didn't know anything. Not about Pocahontas. Not about going cow. And not about John Smith. At least not this one.

"How old?" the man in the front said back.

"I don't know. However old they are in second grade. Eight? Nine?"

John Smith didn't know a lot about kids in school. "More like six or seven," the man in the front said back. "How about a visible man?"

"You mean invisible man?" Pocahontas asked in his squeaky voice.

"He said visible, Mack. Not invisible. What good would it do to give the kid an invisible man?" John Smith said to Pocahontas. Whose name is Mack. "He won't even be able to see it. So, what's a visible man?" John Smith said back to the man behind the counter.

"It's a model of the human body that shows all of the parts. All of the skeleton, the bones and stuff. The boys are crazy about them. Let me show you."

I heard Pocahontas say in his squeaky voice, "I think I prefer the invisible woman," and then he laughed a little like the way Louie Canale laughs. Like a goofball!

"Shut up, would you, Mack!" I heard John Smith say back. Which is rude. My Mother tells me I can never say shut up to my little sister even if she keeps saying the same thing a thousand times and hopping around in front of the TV while I'm trying to watch cartoons. It sounded like they were coming to where we were! John Smith and Pocahontas and the man behind the counter. I pushed Lenny all the way to the back of the store. Which was not easy to do because I had two visible people boxes in my arms. And then we crossed over two rows and then I kneeled down small behind a counter where they had all the comic books. "How much is that?" I heard John Smith say back. I didn't realize it at the Triangle, but he sounds like he has a frog in his voice. It also sounded like they were standing right by the visible people boxes.

"Six bucks," the man in the front said back. Which was almost right.

"Listen," John Smith said back. "The kid is in the hospital with two broke bones already. You know what I mean?" Which I already knew what it means. "This box looks like it has a lot of bones in it. Maybe something else would be better for a kid with broke bones than a whole box of little broken ones." Pocahontas cackled again. Like Louie Canale does.

"Oh, sure," the man behind the counter said back. Except he wasn't behind the counter anymore. "I see what you're getting at."

"And while you're at it," John Smith said again, "maybe something that costs less than a buck."

"Less than a buck?" the man said back. I could hear them walking back to the front of Burdine's. "That's not hard," he said again. "How about a top? Boys are crazy for tops these days." Which is true. Except if you're a boy who lives in a house where they have brick sidewalks and the top spins only a few times and then falls into a crack. Or sometimes your top just lands in the crack between two bricks right away after you throw it and breaks in half even before it can even spin one time.

"Hey, Jake. I had a top when I was a kid too," Pocahontas said in his squeaky voice.

"When was that, Mack?" John Smith said back. "Last week?" He started laughing, but nobody else laughed back at him. Not Pocahontas. And not the man behind the counter.

"This is the one most boys go for," the man in the front said.

"I had a red one too," Pocahontas said. Who is really named Mack. Now, I know.

"Would you like me to wrap this up in a gift box?" the man in the front asked.

"Sure," John Smith said back. "The kid will like that. What kid doesn't like to open presents?" Which is true. I like it a lot. I heard the bells on the door jingle again. "Hey, Mack," John Smith said again in his froggy voice. "Don't go too far off. We got to get out of here right away." My Mother would punish me if I talked that way. But that's the way John Smith talks.

"If you don't mind me asking," the man in the front said, "is this for the little boy who was hit by the car earlier this week just around the corner?"

Jimmy Broom! Why was John Smith buying a top for Jimmy Broom? And why was he visiting him in the hospital? I was still kneeling on the floor behind the comic books, right in front of a picture of a big green muscle man guy. Lenny was sitting down next to me and was reading one of them. Or maybe just looking at the pictures mainly.

"Why do you ask?" John Smith said back. "You're a very curious guy, you know."

"It's just that you said the boy has two broken bones," the man in front said back. "The one you're giving this top to. And word gets around, you know." Which it does!

"You know him?" John Smith said back.

"He comes in here now and again," the man in the front said back. Which he does. Two times with me. Last summer, Jimmy and I went to Burdine's after I got two dollars from my Grandma for my birthday. "All the boys in the neighborhood do. There's two of them back there some-wheres now. They were making a racket just before you came in."

"You know his father?" John Smith said back. The bells jingled again.

"Wouldn't know him from Adam," the man in the front, now back behind the counter, said. And it made me think, who is Adam?

And then I heard a squeaky voice say, "Who's Adam?" Pocahontas was back. And just like me, he was confused about who was Adam.

"Would you shut up, Mack?" John Smith said again. "Maybe I should buy you a top too. A nice red one." At the Triangle, John Smith was nicer to Pocahontas than he was now at Burdine's. He was nice to me. He was polite to Larry. But he was not polite now. And he was not nice now. I could tell by the way he talked to him that Pocahontas was not his friend. I don't talk to my friends like that. "You know anything about the kid?" John Smith asked. "Anything about his family? His maw? His pop?"

"Not really," the man in the front said. "Here you go. He just comes in here now and again. That's a dollar and two cents."

"Says ninety nine cents on the sign," John Smith said back.

"Tax," is all the man behind the counter said back.

"Oh, right," John Smith said back.

I started to think about that. Tax! How much would the tax be on the two visible people? On eleven dollars and ninety cents? I hoped I had enough money because I only had twelve fifty. One time I went to get the laundry from Mister Lee. Who has a hook where his hand use to be. Like the Captain in Peter Pan. And my Mother didn't give me enough money for the tax and I had to go home and get more and then go back to see Mister Lee's hook twice in the same day. Which I don't like to do! I always wanted to ask him if a crocodile ate his hand like the Captain in Peter Pan. Which I read about. And which I saw on a TV program. And a cartoon movie too.

Anyways, John Smith said to the man behind the counter, "Here's the thing. I don't want anybody to know I'm bringing the kid a present, okay?"

"Right," the man behind the counter said. "I see what you're getting at."

"That's right," John Smith said again. "It's none of your business. Here's your dollar two. That's your business. But that's it. You got me?"

"I got you," the man behind the counter said again. Now, he was talking like John Smith too. "I see what you're getting at. It's none of my business." Then I thought about how people who talk good always talk bad around people who talk bad. But people who talk bad never talk good around people who talk good. It's like smart people want stupid people to think they're stupid. But stupid people never want smart people to think they're smart. I don't know why I was thinking that while John Smith and the man behind the counter were talking about Jimmy Broom and Lenny was reading a comic book and I was hiding right next to him by the shelves in the back of Burdine's. It just popped into my head.

The bells on the front door jingled again. "Thank you for your business, gentlemen," the man behind the counter said.

Then I heard John Smith say, "Right. See you." And then the door closed.

The man behind the counter said, "What a couple of nut jobs." I don't know what that means.

"Lenny," I said in a low voice. "Let's get out of here." But Lenny didn't move. He just kept on reading his comic book. I leaned my head down low, almost with my ear on the floor, and I saw the comic book cover that had a picture on it of a boy eating an apple and two boys painting a fence and said the ventures of Tom Sawyer. "What's that about?" I said again. But Lenny didn't say anything back. "I'm leaving, Lenny. I have to be back before dark." But Lenny still didn't say anything back. "My Mother said I have to be back before dark, Lenny!" So, I just got up off the floor, brushed off the bottom of my dungarees so my Mother didn't see any dirt when I got back home, and then I just left him there reading about Tom Sawyer. Whoever that is.

"You find what you need?" the man behind the counter said when I walked up to the front of the store trying to carry the two visible people boxes. They weren't too heavy for me but they were big. I could barely get them up on the counter, so the man had to help me. Which he did. "Here," he said. "I'll get those for you." And he did. He put them on the counter. Right behind him there was a shelf with a bunch of red tops. There was a sign that said, "Tops" and then right below it "99 cents". I never noticed it before. It was probably like the one he sold to John Smith who was bringing a top to Jimmy Broom. Who John Smith or maybe Pocahontas probably ran over with his black Pontiac!

"How much is the tax?" I said to the man. "Sir?"

"Well, let's see," the man said. "Two times five ninety five is what?" and he started looking at the buttons on a big machine on the counter.

"Eleven ninety," I said back.

The man looked at me. "Don't be so impatient, young man. Let's just let this gizmo do its work now." I liked when the man said to me young man. "I paid a lot of money for it." My Mother says sometimes I'm impatient too. I don't know what a gizmo is. I looked it up in the dictionary when I got home. But it wasn't in there. I saw it written in the Sunday comics once. Which is how I know how to spell it. While he was looking at the buttons on the gizmo, the man said, "So, where's your friend? The one you came in with."

"In the back," I said back. "Sir."

"Okay. Five ninety five once," the man said. He pressed some buttons on the gizmo. I saw four little white squares with black numbers pop up saying $ then 5 then 9 then 5. The one with the first 5 had a little dot after it. "What's he doing back there? Five ninety five again." He pressed the buttons again. I saw the same little white squares with black numbers. Except they were already popped up.

"Reading a comic book about some boy," I said back.

"What?" The man started walking to the back of the store. "This isn't a liberry, kid. Get up here," he shouted at Lenny. "You have to buy it if you want to read it!"

I heard Lenny getting up in the back. "He's thinking about buying it," I said to the man. "He's just seeing if he wants to."

The man looked at me and just stared. "Well, he can see if he wants to buy it after he buys it," he said. "That's the way it works in here. You don't get to decide to buy something until you bought it." He looked back at the gizmo. "So, where was I?" I stood up on my toes and had my chin on the counter and was staring right into the face of the visible woman box. Which was on the bottom now. She looked scary with no hair on her head or over her eyes. The man pressed another button on the gizmo and three other little white squares with black numbers popped up. The ones that already said $ and 9 stayed the same. "Okay," the man said, "that's eleven ninety total." Which I already knew. And now the gizmo knew too. The little white squares with black numbers said $ and 1 and 1 and 9 and 0. He looked over the boxes at me. "How much money you got, young man?" Just then, Lenny walked up. He wasn't holding the Tom Sawyer comic book anymore. The man behind the counter looked at him and said, "What's the matter, kid? You don't want to buy the comic book now?"

"Don't need to," Lenny said. "I finished reading it."

"You think this is a liberry, kid?" the man said again.

I quick said back, "I have twelve dollars and fifty cents." Which I did! The man looked at Lenny and then looked at me. "Which is why I need to know how much is the tax." The man just looked at me. "To see if I have enough money," I said again. I just lifted up my shoulders.

"Right," he said. "Right. I see what you're getting at. How much tax." The man picked up the two visible people boxes and moved them to another part of the counter. And then I could see a little card taped to the top of the glass that was under the visible woman before he moved her. He put his finger on the little card and was talking to himself saying, "Eleven ninety, eleven ninety, eleven ninety," the same way my little sister says everything three times. "Oh," he said again. "Here we go. Eleven ninety? Tax is thirty six cents."

Thirty six cents! "Thirty six cents just for tax?" I said back. It just popped out of my mouth. "Sir?" That's seven cokes with a penny left over! That's what I was thinking when the man behind the counter said thirty six cents. For tax! Whatever that is.

But I knew I had enough money. Because twelve is more than eleven ninety and fifty is more than thirty six. And I had twelve fifty.

"Listen, young man. I don't make up the rules," the man said back. "I just follow them." He pressed some buttons on the gizmo again and up popped more little white squares with black numbers saying $ and 1 and 2 and 2 and 6. "Twelve twenty six, young man. So, let's see your money." While I was digging in the pocket of my dungarees, the man behind the counter said again, "So, you boys know the little guy who was run over by the car last Monday?"

"It was Tuesday," I said back. "Sir."

Lenny said, "He lives on our street."

"Really?" the man said back. "You go to school with him?" Lenny just nodded.

"Here you go," I said to the man. Twelve fifty." And I put the ten, two ones, and two quarters on the glass top of the counter.

"You know his parents?" the man behind the counter said. Same as John Smith.

Lenny just lifted his shoulders. "I'm not allowed to play with him."

I just lifted my shoulders. I just wanted to get my change and go home. It was almost dark.

"So, where did you get this much money, young man?" He called me young man again. "And don't tell me you got it for your birthday because nobody gets that much money for their birthday. At least not around here, they don't." He called Lenny kid whenever he talked to him. "So?" he said again after I didn't say anything.

I didn't want Lenny to know about me going cow, and I didn't want the man behind the counter to know either. And besides, like John Smith said, it's none of his business. But I didn't want to say that. Because it was rude for John Smith to say it. So, instead, I said, "I won it at the horse race track."

Lenny pushed my arm and said, "You did?"

The man behind the counter just laughed at me. "That's quite a story, young man," he said back. "You don't expect me to believe that, do you?"

"It's the truth," I said back. Which it was not. "I go to the horse race track with my father all the time." Which was the truth.

"Young man," the man behind the counter said, "they don't allow children into the horse race track."

"If you just stay outside by the rail, they do!" I said back. Which was also true. I was thinking that if I said more true things than things that were not true, then most of what I said would not be a lie and then I wasn't telling a lie.

"Well, I don't believe a word of it," the man behind the counter said. "But let me get your change." He started pushing coins around in the gizmo. Which I could not see but I could hear. "You got a penny?" Which I didn't. "I owe you twenty four cents but I'm out of pennies. If you give me a penny, I'll give you a quarter."

"I have a penny," Lenny said. "Here." He handed it to the man behind the counter.

Who then took a quarter out of the gizmo and put it on the glass top. "There you go, young man. We're all settled up. You want me to put these in a bag for you?"

"Two of them, please," I said back. "Sir." Which he did. I wanted Lenny to help me carry them home. I picked up the quarter from the counter. And when I was putting it into the pocket of my dungarees, my empty pocket, I remembered talking to my Mother. "Oh, Sir," I said again. "Could you please give me change for this quarter?"

"Young man, I already told you I don't have any pennies. If you want pennies for the gumball machine at Picou's, you'll have to get them somewheres else."

"Oh, no, Sir," I said back. "I just need a nickel and two dimes."

Six, or Rivoli

When I was little like my little sister is little now, we lived in California in a house near the place where Daddy fixed airplanes for the government. Which is far away from the house where we live on Columbus Street now. But I remember a lot about California.

For instance, number one, California is where I started going to school. I went to kindergarden first. Which is not a garden. Even if some little kids think it is. And I didn't know anybody at that school. Because my friend Pepe went to another one. Kindergarden was where I saw a brown boy for the first time. A negro boy. Even now, at home, there are no negro boys at St. Rose de Lima Bean School. But in California, there was one. After that, I started the first grade in California. Which was in another school. The only difference between kindergarden and the first grade is in the first grade my Mother use to make me a sandwhich to take to school for lunch, and in kindergarden I use to just come home for lunch and eat a sandwhich with my Mother. The other difference is that in kindergarden it was just little kids like me. In first grade there were a lot of bigger kids in bigger grades. Even eighth graders in eighth grade! Like Lenny Mahoney's cousin Red, the bigger kids will just punch you in the stomach for no good reason if nobody is looking or maybe even just push you down and pretend like it was an accident. Which it wasn't.

Number two, California is where my Mother use to teach me to read. At first all I could read were little words like bat, cat, fat, hat, mat, pat, rat, sat, and vat. Also words like bit, fit, hit, lit, sit, and wit. And I didn't even know what all those words mean. Even now I still don't know what wit means. My Mother use to say it doesn't matter if I don't know what every word means so long as I can read them. But now that I'm in second grade, she says I have to know what words mean too. Which mostly I do. And when we were in California, my Mother too taught me how to read bigger words like another, brother, other, and of course mother. When she was teaching me a lot of words, all of them looked like each other. That made it more easy for me to learn a lot of words. And then when I was able to read a lot of words, my Mother made me read the newspapers every morning before I went out to school or to play with Pepe or with my cousin Willy or other kids. My Mother made me read the newspapers to her while she was making me and Daddy breakfast. This was before my little sister even was eating breakfast. Which she still doesn't do even if my Mother gives it to her now. Unless it's a doughnut! Anyways, this is why I still like to read newspapers.

Number three, we use to visit my cousins who live in California. I have a lot of cousins everywhere. Here, for instance. I already told about a lot of them. It's because my Mother has a lot of brothers and sisters. So, I have cousins in other places too. Like in Alabama. And even in California too. I have mostly girl cousins there. The big ones are older than me and just talk to my Mother. Their mother is my mother's sister too, and her name is Aunt Tea. Like the drink. The little ones are little like my little sister is little, and they all play together mainly goofy girl games. Which is dolls and sometimes jacks. Except their hands are too small to play jacks good. And there is only one boy. Who is my cousin Willy. I think he is one year older than me. Or maybe one year younger.

Number four, there was my best friend there. Who was Pepe. His daddy worked at the same place as Daddy, and his daddy and mother and baby sister, just like mine, lived right next to us. Pepe and I played baseball all the time or sometimes army or sometimes cowboys and indians or sometimes just with toy soldiers and tanks and trucks. Also, Pepe showed me Mexican jumping beans for the first time ever.

And for instance, number five, we use to go to the beach a lot. We even sometimes went to the beach with Pepe and his daddy and mother and baby sister. Not every day. But a lot. And the waves at the beach in California were about ten times taller than me! I didn't even go in the water. At least not without Daddy. Because the waves were so tall. The waves were even taller than Daddy!

Number six, we use to go to this farm where pretend robbers would get on this train where we were and pretend like they were going to take all our money. All Daddy's money, I mean. Because I didn't have any money and my little sister was just my baby sister then and she didn't have any either. And she doesn't even have any money now! At the end of the train ride, always a pretend sheriff pretend shot at pretend robbers and then pretend took them to a pretend jail. It was pretending, Daddy said, so it wasn't a lie.

And number seven, the last thing I remember about California, a jet plane crashed one day right near our house and burned into little pieces. The pilot jumped out before it crashed, so he was okay. Just a hurt leg, Daddy said. Which is what happened to Jimmy Broom too. Except Jimmy was not in a jet, and the pilot probably didn't get a broomstick through his arm. Because they are too long to fit in a jet. And besides, why would a pilot have a broomstick? I heard the jet plane crash and saw the black smoke by my house where I was playing baseball with kids and even Pepe. I was afraid the pilot was dead. Except he wasn't. Daddy said the pilot walked away from the jet plane. Even with his hurt leg. Jimmy wasn't able to walk away from the black Pontiac. Because his leg was broken. He might even die!

Anyways, when Lenny and I were coming back from Burdine's, while we walked down Bayou Road to the corner of Dorgenois Street where Picou's bakery is and then turned there to walk up to Columbus where I live, I saw the price of the visible woman on the end of the box in the bag I was holding. Lenny carried the visible man in the other bag. The visible woman box was too big for me to carry by myself with the visible man box. Which Lenny called the invisible man no matter how many times I told him that it wasn't the name. When I saw the price of the visible woman on the end of the box in the bag I was holding, it said five ninety five. And I knew my Mother was going to ask me where did I get twelve dollars and twenty six cents to pay for two visible people. Because there was thirty six cents tax. Which is a lot! Twelve dollars and twenty six cents is a lot. Not thirty six cents.

So, while we were coming back to my house from Burdine's, while I was looking at the price on the visible woman box, I thought about how when you tell a lie it's easy to keep telling lies. Which you have to do! When my Mother said to me what took me so long at the Triangle, I didn't tell her about me betting by going cow with John Smith, so I didn't tell her about where my two dimes from Uncle Martin's quarter were or about winning twelve dollars and fifty cents, so I didn't tell her about how I wanted to go to Burdine's to buy something but I told her only I wanted to just look at things, and so now I can't tell her that I bought two visible people because then she would ask where did I get that much money. The price was right there on the visible woman box. And my Mother is very smart! Also I have a visible man to explain too.

Then I had an idea. I said to Lenny when we got to the corner of Dorgenois and Columbus in front of the snowball stand where second base is, catty corner from Bruno's, "Hey, Lenny. Why don't you take the visible man box to your house with you? You could hide it under your bed, for instance."

Lenny looked at me the way he sometimes does when what I'm saying doesn't make sense. Which sometimes it doesn't make sense to Lenny or to anybody else, and sometimes it doesn't make sense just to Lenny. "Why?" is all he said back.

I didn't even have to think about it before I told Lenny another lie because I didn't tell my Mother about me betting by going cow with John Smith. It just popped out of my mouth. Telling a lie now was as easy as thinking about something. I couldn't stop. It just happened! "My Mother doesn't like me having more than one model in my house at the same time," I said back to Lenny.

"Why not?" Lenny said back again.

He was looking at me like I had a good reason for saying what I did. Which I did. But which I could not say. And I like Lenny. I like him a lot. My Mother says she likes him because he is a calm boy. And I like him because he is a calm boy and because he never makes any trouble for other kids. He never makes any trouble for me. Which his cousin Red does all the time. And which Lenny's big sister does too. Can you believe that Lenny's big sister has the same name as Sharon the Roach? Which my little sister does too! But even if he doesn't make any trouble for me, Lenny always wants to know the whys and the wherefores. And my Uncle Martin said sometimes it makes sense not to ask too many questions. Leave the whys and the wherefores to other people. So, I said that back to Lenny. Which is that he asks too many questions.

"Too many questions?" Lenny said back. "I just asked one question!"

Which was not true. He asked two questions. He asked why I wanted him to take the visible man box to his house and hide it under his bed.

And he asked why my Mother did not want me to have more than one model in my house at the same time. But instead of saying so, I just said again to him, "Maybe you did, Lenny. But sometimes it's better to just leave well enough alone." Which my Uncle Martin also said.

We were stopped on the corner waiting for a car to pass. It was almost dark. Lenny was still looking at me like I was not making sense. Which I wasn't to him. I just wanted Lenny to take home the visible man box so I didn't have to talk to my Mother about him. About the visible man. Not about Lenny.

Then I had another idea. "What do you think about what happened to Jimmy Broom?" I said to Lenny.

"My mom says he might die," Lenny said back.

If we talked about Jimmy, maybe Lenny would stop asking me questions about why I want him to take home the visible man box. "I know," I said back. "His leg is broken."

"My mom says he broke his arm too," Lenny said back.

"Right," I said. "My Uncle Martin saw everything. He saw the whole incident happen when he was coming home from work." Sometimes I say things to kids so they think I know a lot. For instance, I would tell kids if Daddy killed two thousand Germans like Red's pop did instead of being a newspaper boy in the war. When Red said his pop killed two thousand Germans in the war, he did it to make me think he's better than me. Or at least his pop is better than Daddy. Which he is not. Also, I like to say things to kids that they don't know. It's news to them. It's something I know that they don't know. I know more than they do. For instance, I said to Lenny while we were standing at second base in front of the snowball stand, "My Uncle Martin says it looked to him like the driver tried to hit Jimmy!"

Lenny was surprised. "Really?" he said back.

So, I kept going. "And the police didn't even ask him any questions."

"The driver?" Lenny said back.

"No!" I said back. "My Uncle Martin, Lenny!" Who he already knows because Lenny's house is between my house and my Uncle Martin's house. "The police are investigating the incident, Lenny!" I said again. "It was in the newspapers!"

"Your uncle saw the accident?"

I didn't have time to tell Lenny the difference between an accident and an incident. I just said back, "Sure! And that kid who plays stickball here all the time. He saw everything too. He was standing right here when it happened."

"Who?" Lenny just kept asking questions.

"You know that kid Bobby. Or maybe Robby. The publican. He goes to public school."

"I don't know him," Lenny said back.

"Anyways, he said the same thing to me today. He said the guy in a black Pontiac was aiming right at Jimmy. Right at him!"

"Really?" Lenny said again.

"And he got him!" I said back. "You see there?" I pointed at the place in the street between third and home where you can't even see Jimmy's blood anymore. "Not even a skid mark in the street. He never even touched his brakes. Just kept on going."

Lenny looked in the street like he was looking for a skid mark. And then he held up the bag that had the visible man box in it. "So, why do you want me to keep this at my house under my bed?" he said again.

Lenny doesn't know Jimmy Broom like I do. He probably won't even cry if Jimmy dies. He is a calm boy just like my Mother says. And so I had to think up another idea. "Hey, Lenny. You want to go to the movies tonight?" I said back.

"My mom won't let me go to the Bell by myself at night," Lenny said back.

"Not the Bell," I said back. "The Rivoli." Which is only one street away, just across from the Triangle. My Mother lets me go there if I'm not back too late. Even at night.

"What's playing?" Lenny said back.

"I don't know, Lenny," I said back. "I can look at the newspapers when we get home. Maybe you can give me back the visible man box then," I said again. "After supper, before we go to the movies." I had to get Lenny to keep the visible man!

"Sure," Lenny said. "Okay. I can hide it for you just until tonight. So, do you think Jimmy Broom is going to die like my mom said?" I heard a bicycle on the sidewalk behind us coming from where the church is. So, I turned around. It was the brown boy I saw when I was coming back from the Triangle with the roast beef poor boy. The negro boy who smiled at me and waved too. When he was getting closer, he smiled at us again and then he took one hand off the handlebars to wave at us. "You know that kid?" Lenny said.

Before I could say anything back, the brown boy and his bicycle were stopped right next to us, right at second base in front of the snowball stand. All he said was, "Hi! What's your name?"

I know what Daddy said, but I just said back, "Who are you?"

"You know that kid?" Lenny said to me again.

"I'm Henry," the brown boy said back. "I live over there." He pointed down Dorgenois to the street behind Columbus. He was wearing dungarees and a polo shirt. Just like me and Lenny. "I think it's called Harp Street. I just moved here from California."

California! I was thinking about what Daddy said. But I said back anyways, "I use to live in California too!"

"Where?" the brown boy said.

"When I lived in California, I use to live by the place where my daddy fixed airplanes for the government."

"I don't know where that is," the brown boy said back. "I use to live on Jackson Street. Did your daddy use to fix airplanes for the government by Jackson Street?"

I just lifted my shoulders. I didn't know. But I don't think Jackson Street was by us. And I was still thinking about if Jackson Street was by us in California when I saw behind Lenny a black Pontiac coming right down Dorgenois Street again.

"Lenny!" I said. "The black Pontiac!"

"Is that the one that hit Jimmy?" Lenny said back.

And then I saw John Smith driving the black Pontiac, and I saw Pocahontas sitting right next to him. "I have to go," I quick said to the brown boy. Who is Henry. "Let's go, Lenny!"

"See you around," Henry said. He stepped on his bicycle pedal like he was going to ride away.

"You know that kid?" Lenny said again.

"Now, I do," I said back. "Let's go!"

But the black Pontiac pulled up right at second base and turned like he was going up Columbus Street to the church and stopped all of a sudden in the middle of the street and blocked Henry and trapped us all. The car window was rolled down and John Smith said to Henry, "So, where do you think you're going, punk?" I hope my Mother doesn't even find out I had to write that word. And it's not even what John Smith said. What John Smith said to Henry was worse even than punk. Which now I wrote two times.

Henry just lifted his shoulders up and down, and he said back, "Home, Sir."

"What are you boys doing talking to this punk?" John Smith said again to Lenny and me with his frog voice. Except he didn't say punk again.

"I didn't say anything," Lenny said. "My mom won't let me talk to them."

At first John Smith pretended like he didn't know me. I was hoping he didn't say anything about me going cow with him at the Triangle because I didn't want Lenny to know about it. Or even Henry. I didn't want anyone to know about it. John Smith looked at Henry and shouted, "Scram, punk! Get your black behind out of here!" Which in his froggy voice was very rude. And he didn't say punk even again. And he didn't say behind either!

Pocahontas yelled from the other side of the car. "Scram, punk!" Which even in his squeaky voice was very rude.

Then John Smith pointed at me. "Come here, kid. You still got my twelve fifty?"

Henry, the negro boy, jumped up on his bicycle pedal again and rode back down Columbus Street to where the church is. Without turning around, he waved at us, only one hand on the handlebars.

Lenny leaned over to me and whispered, "What's he talking about, Vonny? Twelve fifty what?" Lenny is always asking about the whys and the wherefores. Like me.

So, I lied again. "I don't know what he's talking about!" I said back. It just popped out. I was looking at John Smith. I was not going anywheres near that black Pontiac. John Smith looked angry. And Pocahontas was staring at us too from the other side of the car. They ran over Jimmy Broom, and now they were going to the Hotel Dieu to bring him a stupid red top that only costed a dollar two. With tax! And then they were probably going to finish him off the way Travis finished off Old Yeller in that movie where I cried almost all night after it.

"Do I have to get out of this car to get an answer, kid?" John Smith said again. "I have a feeling you know more about this accident here than you're saying." He pointed behind him at Bruno's and where Jimmy was hit. "And either you tell me what you know or else!" He pointed his finger at me. "And I want my twelve fifty back too. Don't you hold out on me, Vonny Foster!"

"Holding out?" Lenny whispered to me again. "What does that mean, Vonny? How does he know your name?"

I didn't say anything back to Lenny. I know my Mother is right about me not talking to strangers. Now John Smith wanted his money back. And I didn't have the money because now all I had was two visible people in boxes in the Burdine's bags Lenny and I were holding. And I knew John Smith doesn't even like visible people because he didn't buy one for Jimmy. Who he was going to finish off!

"Well," John Smith finally said, talking like they do in the Dick Tracy cartoon, "I guess I'm gonna have to get out of this car after all." I heard the door click. "Don't you think about running away either!" he said again.

But just then I heard another car honk its horn. It was across the street coming up on Columbus Street at the stop sign between third base and home. The black Pontiac was blocking its way. The other car pulled into the middle of the two streets and honked its horn again for John Smith to move so it could go down the street where the church is. The two cars were one right behind the other with the black Pontiac in front. Pocahontas started to get out of the other door but then even another car pulled up on Dorgenois Street and honked its horn because the car behind John Smith's car was blocking it from going down to where Picou's and the Triangle are on Bayou Road. Then both of the cars were honking at the same time, and Pocahontas was out of the black Pontiac yelling at them in his squeaky voice.

"Shut up!" he shouted. "Shut up!"

"Let's run!" I said to Lenny. So, we did. We quick ran across Dorgenois to third base where the black and brown dog was barking like crazy from all the honking noise on the corner. Just like Jimmy Broom did when the black Pontiac hit him, we ran across Columbus from third base to home plate in front of Bruno's.

Behind us I heard Pocahontas yelling with his squeaky voice. And then, John Smith was yelling with his froggy voice. "Where do you think you're going?"

The other cars were still honking, and the black and brown dog was still barking when we got to my house. I was out of breath. While I was trying to catch it, I said to Lenny, "I'll look at the movies in the newspapers and then come by your house later after supper. Ask your mom if you can go to the Rivoli tonight."

But I never did look at the movies in the newspapers that night and I never did go by Lenny's house later after supper. The sky was dark when I got home and was still getting darker and darker. I ran around the alley and went into my house through the back door in the kitchen. I already knew that Daddy was frying the fish he caught because I could smell it all the way outside.

"Vonny! Vonny! Vonny!" My little sister hopped over and hugged me around my belly.

My Mother said, "She loves you so much, Vonny." My Mother was cooking the fish. It wasn't Daddy. Usually I say she is cooking the fish. But whenever I call my Mother she, my Mother always says, "Who's she? The cat's mother?" I don't understand what that means. Except I know I'm not suppose to call my Mother she. At least not to her face.

Anyways, I said to my Mother, "What are we eating?" Because nobody in our house eats fish except Daddy and her. I love the way fried fish smells. But I don't like to eat anything that has eyeballs and whenever Daddy brings home fish that he caught they always have eyeballs that follow me around the room no matter where I go. And my little sister doesn't eat anything almost, so she never eats fish. And my baby brother doesn't even have teeth to eat fish with. So, it's just Daddy and my Mother.

"What's all that racket outside, Vonny?" my Mother said again, standing by the stove and moving the fish around in the pan while they were frying the way Charly moved the doughnuts around in the same pan last night. "Daddy's trying to get some sleep, and I just put your baby brother down for a nap." She kissed me on the forehead. And then she looked down at my Burdine's bag. "So, Vonny," my Mother finally said, and I already knew what she was going to say. "You never showed me the two dimes you got back from the quarter your Uncle Martin gave you because you were his caddy this morning."

"Oh," I said back. "They're right here in my back pocket, Mama." Which was true. And I said again, "They were there the whole time." Which was not true. "I just forgot where I put them." Which also was not true. For a good kid like me who is making a confession list, where you cannot lie unless you want to go straight to hell when you die, I was doing a very good job of having a very big list. It was probably up to about three pages now with two whole pages just for today. And it all started with me going cow with John Smith at the Triangle.

After I said this, still standing by the stove, my Mother closed one of her eyes and twisted her mouth a little. She wasn't smiling. When she did that, it made me think about the very first time I lied to my Mother. Which I didn't want to do, but then I did it anyways. It was when we lived in California, and my Mother always told me there what she always tells me now here. Which is I am not suppose to go into any other kid's house unless my Mother tells me I can. Except I can go into my cousins' houses. Like my cousin Pia's house. Which is where my Uncle Martin and Aunt Audra live. Or like my Uncle Roger's house. Who is really my cousin. And who lives just next door to Jimmy Broom. And where I went the night I sleepwalked. Or like my cousin William's house. Which is on Broad Street. But for everybody else, I am suppose to ask my Mother first. Which I always do.

Except in California, this one time, when this kid was playing baseball with me and with Pepe, and the kid said did we want to see a snake that his daddy bought and kept at his house. I wanted to. I wanted to a lot, and I told him so. And after we played baseball all morning and after I had lunch and after my Mother made me take a nap because I was still a little kid then and wasn't even in kindergarden, or maybe just starting kindergarden, we met up behind the houses like we were going to play baseball again. Except we went over to this kid's house instead. His parents weren't at home because his mother was visiting somebody and his daddy was working at the same place where Daddy worked. Which everybody who lived by us in California did. I was afraid when we went in his house to see the snake. I was afraid a little because of the snake, but I was afraid mostly because I did not want my Mother to know that I didn't ask her first like I was suppose to. I didn't ask her first like I was

suppose to because I knew my Mother was going to say no. She was probably going to say something like, "No, you cannot, Vonny! Are you crazy?
A snake?" And so that was the first time I lied to my Mother, and it is the
first thing I had to write on my confession list. Which Sister Marianna
says is secret. Except now you know too!

So, when my Mother asked me about the dimes and where were they
and I said they were in my back pocket all the time, she just closed one
of her eyes and twisted her mouth a little. My Mother is very smart.
Very, very smart! I knew she was thinking about what happened when
we were eating the roast beef poor boy and what she said then about the
two dimes and what I said then about the two dimes and what I was saying now about the two dimes. She was thinking about the whys and the
wherefores. My Mother was not going to leave well enough alone. But
then, she surprised me. "Oh," my Mother finally said back after I lied
about the two dimes being in my pocket the whole time. "I see."

Which I did not understand what my Mother was saying. Did she
see I was not telling the truth or did she see I was telling the truth and
anybody can forget what pocket they put two dimes in? But I didn't want
to ask her. And then I thought about my Uncle Charles, my Mother's
brother who played golf with my Uncle Martin this morning. Whenever
anybody says, "I see" around my Uncle Charles, he always says back,
"Said the blind man."

For instance, somebody says something to some other person. Like,
for instance, "The second race will be run at a distance of six furlongs."

And then the other person nods his head and says back, "I see."

And then my Uncle Charles says back again, "Said the blind man."

It doesn't make sense to me, but like a dope, after my Mother said, "I
see" when I said about the two dimes being in my back pocket the whole
time, I said back, "Said the blind man."

My Mother all of a sudden unclosed her closed eye and untwisted her
twisted mouth. "Vonny Foster!" she said in a mean voice. "Are you making fun of your mother?"

"No!" I said back. Which was true.

"No, what?" she said back.

"No, I'm not making fun of my Mother," I said back. "I'm not making
fun of you, Mama."

"Vonny?" I knew I was in trouble because my Mother was smiling with all her teeth and then she pretended like she was biting her knuckle like she does when she's not really smiling at all. "No, I'm not making fun of you, Mama, what, Vonny?" my Mother said back again.

"Oh," I said back. "No, I'm not making fun of you, Mama," I said again, "Ma'am!"

"That's better," my Mother said back. "Well, I'm glad you found your dimes. Now go and put them in your piggy bank with this nickel that your Uncle Martin brought you this afternoon." Which my Mother handed to me and which I went and put in my piggy bank with the two dimes I got from Burdine's. Which my Mother thought was my change from the quarter than Uncle Martin gave me for being his caddy. And that was the end of it. It was a miracle! Just like that, my Mother didn't care about my two dimes anymore. But then she said, "So what's in the Burdine's bag?" Which I put on a chair by the kitchen table when I came in the back door.

"Oh, it's a visible man model," I said back.

"You mean the invisible man?" my Mother said back.

So, it isn't just Lenny Mahoney. A lot of people saw that movie. Which is old anyways. "No, Ma'am," I remembered to say back. "A visible man, Mama. You can see right through him."

"Oh, my smart little Vonny," my Mother said back. "Are you going to be a doctor when you grow up?" My Mother rubbed me on the top of my head. "Doctor Vonny Foster."

For now, I just want to play baseball when I get bigger. Like Mickey Mantle. Who is my favorite baseball player! Or maybe like Bobby Richardson. Because he's smaller like me. Maybe I can play baseball and be a doctor when I get bigger. Besides, I don't know why my Mother always says when I grow up. Because I already grew up. I'm in second grade already. I'm just going to get bigger now. Anyways, I just lifted up my shoulders. "Maybe," I said back. But I know I'm going to play baseball.

Then my Mother pulled the visible man box out of the Burdine's bag. "Vonny!" she shouted in a mean voice again. This time very loud. I thought she saw the price. Which was five ninety five. So I was glad that Lenny took the other visible person. Then my Mother said, "This is disgusting, Vonny!"

"It's just a model of a visible man, Mama." I thought maybe my Mother didn't like to see the man's bones and guts like I don't like to see the bones and guts at the disgusting meat shop where they sometimes even have a baby cow's head.

"You bring this back to Burdine's right now, Vonny! Right now! What if your sister sees this?"

"I want to see! I want to see! I want to see!" My little sister hopped around the kitchen waving her little arms above her little head like my Mother was going to hand her the visible man box when she just said she didn't even want her to see it.

"Why would you ever think you could bring such a disgusting thing into this house?" my Mother said again.

"But, Mama," I said, "if I'm going to be a doctor, I have to know about all the bones and the artries and other things that are inside a man's body."

"A man's body?" my Mother said again. "A man's body? This is not a man's body, Vonny Foster!" She put the box back in the Burdine's bag and handed it back to me. "That is a woman's body. A naked, invisible woman!"

My little sister kept hopping around. "I want to see! I want to see! I want to see!"

My Mother put her hands over my little sister's little ears, and then she said, "It even has breasts, for goodness sake!"

"Like chicken breasts?" I said back. When my Mother makes fried chicken on Sunday, I just eat the legs and the thighs. They're the best! At least that's what I think. My Mother likes the breast meat. Daddy will eat anything. Even the chicken bones!

"Are you making fun of your mother, Vonny?"

"No, Ma'am!" I said back right away. "No, Ma'am! No, Ma'am!" I was starting to talk like my little sister. "I promise. I promise. I promise. I'm not making fun of anybody." Which I wasn't.

"I want you to take this disgusting thing back to Burdine's right now. Don't they have a model of a man? Don't they? Why didn't you buy a model of an invisible man, Vonny?"

Like a dope I almost told my Mother that they do have one and that I did buy one too and that it is next door under Lenny Mahoney's bed. But I didn't want to tell her the whys and the wherefores. I decided to try to leave well enough alone. "I think it's closed now, Mama," I said back. Which it was. Because I saw the clock in the kitchen say it was after five o'clock. So, just like I did with Lenny, I tried to talk about something else. "So, Mama, do you think I could go to the Rivoli with Lenny Mahoney tonight to see a movie? Do you, Mama?" My Mother almost always lets me go places with Lenny because she likes him.

But not this time. "Don't try to change the subject, Vonny." My Mother is smarter than me. "After school on Monday, you are going to walk back over to Bayou Road and either get your money back or get an invisible man at Burdine's. You tell them that your mother will not have such a disgusting thing in the house. Tell them you have a sister, for goodness sake! A little sister." Which I do.

"I want to see! I want to see! I want to see!"

Just then, my cousins Charly and Marly were at the back screen door. "Hey, Nanny," they both said at the same time to my Mother. Who is their godmother. "We're going to see a movie at the Rivoli with the boys. So we stopped by to say hello first."

"What's playing?" my Mother said back.

"The Tingler," Charly said back. I knew that movie because I saw the sign last Saturday when Lenny and I were at the Rivoli in the afternoon watching a movie about guys going into outer space where one guy was turned into smoke when he took his space suit off.

"Oh, you girls and your horror movies," my Mother said back. "You really love that trash, don't you?"

"We do, Nanny," Marly said.

"We really do!" Charly said.

"We love those scary movies, Nanny," Marly said again.

Which I do too! The Rivoli movies is not too far away from us and is close enough that my Mother lets me go there by myself. Sometimes even at night. That's because the Rivoli is right next to a big house that my Mother use to grow up in with all her brothers and sisters and with my Grandpa who died when we lived in California and with my Grandma who died when she was a girl. When my Mother was a girl. Not my Grandma. My Mother grew up right across the street from the Triangle. Which is why she knows they have the best roast beef poor boys in the whole wide world.

When she was a girl, my Mother use to go to the movies at the Rivoli all the time too. She said she was lucky. All her sisters and brothers were bigger than her and were never home, and her parents didn't know what to do with a little girl like her, so the people at the Rivoli just let my Mother go to the movies by herself, because they knew her because she lived right next door, without even having to pay a penny or whatever it cost to go to the movies then. And then they even gave her free candy too!

Lenny and I are not that lucky. There are only two people who always work at the Rivoli now. There is a lady who wears a dress with pink or purple or red flowers on it. It's not the same dress all the time. But the different dresses always have flowers on them. And then there is a man who looks like my Grandpa who died. He is short and has wavy hair like me and has crocodile skin like the men at Bruno's who raise their glasses of beer at me when I go there. The Rivoli is a very old building and sometimes doesn't smell so good. And it's always dark inside. Always! I don't even think they have any lights in the whole place. The floor sticks to the bottom of my sneakers from people dropping candy and drinks. And the seats squeak! Even when you sit still and don't move around a lot. Which we don't! The lady and the man are never nice to us. Sometimes they are even very rude. Whenever I buy a pickle and ask "How much?" the man just looks at me and says, "Same as last week, kid." Which is a nickel. There is a funny sign on the jar on the counter that says "NICKEL PICKLE" in black block letters. Just like the way I just wrote it. And one time I dropped my popcorn by accident in the lobby, and the man called me a bad name that I can't even write in case my Mother reads this. Even if I knew how to spell it. Which I don't.

But most of the time, especially on Saturday afternoon, Lenny and I are the only two people who even go to the movies at the Rivoli. That's because they mainly show scary movies there. Like the Tingler. And most kids don't like to go to scary movies. Except for me and Lenny. Because we both know better. Lenny and I both know now that the scary things in the scary movies are not for real. But a lot of kids don't know better.

For instance, a lot of time scary movies are about dead people. One time when I wasn't able to sleep one night after I saw a scary movie on a TV program, I told Daddy I was afraid of dead people. Right away, Daddy said back, "Vonny, my boy, don't you ever worry about dead people. They can't hurt you. They can't even move!"

"But in the movies dead people are always moving, Daddy," I said back. Which they are. "They hide in the dark and walk around all over the place and try to get you." Which they do. "In the movies, dead people run faster than live ones," I said again. "And ghosts, who are very dead people, don't even need legs to run after you!"

Daddy laughed. "Don't you ever worry about dead people, Vonny, my boy," he said again. "It's live people you have to look out for. They can do more than just run after you." Which reminded me about Red and the other kids who just punch you in the stomach for no good reason. "If you're going to be afraid of anybody," Daddy said, "be afraid of live people." Which reminded me about John Smith and Pocahontas.

Anyways, ever since then, I don't even worry anymore about dead people in the scary movies at the Rivoli the way other kids do. And Lenny doesn't either. Because I told him what Daddy said. So, we both know better.

The other kind of movies they always show at the Rivoli that we like are about guys going into outer space on rocket ships. I was in a airplane one time, but I was never in a rocket ship. And I went to Florida once and to California too. But I was never in outer space. Which is where I want to go if I ever get enough money to buy a rocket ship. Which I might when I get bigger.

"Are you going to the movies alone?" my Mother said back to Marly.

"Oh, no, Nanny," Charly said back. "Like I said, the boys are waiting for us outside in the car. We just stopped in to say hello. And I wanted to see if the little monkey is better after eating all those doughnuts."

"Can I go? Can I go? Can I go?" It was the little monkey.

"Not tonight, baby," Marly said, and she picked up my little sister. "Besides, I heard you ate too many doughnuts last night."

"Doughnuts! Doughnuts! Doughnuts!" the little monkey shouted. "Can I go? Can I go? Can I go?" she said again.

"We'll take you and Vonny to see another movie some other time," Charly said.

"You girls are too sweet," my Mother said back. "Don't keep the boys waiting. Give me a hug and get going now." Which they did. Both of them hugged my Mother and then they kissed my little sister and then me and then they went away to the Rivoli with their boyfriends. Because they're old enough to have boyfriends now. Which they weren't before, my Aunt Gwendolyn use to say. I don't know why.

Anyways, after Charly and Marly left, I said, "Mama, I like scary movies too. Can I go to the Rivoli tonight too? Can I ask Lenny to go with me?"

"It's late, Vonny," my Mother said back. "Aren't you tired?"

Which I was. I was up very early to go caddy for my Uncle Martin at City Park. And then I went to the Triangle for sandwhiches. And then I went to Burdine's to get the visible people and two dimes. I was very, very tired.

"No, Ma'am," I said back. "I'm not tired. Lenny and I talked about going to the movies tonight. Can we go, please? Can we?"

"What does Lenny's mother have to say about it?" my Mother said back.

I just lifted my shoulders. "You want me to go and ask her?" I said back.

"Vonny, no," my Mother said. "You need to stay home tonight. Your Uncle Martin and Aunt Audra and Uncle Roger and Aunt Anna are all coming over to play cards. Daddy is sleeping. I have to feed your baby brother. I have to fry this fish. Somebody needs to take care of your little sister while I do everything here. And you must be very tired after the day you had. Very, very tired. Why don't the two of you just go in your room and play a game? Play pick up sticks. Or go fish."

"Pick up sticks! Pick up sticks! Pick up sticks!"

Which is what we did. My little sister was more very, very tired even than me, and she fell asleep very early without even eating supper. While we were playing pick up sticks, she just put her little head down and fell asleep on the floor. After my Mother fed my baby brother and put him in his crib, she made me a peanut butter and jelly sandwhich. Another one! While I was eating it, I was thinking about Lenny and if he was able to hide the visible man box under his bed without his mother asking him about it. I wanted to talk to him. But my Mother didn't let me go outside after I put on my pajamas. Which was right after I finished eating and when my tongue was still sticking to my mouth.

Then, Daddy finally woke up after a while and took a hot shower. After that, he looked even more like a boiled crab. And when everybody came over to play cards, which they did at the kitchen table in the back of our house, my Mother said I could bring my pillow up to the front room and watch a TV program on the sofa by myself so long as I didn't put the sound up too high and wake up my little sister and baby brother. Which I did not do. But I was very, very tired. And the TV program was a movie that I already saw with Charly last year at the Bell, which is the other place that has movies and that is near the horse race track, about a boat that runs into ice in the ocean and then a lot of people are killed. I kept falling asleep on the sofa. So, instead of watching the TV program, after a while, I just took my pillow and walked back to the room where my little sister and I have our beds and I got into mine. I didn't even tell Daddy or my Mother. I didn't even call them to tuck me in. I just went to bed by myself.

It was dark in my room, darker than in the parlor. But for some reason I wasn't able to sleep right away. Even if I was very, very tired. Which I was. Daddy and my Mother and my Uncle Roger especially and my Uncle Martin were talking while they were playing cards and it kept me up. So, I just listened to them talking while I was trying to go to sleep.

My Mother said, "Vonny was very upset by what happened to that little boy who lives next door to you." She was probably talking to my Uncle Roger and my Aunt Anna. Who live next to Jimmy and his parents.

"He's still in the hospital," Uncle Roger said. "The light is on at their house all night. I don't think they ever sleep."

"Would you sleep if that was your boy?" my Mother said. "No wonder the light is on all night."

"Sure," Uncle Roger said back. "But the light is on all night at their house all the time, people coming and going all night. Even before the accident."

"Well, it's a terrible thing that happened," my Mother said again. "That's why Vonny was sleepwalking."

"Oh, Irene!" Daddy said out loud. "Don't be so dramatick."

"Dramatick?" my Mother said back. "Our boy, your son, walked right out into the street in the middle of the night, for goodness sake. While he was sleeping. Right after that poor little boy was run over by a car. We're lucky he didn't get run over too!" Which I am lucky I didn't too.

"He's not such a poor little boy," Uncle Roger said.

"Roger!" my Aunt Anna said.

"Not Vonny!" Uncle Roger said. "The kid next door. He's always making trouble, that kid. Making a racket. He's a problem." I never heard Daddy or my Mother talk about Jimmy that way.

"Roger!" my Aunt Anna said again.

"I'll take two cards," Daddy said.

My Aunt Anna said again, "He's just a little boy, Roger." Which he isn't! Because Jimmy is in second grade just like me. Except he's even smaller than me. "His parents are no good to him, always yelling and carrying on." My Aunt Anna is from some other country. Like Aunt Audra is from Australia. So, my Aunt Anna talks funny sometimes too. And she talks funny like Aunt Audra talks funny but not the same way. Not Australian. Then, Aunt Anna said, "One card, please."

"I smell a straight," Daddy said. Whatever that means.

"Well, he's got a mouth on him, that kid," Uncle Roger said back.

"And what about the boy's father?" my Aunt Anna said back. "He's a pig! Roger had to say something to him one day about the way he talks in front of the children, in front of our girls." Uncle Roger and Aunt Anna have two baby girls who are not even as little as my little sister yet. They are very small. "The language he uses! He's so rude!"

Daddy said, "I see him at the barber shop all the time."

"He's almost bald!" Uncle Roger said. Which is true. Jimmy Broom's daddy hardly has any hair at all. And he's always wearing an undershirt. Even outside. "What's he doing spending a lot of time at the barber shop?" Uncle Roger said again. Then, he said, "I'm good."

"No cards, Roger?" my Mother said.

"No. I'm good," Uncle Roger said back again.

"I've got my eyes on you, Roger," Daddy said. "He's bluffing over there." Whatever that means. Then, Daddy said again, "I think he runs a book for the barber." Daddy was saying a lot of things I didn't understand.

"The kid's dad?" Uncle Roger said.

"Three cards," my Aunt Audra said.

"Sounds like a small pair to me," Daddy said.

"Just pay attention to your own cards, you bugger," Aunt Audra said back. She talks Australian. It's like the way we talk except some words are different. Like bugger. Which I think is like when I say Sharon the Roach.

"Sure," Daddy said again. "Why else would a bald guy spend so much time at the barber shop?"

"I've seen him there too," Uncle Martin said.

"Unless the bald guy is the barber," Uncle Roger said, and everybody laughed.

"One card," Uncle Martin said again.

"I hope that's not an inside straight you're working on," Daddy said.

"You bugger!" Aunt Audra said again. More out loud than before this time. "Just mind your own business over there, would you?"

Uncle Martin said, "I think Vonny heard me talking to Stephen this morning about the accident."

"Why do you say that?" my Mother said back. And then she said again, "These cards are terrible. None of this is worth keeping. I'm out. Anybody need something to drink?"

"Well," Uncle Martin said back, "on the way to City Park, I told Vonny that I saw the accident happen just as I was coming home from work. He wanted to know what I saw and whether the police asked me to tell them what I saw."

"He's a curious boy," my Mother said. I could hear her moving glasses around in the kitchen. "Does anyone want some coffee?"

"And then," Uncle Martin said again, "when we were golfing, I was telling Stephen this morning that the car didn't even try to slow down while the kid was crossing over and it almost looked like the guy went out of his way to try to hit the kid."

"Oh, my God!" my Mother said. Which is taking the Lord's name in vain!

"Martin, you don't know that's what happened," my Aunt Audra said.

"Well, it's what I saw," Uncle Martin said.

"It's what you think you saw," my Aunt Audra said back.

"A nickel," Daddy said.

"And you know Vonny," Uncle Martin said again. "Always with the questions. Always wanting to know the whys and the wherefores." Which is true. "He was standing by Charlie and Gauthier while I was talking to Stephen. But he was listening to me the whole time. Because on the way home he asked me did I think the guy in the black Pontiac really tried to hit the boy on purpose." So Uncle Martin did know I was listening!

"What black Pontiac?" Uncle Roger said.

My Aunt Anna said, "The one that ran over the boy, Roger. I'm out too."

"How am I suppose to know?" Uncle Roger said back. "I see your nickel and raise you a dime," he said again.

"You think that bluff is going to work on me?" Daddy said.

"It was in the newspapers," Aunt Anna said again.

"I'm out," Aunt Audra said. "You need some help, Irene?" I heard a chair scratch on the kitchen floor.

Then, Uncle Martin said, "What's it to me?"

"What's it to you?" Aunt Audra said. "A little boy is run over right in front of your eyes, right on the street where you live, and you want to know what's it to you?"

"No!" Uncle Martin said back. "I mean how much do I have to put in to keep playing?"

Daddy laughed and said, "Fifteen cents to you."

"What am I suppose to do?" Uncle Martin said again.

"You either call, raise, or fold," Daddy said again.

"Not that, brother in law," Uncle Martin said back. "I'm out too. I've got nothing. I mean, how do I know for sure that the guy was trying to run over the boy? What am I suppose to tell the police?"

"I see your dime and call you," Daddy said. "Turn them over and meet your maker." And then, nobody said anything else. After a while, Daddy and Uncle Roger started laughing very loud.

"What's the matter?" my Mother said.

"What's so funny?" my Aunt Audra said.

"Who's bluffing who?" Uncle Roger said in a loud voice.

Uncle Martin laughed too. "Well, you're both full of baloney," he said. "But Albert's jack beats your ten." Which I don't understand either.

I could hear coins jingling on the table. "Come to daddy," Daddy said. "But why would a grown man want to run over a kid? It doesn't make any sense. None at all. Whose deal is it?"

"Maybe it has something to do with the barber shop," Uncle Roger said.

"How do you figure?" Uncle Martin said back.

"What if the kid's dad is running a book for the barber shop?" Uncle Roger said again. I was thinking what running a book means.

"I see him in there all the time," Daddy said. "And I know they're running a book there. Because they take mine when I don't have time to get to the track." I was thinking what kind of book. A book about barber shops?

"What barber shop doesn't book bets?" Uncle Roger said. Bets? Booking bets?

"So a guy gets behind and you run over his kid?" Uncle Martin said.

"Who knows?" Daddy said. "There are some bad people in this town." It reminded me about Daddy saying it's the live people you have to look out for. Then Daddy said again, "I just hope the kid gets better."

"I just hope they all leave," Uncle Roger said.

"Roger!" Aunt Anna said back. "Don't be rude!"

"Well, I do," Uncle Roger said. "The kid's nothing but trouble. The old man is nothing but trouble. And the mother is a witch. All she does is scream at the two of them day and night."

My Mother said, "That's an unkind thing to say."

"Well, it's true," Uncle Roger said back.

"She may not be the best mother, but she cares about her boy," my Mother said again. "I saw her this morning, and she's worried to death about that boy."

"If she spent more time caring for him, he might not be in the Hotel Dieu now," Uncle Roger said back. "We live next door to them. We know what kind of people they are."

Aunt Anna said, "Keep your voice down, Roger, will you? Irene's got children sleeping."

"Oh, Albert," my Mother said. "That reminds me. Can you go check on Vonny? I think he was on the sofa in the parlor watching TV. If he fell asleep, please just carry him to bed. And make sure you tie his foot to the bed post."

I quick turned over in bed and closed my eyes like I was sleeping. I didn't want Daddy to know that I heard everything they were talking about. About Uncle Martin seeing what he saw and not saying anything to the police. Which Uncle Martin knows I know. And about Jimmy's daddy always being at the barber shop where people bet on horse races. Which Daddy does too. And about Jimmy's dad being a pig and being so rude. Which my Aunt Anna said. And about Jimmy's mother being a witch and screaming at Jimmy and his dad day and night. Which my Uncle Roger said.

Daddy came out of the kitchen and walked through the room where my little sister and I sleep. Or for me, the room where I try to sleep. I knew Daddy was not going to find me on the sofa in the parlor in front of the TV. But I didn't want to say anything because I didn't want him to know that I heard everything they were talking about. After a while, Daddy walked back through the same room and back into the kitchen. "That's strange," he said.

"What's that?" my Mother said back.

"Now, don't be dramatick," Daddy said.

"Is something wrong, Albert?" my Mother said back in a loud voice.

"Well," Daddy said again, in a calm voice, "Vonny's not in the front room."

"Oh, my God!" my Mother said again in a very loud voice. Which is taking the Lord's name in vain again! "Did you check the bathtub?"

"The bathtub?" my Aunt Audra said while she was laughing.

"He likes to take a hot bath at night," my Mother said back. Which I do. "When he sleepwalks." Which I do too.

"Not there either," Daddy said back again.

Then I heard a lot of the chairs scratching against the floor in the kitchen and my Mother said again, "Oh, my God!" Which is breaking a commandment again. It sounded like everyone was standing up. I heard my Mother and then Daddy and then Aunt Anna and then Aunt Audra all rushing through the house from the kitchen through the room where my little sister and I sleep through the hallway by the bathroom through the room where Daddy and my Mother and now my baby brother sleep through the parlor and then out through the front door. "He's sleepwalking again," my Mother said. "In the street!"

It was too late for me to do anything. I just kept my eyes closed and didn't move. I knew they would find me. I wasn't lost. Even if they thought I was. I wasn't sleepwalking. Even if they thought I was.

After a little while, I heard another chair scratch on the kitchen floor and then I heard someone walk into the room where I was and I could feel someone standing by my bed. But I didn't look. I knew it wasn't a dead person. I could hear him breathing. I knew it was a live person. I could feel him leaning over my bed. He could see me. After a while, he went back into the kitchen and I heard the chair scratching on the kitchen floor again. I was very, very tired. And just before I fell asleep, I heard my Uncle Martin say, "She really can be dramatick sometimes."

Seven, or
St. Rose de Lima Bean Church

Henry is the negro boy that I saw on Saturday, the first time by my-self on the way back from the Triangle and the second time with Lenny Mahoney on the way back from Burdine's when John Smith and Pocahontas tried to trap us at the corner of Columbus and Dorgenois.

Henry is a kid who looks almost just like me. Almost exactly just like me!

For instance, Henry is a very skinny kid. Just like me. And he's not very tall. Just like me. Most kids in my class are taller than me. Even some of the girls are taller than me. Even Sharon the Roach is taller than me! Also, Henry has dark brown hair like I do. Except his hair is very short and is real close to his head. Mine is longer and has waves in it like Daddy's hair and like that guy named Rock. My hair is easy to mess up. Which Daddy does sometimes. Henry's hair is hard to mess up. Because it's so short. He also has very brown eyes like me that look like they might jump out of his face. Also, he is missing a few teeth, but he already has his new front teeth. Which are very large. Just like my new front teeth. So, he has a very big, white smile. Just like mine!

Like I already told, Henry looks almost just like me. Almost exactly just like me!

I only saw Henry those two times before I saw him again when me and Daddy and my Mother and my little sister and my baby brother were all walking down Columbus Street to St. Rose de Lima Bean Church for Mass on Sunday morning, the one after the Saturday when I first saw Henry, which was the Saturday when I went to caddy for my Uncle

Martin at City Park where I got two dimes and then I walked to the Triangle for my Mother where I went cow with John Smith and gave the two dimes away and then I went to Burdine's to buy the visible people so my Mother wouldn't know about me betting and where I got two dimes back again.

On that Sunday morning, the one after that Saturday, we were all walking to Mass on Columbus Street. Except my baby brother wasn't walking to St. Rose de Lima Bean Church because Daddy had to carry him. My baby brother doesn't know how to walk yet. He doesn't even know how to crawl yet. He just lies around and smiles most of the time. So, somebody has to carry him and put their hand under his head because he's not strong enough to hold it up himself.

Both times I saw Henry before, on Saturday, he was wearing dungarees and a polo shirt. Just like I always do! When I saw him again, on Sunday, while we were walking to church, Henry had on dress up clothes. He was wearing a bow tie and a jacket. Just like I always do too!

And when I saw him again, on Sunday, he was walking on the other side of Columbus Street, the side where my school is, with a very tall negro man and a tall negro lady and a little negro girl. The tall negro man was wearing a regular tie and a jacket too. The tall negro lady had a bump in front of her stomach like my Mother did when she was pregnant and my baby brother was inside her. She was dressed just like my Mother in a shiny dress with a little hat on her head and long white gloves on her hands and wrists. And the little negro girl was wearing a little pink dress and a little pink hat and little white socks and little white shoes. Just like my little sister! And while they were walking on the other side of Columbus Street, the little negro girl was hopping along the sidewalk just like my little sister does. Not skipping, but hopping. Like a Mexican jumping bean! Exactly like my little sister was doing while we were walking to Mass too.

Except we were on two different sides of Columbus.

"Hi, Henry!" I called across the street, and then I waved at him. I knew him from the day before. So, I just said hello.

The negro people were all walking a little ahead of us, and Henry had to turn around his head to see who I was. And then, all of the negro people, the very tall man and the tall lady and the little hopping girl stopped walking and hopping, all at the same time, and all of them turned around with Henry to see who I was.

"Who is Henry?" my Mother said. We didn't stop walking but just kept going on our side of the street.

"That boy over there," I said back, and I pointed at him.

"Oh," Henry said back after he saw me. And then he said to me, "How are you doing, California?"

"You know that kid?" Daddy said.

"Why did he call you California?" my Mother said again.

"We're just going to church," I said back to Henry.

"Us too," Henry said back again.

The tall negro lady looked at me and then looked at Henry and said, "Who is that boy, Henry? What did I tell you?" She was talking in a low voice. But I could hear her. Because we caught up to them on our side of the street and because it is always very quiet on Columbus Street on Sunday morning. Because school is closed.

"You know that kid?" Daddy said again. Except at the same time, Daddy looked over at the negro people and waved at them while we were walking ahead of them on our side of the street. Like he knew them. Daddy even smiled and then waved again.

The very tall negro man nodded his head at Daddy, and the tall negro lady raised her hand and smiled.

"Good morning," my Mother said to them, and she also raised her hand. But she didn't wave.

"Do you know them, Mama?" I said just about when we turned off of Columbus Street and started walking down the alley on the side of the St. Rose de Lima Bean Church that leads to Bayou Road.

"See you later, California!" I heard Henry shout behind me.

And then I heard the tall negro lady say, "Henry!"

I knew they were going to a different church because they had to cross the street and walk down the alley behind us if they were going to St. Rose de Lima Bean Church. Which they didn't and which they weren't. "How do you know that boy?" Daddy said while we were walking in the alley.

"From around," I said.

"Around?" Daddy said again. "Around where? You remember what we talked about, don't you, Vonny, my boy?"

"Calm down, Albert," my Mother said back. "They seem like a nice family to me." Nobody said anything for a while. I was thinking about why Henry called me California. I guess I didn't tell him my name before John Smith and Pocahontas trapped us. I liked being called California. I never had a nickname. Like Red, for instance. My Mother said again, "It's good for Vonny to make new friends." She put her hand on my shoulder. "Anyways, they have to be better than that kid you call Jimmy Broom." My Mother doesn't like Jimmy. "And those parents of his!" She doesn't like his parents either.

My little sister was still hopping when we came out the other end of the alley and then walked in front of the church on Bayou Road. There were a lot of people standing around, talking, every one of them dressed up and waiting to go inside for Mass. Little kids like my little sister were running around chasing each other. I knew better. Even my little sister knew better.

"We'll talk later," Daddy said back. Which we didn't.

I could see Burdine's down the block on the corner of Broad Street. And it made me feel bad because it made me think about all the lies I made up yesterday. Especially because now we were going into church where there were the little rooms where you have to say your confession to Monseigneur Deutsch or to Father Roy, and you have to tell about all the bad things you did and all the mean words you said and all the impure thoughts you had. "Wait here a minute," Daddy said again. "I'll be right back." And then he walked away to talk to a man I didn't know.

"Who's that man?" I said to my Mother.

"What man?" my Mother said back.

"The one talking to Daddy," I said back.

"I don't know him," my Mother said again.

"Is he my cousin?" I said back again.

"Vonny!" my Mother said back. "Don't be so silly. Not everybody is your cousin, you know."

Which is not true. Almost everyone I know is my cousin! Except Lenny and Jimmy Broom and Bobby Robby. And now Henry. Almost everyone else is my cousin.

"Mama," I said back. "He could be." Which he could. She looked at me. "He could!"

My Mother laughed. "He's not your cousin, Vonny," she said again. "At least I don't think he is. Unless he's your cousin on your Daddy's side." My Mother still had her hand on my shoulder, and my little sister stopped hopping because there were a lot of people in front of the church. My little sister doesn't hop so much when there are a lot of people around. One time someone pushed her down by accident when she was hopping in a crowd. "So, tell me, Vonny," my Mother said, "where did you meet that little boy? That little boy Henry."

I looked around in front of the church. The sky was very blue. It was very, very blue. The sky was so blue I had to almost close my eyes because the light was hurting them. And there were a lot of people in front of the church. I saw a lot of the kids who go to my school. And I saw their parents. Who were older people and who I knew from school too. The man from behind the counter at Burdine's was there to go to Mass. Not to go to Burdine's. Which was closed on Sunday. I turned around so he didn't see me because I was afraid he might ask me in front of my Mother about the visible people and where did I get the twelve dollars and fifty cents and why did I ask for two dimes. He went in the church while we were still outside waiting for Daddy to talk to the man we didn't know. Larry the cook from the Triangle was there too. I turned around from him too because I was afraid he might say something in front of my Mother about how I went cow with John Smith. And there was even one of the old crocodiles from Bruno's standing outside with a lady in a dress with flowers on it. I turned around from him too because I was afraid he might ask me in front of my Mother about what did I think about the ladies on the calendar on the back wall at Bruno's. I turned around so much, I was almost spinning.

On the other side outside of the church, I saw Sister Marianna with some other Sisters who I don't know because Sister Marianna is the only teacher I ever have at St. Rose de Lima Bean School. And while I was looking at all of those people in front of the church and thinking about what to tell my Mother about where did I meet that little boy Henry, I saw that none of the people in front of the church, not anybody I knew or even didn't know, not a single person there at St. Rose de Lima Bean Church was a negro.

I was standing right in front of the church, so I told my Mother the truth about Henry. "He waved at me yesterday when I was coming back from the Triangle with our sandwhich."

"Is that why it took you so long to get back?" my Mother said.

I was standing right in front of the church. So I did not want to make up a lie when my Mother said that. Instead, I said the truth again. "No, Ma'am," I said back. "I didn't stop to talk to him. But I saw him again when I was walking back from Burdine's yesterday. He just waved at me when he was riding his bicycle while I was walking back from the Triangle. And then later he stopped his bicycle to talk to me and to Lenny Mahoney when we were walking back from Burdine's." All of that is true. "I think he likes to ride his bicycle a lot."

"Why does he call you California?" my Mother said back.

"I don't think I told him my name," I said back. Which is true too. "I just said I use to live in California because he said he just moved here from there."

"So you have something in common," my Mother said, and she smiled at me. "You both use to live in California!"

And we are both skinny and not very tall and have brown hair and brown eyes and big, white new front teeth. And we both wear dungarees and polo shirts most of the time and wear bow ties and jackets on Sunday. And we both have little sisters who hop all the time!

"Mama," I said, "why don't they have any negro kids at my school or any negro people here at the church?"

Daddy came up and said, "Sorry." He rubbed my head. "I had to talk to that guy."

"Who is he?" my Mother said back.

"He works at the barber shop," Daddy said back. Which is next to the dead chicken store right across Bayou Road from the front of the church.

"Vonny just asked me a good question, didn't you, Vonny?" my Mother said again.

"Vonny always asks good questions," Daddy said back. "So, what is it this time, Vonny, my boy?"

"Well," I said, "I told Mama that at my school and the church here I never saw."

But before I finished, Daddy said, "We better go in now. Mass is starting. It's almost ten o'clock." So, we did like Daddy said. We went in.

St. Rose de Lima Bean Church is a very, very big place. Bigger even than the Rivoli movies. Which is very, very big too. At Mass on First Friday, every kid in my school and all of the Sisters and all of the other teachers and all of the ladies who work in the cafeteria and all of the guys who clean up the school at night and even a lot of parents who come with their children can all sit in St. Rose de Lima Bean Church at the same time and there is still room for everybody to bring a friend with them too. Because it's only half full even with all of those people.

Mass on Sunday takes a very long time. It takes even longer than on First Friday because Monseigneur is there on First Friday and because everybody wants to hurry up on First Friday so they can go to eat breakfast in the cafeteria and then go to school. On Sunday, nobody is going to school after Mass. So it takes a very long time. Also, when Father Roy is at the Mass, it takes longer because Father Roy just came here from another country and he speaks in a low voice you can't even hear. Because he is from another country, it's hard to tell what he is saying even when he is speaking English. But at Mass Father Roy says words that are not even English words. And because he is from another country and speaks in a low voice, you can't even hear. And because he says words that are not even English words, then nobody can even tell what words Father Roy is saying or if they are English words because nobody can even hear him saying them. So, Mass takes a very long time!

Anyways, while we were sitting in Mass and everybody was trying to figure out what Father Roy was talking about, I heard him say something about paradise and then I started to think about the license plate on the black Pontiac with the little yellow indian on the front that John Smith and Pocahontas were inside of and that ran into Jimmy Broom while he was trying to make it from third to home instead of holding up like he should have. Which was like all the license plates on all the other cars on our street. Blue with white letters. Three numbers, then a pelican bird, and then three more numbers. Three. Six. Seven. Pelican. Four. Seven. Four.

And while I was listening to Father Roy, I remembered seeing something else on the license plate. It was two words that said SPORTSMAN'S PARADISE in little white block letters. Just like the way I just wrote it. Which I don't even know what it means. Sportsman's Paradise? I know what paradise means. It's where good people get to go after they die. Not just people who never did anything bad. Because Monseigneur says nobody is perfect and everybody does something bad sometime. And that's what confession is for. If you do something bad, then you can make it go away by going to confession. And then if you make the bad things go away and then you die before you do something bad again, then you get to go to paradise. It's not so important not to do bad things. It's more important to go to confession so you can make the bad things go away before you die. It's more important to die right after you go to confession and before you can do something bad again. Which is what everybody does sometime. And then you get to go to paradise. Which is where God lives and where all the angels live and where my Grandma who is dead lives. And my Grandpa who is dead too!

So, while Father Roy was talking about something everybody was trying to figure out what he was talking about, I was thinking about paradise and why SPORTSMAN'S PARADISE was written in little white block letters on the license plate on the black Pontiac. And on every other car on Columbus Street too. I didn't try to think about it. The thought just popped into my head. And after a while, I did what I always do when I can't figure something out. I asked Daddy. I pulled on the sleeve of his jacket and when he bended his head down to me, I just said in a low voice, "Daddy, what does it mean, Sportsman's Paradise?"

But he didn't say anything back. Daddy just put his finger on my lips as a way to say I was suppose to be quiet. Which I was. Then, a little while later, when everybody stood up because Father Roy said to and there was a lot of noise, Daddy bended over to me again and said back in a low voice, "It's where we live."

"What?" I whispered back.

"Sportsman's Paradise," Daddy said back again still in a low voice. "It's where we live."

"In paradise?" I said back again still in a low voice. But Daddy just put his finger back on my lips again. So, I was quiet standing in the St. Rose de Lima Bean Church trying to think about how we were living in paradise already even if we were not dead yet. And also thinking about if this is paradise then where is God and where are all the angels and where is my Grandma who is dead? And my Grandpa who is dead too? Monseigneur says paradise is somewheres else. But Daddy says paradise is right here where we live.

That's what my Mother calls a mystery. It's what she always tells me when I don't understand something. For instance, one time I asked my Mother what is a virgin. Like the blessed virgin Mary that Sister Marianna was talking about in school one day. Who is the mother of the baby Jesus. And my Mother said back, "It's a mystery, Vonny." A mystery? "It's just something that can't be explained," my Mother said again. Which I guess is what paradise is too. And what Sportsman's Paradise means. And why John Smith and Pocahontas ran into Jimmy Broom with the black Pontiac while he was trying to make it home instead of holding at third like he should have. These are all mysteries! What is a virgin, where is paradise, and why guys run into kids with their cars.

After Mass, like we always do, we went out of the St. Rose de Lima Bean Church and walked down Bayou Road toward Picou's Bakery.

At first, I was walking ahead of everybody. Because I always walk on Bayou Road by myself when I go to run errands to the Triangle, which has the best roast beef poor boys in the whole wide world, to Richard's Five and Dime, to Picou's, to Mister Lee's laundry, and to the disgusting meat shop, which is the baby cows' head shop. We have to buy things. We don't have anything unless we go and buy it somewheres. And in my family, I'm usually the one who has to go on errands and get it. So, I like walking on Bayou Road by myself, and I'm use to it.

But then, when I was walking alone in front of everybody, out of the corner of my eye, I saw a man waving at me from across Bayou Road in front of the barber shop. Which is next to the dead chicken store across from the St. Rose de Lima Bean Church. The man waving at me from across Bayou Road was talking to the same guy Daddy was talking to before Mass, the guy who works at the barber shop and who my Mother says is not my cousin unless he's my cousin on Daddy's side. And then I saw who was the man waving at me from across Bayou Road in front of the barber shop and talking to the guy who Daddy was talking to before Mass. It was John Smith!

Daddy and my Mother didn't see him waving at me because they were busy with my little sister, who was hopping up the street, and my baby brother, who was crying. When I saw who it was, I quick slowed down and waited until everybody got up to me and then I got on the other side of Daddy while we were walking down the street so John Smith wasn't able to see me. But I had to look back, something made me look back, and when I did I saw John Smith was still waving at me. He was smiling too. Daddy and my Mother still didn't notice him. I thought maybe John Smith might run after us. But instead, the guy who works at the barber shop and who was talking to Daddy before Mass and who was talking to John Smith after Mass just pointed at us while I was looking back at John Smith. And then I saw John Smith writing something on a little piece of paper that he tore in half and he gave one half to the other guy and then both of them put half of the little piece of paper into his pocket. Before I turned back around, I saw John Smith give the guy who works at the barber shop some money. I was too far away, so I wasn't able to see how much money he gave him.

That made me think about Pocahontas and where was he. So I looked around for the black Pontiac. Which I saw was right across Bayou Road from Richard's Five and Dime parked in front of the regular meat shop. Pocahontas was in the front seat of the black Pontiac reading the newspapers, so he didn't see me. I was walking behind Daddy anyways.

When we got to Picou's, I got a jelly doughnut because I love jelly doughnuts and my little sister got a cupcake shaped like some goofy animal that she winds up getting all over her good dress and my baby brother didn't get anything because he doesn't even know what a bakery is yet and, even if he did, he can't see good enough to pick something out of the shop window and, even if he could, he can't talk yet to say what he likes or what he wants. Like we always do! And Daddy and my Mother got cinnamon rolls. Like they always do!

After that, when we came out of Picou's, I thought John Smith or Pocahontas or both of them would be waiting for us. Or following us. But I never saw them again. We just went home and ate everything we got at the bakery. Daddy was teasing my Mother the whole time, and they were laughing with my little sister. All I did the whole time was think about John Smith and the guy who works at the barber shop and whether I had to tell Daddy and my Mother about everything that happened yesterday before John Smith and Pocahontas decided to run into some other kid on Columbus Street with the black Pontiac. But I wasn't able to figure out why the guy at the barber shop was pointing at us and what John Smith was writing on the little piece of paper they put in their pockets and why John Smith gave the man money. And I especially didn't know why did Daddy have to talk to the guy who works at the barber shop in front of the church before Mass and what did he say to him. Even if the guy was my cousin! Which he wasn't.

Anyways, after we finished breakfast, we changed out of our good clothes, and I put on my dungarees and a polo shirt and then we went in Daddy's car to my Grandma's house. The one that is alive. Who is Daddy's mother. Not my Grandma that is dead. Who is my Mother's mother.

To get to the house of my Grandma that is alive, we have to drive through City Park. So I remembered being a caddy yesterday for my Uncle Martin and that made me remember buying my Coke and using my quarter Uncle Martin gave me and getting two dimes back and going cow at the Triangle and losing my two dimes and all of the other bad things I did and the lies I told.

While I remembered all of those things, we came to the place in City Park that we always go to where when you drive fast over a little bridge over some water it makes the hair on the back of your neck stand up and it tickles on the back of your head. "Faster! Faster! Faster!" The little monkey was screaming when we got close to the bridge.

"Go fast, Daddy," I said too. "Go faster!" It's something me and my little sister like a lot.

And Daddy did it! He went fast over the little bridge and then the hair on the back of my neck stood up and I was tickled on the back of my head. My little sister was laughing. "Again! Again! Again!" she was yelling. Because sometimes Daddy drives around in a circle so we can go fast over the bridge again.

"No, no," Daddy said.

"I want to do it again!" my little sister said again.

"On the way home," Daddy said back. "On the way home." And that calmed her down. So she didn't start crying. Which sometimes she does if we don't do it again. "So," Daddy said again, "Vonny, my boy, I forgot to ask you. What were you talking about in Mass?"

"In Mass?" I said back.

"About paradise," Daddy said back. "Something about paradise. What was that about?"

I forgot it at first. I forgot about the Sportsman's Paradise. But then I saw a car in front of us in City Park with its blue and white license plate, and it reminded me. So, I said back, "It was about how on all the cars they have written Sportsman's Paradise."

"Where?" Daddy said.

"On the license plates," I said again. "What does that mean? Sportsman's Paradise?"

"Vonny!" my Mother said back. "You know what paradise means. It's where good girls and boys go. You even know how to spell it." Which I do.

"I know, Mama," I said back. "P-A-R-A-D-I-S-E. Paradise. But what does it mean? What does Sportsman's Paradise mean?"

"It means we live some place where we can catch a lot of fish and crabs and shrimp," Daddy said back. "It means when we get to the real paradise, there won't be any more fish or crabs or shrimp to eat because we have them all right here where we live."

"Well, there might be some," my Mother said back. "Nobody knows what paradise is like. Or if they even have fish or crabs or shrimp. It's a mystery." My Mother likes mysteries.

"Mystery or not," Daddy said. "Whatever paradise is like, there won't be anymore fish or crabs or shrimp than we have right here where we live. This is the Sportsman's Paradise."

"That's your idea of paradise," my Mother said. "Not everybody likes to go fishing. My daddy use to say that paradise is whatever you want it to be." My Mother calls her father daddy too. Just like I do. "Every person makes his own paradise is what my daddy use to say," she said again. "Every person makes his own paradise."

"Sister Marianna says it's where God lives and where all the angels live," I said back. "And it's where my Grandma who is dead lives too," I said again. My Mother always tells me that.

"And your Grandpa too now," my Mother said. Which is true. My Mother's daddy, who was my Grandpa, died too when we lived in California. My Mother cried for a lot of days after we got a letter saying he died. My Mother sometimes shows me pictures of my Grandpa who is dead. Sometimes I was in the pictures with him when I was little like my little sister is little now and when I was a baby like my baby brother is a baby now. And in the pictures my Grandpa looks just like one of the old crocodiles at Bruno's. If I close my eyes hard, I can almost see him raising up a glass of beer at me. Which maybe he use to do.

"Well, I know your Grandpa," Daddy said, "and if his paradise is whatever he wanted it to be, he's probably in a barroom right now."

"Albert!" my Mother said out loud, and then she hit Daddy on the arm with one of her little fists. But not hard.

"And probably with God and all the angels too!" Daddy said again.

"That's not a very nice thing to say," my Mother said again.

"But it's true," Daddy said back. "You know it's true."

"Like your family is any different!" my Mother said back. "Like nobody in your family ever drinks," she said again. Which is not true. Because we all drink. All of us in my family. Even my baby brother drinks milk.

But Daddy's family is different from my Mother's family. For instance, I already told that my Mother has a lot of brothers. Four of them. Which are the ones I saw at City Park when I went to caddy for Uncle Martin. Except for the one who is dead. Which makes five brothers for my Mother.

Daddy doesn't have any brothers. He doesn't even have one brother. A long time ago he had one. But Daddy's brother died when he was just a little boy. Like about as little as my little sister is little now. Daddy says his little brother was very skinny and was always sick. Even when he was a baby boy.

And my Mother has a lot of sisters too. Like Aunt Gwendolyn. Who is Charly and Marly's mother. And like Aunt Tallulah. Who bought red shoes for my cousin Dottie that were too big for her and that my Mother tried to make me wear to school one day. Which I didn't. Because they were girl's shoes. And because they were red! Boys don't wear red shoes. Especially not red girl's shoes. And like Aunt Junie. Who is my Uncle Roger's mother and who dropped him on his head. My Mother says it was an accident. And like my aunt who is a very large lady who my Mother made me buy underwear for at Richard's Five and Dime. And like my other aunt too. Who lives in California with all her girls and with my cousin Willy.

But Daddy has only one sister. Just like me. And the best thing about Daddy's only one sister is that she is my Nanny. Which means she is my godmother. Like my Mother is Charly and Marly's Nanny. She is their godmother. So, they call her Nanny. Like I call Daddy's sister Nanny. And my Nanny is always at my Grandma's house whenever we go there. Which is always on Sunday after we go to Mass and after we go to Picou's.

"Hey, Junior," my Grandma said to Daddy when we went in her house through the back door into the kitchen. "I thought you said you were coming early to help Doc run his boat engine before dinner." For some reason, my Grandma calls Daddy Junior. Who is not little. And she calls my Grandpa Doc. Who is not a doctor. And we always go in the house through the back door into the kitchen. Just like we do at our house. Except my Grandma's kitchen is smaller than our kitchen.

"We got out of Mass late," Daddy said back. Which was not true. "Maybe we can do it later. After lunch." He was just pretending.

"Hey, brother in law," my Uncle Duke said. My Uncle Duke is married to my Nanny. They have two little girls who are even more little than my little sister is little. And who are my cousins too. At my Grandma's house, my little sister and my cousins always play goofy girl games or little kid games together, and I sit in the front room by myself either watching a TV program or sometimes reading a book if I remember to bring one. Sometimes, if I don't like any TV program and I forget to bring a book, then I go into my Grandpa Doc's bedroom where he has a lot of books about policemen and bad guys. Which my Mother says I am not suppose to read. But I do anyways because I know how to read them and because I like when the policemen always catch the bad guys. Or sometimes just shoot them.

When we got to my Grandma's house after Mass and after Picou's, after I hugged my Grandma in the kitchen and then shook my Grandpa Doc's hand, which is very large and which he uses to squeeze my hand until it hurts, I went straight to the front room and sat down on the sofa. There was newspapers there. So I wanted to find the funny pages and look at what the Prince was doing that week. Which is Prince Valiant. But on the sofa there was also one of my Grandpa Doc's books about policemen and bad guys. I picked up the book to read it. But before I could start my Nanny walked into the front room and said, "So, Mister Vonny Foster, do you think you're too old to kiss your Nanny now that you're going to make your First Communion?" Which I didn't think that. "Is that what they teach you in school these days?" my Nanny said again. Which is not what they teach me.

I just didn't see my Nanny when I walked into the kitchen or the front room. So I told her so. And then I said again, "Where were you when we got here, Nanny?" I got up and hugged her. She kissed me on the cheek.

I sat back down on the sofa, and then she sat down next to me and put her arm around my shoulders.

"I was just in your Grandma's bedroom wrapping a present for your baby brother. We're so busy we didn't have time to come by your house since he was born." Which they didn't. They hardly ever come by our house. We almost always see my Nanny and my Uncle Duke at my Grandma's house. Because they live close by to her like we live close by to my Uncle Martin and my Uncle Roger. Except my Nanny and my Uncle Duke don't live on Columbus Street. "So, what's this I hear about your mama tying your foot to the bed?" my Nanny said. She laughed out loud. When my Nanny laughs, she always laughs out loud. Sometimes very out loud. My Nanny has the kind of laugh that makes you want to laugh out loud too. "I think your daddy and mama think you're trying to run away from home!" my Nanny said again. And she laughed again. In the way she does. So, I laughed too.

I would never run away from home! I like my house and don't even want another one. I don't know what I was doing when I sleepwalked. I don't even remember it. It's just something that happened. Like when a thought pops into my head. But whatever I was doing when I was sleepwalking, I was not running away from home. "I just sleepwalked one night," I said back, and lifted my shoulders. "I don't even remember doing it."

My Nanny laughed again. "So, now you get to have your foot tied to the bed like you're a criminal or something," she said again. My Nanny thinks a lot of things are funny. She's happy all the time. And she laughs a lot. So, I laughed too.

Then I remembered. "Last night, Nanny, they tied both of my feet to the bed!" I said back. Which Daddy and my Mother did after Uncle Martin finally went outside and told everybody I was in my bed and not sleepwalking again. That's very funny. So, my Nanny and I laughed more and more.

"Both feet?" my Nanny said back.

"They did, Nanny!" I didn't tell her that I pretended to be sleeping while I listened to them talking about Jimmy Broom and then how Daddy went to look for me in the parlor and then how he didn't find me, even in the bathtub, and then how my Mother was dramatick and then how they all ran out into the street looking for me until my Uncle Martin came and found me in bed and then finally went outside and told them.

"Whose idea was it to tie both of your feet to the bed?" Nanny said. I just lifted my shoulders again because last night before everybody came back inside I was finally sleeping already. The last thing I remembered was Uncle Martin telling Uncle Roger he was going to go out and tell everybody the good news. Then, my Nanny whispered to me, "I bet it was your mama." My Nanny leaned over to me. "You know how dramatick your mama gets sometimes." Which I don't know. Except Daddy and Uncle Martin and now my Nanny say my Mother is dramatick sometimes. "I'll have a talk with your mama and daddy," my Nanny said. "If you're big enough to make your First Communion, you should be big enough to sleep without being tied to your bed." My Nanny laughed, and then she rubbed me on top of my head. "What are you reading there?"

I showed her Grandpa Doc's book that was on the sofa. There was a picture of a lady on the cover of the book who was wearing a red dress that didn't cover all of one of her legs. "It's Grandpa Doc's book," I whispered.

"Oh, my," Nanny said. "One of those. A mystery book. Detectives and such. You know how to read that?"

"I can read almost all the words, Nanny," I said back. "Some of them I have to sound out. And some of them I don't understand even if I sound them out. But I can read them all."

"It's probably better you don't understand them all, Vonny," my Nanny said, and then she stood up. "There's a lot of things I wish I didn't understand myself," she said again. Whatever that means. "Well, don't let your mama see you with that, whatever you do." My Nanny rubbed me on the head again. "And if you read that whole book, you probably will have to put it on your confession list!" she said again. And then my Nanny laughed after she said that, while she was walking back into the hallway to the kitchen. "Junior!" I heard her say out loud. She turned around and winked at me. "When are you going to stop tying this child's foot to the bed?"

I just sat on the sofa looking at the lady's leg in the red dress on the cover of my Grandpa Doc's book. At school, the books are not very big. Not even as many pages as in the newspapers. And the words are printed in big black letters. Much bigger than in the newspapers. But my

Grandpa Doc's books are bigger with a lot of pages. And the words are very, very small. Little black words. And there are a lot of words on every page. And the pages are smaller than in the newspapers. But there are a lot more pages. A lot more! The book with the lady in the red dress on the cover has two hundred seventy two pages. Also, the books at school are different colors. There's a red book, a blue book, a green book. With pictures on the cover of kids running after dogs or of kids running after kids or of dogs running after kids. Sometimes on the cover of the books at school there is a boy running after a girl or a girl running after a boy. The books at school never have a picture on the cover of a lady in a red dress that didn't cover all of one of her legs. Maybe they do in the eighth grade.

Anyways, sitting on the sofa in the front room at my Grandma's house, I forgot all about the newspapers and the Prince, and I started to read my Grandpa Doc's book. Which right away was about a guy named Sam. Who use to be a policeman and who use to be married to a pretty lady that died. Sam's wife was run over by a car and killed in an accident. Just like Jimmy Broom! Except Jimmy wasn't killed. And except the lady wasn't playing stickball and trying to make it home instead of holding at third base when she got run over. She was just crossing the street and carrying a lot of presents for her little children. Because it was Christmas time. And so she didn't see over the top of the packages. Just like me at Burdine's with the two visible people boxes! And she forgot to look both ways before she crossed the street. Which my little sister does all the time. Because she was in a hurry to catch the bus and to get to her house to cook supper for her husband, who was Sam the policeman, and for her little children. Who were a boy and a little girl and a baby boy. Just like my Mother! Except my Mother never catches the bus. Then when the lady was crossing the street a car ran into her right in front of the bus stop. And it didn't stop right away. Just like the black Pontiac! And Sam the policeman saw everything that happened. Because he was working right by the bus stop. He saw the man who was driving the car. Who ran away. But Sam didn't say anything to the other policemen about the accident. He knew what happened, but he didn't want to talk about it. So, he had to stop being a policeman. Just because he didn't say anything. Because everybody knew he saw something. But he wasn't saying what he saw. Just like Uncle Martin! He didn't tell the truth about what he saw. So, the other policemen made him quit being a policeman. Even when his wife was dead. And he had three kids to take care of. So, Sam was angry. And he had to try to figure out what happened to his wife. Where the man went who hit her with the car. And if it really was an accident or an incident. It was a mystery!

"I want to read! I want to read! I want to read!" My little sister ran into the front room at my Grandma's house.

"Why don't you go play with the girls?" I said back. Those are my little girl cousins who belong to my Nanny and my Uncle Duke.

"I don't want to! I don't want to! I don't want to!" she said back. "I want to read! I want to read! I want to read!"

"Here," I said back again. I gave my little sister my Grandpa Doc's book. "You can try to read this." Which she is not able to do.

"No!" my little sister said back again. "No! No! You read! You read! You read!"

"Okay," I said back. "I'll read to you if you want." I took back my Grandpa's book. "But you have to listen. Okay?"

My little sister didn't care about the story. She just wants to listen to me read. "Okay! Okay! Okay!" she said back. She climbed up on the sofa and sat next to me.

"So, here goes," I said, and then I closed my eyes, opened up the book to the middle, and looked at the page. Which was the beginning of Chapter 8. Because that's what it said at the top of the page. It didn't matter to my little sister. She didn't know anything about Sam anyways. And then I just started reading to her. Like I have to do in class sometimes. "Now, listen," I said. Which she did. "Sam walked through the door, tired and wet after a day in the rain hunting his wife's killer, and right away saw a good-looking woman sitting on a stool at the bar, a beautiful woman in fact, alone, a cigarette in her hand, one long leg crossed over the other beneath a smart red dress. What a sight for sore eyes! Sam said to himself as he took off his water-soaked hat. The woman had long auburn hair and bright green eyes that Sam could make out even in the dark room. She was tall, very tall, too tall in fact for the tight crimson dress that clung to her pale, slim body like paint on a fire engine. The beige stockings on her pink thighs peeked out from beneath the too high hem, but the woman didn't care if everyone enjoyed the view. Which Sam surely did."

My little sister put two fingers on her lips and then moved them back and forth from her face like she was smoking. "See, Vonny. I can smoke too," she said. "See! See!"

"I thought you were going to listen," I said back.

"Who's Sam?" my little sister said back.

"I'm not going to read if you don't listen," I said back again.

"What's beige mean, Vonny?" my little sister said again.

Then, my Mother walked into the front room from the hallway. "So, what are you two doing?" she said. "You look so cute together there on the sofa." Which I don't like when my Mother says I'm cute. Because it makes me sound like I'm a girl.

"I was reading to her," I said back.

"You're such a sweet boy, Vonny," my Mother said back. Which I also don't like when my Mother says I'm sweet. Because it makes it sound like I'm a girl too. A cute, sweet girl! "And your little sister loves you so much, Vonny. You know she does! You love your big brother, don't you, you little monkey?"

"Look, Mommy!" my little sister said. Who calls my Mother mommy. Which is what little kids do. "Look, Mommy, look! I can smoke too!" And then my little sister put her two fingers together again like she was holding a cigarette and then moved them back and forth from her mouth like she was smoking. "See! See! See!"

"You're a silly goose," my Mother said back. "You little monkey, you." My Mother walked over to the sofa, bended down, and started to tickle my little sister. "You're too little to smoke. Too little!" The little monkey got up from the sofa and started hopping around the front room and waving her little arms in the air. "You calm down now," my Mother said, and then she sat next to me on the sofa. "Come here and sit on Mommy's lap," she said again to my little sister. "Come over here and let's listen to your big brother read his story to us."

"Mama," I said, "what does crimson mean?"

"It's another way to say red," my Mother said back. "It means red."

"And what about auburn," I said back.

"Same thing," my Mother said back again. "Same as crimson. It means red. Except usually you say someone has auburn hair."

"Can you say people have crimson hair?" I said back again.

My Mother laughed. "Only if you're talking about a circus clown, Vonny. Usually you say people have red hair or maybe auburn hair."

"Can you say a fire engine is crimson?"

My Mother laughed again. "You and your questions, Vonny! I guess you can say a fire engine is crimson. Sure. Why not?"

"Can you say a fire engine is auburn?" I said again.

My Mother didn't stop laughing for about a minute. "Vonny! Stop with your questions, will you?" When she stopped laughing, my Mother said, "No. I think the only thing that is auburn is hair. Just hair. And usually a lady's hair. What are you reading there anyways?" My Mother reached for my Grandpa Doc's book in my hand and turned it over to see the cover. Which was the picture of the lady with the auburn hair in the crimson dress.

"It was just here, Mama," I said. "I didn't go into Grandpa's bedroom. I didn't." Which was true.

"Well, this is not a good story for your little sister, Vonny."

"But it's what I was reading, Mama," I said back. "When she asked me to read to her."

"Well, it's nice of you to read to your little sister. It's very cute. And you're very sweet to do it." Cute and sweet again! "But this is not a good story for her, Vonny. And it's not a good story for you either."

"It was just here, Mama," I said back again. "I didn't go into Grandpa's bedroom." Which was still true. "I promise."

"I believe you," my Mother said back. "I do." Which I want my Mother to believe me. Especially when what I say is true.

"And, Mama, you always say I can only get a better vocabulerry by reading a lot," I said back. Which she does say. All the time.

My Mother laughed again. "That's true, Vonny." She rubbed me on the head. "That's true. I do say that. And it's true that you can only get a better vocabulerry by reading a lot." My little sister was still putting her two fingers together like she was holding a cigarette and then moving them back and forth from her mouth like she was smoking. "Stop that, you little monkey!" my Mother said to her.

"And the books at school are too easy, Mama," I said back. "They're just for little kids." Which they are!

My Mother put her arm around my shoulders and hugged me. "I tell you what," she said back. "I'll come to school and talk to Sister Marianna about getting you some liberry books to read so you can get a better vocabulerry."

"Liberry! Liberry! Liberry!" is what my little sister started saying out loud.

Just then, my Nanny walked into the front room and said, "Okay, everybody. Dinner's ready."

Most of the time, I like when we go to my Grandma's house on Sundays after Mass at St. Rose de Lima Bean Church after we get jelly doughnuts at Picou's Bakery. Everybody leaves me alone at my Grandma's house. My little sister plays with my little girl cousins. Daddy and my Mother sit around talking to my Nanny and my Uncle Duke, and to my Grandma and my Grandpa Doc. And I can just sit in the front room by myself. Where I can just read. Or sometimes just do nothing.

But what I don't like about when we go to my Grandma's house is when we eat dinner. Which is always very good! Because my Grandma cooks the best red gravy. But which I have to sit at a little table in the kitchen with my little sister and my little girl cousins while everybody else sits at the big table eating and talking. What do I have to say to my little sister and to my little girl cousins? Nothing! I'm not little like them. I'm in second grade, and they're not even in school. Also, they are girls!

Which is why I don't like eating dinner at my Grandma's house. Except the food is very good. When I am sitting at the little table in the kitchen, I don't even look at my little sister and my little girl cousins. I just eat, and I just look at the big table where almost all the time everybody is talking all at the same time. Daddy and my Mother. My Nanny and my Uncle Duke. And my Grandma and my Grandpa Doc. All of them talking almost all the time at the same time. Which was hard to listen to. So, I just eat as fast as I can before asking my Mother if I can go back into the front room. Where I can just read. Or sometimes just do nothing. Which is what I did on that Sunday too.

I was tired after eating. I sat down on the sofa in the front room and read a little more of my Grandpa Doc's book about Sam the policeman and about him trying to find the guy who ran over his wife when she was running for the bus to go home and cook supper for her husband, who was Sam the policeman, and for her little children. When she was just crossing the street and carrying a lot of presents for them. Because it was Christmas time. And because I was tired, I took off my shoes and just lied down on the sofa and kept reading my Grandpa Doc's book. About how Sam the policeman lost his job. How he was angry. How his little children barely had anything to eat. How his pretty wife was dead now. And the more I read, the more I was tired. Because my Grandma's red gravy makes me tired if I eat too much of it. Which I did. Because it is good!

I was very tired. But I could hear everybody in the back of my Grandma's house talking almost all the time at the same time. It was hard to hear what they were saying. But I heard Daddy say, "My brother in law Martin saw everything. Everything! The guy driving the black Pontiac ran right over the kid. Didn't even try to miss him. He wanted to kill him. Kill him right there on Columbus Street. The police are looking for him."

"For your brother in law?" I heard my Nanny say.

"No!" Daddy said back. "Not Martin. They're not looking for Martin. They're looking for a guy named John Smith. He's the guy who ran over the kid! Him and his buddy Pocahontas."

My Nanny laughed, and then everybody laughed. Because whenever my Nanny laughs, it makes everybody want to laugh too. "Pocahontas?" she said out loud. "That's a funny name!"

"So," my Uncle Duke said, "did your brother in law Martin tell the police what he saw?"

"They never asked him," Daddy said back. "And he saw everything! Everything there was to see. He even saw that the kid should have held at third instead of going for home."

"Why doesn't he call the police up and tell them what he saw?" my Uncle Duke said again.

"Well," Daddy said, "sometimes you see things and are not sure about what you saw. And even if you are sure about what you saw, it's not always clear what the meaning is of what you saw."

"That's what I call a sin of omission," my Uncle Duke said back again.

"A what?" Daddy said back.

"It's when you don't do something you're suppose to do," my Uncle Duke said. "It's as bad as a lie."

Daddy laughed out loud. And everybody else laughed out loud with him. Then a man opened the door of my Grandma's house and walked into the front room with me. But I didn't look at him. Because I was listening to what Daddy said. "That's not a lie!" Daddy said back. "It's just pretending!"

"Pretending?" my Uncle Duke said again.

"Right!" Daddy said again. "He's just pretending he didn't see anything." The man who came into the front room of my Grandma's house while I was reading my Grandpa's book and listening to Daddy talk sat down on the end of the sofa where my feet were. I didn't move because I was very tired. Very, very tired.

"That's a lie!" my Uncle Duke said. "A sin of omission. He's not doing something he's suppose to do. Which is tell the police what he saw."

The man sitting on the end of the sofa said to me, "What are you reading, Vonny?"

I didn't even look at the man. I was so tired. "It's a book about a Sam the policeman," I said back. "Whose wife was run over by a car and killed in an accident. And about a lady in a tight crimson dress. Like a fire engine." It was dark in the front room of my Grandma's house.

"But sometimes you see things and are not sure about what you saw," Daddy said back.

"Except your brother in law knows what he saw," my Uncle Duke said back. "He saw this John Smith. And this Pocahontas. He saw them run over the kid!"

The man sitting on the end of the sofa where my feet were said, "Did that guy say something about John Smith?"

"That's my Uncle Duke," I said back. I was very, very tired. I could barely keep my eyes open. So, I just said back again, "She was just crossing the street and carrying a lot of presents for her little children. Because it was Christmas time. And so she didn't see over the top of the packages. Just like me at Burdine's with the two visible people boxes!"

"So that was you in the back of Burdine's after all, wasn't it?" the man sitting on the end of the sofa said. I just nodded. "I was looking for you, kid."

I heard everybody in the back of my Grandma's house talking all the time at the same time. My Nanny was laughing louder and louder. Daddy was talking about what Uncle Martin saw. My Uncle Duke too. Even my little sister was saying, "I saw it too! I saw it too! I saw it too! Jimmy! Jimmy! Jimmy!"

The man sitting on the end of the sofa bended over and said in a low voice, "I want my twelve dollars and fifty cents back, kid. Before I do to you what I did to that Jimmy Broom!"

It was John Smith! At my Grandma's house!

I tried to call Daddy. I tried to call my Mother. But John Smith just put his hand over my mouth. And then he used his thumb and a finger to pinch my nose closed. I wasn't able to breathe. I wasn't getting any air! He was choking me! "Please, stop!" I tried to say. Which it was not possible to do because I didn't have any air in my throat.

"You and your Uncle Martin and your Bobby Robby and your little punk friend Henry." Except he didn't say punk. He said something worse. "You think you saw what happened. You think you know what happened. But I'll get every last one of you! You think I'm going to let some kid ruin my life? Some kid who can't even tell his mother the truth about what he does? About going cow? About buying visible people? About where he got two little dimes?"

"Daddy! Daddy! Daddy!" I tried to cry out. But John Smith had his hand over my mouth. He pinched my nose closed with his thumb and a finger. "Daddy! Please! Help!"

"Maybe if you told the truth, you could get away," John Smith said. He put his other hand behind my head and started to press his two hands together. Like he was trying to crush my head.

"Please, stop!" I tried to say. Then I tried to get up. But my feet were tied to the sofa. Like at my house at night. I tried to push away John Smith's hand from my face. But the harder I pushed, the more he pinched my nose closed. I pushed and pushed, and he pinched and pinched. I tried to get my feet loose. But they were tied to the sofa. "Daddy! Please! Help!" I tried to say again. I tried again to push away his hand from my face.

And then John Smith said, "Vonny, my boy. Calm down. Just calm down, Vonny, my boy! You're alright. You're okay." And I felt somebody rubbing my head.

"My feet are tied to the bed," I said back. "My feet are tied! I can't move! I can't move!"

And then a lady laughed out loud and said, "I told you it wasn't a good idea to tie his feet to the bed. You see what you get?"

I finally pushed away John Smith's hand from my face and sat up on the sofa. My feet were untied. I sat up and Grandpa Doc's book fell on the floor. I could hear my Nanny laughing. Daddy was leaning over me. And my Mother too. "You're alright, Vonny, my boy," Daddy said. "You'll be just fine."

"Oh, Vonny!" my Mother said out loud. "You're still worried about that little boy, aren't you? I knew you were. That's why you went sleep-walking!" My Nanny and my Uncle Duke were in the front room now, and my Grandma and my Grandpa Doc too. Even my little sister and my little girl cousins.

"Where's John Smith?" I said back.

"John Smith was here?" my Nanny said. "What about Pocahontas?" Everybody laughed.

"No," I said back. "Just John Smith." And everybody laughed even more out loud.

"You fell asleep on the sofa, Vonny, my boy," Daddy said. "No cowboys and indians here." My Nanny laughed again when he said that. And then everybody else laughed too.

Even my little sister laughed. "Cowboys and indians! Cowboys and indians! Cowboys and indians!"

Eight, or
St. Rose de Lima Bean School

I have a lot of cousins. Like I already told. Not just my little girl cousins that belong to my Nanny and my Uncle Duke. But all the cousins I have because my Mother has a lot of brothers and sisters. And almost all of my cousins live right by us.

For instance, I already told about my Uncle Roger. Who lives next to Jimmy Broom and who is not my uncle but is really my cousin. And my Uncle Roger has a brother and some sisters too. And there are my girl cousins who live with my Uncle Martin and my Aunt Audra. Who live in the house on the other side of Lenny Mahoney. Who are Pia and Suzette. And they have a big sister and a baby sister too. Over on Broad Street is where my cousin William lives. Who is bigger than me and makes sure that big kids at school don't give me any trouble. He has so many brothers and sisters I can't even remember them all. And I already told about my cousin Earl. Who went to the football game with me and Daddy that one time. And his big brother is Uncle Dingle. Who also is not my uncle but is really my cousin. And they have a big sister and a little sister. Who is Dottie. Who lives by the horse race track and use to have red shoes. And there is my cousin Floyd. Who I went to the new hamburger shop with. He has two brothers too. Who only sometimes live by us because their daddy, who is my Uncle Charles, is in the army and has to live all over the place.

That's just the cousins who almost all live right by us.

I already told about Charly and Marly. Who don't live in our neighborhood. Even if they don't live far away. And they have some brothers too. And then there are other cousins who live somewheres around us. Who their daddy is my Uncle Gauthier. But I don't know where because they are all too little for me to even play with. They are babies like my baby brother is a baby. I don't even know their names sometimes. I just see them when they get baptized or somebody gets married or has a birthday. All I can do is just try to figure out who they are. But it's not easy.

That's just the cousins who live in our town. Which is New Orleans.

I have a lot of cousins who live somewheres else too. For instance, I have a lot of cousins who live in Alabama. Wherever that is. Whose mother is my aunt who is a very large lady that my Mother sent me to the Richard's Five and Dime on an errand to buy underwear for. And I already told about my cousins in California. Who are all girls. Except my cousin Willy. And I have even some more cousins who live somewheres I don't even know. Because their daddy died before I was even born and I don't know what they look like or even what grade they are in.

My Mother has so many brothers and sisters, I don't even know who everybody is. And that's why sometimes I think everybody is my cousin. Or at least maybe is.

Anyways, on Monday morning, like almost every morning when I go to school, I walked with my cousin Pia. Who is my age and is in the second grade and who lives with my Uncle Martin and his wife. Who is my Aunt Audra. Who talks Australian and makes my Mother laugh all the time. Like I already told. My cousin Pia is not my only cousin who is my age because my cousin Queenie in Alabama is and my cousin Dottie by the horse race track is too.

Dottie is my cousin who one time got some red Buster Brown shoes that were too big for her and that my Mother thought would be a good idea for me to wear to school. Red shoes! Girl's shoes! That was last year when I was in first grade. When I was a new kid at St. Rose de Lima Bean School. A new, little kid!

"I can't wear those shoes to school," I told my Mother. "Those are girl's shoes!"

"Don't be so dramatick, Vonny," my Mother said back. "Nobody can tell they are girl's shoes. They're just shoes. And they fit you."

Which was not true. They were tight. "They hurt my feet, Mama," I said back. "My toes are all pinched inside. I'll get a blister."

"Well, if you get a blister, we'll put a bandage on it," my Mother said back. She is very smart, my Mother. She thinks of everything. If I contradict her, I get in trouble. But she contradicts me all the time!

"But they're girl's shoes!" I said again. "And they're red!"

"I know," my Mother said back. "Think of how special you'll be at school. The only boy in school with red shoes."

"That's not special!" I said back. I was whining. "Mama!" I said again. I don't like to whine. But my Mother was not leaving well enough alone. Everybody was going to laugh at my red girl's shoes. Everybody was going to laugh at me!

"Do you want me to punish you, Vonny Foster?" my Mother said back again.

"But the kids at school are going to think I'm a girl," I said.

"Who's going to think you're a girl, Vonny?" my Mother said back. "Sister Marianna? Monseigneur Deutsch? Don't be ridiculous."

"But already some kids think my name is a girl's name!"

"What do you care about what other kids think?" my Mother said back again. "Besides, Vonny is a perfectly good boy's name. Which everybody already knows anyways."

"Mama!" is all I could say back again. No matter what I said, my Mother was going to make me wear my cousin Dottie's red Buster Brown girls shoes. To St. Rose de Lima Bean School! Which my Aunt Tallulah bought on sale at the shop on Bayou Road and that were too big for my cousin Dottie and that she didn't keep the receipt and so she couldn't take them back and so now I had to wear them because it was a bad thing to waste good shoes. Which is what my Mother said. Even if I had to look like a dope. Which is what I said. "But, Mama, the other kids are going to think I'm a goofball!"

"Well, do you think you're a goofball, Vonny?" my Mother said back.

"Of course not!" I said back out loud.

"You watch your tone, young man," my Mother said back. "I'm not one of your little friends." Which my friends are not little. They're in the second grade. Like me. "I'm your mother!" my Mother said back again. "And if you know you're not a goofball, what do you care about what the other kids think?" my Mother said. "Just because other kids think things about you doesn't make them true."

My Mother is too smart for me. She's not like Lenny Mahoney. Who does what I ask him to do after I say something to him about why it's a good idea. My Mother has too many good ideas of her own. She's always thinking about the whys and the wherefores.

"But, Mama!" I said. I was whining even more. I didn't know what else to say. "Mama!"

"Don't wait until you grow up to become who you are, Vonny. Be who you are now," my Mother said. Whatever that means.

I just said back, "Mama, if I wear those red girl's shoes to school, the big kids are going to beat me up."

"Well, you just get your cousin William to stand by you in the school yard."

"What if he's sick today, Mama? What if he misses school?"

"Your cousin William is just fine, Vonny. I talked to parain last night on the telephone." My Mother calls my parain her parain too. Because my Uncle Stephen, who is my parain, is her godfather too. "He said William is just fine. You know I'm his Nanny too." Which is true. My Mother is my cousin William's godmother too. Who is the son of her parain. And my parain too.

Anyways, my Mother is too smart for me. If I say anything, she says something better back. It's the way she is. She's not like Lenny Mahoney. She never leaves well enough alone.

So, on that morning last year, when I was in first grade, I finally put on the red Buster Brown girl's shoes that were so tight they pinched my toes. And like I always do, like I still do, I met my cousin Pia out on the brick sidewalk in front of our house on Columbus Street to walk to school.

When Pia saw my red girl's shoes, she started laughing. Which I knew everyone was going to do if I wore them to school. "Why are you wearing those girl's shoes?" Pia said. She was laughing and laughing. "Red ones!" she said again. "They look very cute on you."

"They belong to Dottie," I said back.

"Then why are you wearing them?" Pia said back again.

"My Mother is making me wear them," I said back again.

We started walking to school. "Are you really going to wear those little red girl's shoes into the classroom?" Pia said back again. "Red girl's shoes!" She was still laughing and laughing. Walking on Columbus Street, I was thinking that I looked like a circus clown in my khaki shirt and khaki pants and red girl's Buster Brown shoes. "Are you wearing little white frilly socks with those girl's shoes too?" Pia said again. Who was still, still laughing and laughing.

So, on that morning last year, when we got to the corner of Dorgenois in front of Bruno's, a thought just popped into my head. Which was I needed to get an upset stomach. I don't know where it came from. But when we got to the corner, I just made myself get an upset stomach. Right on the street. Just like that. "I feel terrible!" I said to Pia. And then I bended over, and I just made myself get an upset stomach right in the gutter.

"That's disgusting," Pia said back. "I think you just got throw up all over your little red girl's shoes!" And she kept laughing and laughing and laughing. "And maybe even your little white frilly socks too." I just turned around and ran home.

But this morning, when I am in second grade, on the Monday after the Sunday when I dreamed on the sofa in the front room at my Grandma's house about John Smith trying to smother me, I was wearing plain old boy's brown shoes when I met my cousin Pia out on the brick sidewalk in front of the house on Columbus Street to walk to school.

"Are you still walking outside in your sleep?" my cousin Pia said.

"I only did it once," I said back. Which is true.

"Are they still tying your feet to the bed?" she said back.

"They only tie one of them to the bed," I said back again. Which is also true. Except for one time they tied both. "And they still do. Because that's what the doctor said to do. I think they think I'm going to walk out into the street and get hit by a car."

We were walking right in front of Bruno's. I looked over into the street to see if there was any of Jimmy Broom's blood left in the street between third and home. But it was covered over with dirt. It was invisible. The stupid black and brown dog across the street at third base was barking and clapping his teeth at all the kids who walked by. A lady was standing in the middle of Dorgenois Street holding up a stop sign in case any cars tried to run over kids walking to school.

"Hey, California." Just as we were walking into the street I turned around and saw Henry. Who was sitting on his bicycle. He was in the little alley that is in the back of Bruno's, on Dorgenois Street. Which is on the other side from the back door that I usually go in when I buy my Mother's cigarettes. "Hey, California!" Henry said again.

Pia turned around and saw him. "You know that kid?" she said.

I told the truth. "I do," I said back. "I saw him yesterday morning with my family when we were walking to Mass. He was on Columbus Street. You go ahead. I'll catch up." Which Pia did. Go ahead, that is. Except I didn't. Catch up, that is. Instead, I went back to see Henry. "Hi, Henry," I said. "Don't you go to school?"

"That's what I'm doing now," Henry said back. "Riding my bike to school."

"Why don't you walk?" I said back.

"Too far away. My school is way far away. It's over the other side of the race track."

"I walk to the horse race track with my daddy sometimes," I said back again.

"Right," Henry said back. "But my school is way the other side of the race track. Way the other side! Anyways, we have to talk after school," he said again. "That's why I came over here."

"We do?"

"Right!" Henry said. "Today. Before somebody gets hurt."

"What do you mean?" I said back.

"That man came over to my house last night to talk to my daddy," Henry said back.

Then the lady in the middle of the street with the stop sign saw us talking and said out loud, "Hey! What are you two doing in that alley? What kind of trouble are you up to over there?"

"Just meet me after school down the block," Henry said. "At five thirty. Six at the latest."

"Today?"

"Yes," Henry said out loud. "Today!"

"Where down the block?" I said back.

"Down there," he said. Henry pointed down Dorgenois at his street, the one behind Columbus. "Harp Street." But then he just shook his head. "Forget it, California. My daddy might be on our porch and see us. Just meet me here in this alley," he said again.

"Hey, you two. Let's get a move on!" the lady in the street said again.

"I have to go," Henry said again. And then he hopped up on a pedal and rode his bicycle back along Dorgenois Street, away from Bruno's, back to where his house is.

Right when I got back to the corner to cross the street, Lenny Mahoney walked up behind me. "You have to come and get that invisible man from me this afternoon after school," Lenny said in a low voice. "You said you were going to come over Saturday night to get it. That's the only reason I took it home. We were suppose to go to the movies at the Rivoli."

"My Mother didn't let me," I said back. "She didn't even let me go outside." I was just making excuses. "And I was tired. Very, very tired. I got up too early Saturday to caddy at City Park for my Uncle Martin when he played golf." As many as I was able to think of. "And then I was at my Grandma's house all day yesterday too."

"I need to get it out of my house today before my mother finds it," Lenny said again in a low voice. "If she finds it under my bed, I'm going to get in trouble."

"Okay," I said back. We were walking past second base in front of the kindergarden.

"Big trouble!" he said again.

"Okay," I said again. "Meet me in the alley over there right after school." I turned around and pointed at the alley where I just talked to Henry on his bicycle. "You can give it to me over there."

"Right after school," Lenny said. "Right after!"

"Okay!" I said back again. "We'll meet in the alley behind Bruno's right after school. You bring the invisible man, Lenny." Which even if it was a visible man, I said it the way Lenny does just that one time so he knew what I was talking about.

School was not fun on Monday. Sharon the Roach was still sick with her rabbity pink eyes. So, she didn't come to class. Even Louie Canale didn't come to school because his daddy's car was broken. He lives too far away from school to walk. Like Henry. We didn't have any contests in class. And we didn't learn anything new. Monseigneur Deutsch was suppose to come and talk to us about how to make our confession. But he had a cold and didn't even come to our class either. Then, it started raining sometime in the morning. So, we didn't get to go outside at recess or even at lunch time. We just stayed inside and played goofball games.

I asked to go to the liberry to get some books. But Sister Marianna said that there were too many other big kids already in the liberry. Because it was raining. So, she didn't let me go there. And then, to make it as bad as possible, right after lunch time was over and we weren't able to go outside because it was raining, right after we started doing some work in the afternoon, the sun came out. At recess and lunch time, it rained all day. Then after when we didn't have any recess or lunch time, the sun came out. School was not fun on Monday.

Anyways, all day in school I was thinking about what I had to do right after. Which was go home and get the visible woman. Which my Mother thought I was going to trade her for a visible man at Burdine's. The visible woman. Not my Mother. And then instead, take her back to Burdine's and get my money back. The visible woman. Not my Mother. And then meet Lenny in the alley behind Bruno's to get the visible man. Which my Mother thought I was going to get from Burdine's. Then bring back the visible man to my house. And then eat supper and meet Henry back in the alley behind Bruno's again. Which I didn't say to anybody.

That was what was suppose to happen. But here's what happened instead.

When I got home from school, as usual, my Mother hugged me and gave me a kiss on the forehead and my little sister hopped around the kitchen, waving her little arms in the air, and said out loud, "Vonny! Vonny! Vonny!" My Mother asked me if I wanted a snack like milk and cookies. Which I usually do. But I said no instead. I mean, I said no, Ma'am! I told my Mother I had to take the visible woman back to Burdine's to trade for a visible man. Which she told me to do. But which I was not going to do.

"Oh, you're right, Vonny," my Mother said. "I forgot all about that. You're such a smart little boy." Which I am smart and am not little and am a boy. My Mother got most of it right. "What time does Burdine's close?" she said again. I told her five o'clock. Which means I had to go right after school because it was closed after supper. Which is usually when Daddy gets home from work at four o'clock. Unless we go to the horse race track. Which we didn't do on Monday because the horse race track is closed on Monday. Because it is open on Saturday. And the people who work there need two days to rest. The horses too! So, I had to go to Burdine's before supper, I told my Mother. "Be sure you're back here by four o'clock, Vonny," my Mother said again. "Don't stop to talk to any strangers. Or to anybody else!"

So, now that my Mother knew that I had to go to Burdine's right away, I was going to take the visible woman to Burdine's, get my money back, meet Lenny in the alley behind Bruno's, get the visible man back from him, and then go back home for supper with Daddy before I went back out again to meet Henry. Like he told me to that morning.

"No receipt, no refund." That's what the man behind the counter at Burdine's said to me when I went to return the visible woman.

I took off my cap so he could see my face. "Don't you remember me?" I said back. "I was just here on Saturday. Just two days ago! My friend was reading comic books in the back. I bought a visible man and a visible woman. But my Mother won't let me keep the visible woman. Because I have a little sister. And because the visible woman has breasts!"

The man behind the counter laughed a little bit. "What I remember doesn't matter, my little friend." I don't like it when people call me little. I'm in the second grade! "But no receipt, no refund! That's all I can tell you, kid. I don't make up the rules. I just follow them."

"But it's still in the box!" I said back. "I didn't even take the plastic off."

"For all I know, kid, that invisible woman fell off the back of a truck," the man behind the counter said back.

"But," I tried to say back.

He didn't let me finish. "But nothing, my little friend," he said back again. "If you bought it here, where is your receipt?"

"I'm not sure you even gave me one."

"I put it in the bag, kid. I always put the receipt in the bag." Then, I remembered. The receipt must be in the bag that Lenny took, the one with the visible man in it.

"Okay," I said back again to the man. "I'll be right back." And then I walked very fast down Bayou Road to Dorgenois, then down Dorgenois to Columbus, then in the alley behind Bruno's to meet Lenny to get the receipt from the bag with the visible man in it.

That was what was suppose to happen. But here's what happened instead.

"You threw the bag away?" I said to Lenny. "What did you do that for?"

Lenny just moved his shoulders up and down. "Why do you need the bag?" he said back. "It's just a bag. I thought my mother would see it under the bed. So, I just put the invisible man box under my bed and threw the bag in the garbage can behind the house."

"Garbage can?" I said back.

"Sure," Lenny said. "We can go look for it now."

"No, we can't, Lenny," I said back again. "Didn't you notice all the garbage cans on the street this morning when we were walking to school? Monday is the day when they pick up the garbage cans. Now I'm stuck with a visible woman I don't need!" Lenny just moved his shoulders up and down. I didn't even think about it for one minute. "Listen, Lenny. You have to keep the visible woman at your house until I can think about what to do now that I don't have a receipt and can't get my money back. I can't go back into my house with two visible people. I'll be punished forever. Especially if one of them is a visible woman. With breasts!"

"I can't take the invisible woman box home," Lenny said back. "I only was suppose to have the invisible man box for one night. But I had it for two nights! That's all I can do."

"Lenny," I said, while thoughts were popping into my head a thousand at a time, "you have to take the visible woman. You have to! You're the one who threw away the receipt." Lenny just moved his shoulders up and down. "Lenny," I said again, "don't wait until you grow up to become who you are. Be who you are now!"

Lenny blinked at me a couple of times. Which I think means he didn't know what I was saying. Which I didn't know what I was saying too. But then Lenny reached for the Burdine's bag and took it from me, the one with the visible woman and no receipt in it. And then he handed me the visible man box. But he took the visible woman out of the Burdine's bag and handed it back to me. Which was the bag. And then Lenny said back, "But you have to take the bag. It's too hard to hide under my bed."

"Sure," I said back. "Sure, Lenny. I'll take the bag back." Which I did. I put the visible man in it.

"And you have to take the invisible woman back by tomorrow night," Lenny said back. "Or else!"

It was like when John Smith told me I had to tell him everything I know about Jimmy Broom or else. Except I don't know what or else means to Lenny. And I didn't want to ask what or else means to Lenny.

Because I didn't want to know what or else means to Lenny. I just repeated it. "Or else," I said back. "I get it, Lenny. Or else."

I ran back up Columbus Street to my house, went up the alley, through the back door into the kitchen, hug, kiss, hug, kiss, "Vonny! Vonny! Vonny!" hop, hop, wave, wave, "Hello, Daddy," "Vonny, my boy," put the visible man box in my room, change into dungarees and polo shirt, sit at the kitchen table, eat, laugh, eat, laugh, finish supper, clear kitchen table, stretch, and then to the back door. "I'll be right back," I said to Daddy and my Mother.

"Where are you going in such a hurry, mister ants in your pants?" my Mother said.

"I just have to run an errand," I said back.

"Run an errand?" Daddy said. "Who are you running an errand for?"

"Just for me," I said back. "I'm running an errand for me."

"So, where are you going on this errand?" my Mother said back.

"Not far," I said back again.

"Well, what kind of errand is it?" Daddy said back.

I just lifted my shoulders up and down, and then I said, "It's a mystery."

Daddy and my Mother laughed for about a minute after I said that. "A mystery because you don't know where you're going?" Daddy said. "Or a mystery because you don't want to tell us?"

I just lifted my shoulders up and down again, and then I said again, "That's a mystery too!" And then I just went out the kitchen door in a hurry, ran back down the alley onto the brick sidewalk in front of the house, and then down Columbus Street to the corner, and then around the corner to the alley behind Bruno's on the Dorgenois side. Henry was already there sitting on his bicycle reading a comic book. "Hi, Henry," I said. "What's that?"

"It's a picture story about a girl and a boy," Henry said back.

"What's it about?" I said back.

"About a boy and a girl who like each other but their parents don't like the boy and the girl to talk to each other because everybody is different," Henry said back. "They are from two different families who don't like the other family. And then the boy makes a mistake by accident and kills the girl's brother. But not on purpose. He just stabs him in the chest by accident."

"With an ice pick?" I said back. I don't know why that popped into my head.

Henry looked at me funny. And then he laughed. "No!" he said back. "Not with an ice pick. With a sword. In a sword fight!"

"A sword fight?" I said back again. "Who fights with swords anymore?" Except the Prince in the Sunday newspapers.

"The boy and the girl lived in olden times," Henry said back. "When people had fights with swords."

"And then what happens?" I said back again.

"I don't know," Henry said back again. "That's as far as I got."

"Oh," I said back. Then I said again, "Daddy says I'm not suppose to talk to you either, Henry." I don't know why I said that. "Because he thinks we're different too."

"That's funny," Henry said back. "Because that's what my daddy says too." Henry was small like me. But when he talked, it was like talking to somebody older. Henry acts like nothing is the matter. Like he isn't afraid of anything. "My daddy says talking to white people here is dangerous," he said. Henry talks just like he is a teacher. Like he knows everything.

"Just here?" I said back. "What about when you lived in California?"

Henry rolled up the comic book and then put it in the back pocket of his dungarees. "I don't know," he said back. "I didn't see a lot of white people when we lived in California."

"You read a lot?" I said back. "I like to read. I go to the liberry at school to get books all the time. About the war. And science."

"Liberry!" Henry laughed. "Did you say liberry? Like L-I-B-E-R-R-Y?" He spelled it. And he was laughing and laughing when he spelled it out. "Like a strawberry?" Henry said again.

"Sure," I said back. "Don't you have a liberry in your school?"

"We have a library," Henry said back. Then, he spelled that out too. "L-I-B-R-A-R-Y. We have a library. But we don't have any liberry. Or even any strawberry!" Henry laughed again.

"I think it's liberry," I said again. I wanted to tell Henry that I always win the spelling bee at school every week. But it's not true. I just come in second every week. Except when Sharon the Roach has rabbity pink eyes and that one time I spelled furlong. So I just said, "I'm a very good speller, Henry."

"Well," Henry said back, "I'm a good speller too, California. And my mother works in a library. So, I at least know how to spell that!" Which I later went home and looked it up and found out that Henry is right. "Anyways," he said back, "I like to read a lot. But I like to read stories. Made up stories. Not stories about the war or about sports. But pretend stories about people who are just pretend people. Not real people."

"Like in the movies?" I said back.

"Sure," Henry said back. "Stories like in the movies. Where somebody just makes up a story. Where the story is not real. And the people are not real. And the places are different from regular places. Different from California where I use to live. And different from here."

"Right," I said back. But I just like real stories and real people. So, I changed the subject. "So, will you get in trouble for talking to me today?"

"Not if nobody knows about it," Henry laughed. Which is a sin of omission, I think. "But, listen." Henry started talking in a very low voice. "You know that guy in the car Saturday?" He pointed across the street to second base where John Smith and Pocahontas trapped me and Lenny Mahoney at the corner on our way back from Burdine's just when Henry rode his bicycle up the street.

"You mean John Smith?" I said back.

"John Smith?" Henry said back. "Who's that?"

"He's the guy who was in the black Pontiac on Saturday!" I said back again. "Him and Pocahontas."

"Pocahontas?" Henry said back while he was laughing. "You mean the white men in the car on Saturday?"

"Sure," I said. And I almost told Henry about going cow with John Smith and the whole real story about the dimes and the visible people and them running over Jimmy Broom because he tried to make it home instead of holding at third.

"Well," Henry said back, "the only John Smith and Pocahontas I know about died a long time ago. Those two men who you ran away from on Saturday are called Jake and Mack." Which I remembered is what they said at the Triangle. And maybe at Burdine's.

"Jake and Mack?" I said back.

"That's right," Henry said back. "And they were at my house last night."

"Your house? Why at your house?" I said back again.

"Because for some reason they know my daddy," Henry said back again. "They just showed up on the porch last night after we had supper and knocked on the door and my daddy had to go out on the porch to talk to them."

"I saw them in front of church yesterday," I said back. "John Smith, that is. I mean the one you call Jake. Who was talking to a man at the barber shop, the one who was talking to Daddy before Mass." Then I remembered we saw Henry and the other negro people on Columbus Street yesterday. "Was that your daddy with you yesterday?" I said again. "On Columbus Street?"

Henry nodded his head. "And my mother too," he said back.

"So, you have a little sister too?" I said back again. Henry nodded his head again. "Do you like her?"

Henry just lifted his shoulders up and down. "My mother always just says she loves me so much," he said back.

"So does my Mother say the same thing," I said back.

"But she always just gets me in trouble!" Henry said again.

"So does my little sister do the same thing!" I said back again.

"Well, anyways," Henry said, "I sneaked into the front room and hid below the sofa by the window. So, I was able to listen to my daddy talking to Jake and Mack on the porch. Because the window was open."

"About what?"

"Something about that barber shop," Henry said back. "The one on Bayou Road. And about that kid Jimmy's daddy. Who works at the barber shop."

"Jimmy's daddy isn't a barber!" I said back. "He just fixes tires all the time. In front of his house."

"Jake and Mack think he works at the barber shop. The one where me and my daddy can't even go," Henry said.

"Why not?" I said back.

"You know," Henry said.

But I didn't know. "I don't," I said back. "I don't know, Henry. Why can't you and your daddy go to the barber shop?"

Henry just pointed at his arm. "You know," he said.

"You mean the one on Bayou Road, right?" I said back. "The one across from the church?"

"Yes," Henry said. "We can't go there because. You know." But I still didn't know. Henry just pointed at his arm again. And then he said out loud, "Because they would just call us names. And maybe even just punch us in the stomach for no good reason!" When Henry said that, it made me think about how there are never any negro people at St. Rose de Lima Bean Church. And how there are never any negro children at St. Rose de Lima Bean School. And how I never see any negro people. Except Henry. Then he said out loud, "All Jake and Mack kept saying last night was calling my daddy names. It makes me mad. Very mad!"

"My Mother says people who call other people names are dopes," I said back.

"Well, maybe," Henry said back. "But, listen. When they weren't calling my daddy names, all they were talking about was your daddy and Jimmy's daddy and the barber shop."

"My daddy?" I said back.

And then Henry pointed at me. "And you too!"

"Me?" I said back. "What about me?"

"They think you know what happened to that Jimmy kid."

Which is true. I do know what happened to Jimmy Broom. John Smith and Pocahontas ran over him with their black Pontiac with the little yellow indian head on the front while he was trying to make it home instead of holding at third base. So I told Henry. "I do know what happened to Jimmy Broom. They tried to kill him!"

"Who?"

"The ones you call Jake and Mack. The ones who talked to your daddy last night," I said back. "They ran into him with their black Pontiac. License plate three, six, seven, pelican bird, four, seven, four. Sportsman's Paradise."

"What are you talking about?"

"My Uncle Martin saw it," I said back. "On his way back home from his work. But he says sometimes you see things and are not sure about what you saw. And even if you are sure about what you saw, it's not always clear what the meaning is of what you saw." I was talking out loud. Too out loud!

"Calm down, California!" Henry said back.

"My name is Vonny!"

"Vonny?" Henry said back. "Okay, Vonny. Just calm down. I just wanted to let you know that those guys from the car came by my house yesterday and talked to my daddy about you and your daddy and this Jimmy kid and his daddy too. That's all."

"Okay," I said. "Okay." Sometimes I just say okay when I'm trying to think about what to say different from okay. But I was also thinking about if I have to tell Daddy now about John Smith and Pocahontas and about Henry's daddy. About Henry too. And about how I was investigating the incident. So, like with Lenny Mahoney, I just tried to change the subject and said, "So, why does your daddy say you're not suppose to talk to me either?"

Henry just moved his shoulders up and down. "I think because you're white," he said back. "Because my daddy thinks talking to white people here is dangerous." Which is true. For instance, Red is dangerous to me and Lenny Mahoney, who is even his cousin, because sometimes Red just punches you in the stomach for no good reason. And Red is white. Then Henry said again, "So, why does your daddy say you're not suppose to talk to me either?"

I just moved my shoulders up and down. Daddy never said why. "I think because you live on another street," I said back.

"Does your daddy think I'm dangerous?" Henry said back.

I just moved my shoulders up and down again. "He never said so," I said back. Which he didn't. Daddy just says I can't go on the streets in our neighborhood where all the people who live there are negro people. "Do any white people go to your school?" I asked Henry.

"Not one," Henry said back. "No white kids."

And no negro kids go to the St. Rose de Lima Bean School too. That made me think about what the man at Burdine's said. "Well," I said back, "I don't make up the rules, Henry. I just follow them."

Henry laughed and laughed. "What does that mean, California?" he said back. "I mean, Vonny?"

"It means I don't know why no white kids go to your school," I said back. "They just don't."

"Or why I don't go to your school," Henry said back. "I don't know why I don't go to your school. I just don't."

"Maybe because you're a publican," I said back.

"A what?"

"A publican!" I said back again. "You know? Somebody who goes to public school."

"I can't go to public school either," Henry said back. "Not here I can't."

It was getting dark. Daddy and my Mother didn't know where I went on my errand. "I need to go back home," I said.

"Me too," Henry said back. "You want this comic book?" he said. He pulled it from the back pocket of his dungarees. "It's a sad story. My mother told me that it has a sad ending. Because everybody dies."

Just then, I heard a car stop in front of the alley behind Bruno's. And then I saw it was a black Pontiac! "Hey, kid! Come here!"

"It's John Smith and Pocahontas!" I said in a low voice.

"It's Jake and Mack!" Henry said out loud.

"Don't even think about running, kid!" I heard John Smith say in his froggy voice.

But that's what we did anyways. Out of the alley, down and across Dorgenois, and then down Columbus Street in front of the kindergarden. Before either of them was even able to get out of the car. We were both heading away from our homes. Henry riding his bicycle, me running behind him as fast as I can. Which is fast! Down to Broad Street. I heard the black Pontiac start up behind us and drive up near us just when we got in front of the school.

"You can't run forever, kid!" Pocahontas said out loud in his squeaky voice.

They were driving right by us when we got to the corner. "Let's go this way," Henry said. He pointed to the left. And so we crossed Columbus at Broad Street right in front of the black Pontiac. Which was stopped at the stop sign. "Hop on the back," Henry said again. Which I did. I got on Henry's bicycle where there was a little place to sit. My legs and feet were just hanging down. And then he pedaled fast on the sidewalk in front of Mister Lee's laundry and then Burdine's. And then we crossed over Bayou Road and then in front of the hamburger shop and then across another big street and then across another small street and another one and another big one and then maybe five or six other smaller streets after that. Which I never went to.

Because Broad Street is very wide and there is some grass in the middle of it, John Smith and Pocahontas had to turn the black Pontiac the other way first and then go up the block the wrong way and then turn around and come back the right way and try to catch us. Even if we were on the sidewalk on the other side of the street. Because their car wasn't able to go down the side of the Broad we were on without running into other cars going that way.

So, we got a head start by staying on the sidewalk on the other side of the street from where they had to drive. But we were on a bicycle and they were in a car. And after a while, they caught up to us and tried to turn in front of us. But the light was red at that corner too and another car got in their way, and we were able to get to another street where we turned off of Broad Street and down it. Henry was going as fast as he could. But the bicycle started to go all over the place. "I'm tired," he said after a while.

"You want me to pedal, Henry?" I said back.

"No," he said back. "No! Anyways, we're almost there!"

"Almost where?" I said back. I didn't even know we were going anywheres. I was thinking we were just running away from John Smith and Pocahontas. As fast as Henry was able to pedal!

There were houses on both sides of the street we were on. Which was a lot like on Columbus Street. And the sidewalks on both sides of the street were made out of brick. Which was a lot like on Columbus Street too. But on the porches of all of the houses there were a lot of people sitting outside talking to each other. Negro people. Which was not a lot like on Columbus Street.

After a while, I saw that there were no white people at all on the porches or on the sidewalks or on the street. I was the only white person on the whole street and it made me think that maybe, like Henry's daddy said, everybody there on that street thought I was dangerous. Because I'm white. "Let's ride in the middle of the street!" I said out loud to Henry. I didn't want to scare anybody.

"Too dangerous, Vonny," he said back. "We're almost there." And so Henry kept riding the bicycle on the sidewalk.

We went through another corner and when we did I looked to the left and saw the black Pontiac turning a block away and heading at us. "They're over there!" I said to Henry.

He stood up on the pedals and went as fast as he can go. This block had the same houses and the same sidewalks and the same negro people sitting on the porches talking. Except at the end of the block was a large white building made out of wood with a sign on it that said in very fancy script letters Trinity Zion African Methodist Episcopal Congregation Church – All Are Welcomed. Which I don't even understand. Except for all are welcomed. Which I understand.

When we got in front of the large white building, Henry stopped the bicycle and we got off. "Follow me!" he said. I looked back and saw the black Pontiac turning again onto the street where we were. John Smith and Pocahontas were coming to the Trinity Zion African Methodist Episcopal Congregation Church too! Henry just left his bicycle in the middle of the sidewalk, and I followed him down an alley along the side of the church. "Let's go!" Henry said out loud.

"Why did we come here?" I said to Henry while we were running down the alley. Where it was dark.

"We'll be safe," Henry said back. "They'll never find us here."

"They're going to see your bicycle on the sidewalk," I said back. "They're right behind us!"

"It's too dark," Henry said back. "Just follow me." Which I did.

But then, behind me, I heard the black Pontiac stop on the street in front of the church. "They saw it," I said in a low voice. While I was running, I was looking back and I saw the white lights from the black Pontiac lighting up the street in front of the alley.

I heard John Smith's froggy voice. "You go in the front door, Mack. I'll check out this alley."

"This way!" Henry said. "Hurry up!" We ran all the way to the end of the alley. Just like my house, the church was built up on top of little squares of bricks so you can crawl underneath it. Which I don't like to do because one time I did and a worm got in the pocket of my dungarees. "Down here, California," Henry said again. And then he just fell on his knees, got down on his belly, and slided underneath the church. I looked behind me and saw a flashlight shining up in the air all the way down the alley by the street. So, I did the same thing before John Smith saw me. "Just stay with me," Henry said in a very low voice. Which I did. Even when he crawled into what was a little box underneath the church, a little box that had a little door in it that we could close. In case John Smith put his flash light down there and tried to see us.

At first, it was so dark that I wasn't able to see anything in the little box under the church. But then, little by little, I was able to see everything.

Not very good. But good enough. I saw that the little box we were in was only big enough for maybe four kids like me and Henry. Or maybe only one man like Daddy. And it wasn't very high. If Daddy was in the little box, then there wasn't enough room for him to sit up straight. But it was high enough for us to sit up in it. Which we did. And when Henry closed the little door, nobody was able to see us under the church. It was perfect for playing hide and seek! Except John Smith and Pocahontas were not just kids in a game with us. They were the kind of people who run over kids in their car!

"We're going to find the two of you sooner or later!" John Smith said out loud in his froggy voice. "We know you're here somewheres."

We heard someone else running in the alley. "I can't get in the church, Jake. The front door is locked," Pocahontas said in his squeaky voice.

"Well, then break it down!" John Smith said.

"Can't do that, Jake," Pocahontas said again. "The neighbors are starting to come out on the street. Anyways, if the door is locked, that means they have to be somewheres out here then."

"You're not so dumb after all, Mack," John Smith said back. "They must have crawled underneath the church. Those kids!" But he said another word too, a word between those and kids. Which was taking the Lord's name in vain. "Get down on your knees and get under there, Mack," John Smith said again.

"What?" Pocahontas said back.

"I said, get down on your knees and get your fat self down there, Mack." Except John Smith did not say self. I can't even write the way John Smith talks all the time.

"But, Jake," we were able to hear Pocahontas say, "it's dark down there. Really dark! There may be rats too."

I could see Henry shaking his head from side to side. He said in a very low voice, "Not under here." And then he smiled. "Only in the alley!"

I almost laughed. But I just put my hand over my mouth instead. And then we heard John Smith say, "Mack, either you get down on your knees and get your fat self down there on your own. Or I'm going to make you do it."

"Put that back in your holster!" Pocahontas said out loud.

"So, it's either the rats or me, Mack," John Smith said back again. "The rats or me! Besides, the only rats down there are those two kids. You come out of there right now, you rats!"

But Henry and I are not rats. We're just kids. Kids sitting in the dark in a little box underneath a church being chased by two men.

We didn't hear anything for a while. It was very quiet. Then we heard Pocahontas say in his squeaky voice, "Hand me your flashlight, Jake."

"Here," John Smith said back. "You see anything?"

We didn't hear anything for another while. Then we heard Pocahontas say again, "They're not down here, Jake. I looked everywhere with the flashlight. They're not in there, underneath the church." Which was not true.

"Well, they didn't disappear into thin air," John Smith said out loud. "They're not invisible!"

"Unless," Pocahontas said back.

"Unless what?"

"Unless," Pocahontas said back again.

"Unless what?" John Smith said again.

"Well, it looks like there's a little room under there," Pocahontas said again. "With a door in it. Like a little room. Maybe they're hiding in that little box behind the door."

"So, what are you waiting for?" John Smith said back. "Get your self in there!" Except he didn't say self again.

I saw Henry start to feel around above us in the dark. I was now able to see just like I was outside on a sunny day. Even if it was dark down there. "Come on, Jake," Pocahontas said. "Can't we just go to the kid's house and pick him up there?"

"Great idea, stupid," John Smith said back. Except he didn't say stupid. My Mother always told me it's rude to call people stupid. But what John Smith called Pocahontas is even ruder. "Let's just go to the kid's house on Columbus Street and ask his parents to turn him over to us so we can twist his thumbs and find out what he knows about the kid in the hospital." Twist my thumbs? "Nobody will think that's unusual, you stupid dope!" Except he didn't say stupid again. Or dope. I can't even write the way John Smith talks! "Now get under there, Mack, and find those two little rats. You come out of there, you rats!"

"Here it is!" Henry said. Except in a low voice. I heard a little snap. And then I saw Henry pushing up on the top of the little box. Which was also the bottom of the church floor above our heads. He pushed very slowly. And then I saw a tiny crack of light coming from above us. And when Henry pushed even more, I saw even more light. "Come on, California. Let's go! Follow me." And then I saw there was a little door above us in the top of the box. After Henry opened it, we were able to stand up, half underneath the floor and half above it, and then we were able to climb out into a little room in the church. "Where are we?" I said to Henry.

"I think it's a closet," he said back. "Step over here behind me." And then Henry slowly closed the door over the little hole that we just climbed out of. The room was also dark. Except there was more light than in the little box under the building. "We have to be quiet, California. Take off your shoes." Which I did. And Henry did too. "They won't ever see this door in the dark down there. You have to know it's there." Then Henry went over to a wall in the closet where we were and took down a key from a hook near the corner. He came back, put the key in a little metal lock on the door in the floor, and then turned it. "And even if they do find it, now they can't open it," Henry said again.

"What do we do now, Henry?" I said back in a low voice.

"Let's just sit here quiet for a little while," Henry said back again.

I didn't know what John Smith was doing. We weren't able to hear him anymore. But after a while, we were able to hear Pocahontas and his squeaky voice while he was crawling underneath the building and trying to get into the little box. "Ouch!" he said out loud. Then he said a lot of words I can't even write again. In case my Mother ever finds this and sees what I wrote. Then we heard him crawling around right underneath the closet, probably right in the little box. He was talking to John Smith, but we weren't able to hear what John Smith was saying back. We were only able to hear what Pocahontas was saying.

"I tell you, Jake, there's nobody down in here."

"Of course, I'm sure. I'm as sure as I can be. It's dark in here."

"Even with the flashlight."

"No, I don't see any doors down in here. There's not enough room anyways."

"How am I suppose to know where they went?"

"Ouch! What was that? Jake! Jake, I think I'm bleeding. Jake! Jake! Help! Jake!" That was just after we heard Pocahontas bump his head against the bottom of the floor. Henry and I started laughing. But without making any noise.

And then we didn't hear anything for a while again. "Do you think they left?" I said after another while.

"Not yet," Henry said back. "They're looking for a way to get in here now," he said again. "They know we're here. Except all the doors and windows are locked from the inside."

"How did you know about that secret door?"

"Everybody knows about it," Henry said back.

"Why is there a secret door to get into a church?" I said back.

"We're here, aren't we, California? There's a secret door to get into church just in case people like us need to get into church."

"Because somebody is chasing us?"

"That's one reason," Henry said back. He put a finger on his lips. "Listen," he said in a low voice. We were able to hear somebody hitting the side of the church from the alley. "Let's go," Henry said.

We went out the door of the closet into another room. Which was a much bigger, white room that had a lot of pews in it. Or just benches. There were no pictures on the wall like at St. Rose de Lima Bean Church. And there was no altar like at St. Rose de Lima Bean Church too. And I didn't even see any confession boxes anywheres too. It was a big white room with a lot of benches in it. A plain big white room.

We were able to hear a noise outside, like somebody was walking down the alley hitting the outside of the church now and then all the way from the back where we were before up to the front by the street where the Trinity Zion African Episcopal Methodist Congregation Church – All Are Welcomed sign is. And where Henry's bicycle still was on the sidewalk. John Smith started saying out loud in his froggy voice, "I'm going to get the two of you. You know I am. And when I get my hands on you, you're both going to stay got." Whatever that means. The noise from somebody hitting on the outside of the church followed John Smith's froggy voice all the way to the street. And then somebody started knocking very loud on the front door of the church. Which was very tall and very black. "You know I'm going to get the two of you. So, why not come out and make it easy on yourself? Just open the door," he said again. "Just open the door!" John Smith said out loud.

"You think they will ever leave?" I said to Henry.

"Follow me," Henry said back in a low voice. Which I did. We both just had on our socks with no shoes. So, we didn't make any noise on the wood floor. I followed Henry across the room to some stairs that were near the front door.

"Open this door!" John Smith said out loud again. Only he used the Lord's name in vain again right between saying this and door.

"Up here," Henry said in a low voice, and he started up the stairs. When we reached the top, there was another smaller room with more benches in it. And there was a round window in the room in the front of the church. Which, if we got up on our tippy toes, we were able to look out of and see the street below us. Except the people outside were not able to see us because it was still dark inside the church. "Look at all those people out there," Henry said. And just when he said that, there was a police car that drove up. It was black and white with a red light on its top that was turning around and lighting up everything. It was lighting up John Smith. Who was standing on the sidewalk looking at the front door. It was also lighting up Pocahontas. Who was standing on the sidewalk talking to some negro people. It was also lighting up all of the other negro people too. Who were standing on the sidewalk talking to each other and pointing at the church and pointing at John Smith and at Pocahontas.

"Do you think we need to go outside and talk to that policeman?" I said in a low voice to Henry. "To tell him about John Smith and Pocahontas?"

"You mean Jake and Mack?" Henry said back.

"Right," I said back. "Jake and Mack." But for me, they are John Smith and Pocahontas.

"No," Henry said back in a low voice but out loud anyways. "You think that policeman is going to believe two kids like us?"

I was surprised when Henry said that. "But he's a policeman!" I said back. "He's suppose to catch bad guys like John Smith and Pocahontas. I mean, Jake and Mack."

Henry just shook his head. "Look down there, California," he said back. "What do you see out there?"

Sitting up in front of the round window in the little dark room at the top of the Trinity Zion African Episcopal Methodist Congregation Church, it was like being able to see what God is able to see. Henry and I were able to see the whole wide world from up there. We had started out being chased by John Smith and Pocahontas from the alley behind Bruno's all the way down Broad Street to the church, and then we were below the bottom of the church, in the dark, in the dirt, in a little box, and now, we were high up above everybody, out of danger, and maybe even safe. Almost like in paradise. And we were able to see everybody and see what they were doing and see who they were talking to and see where they were going. We were two little kids, who are exactly alike, and we were able to know almost everything about everybody without having to tell anybody what we saw. Except each other.

"There's just a bunch of people out there," I said back. "A bunch of people standing around out there talking."

"And what do you think they are talking about, California, all those people standing around out there?"

"They're probably talking about us, about you and me, and about where we are, and about what we're doing, and about why we're doing it," I said back. "They're probably just talking about you and me!" I said out loud.

Henry put his hand over his mouth. But I heard him laugh anyways. "You're funny," Henry said back. "You're a very funny kid, California." He turned his back to the wall under the window, slided down it until he was sitting on the floor below it, and then waved his hand for me to do the same thing. Which I did. "Listen, Vonny. Only three people out there are talking about us," he said again. Which was almost the only time he ever said my real name. "Just Jake, Mack, and maybe that policeman. The rest of the people out there don't care about us. They don't even know about us."

"Maybe," I said back. Because I thought maybe it was true. Only John Smith and Pocahontas knew about us. Not even the policeman did. Unless they told him. Which they maybe didn't even do.

"Do you know what all those other people out there are talking about?" Henry said again. I just moved my shoulders up and down. "All those other people out there are talking about why there are two white men in a black Pontiac and a white policeman standing around outside in the dark in front of a church where white people don't ever even go. All those other people out there are trying to figure out who is in trouble, and what they did, and where they are, and what those white men in the black Pontiac and that white policeman are going to do to them if they catch them, and why. Because all those other people out there know about the door underneath the church. Jake and Mack don't. And the policeman doesn't. But all those other people out there do. So, they're talking about who used the door to get away from them."

"Which is you and me!" I said back.

"But all those other people out there don't know that, Vonny. They just know somebody is in trouble. Maybe it's somebody they know. Maybe it's their daddy. Or their son. Or their brother," Henry said back. "And now they know the police are out there too."

"But John Smith and Pocahontas aren't policemen," I said back.

"All those other people out there don't know that, Vonny," Henry said back. "Most of them think every white man is a policeman." We could hear car doors opening outside. People were talking, but I wasn't able to hear what they were saying. "Let's see what they're doing," Henry said, and we both stood up again, and leaned up on our tippy toes again, and peeked up over the edge of the bottom of the round window in the front of the church again. Which made me think again that it was like being able to see what God is able to see.

And if God was looking then when Henry and I were high up above everybody, then the last thing that God was able to see before we went downstairs to finally go home was Pocahontas picking up Henry's bicycle and putting it in the back of the black Pontiac that ran over Jimmy Broom. Which means Henry and I had to walk home. And then God was able to see the policeman going over to John Smith and pointing up the street. Like the policeman was telling John Smith to move his car somewheres else. And then God was able to see John Smith and Pocahontas getting into the black Pontiac and them driving away in it. With Henry's bicycle in the back. But without us. And then God was able to see the policeman standing around talking to a lot of other people out there who were also standing around talking to the policeman and even talking to other people out there. And then, after a while, God was able to see the policeman turning off the red light on top of his black and white car, and then him driving away down the street too. The same way where John Smith and Pocahontas went before.

Which was all of what Henry and I were able to see too.

"Okay," Henry said. "I think we can head for home now." He walked over to the stairs and started down. "Follow me."

Which I did. And on the stairs, while I was walking down, I saw the whole big white room in front of us. So I said to Henry, "If you don't have a confession box in this church, where do you make your confession anyways?"

Henry stopped at the bottom of the stairs and just blinked the way sometimes Lenny Mahoney does when I say something. And then Henry just said back, "California, what's a confession?"

Nine, or Baby Cows' Head Shop

Then, everything turned into a mess on Tuesday. Which was the day after Monday night when John Smith and Pocahontas chased Henry and me all the way to the Trinity Zion African Episcopal Methodist Congregation Church. And also the day after Monday night when I didn't get back home until way after dark when it was already eight o'clock.

"Where were you, young man?" my Mother said on Monday night when I walked into the parlor from the porch after walking back with Henry. I didn't want to go down the alley to the back door into the kitchen because it was too dark. I was afraid maybe somebody was back there. When I went in the front door, my Mother was watching a TV program I like a lot too about a man who always helps different people who the police are always trying to put in jail for killing a dead person. But who the police never are able to put in jail because somebody else always killed whoever is the dead person.

I just moved my shoulders up and down. Daddy walked into the parlor from the back of the house carrying a bowl with some popcorn in it. "Hi, Daddy," I said. "Can I have some popcorn?"

"Vonny Foster!" my Mother said out loud. She was trying to talk in a low voice so my little sister and my baby brother stayed sleeping. Which they were. But instead, my Mother said out loud in a very mean voice, "First of all, it's may I have some popcorn. Not can! Second of all, it's may I have some popcorn, please! And third of all, it's may I have some popcorn, please, Sir!" My Mother likes to count things she says. Which I do too. "And finally, where have you been for the last two hours, Vonny Foster?"

I just moved my shoulders up and down again. Daddy sat down next to my Mother on the sofa across the parlor from the TV. All the lights in the house were off all the way to the back. Except the kitchen light all the way in the back. Which I saw only a little in the hallway by the bathroom. So, it was very dark in the front room except for the light that came from the TV program. Even in that little light I saw Daddy smiling. "So," he said, "how did your errand go?"

My Mother said back, "How did his errand go? What are you talking about, Albert? I don't want to know how his errand went. As far as we know, there wasn't even any errand." I wanted my Mother to believe me. "He just can't be believed anymore. All he does now is make things up." Which was true. But I wanted my Mother to trust me. "Who does that remind you of?" she said to Daddy. "He just can't be trusted anymore!"

I didn't want to do it. But when I heard what my Mother was saying, it made me very sad. I wasn't afraid anymore. I was just very sad. And so I just started crying, standing right there in the middle of the parlor.

Daddy said, "You upset him."

My Mother stood up and stepped across the room to me. "Come here, Vonny," she said in a low voice. But I just ran past her and rushed through the room where Daddy and my Mother and now my baby brother sleep. Which is where my baby brother was sleeping. And then through the hallway by the bathroom and through the room where my little sister and I sleep. Which is where my little sister was sleeping. And then into the kitchen. If I wasn't so afraid about John Smith and Pocahontas being in the dark in the back yard to get me, I probably was going to go right through the kitchen door out the back of the house. But instead, I stopped in the kitchen, pulled out a chair from the table, sat down, and then put my head down in my arms on the table the way we have to do at school when Sister Marianna goes out in the hall to talk to somebody in the middle of class. The tears from my face were dripping onto my arms.

Right away I heard somebody walk into the kitchen. "Why are you so upset, Vonny?" my Mother said. "What's the matter?"

"You don't trust me!" I said out loud. Which she didn't. My head was still face down on my arms.

I felt my Mother put her hand on the back of my head. "Hush now," my Mother said back. "Your little sister and baby brother are sleeping." I heard her pull another chair out and sit down next to me. She was rubbing the top of my head. "Don't you expect me to be worried if you're not home by eight o'clock, Vonny? What kind of mother isn't going to be worried about their son who is out in the street after dark?"

"I know!" I said back. Which I do. "But you said you don't trust me!" Which makes me mad. But everything I say to her now is a lie. Which makes me even more mad.

"Maybe I didn't mean that, Vonny," my Mother said back. "Maybe I was just worried about you." She put her hand under my chin and tried to lift my face up. "Look at me, Vonny. Let me see your big brown eyes." But I didn't let her lift my face up. I didn't let her see my eyes. I was too ashamed. If I looked at my Mother now, I was going to tell her everything. About going cow and betting with John Smith. About how I lied about where I got the dimes. About buying two visible people and getting Lenny to help me lie about it. About how Uncle Martin didn't talk to the police about what he saw. About how John Smith and Pocahontas ran over Jimmy Broom. About how I didn't run an errand but just met Henry in the alley behind Bruno's. And about how Henry and me got chased too!

I heard Daddy walk into the kitchen and say, "Well, whatever it was, I guess it wasn't a happy errand, was it?" Daddy was laughing. But that made me cry out loud.

"Just be quiet, Albert," my Mother said. "Just leave us alone, will you?"

"I'm just trying to help," Daddy said.

"Well, you're not," my Mother said. "You're upsetting Vonny." Which was not true. I was mad because my Mother said she doesn't trust me.

"Well," Daddy said, "I'll let the two of you talk. But, just so you know, it was the detective who killed the maid."

"I knew it!" my Mother said.

"You said it was the insurance agent," Daddy said back.

I still had my head down on my arms on the table.

"Just go," my Mother said back. "I'll be up front in a minute."

"I'll keep the seat warm," Daddy said back.

"Now, let's see those big brown eyes, Vonny," my Mother said.

I just shook my head. "I don't want to."

"Do you have something you want to tell me?" my Mother said back.

I just shook my head again. I had a lot I wanted to tell her! But I wasn't going to. At first, when I just got home, I was still afraid about whether John Smith and Pocahontas were out to get me and Henry like they did Jimmy Broom. But now I was just mad about my Mother not trusting me anymore. And I was tired. Very tired. "I'm tired, Mama," is all I said. Which is all I wanted to tell her.

I heard my Mother stand up, take a glass from the cabinet, and then heard the faucet running. "Here's a glass of water for you, Vonny," she said. "Now drink this to cool yourself down. And then go and put on your pajamas, and then hop in bed. I'll come and tuck you in later on. I may be upset with you, Vonny, but I still love you," my Mother said again. "You are a special boy." Which is true. I am a special boy. Because I am a liar!

Then my Mother went up to the front room and I did what she said. I was still upset after I got in bed. Which is why I was even crying there. But after a while, I just fell asleep and didn't even feel my Mother tuck me in under the covers or hear Daddy when he tied my foot to the bed like the doctor said to do. I just woke up the next morning, Tuesday, tucked in under the covers with my foot tied to the bed. Which is how I know they did it.

Before I went to school the next morning, Tuesday, which is today, my Mother didn't say anything about me being out late Monday night. She just said right before I left to go outside to meet my cousin Pia again to walk to school, "Let's you and me have a little talk tonight after supper, okay?" I just nodded my head. Then my Mother kissed me in the middle of my forehead. "You're my special boy, Vonny. Be careful on the way to school." Which I was.

But then, after a very quiet day in school on Tuesday, after a day when I didn't even have any homework, everything turned into a mess. Without me even knowing how it happened.

At first, it was a normal day. Like everything was going to be okay. When I got home after school, my Mother wasn't even upset anymore about me being out late the night before. Also, I had the visible man at my house. Which my Mother thought I traded at Burdine's for the visible woman. Which Lenny still had at his house under his bed until I figured out how to turn it back in to Burdine's. And Henry and I decided Monday night to meet up Friday at the Bell where I am going with Charly after Henry has time to figure out what his daddy has to do with the guy who works at the barber shop and after I have time to talk to Daddy about what he has to do with the guy who works at the barber shop too.

I might even be able to talk to Jimmy Broom tomorrow about why John Smith and Pocahontas ran into him. Because on the way back from school, when I was walking just past the back door at Bruno's, I heard Jimmy's daddy on the street screaming up at his mother that she better make up his bed and clean up his bedroom because Jimmy is coming home tomorrow. Jimmy Broom is coming tomorrow! Wednesday! Which is tomorrow! Jimmy isn't going to die after all! I wanted to run into Bruno's to tell all the old crocodiles. But I didn't.

When I got home on Tuesday after school, I came through the back door into the kitchen, like I usually do, and my Mother gave me a hug and then she kissed me on the forehead, like she usually does. "I want to kiss Vonny on the head too. Me too! Me too! Me too!" Also, my little sister was hopping around like a Mexican jumping bean, waving her little arms in the air, like she usually does.

"She loves you so much, Vonny," my Mother said. "You're so lucky to have a little sister who loves you so much." Sometimes I think that's true. That I'm lucky.

So, I bended over and my little sister walked over to me and then I thought she was going to kiss me. But instead, she just hit me in the middle of my forehead with her little hand. And then she laughed! It didn't hurt. But I was surprised. "Hey!" I said in a loud voice.

My Mother said back, "Don't talk to your little sister that way, Vonny." Her back was turned so she could heat up some milk for my baby brother. So, she didn't see my little sister hit me in the middle of my forehead with her little hand. "She's just a little monkey who loves her big brother so much." The little monkey was laughing and ran into the next room.

"But she hit me in the head, Mama!"

"Don't be a baby, Vonny," my Mother said back. "You always tell me you're a big boy now. Your little sister can't hurt you. It's just her way of getting you to pay attention to her. She loves you so much!" Sometimes I think my little sister could stick an ice pick in my chest, and my Mother would think it was because she loves me so much. Or it was just her way of getting me to pay attention to her. Which I would pay attention if she stuck an ice pick in my chest!

I said back, "Mama, is it okay if I try to put the visible man together today? I wanted to try to figure out what bones Jimmy Broom broke if I can." Which I did want to do. And I wanted my Mother to forget that I was out late the night before. Which she did.

"Of course, you can," my Mother said back. "But only after you finish your homework."

"No homework tonight, Mama," I said back. "I already did it." Which I did. We were suppose to read a story in the reading book about a kid who loses his dog. But I already read the whole book way back before last Christmas. "We just have a story in the reading book, Mama, and I already read the whole book." Which she knew I did because she already asked me questions about all the stories in it, and I knew them all, front to back. Even the one about the kid and his lost dog.

"Okay," my Mother said back. "But I want you to do it on the kitchen table. I don't want to see little pieces of that invisible man all over the house."

So, I ran into the next room where I put the visible man on a shelf the day before after I got it from Lenny, got the bag down, and then came back into the kitchen to put it together on the table. But when my little sister saw me get the bag, she followed me back into the kitchen. "I want to play! I want to play!" she was singing. "I want to play!"

"Mama," I said. I knew I sounded like I was whining the way I said it, but sometimes I just can't help it. "There's a lot of little parts, Mama. Little bones and little parts she will put in her mouth." Which she will! "And then maybe choke!" Which maybe she will. I can be dramatick too. It's not just my Mother. "I don't think it's such a good idea if she."

But before I even finished, my Mother said, "Okay, Vonny." She brushed her hands together like she was cleaning something off of them. Then my Mother turned off the gas fire under the pot with my baby brother's milk. "Just keep an eye on your baby brother for me. He's up front sleeping in his crib." Then she turned to my little sister. "Let's go, Sharon. Why don't I take you over to Aunt Audra's house to play with Suzette until Daddy comes back from work. Isn't that a good idea?"

It was a great idea! And a surprise idea too! My Mother was going to help me out. "Thanks, Mama," I said back. "Thanks a lot!"

But before I even finished, the little monkey was crying and laughing at the same time. "But I want to play with Vonny! Vonny! Vonny!" And then she said, "Can we go? Can we go? Can we go?" She was hopping around again, waving her little arms in the air again. "Suzette! Suzette! Suzette!" She didn't know if she wanted to stay with me or go to play with our cousin Suzette. Who is also a little girl like the little monkey. Except she doesn't cry as much.

"Let's go, you!" my Mother said. "Here. Take my hand. Let's let your big brother learn all about his invisible man." And just like that, out the back door they both went.

I walked up to the room in the front of the house, the one right behind the parlor, the one where Daddy and my Mother and now my baby brother sleep, and I looked into the little crib by the window where my baby brother was. He was very quiet. He had a little white cap on his head, and he had his little thumb in his little mouth. He's cute too when he's sleeping. Even the little monkey is cute when she's sleeping. Probably everybody is cute when they're sleeping.

Then I went back to the kitchen and took the visible man box out of the Burdine's bag. After I put it on the table, I looked at the visible man picture on the cover. He was a little scary! Because he just had a skeleton and all of his organs showing, like at the disgusting meat shop, with blue and red lines all over his body. Which was suppose to be his artries I found out. And he didn't have any hair on his head or on his face and his eyeballs just looked right at me wherever I went in the kitchen. The way the picture of Jesus does in the room where Daddy and my Mother and now my baby brother sleep. The way the eyeballs do in the fish that Daddy catches. Which is why I won't eat them!

I wanted to open the box right away so I didn't have to look at the visible man picture. But I wanted to read the box too. So, before I took off the plastic wrapper and opened it, I looked at all the words on it. Which on the side in big yellow letters it had the word incredible! Just like the way I just wrote it. And when I did finally open the visible man box, it was incredible! It looked like there was a hundred parts in it at least. Maybe two hundred. Maybe a thousand! I didn't know how many little bone pieces they had. Everything was wrapped in small plastic bags. There was a bag with all of the organs in it. And another bag with all of the bones in it. And then even another plastic bag with little metal pieces. And there was even another bag with the whole outside of the visible man in it. Who you could see right through him. He was in two pieces. A front and a back. And all of the organs were in two pieces that you have to glue together. And some of the bones were in two pieces too.

In the bottom of the box there was a little book that said how to put everything together. Right on the cover of the little book, it said in black block letters EASY TO ASSEMBLE. Which even I knew it was not. It was going to take forever!

I didn't know where to start. So, I just took all the plastic bags out and put them on the kitchen table first. Which I also did with the little book that said EASY TO ASSEMBLE. Then I saw that there was another book, only smaller than the little book, that had on it An Introduction to Anatomy. I didn't even know what that means. So, I started to read it. The smaller book. When I opened up to the first page, there was two pictures of a skeleton, one facing the front and the other facing the back. There were a lot of little arrows pointing to all of the bones in the visible man with their names on the other end of the arrows. Which were not normal names. Almost all of the names were new to me. The bones in my legs I just use to call leg bones. But the smaller book had different names for all of them. Like tibia. And femur. Which I have to look at the book just now to know how to spell them while I'm writing this. Because before I looked at that smaller book, the only bone I knew its name was the skull bone. Which is in your head.

Also in the smaller book were pictures of all of the organs and what they do. Like your heart makes blood go around your body. And your liver makes you be able to eat food. And your lungs get air in your body so you can breathe. Which everybody has to do or they die. And your brain makes all the other organs work together. Like the boss of everything. I read about all of the other organs too. Which a lot of them are disgusting. Just like at the disgusting meat store. And I read about what all of those organs do too. Which a lot of that is disgusting too. Even more disgusting than the disgusting meat store!

But then, while I was looking at the pictures of the organs in the smaller book and seeing what each of the organs does, a thought popped into my head. Which was I wanted to know what part of the body makes thoughts pop into your head. I looked and looked and looked all through the whole smaller book, looking at all of the organs, and looking for the one that makes thoughts pop into your head. I didn't find it. I know my heart makes my blood go around my body and my liver makes me be able to eat food and my lungs get air in my body so I can breathe and my brain makes them all work together. But, I was thinking, what organ makes thoughts pop into my head? Is it some invisible organ? Is the part that makes thoughts pop into my head the only invisible part of the visible man? Or is it a just mystery? Like my Mother says some things are.

I closed the smaller book and put my head down on the kitchen table on top of my arms like Sister Marianna tells us to do at our desks in school sometimes when she has to talk to somebody at the door. A lot of thoughts were popping into my head after I looked at the smaller book. I know my eyes let me see things I can see. And my mouth lets me taste things I can see. And my fingers let me feel things I can see. And my nose lets me smell things I can see. And even my ears let me hear sounds even if I can't see them.

But what makes me think things? What makes thoughts pop into my head? And where do they come from? And why can't I see them? Why do words pop into my head? And where do they come from? And why can't I see them? The words I think. And where are they after I think them? Where do the thoughts and the words go after I think them? Where do they go?

Bad actions I do come from my hands, which I can see. And mean words I say come from my mouth, which I can see. But where do impure thoughts come from when they pop into my head? Why can't I see them? Do those thoughts come from the brain in my head? That's what everybody says. Like the scarecrow in that wizard movie. But then, why do people eat baby cows' heads? Brains and all. Which is disgusting! If you eat a baby cow's head, are you eating the baby cow's thoughts?

I was trying to figure it out. Just like my Mother makes me sound out words that I don't know how to read, I was trying to sound out why do thoughts just pop into my head.

When I was reading the smaller book, it reminded me about what Sister Marianna said in class today about what a verb is. "A verb is an action word," she said. And she wrote VERB on the blackboard. Just like the way I just wrote it. Except in white block letters she made with chalk. "Like run," Sister said again. "Or walk." Sister turned around and winked at all of us. "Or wiggle!" she said again. All the girls in class laughed when she said wiggle and some of the boys even. But not me. Sister Marianna said, "Who can think of another verb?"

I raised my hand right away. But of course, Sharon the Roach, who came back to school from her rabbity pink eyes this morning, raised her hand right away too. And of course, Sister Marianna called on her first. So, I put my hand down. Sharon the Roach stood up near her desk very slowly, like she was going to answer some mystery, like she was going to tell us finally what a virgin is, and she looked around the classroom to make sure everybody was looking at her. Which I was not. And then she said, "Dance."

"Very good!" Sister Marianna said. "You may sit down, Sharon. You are correct. Dance is an action word. Dance is a verb." Sister Marianna said every word very slowly. Like we weren't paying attention. Sister always talks very slowly. And whenever Sharon the Roach says anything, Sister Marianna always acts like it's the smartest thing anybody who ever lived ever said. Like Sharon the Roach is the smartest person ever. Which she is not! For instance, in the morning whenever Sharon the Roach walks into the classroom, Sister Marianna always says to her, "So, how are you this morning, Sharon?" And Sharon the Roach says back, "Fine, Sister. I'm fine today." Then Sister Marianna says back, "Very good, Sharon! Very good." Like she just answered the hardest question ever. Which she didn't. She only answered how was she!

Then, back in class this morning, goofy Louie Canale raised his hand after Sharon sat down, and some of the boys started laughing even before he said anything. "Yes, Louis," Sister Marianna said. She didn't ask him how he was. She just asked Louie, "Can you think of another verb?"

Louie put his hand down and stood up. He looked around the room to make sure everybody was looking at him too. And then very loud he said, "Sleep!"

A few boys laughed. One of them behind me said in a low voice, "Sleeping is not an action word."

And another boy said, "You don't move when you're sleeping!" He probably never sleepwalked like I did.

But Sister Marianna just said, "Good, Louis." She didn't say very good. She just said, "That's good. Of course, sleep is a verb. It's an action word. Sleeping is an action. It's something we do." Which maybe is true. Because at least you can see somebody sleeping. "Anyone else?" Sister said again. "Can anyone else think of an action word?" Then Louie sat back down.

I raised my hand and Sister called on me. I stood up. I didn't care if anybody was looking at me. I just said right away, "Sister? I have a question."

Sister Marianna smiled. "Of course you do, Vonny," she said back. "When don't you have a question? But let's be quick about it."

"Sister, is think a verb?" I said back. "Is thinking an action?"

"Well, of course, it is, Vonny," Sister said back again. "It's something we do." And then I think I saw her look at Louie. "At least, most of us do. Think is an action word."

I was still standing. "But, Sister," I said back again. "That can't be true. It doesn't make any sense."

"Just because it doesn't make any sense to you, Vonny, doesn't mean it's not true."

"But, Sister," I said back, "I can't see somebody thinking. I can see other things people do. Other verbs. Other action words. Like run or walk or dance. Or even wiggle!" The same girls who laughed before laughed again. Even Sister Marianna was smiling. "I can even see people sleeping. Like Louie said." He cackled like he always does and a few more boys laughed too. "But I can't see if somebody is thinking. It's invisible. And it just happens. Thinking just happens to people. It's not something people do. It just happens. People don't do it!"

"Well," Sister Marianna said, "that may not be the best way to explain it, Vonny. Do you have to be able to see something for it to be an action?"

"I think so, Sister," I said. "You said a verb is an action word. It's something you do. It's like a incident." Then I remembered what Uncle Martin said. "I mean, it's like an incident. When you do something, you do it on purpose. It's an action. It's a verb. But thinking is not something you do on purpose. It just happens to you. You just think even if you don't want to. Thoughts just pop into your head! Thinking is like an accident. It doesn't always happen on purpose!"

After I said that, right away Sister Marianna started laughing. And she didn't stop laughing for about a minute. She even had to go outside the classroom because she was laughing so hard. "Wait one minute, children," Sister said while she was laughing. "Just put your heads down on your desks for a minute," she said again, and then she walked out of the classroom. I sat down and put my head down on my desk like everybody else did. A kid in front of me turned around and looked at me. I just lifted my shoulders up and down. After a while, Sister Marianna came back into the classroom and went up the blackboard. And then she said, "Children, let's get out our readers and start the story about a little boy and his lost dog." And then we didn't talk about verbs anymore.

Anyways, at home in the kitchen, I looked at the smaller book that came with the visible man for a while, and then I opened up one of the little plastic bags that had the leg bones in it. The tibia bone too. And I was thinking about if it was Jimmy Broom's tibia that was broken or some other leg bone. And I was thinking about if it was broken in half or just a little broken. I was happy that Jimmy wasn't going to die after all. And that he is coming home tomorrow.

I heard the front door open and then heard Daddy say out loud, "Hello!"

"I'm back here, Daddy," I said back. I ran to the front of the house. "But the baby is sleeping," I said again in a low voice.

"Oh," Daddy said in a low voice too. "Where is your mother?"

I told him where she was. "Are we going to the horse race track today, Daddy?" I said. "Can we go to the Fair Grounds?"

"Not today, Vonny, my boy," Daddy said back. "I got home too late. Had to stop at the barber shop for a haircut." Daddy's hair is very black. Blacker than my hair. Which is brown. And it's very wavy. Just like mine. We were in the room where Daddy and my Mother and now my baby brother sleep and where my baby brother was still sleeping. Daddy was taking his shirt off. "You want to come run an errand with me to get supper?"

"I have to keep an eye on him for Mama," I said back, pointing at my baby brother in the crib.

But just then, my Mother walked in the front door into the parlor. "Is the baby still sleeping?" my Mother said. Daddy nodded and put one of his fingers on his lips. And then she said in a low voice again, "Did you get the liver yet?"

"No," Daddy said back. "I was just going to walk over there with Vonny."

My Mother said back, "Why don't you let him go by himself?" My Mother thinks I'm the only person in my house who can go on errands to get things. But I don't like to go to the disgusting meat shop by myself.

"You can cut up the onions and make a salad while he's doing that. I have to feed the baby."

But Daddy said back in a low voice, "I can do all that when we get back. It won't take a minute. Besides, Vonny and I need some time to visit."

"About what?" my Mother said back. "About his coming back after dark last night?" She picked up my baby brother. Who started to wiggle in her arms.

"Nothing special," Daddy said back. "Can't a father have a talk with his son now and then?" Daddy rubbed the hair on my head.

"Okay," my Mother said back again. "But don't stop anywheres else. I'm starving. I missed lunch today."

"We'll be right back," Daddy said back again. "Won't we, Vonny, my boy?" My Mother walked to the back of the house with my baby brother in her arms. Daddy put another shirt on, one that didn't have buttons on it and he had to slip it over his head like an undershirt, and then we went out the front door, down the stairs, and onto the brick sidewalk in front of the house on Columbus Street. Daddy said, "You want to walk or take the car?"

"Let's walk, Daddy," I said back. I knew if we walked, we can talk longer too. So, we headed down our street toward the corner where Bruno's is.

Jimmy Broom's daddy was still working behind the red truck he always parked in front of his house. He always was working on car tires. Daddy stopped when we got near to him. "I hear your son's coming home from the hospital tomorrow," Daddy said.

Jimmy's daddy turned around and said, "Oh. Yes. Hi. He is. Coming home tomorrow."

"Is he doing okay?" Daddy said back.

"Better than last week," Jimmy's daddy said back.

"It's tough luck," Daddy said. Which isn't true. It wasn't luck at all. Because John Smith and Pocahontas ran into Jimmy on purpose. "I hope he gets better soon," Daddy said again.

"Thanks," Jimmy's daddy said.

"See you," Daddy said. And then we started to walk down Columbus Street again toward Bruno's on the corner when Daddy stopped, turned around, and said back again to Jimmy's daddy, "Oh, by the way, I was over at the barber shop on Bayou Road for a haircut this afternoon, and Buck asked me to tell you if I see you that it would be good if you could stop over there sometime soon. He knows about your son. But he said he needs to talk to you about something. I'm just saying what he said."

"What?" Jimmy's daddy said back at first. Like he didn't know where the barber shop is or who Buck was. But then he said again, "Oh, sure. I'll go over after my kid's back from the hospital."

Daddy waved at him, and we started walking again. When we were in front of Bruno's at the corner, I said, "Who is Buck, Daddy?"

"Let's cross here," Daddy said. "Give me your hand." I don't know why Daddy makes me give him my hand when we're crossing Columbus Street. Because I always cross it by myself whenever my Mother sends me to the Triangle or to Richard's Five and Dime or to Mister Lee's or whenever I go to the Rivoli with Lenny Mahoney. But Daddy does. So, I do. I give Daddy my hand.

"But can we go to the other side of Dorgenois first?" I said back. I didn't want to walk in front of the house where third base was, where the black and brown dog was.

"It's shorter this way," Daddy said. And he pulled my hand. So, we just walked across Columbus Street. And when we were across it, the black and brown dog started barking, clapping his teeth at us and biting the fence. "I don't know what's wrong with that dog," Daddy said. "He sure makes a lot of racket."

I told Daddy about what Bobby Robby does. "This kid I know," I said, "just goes over to the fence and kicks him right in the mouth."

"He does?" Daddy said back. "What about you, Vonny, my boy? Do you try to kick him too?" I just shook my head. I didn't want to tell Daddy that I don't even walk on the same side of the street as the black and brown dog, that I go around on the other side of Dorgenois by second base. "Well," Daddy said again, "let's walk over to the fence together." And I thought Daddy was going to kick the fence like Bobby Robby did. So I moved to his other side so that Daddy was between me and the fence and the fence was between him and the black and brown dog. But Daddy just stopped in front of the dog. Who was still barking, clapping his teeth at us and biting the fence. I stayed behind Daddy. "Come over here, boy," Daddy said. "Come here." Daddy reached his hand over the fence and bended over it. The dog stopped barking, stopped clapping his teeth at us and stopped biting the fence. "Here, boy," Daddy said again. "Here you go." Daddy leaned over and rubbed the black and brown dog on top of his head. "You need to calm down, boy. We're the good guys. We're not going to hurt you." Daddy turned around to me and said, "You want to pat him on the head, Vonny, my boy?" I just shook my head and backed away. Daddy laughed, "I didn't think so. But, you see. He's just a puppy dog after all. A big puppy dog who is as scared of you as you are of him." Which is not true. I'm a lot more scared than the dog is. "He's not a monster. He's just afraid." Daddy rubbed his head some more and then said, "Okay. Let's get going." And the minute Daddy stopped rubbing his head, the black and brown dog started running up and down again, barking at us again, clapping his teeth at us again and biting the fence again.

I could smell something good from Picou's Bakery. "What's that, Daddy?"

"Smells like something fried," Daddy said back. "Probably doughnuts," he said again. And then he smiled at me. "Or maybe just doughnut holes." He rubbed me on the head and winked at me. "I think they make doughnut holes on Tuesdays."

Then I remembered what I wanted to know before. "Who is Buck, Daddy?"

"Who?" Daddy said back. We were at the corner of Bayou Road across Dorgenois from Picou's now, on the K street where the Rivoli movies is across from the Triangle, right where all of the streets come into Bayou Road. We started walking across the K street to where we had to cross Bayou Road so that we would be at the disgusting meat shop.

"Buck!" I said back out loud. "The man on Bayou Road who asked you to tell Jimmy Broom's daddy if you see him that it would be good if Jimmy Broom's daddy could stop over at the barber shop sometime soon. The man on Bayou Road who knows about Jimmy Broom. But who said he needs to talk to Jimmy Broom's daddy about something."

"Oh," Daddy said back again. "That Buck. He's the barber down there on Bayou Road." Daddy pointed down the street past the Richard's Five and Dime and past the dead chicken store to where the barber shop was across Bayou Road from the St. Rose de Lima Bean Church. "He's got some business with Jimmy's daddy. Why do you call him Jimmy Broom?" Daddy said. "I don't think their name is Broom."

"It's not," I said back, and I told Daddy why Jimmy Broom is called Jimmy Broom. And then, after we crossed the K street and walked in front of the Triangle and walked across Bayou Road, we walked up to the disgusting meat shop. When Daddy opened the door, a little bell rang and we walked in. I had to put my hands over my eyes. "I can't look," I said to Daddy.

"What's the matter with you?" Daddy said back. "It's just meat." Which is not true. It's not just meat in the disgusting meat shop. It's disgusting meat!

The man who works at the disgusting meat shop wears a white apron just like the one that the lady who works at Picou's Bakery wears. Except the apron of the man who works at the disgusting meat shop is always covered with blood. Which comes from the organs that he takes out of the cows and the pigs and the other animals that go there. The man who works at the disgusting meat shop stands behind a white case that has windows in it just like the white case at Picou's Bakery. Except the white case that has windows in it that the man who works at the disgusting meat shop stands behind has in it cow livers and pig hearts and cow tongues and pig kidneys and all kinds of animal bones and even baby cows' heads. With the eyeballs still in them! Sometimes I uncover my eyes just a little and if I look at the eyeballs in the baby cows' heads they follow me around the shop. Like the visible man picture on the box. Like the picture of Jesus in the room where Daddy and my Mother and now my baby brother sleep. Like the eyeballs do in the fish that Daddy catches. Except if I see the eyeballs in the baby cows' heads at the disgusting meat shop, I think maybe they're going to chase me. Even if I know the baby cows are dead and they don't even have any legs anymore. It's disgusting!

"What can I help you with today?" the man behind the white case said to Daddy.

"Need some liver," Daddy said back. "About a pound."

"Beef or veal?" the man said back.

"Veal," Daddy said back again.

"Pound of veal liver coming up," the man said back again. I was just listening to them talking because I still had my hands over my eyes. I didn't see anything. "What's the matter with him?" the man said.

"He thinks meat grows on a bush," Daddy said back. Which I do not. I know it grows on cows. And on pigs too.

But I still didn't uncover my eyes. "What's veal?" I said to Daddy.

"Veal is meat that comes from a baby cow," Daddy said back.

"Like the baby cows' heads over there?" I said back. I pointed to where I know they were in the white case. But I didn't uncover my eyes still.

"He's very curious, isn't he?" the man behind the white case said.

"Mike, you don't know the half of it," Daddy said back. Whatever that means. The little bell on the door rang again and I heard somebody walk in.

I still covered my eyes. But I heard a voice say, "Haven't I seen enough of you for one day?"

"Hi, Buck," Daddy said back while he was laughing.

"Hey, Buck," the man behind the white case said. "How are you?"

"Who's this?" I heard Buck say back.

"This is Vonny," Daddy said. "He's not much on organ meats."

"I can see that," Buck said.

"Hey, Vonny, my boy," Daddy said. "Turn around and say hello to my friend Buck."

Which I did. I turned around so the white case was behind me and uncovered my eyes and looked up and held out my right hand. Like Daddy taught me. Then I said, "Nice to meet you, Mister Buck." Like my Mother taught me. But then I made a stupid face because Buck was the same man who Daddy had to talk to in front of the St. Rose de Lima Bean Church before Mass on Sunday. Which was the same guy who John Smith was talking to in front of the barber shop on Bayou Road when he was pointing at me while we were walking to Picou's Bakery after Mass on Sunday.

"How come I never see you in my barber shop?" Buck said to me.

"His mother cuts his hair now," Daddy said back. "But he's making his First Communion in a couple of weeks, so we'll be in this weekend for his first real haircut."

"We will?" I said back.

"Of course we will, Vonny, my boy," Daddy said back again.

"Sure," I said. "For my First Communion." And then I had a sad thought. Which was my confession list. Which I had to write again because there is so much more on it now.

Buck said back while he was shaking my hand, "Well, pleased to meet you, Vonny." He turned to Daddy. "I saw you from down the block, so

I thought I might catch you." He pulled two white envelopes from his pocket and handed one to Daddy. "Your thing happened this afternoon," Buck said. "Here's one for you too, Mike." Buck handed the other white envelope to the man behind the white case.

"Thanks, Buck," the man behind the white case said.

Daddy laughed. "Well," he said. "Looks like I can pay for the liver now, Mike. I was going to have to buy it on credit." Whatever that means.

The man behind the white case laughed too. "Not a minute too soon, right?" he said back.

"Well, I need to get back to the shop," Buck said. "Nobody there but me." He opened the door and the little bell rang again.

"Wait!" Daddy said. Buck stopped and turned around. The door was open so I could see Bayou Road behind Buck in the door. Daddy said again, "I talked to your friend over on Columbus Street."

"Friend?" Buck said back. "Oh, right. What did he have to say?"

"His kid's coming home from the hospital tomorrow," Daddy said back again. They were talking about Jimmy Broom's daddy!

"How does he look?" Buck said back again.

"Well, the kid's okay," Daddy said back, "but it was a bad week for them."

Buck looked at me. And then he looked at Daddy. I looked out the door on Bayou Road and saw a black Pontiac driving very slowly behind Buck in front of the disgusting meat shop. "Well," Buck said back, "I feel as bad as the next guy. But there are a lot of sad stories in this town." Buck walked back into the disgusting meat shop and closed the door again. Then he said in a very low voice, "But it won't get any better for him if he don't talk to me soon." I know that's not the right way to talk. But that's how Buck said it.

"He knows you're waiting for him to drop by," Daddy said back.

"Well, thanks for that," Buck said. And then he turned again, opened the door again, and the little bell rang again. After he walked out of the disgusting meat shop and before the door closed all the way, I saw Buck turn to walk down Bayou Road to his barber shop across the street from the St. Rose de Lima Bean Church. I saw him waving his hand over his head like he was trying to get somebody's attention. Like my little sister always does. And then I also heard Buck say out loud, "Hey, Jake! Jake! Wait up!" I thought about the black Pontiac because that's the same thing

Pocahontas called John Smith at the Triangle. And what Henry calls him too. Jake!

"It's a tough situation," Daddy said to the man behind the white case. Who just lifted his shoulders up and down.

"Don't know the guy," the man said back. Then he put a white package on the counter and wiped his hands on the bloody apron he was wearing. "That's six bits," he said. Whatever that means. Daddy opened the envelope that Buck just handed him, took out a dollar bill, and gave it to the man behind the white case. The man put it in a box on the counter in front of him and then reached over to Daddy. "Okay, here's two bits," the man said back. But instead he gave Daddy two dimes and a nickel.

I had my hands back over my eyes again. But I felt Daddy put something into my khaki shirt pocket. Which is the one on my chest. "Don't tell your mother," he said. "This is for helping me run this errand, Vonny, my boy. A nickel for walking me here and back." Then Daddy said to the man behind the white case, "See you, Mike. Take care." I turned around, uncovered my eyes, ran to the door, and then opened it. The little bell rang and then we were finally back out on Bayou Road where Daddy said, "That wasn't so bad, was it, Vonny, my boy?" I just lifted my shoulders up and down. "Remember what I told you about dead people not being dangerous?" Daddy said again.

"Sure, Daddy," I said back and nodded. "Don't ever worry about dead people. It's the live people I have to look out for."

"Well, that goes double for dead cows," Daddy said back. And then he laughed and rubbed my hair and put his hand on my shoulder.

Daddy and I walked across Bayou Road and were walking on the sidewalk in front of the Triangle when I all of a sudden saw two live people that I do have to look out for. The black Pontiac was parked on the wrong side of the street in front of the barber shop down the block on Bayou Road. I saw John Smith was on the sidewalk talking to Buck. Somebody, probably Pocahontas, was still in the car. I saw John Smith give Buck a hard push and then he punched him in the stomach. Just like the way Red does with me and Lenny for no good reason. Buck at first just covered up his stomach. But then he held his hands up. Like he didn't want to fight. John Smith told me at the Triangle that he never went to school for a long time. But I was thinking he never went to church too. Because he was punching Buck in the stomach for no good reason right across the street from St. Rose de Lima Bean Church! Which it is a sin to fight anywheres. But even more in front of a church.

While we were walking back across the K street, I said, "Daddy?" I only said that one word. I wanted to tell Daddy about how I was investigating the incident. And how John Smith was punching his friend Buck in the stomach for no good reason. And how John Smith and Pocahontas chased me and Henry the night before and tried to do to us what they did to Jimmy Broom. But Daddy didn't know that I know John Smith. Or Pocahontas. Or where I met them. Which was the Triangle we just walked in front of. Or what I did when I met them. Which was that I went cow with John Smith. Or that they were after me. Which was because I know they tried to kill Jimmy Broom.

"What, Vonny, my boy?" Daddy said, and I saw that Daddy saw Buck in front of his barber shop when he was just talking again to John Smith. Which was after John Smith just punched him in the stomach for no good reason.

I just lifted my shoulders up and down. "Nothing," I said. "I mean, I guess I don't need to be afraid of dead cows after all."

Then Daddy said back, "That's what I was telling you, Vonny, my boy." Daddy rubbed the top of my head again. "But now that we're talking about cows, when were you going to tell me about how you learned about going cow at the Triangle this past Saturday while I was fishing?" Just when Daddy said that, I tripped over the curb stepping from the street to the sidewalk after we crossed the K street. I didn't fall because Daddy was holding my hand. Which he always makes me do even if I am not a little kid. So, I didn't fall when I tripped. "I hear you made over ten dollars while you were waiting to buy a roast beef poor boy for your mother," Daddy said. I just lifted my shoulders up and down. We kept walking along Dorgenois. "Is it true what I heard, Vonny, my boy?"

Was it true what Daddy heard? Was it true? Almost nothing I said for a week was true! I pulled my hand away from Daddy. "I was afraid not to do it!" I said back.

"Not to do what?" Daddy said back.

"Afraid not to go cow," I said again.

"Afraid not to do the right thing?" Daddy said back again.

"No, Daddy," I said back. "I was afraid not to go cow with that man. I was afraid of him."

"All you had to say was no, thank you," Daddy said back. "He didn't have a gun to your head, did he?"

"Who told you?" I said back.

"It doesn't matter who told me," Daddy said back. "And I don't know why you're upset with me. You're the one who was talking to a stranger," he said again. "You're the one who was betting with a stranger."

"Does Mama know?" I said back.

"No," Daddy said back. "It's just between you and me." We were walking in front of the black and brown dog again. Who was doing what he always does. "Calm down, boy," Daddy said as we were walking by third base at the corner. And I didn't know if he was talking to the black and brown dog again or if he was talking to me.

"He's bigger than me," I said.

"Who's bigger than you?" Daddy said back.

"The man who I went cow with," I said back. But then I was thinking, everybody is bigger than me. Even if I am in the second grade. I am smaller than everybody.

"Did he tell you he was going to hurt you if you didn't go cow with him?"

"No!" I said out loud. We were in front of Bruno's now. I saw that Jimmy Broom's daddy wasn't working in front of his house anymore. "He didn't," I said again. "I wanted to go cow with him. I had two dimes from when I was Uncle Martin's caddy at City Park Saturday morning. They were my dimes!"

"Calm down, Vonny, my boy," Daddy said. "You need to be careful is all. You can do what you want. Not everything you want. But you just have to be sure you know who you're dealing with." We got to the gate in front of our house and walked through it. Daddy stopped and then, instead of going up the stairs to the porch, he turned around and sat down on one of the steps. Where I was standing in front of him. "So, what did you do with the money you got from going cow? I heard it was twelve fifty," he said again. "Is that right?"

I just nodded. I put my eyes down. I didn't want to look at Daddy. I wanted to be anywheres except in front of my house with him just then. Then I said in a low voice, "I went to Burdine's."

"You spent all that money at Burdine's?" Daddy said back. I just nodded again. Daddy smiled. "I looked at that invisible man you brought home, Vonny, my boy. He didn't cost you twelve fifty." I didn't say anything. "Not at Burdine's." Daddy put his hands on my shoulders. "You have anything else you want to tell me, Vonny, my boy?" I just shook my head. "About where you spent that money? Or about where you were last night? About your errand last night? Your mystery errand? About who you were with last night? Why you were out so late?" I just pulled away. I didn't want to tell Daddy about where I spent the money. I didn't want to tell him about where I was last night. I didn't want to tell him about who I was with. I didn't want to tell him about why I was out so late. Daddy stood up and started up the stairs. And I followed him up and onto the porch. Where he turned around and bended over again to talk to me. "It will be our secret, Vonny, my boy. I won't say anything about any of this to your mother. Or to anyone." Daddy opened the door into the parlor. But just before he stepped inside, he said again, "But maybe you will want to say something to your mother. Maybe you will want to tell her about all this." He turned around, looked down at me, and said again, "Before you make your first confession next week."

Everything was turning into a mess!

"Is that you, Albert? Vonny?" my Mother said out loud from the back of the house when we walked in the front door. My little sister ran up the hallway and wrapped her arms around one of Daddy's legs.

"Hello, precious!" Daddy said. "You want some liver?"

"Liver! Liver! Liver!" my little sister said.

"Daddy," I said, "if your liver makes you be able to eat food, what makes you be able to eat liver?"

"Lenny's here! Lenny's here! Lenny's here!" my little sister said again.

"Vonny, my boy, I don't know how you come up with these questions," Daddy said back.

"Vonny? Are you coming back here?" my Mother said out loud again from the back of the house, from the kitchen.

"We're coming. We're coming," Daddy said back. He had to walk slowly because he was dragging my little sister on his leg. He handed me the white paper package of liver. "Here, Vonny, my boy. Hold this so I can get this little monkey off of my leg." And then he laughed.

When we got to the room where my little sister and I sleep, I saw in the kitchen the back of a lady's head. But I didn't see who it was. It didn't look like my Aunt Audra or my Aunt Anna or any of my other aunts who didn't live on Columbus Street. Like Aunt Tallulah or Aunt Gwendolyn. It was a lady with yellow hair. Hair like Lenny Mahoney's. And then when I got to the door to the kitchen, I saw Lenny himself standing in the corner of the kitchen all the way the other side. "Hi, Lenny!" I said. But he didn't say anything back. He just looked up at something on top of the refrigerator. I did too but it was too high to see from where I was standing.

When I walked into the kitchen, I saw my Mother standing in another corner. She was pouring milk into a cup of coffee. "Do you take sugar too?" she said to the lady. Who I saw when I was in the middle of the kitchen was Lenny's mother.

"Hi, Lenny," I said again. I turned around to Lenny's mother and said to her, "Good afternoon, Missus Mahoney." Which I don't know if that's how you write that. "How are you today?" But Lenny's mother didn't say anything back too. She just sat by the kitchen table with her hands in her lap. Lenny's mother just looked at me the way Sister Marianna sometimes does when I ask a question that she doesn't want to answer or talk about.

My Mother walked over to the kitchen table and put the coffee cup in front of Lenny's mother. All of the parts for the visible man were missing. Because I didn't see any of them on the table where I left them before I went with Daddy to the disgusting meat shop. I didn't see the two little books too. I just saw the visible man box sitting on the kitchen table. Closed up. I was going to ask my Mother about it. But then Daddy came into the kitchen.

"Hello, ladies!" Daddy said after he finally made it back to the kitchen. But nobody said anything back. "What's the matter?" Daddy said again. "Somebody lose a kitten?" And then he laughed.

My Mother reached on top of the refrigerator. "So, Vonny," she said, "maybe you have a better explanation for this than Lenny here." She put the visible woman box on the kitchen table on top of the visible man box. "Who for some reason seems to think this belongs to you even though Missus Mahoney found it under his bed."

Ten, or Fair Grounds

I like horses. I like horses a lot! I only ever rode on a horse one time that I know. But I like horses a lot anyways. It's because of the way they hold up their heads. Which they move up and down. Even when they're standing still. Except they keep looking at you even if their eyes are moving up and down in their head. They are always looking at you. Horses are always paying attention. No matter what! They are observant.

Dogs are different. Dogs only look at you if they want you to give them some food. Dogs look at you and try to make you think they like you. Because they look at your eyes. But I know better. When a dog looks at you, it's not paying attention. It's not being observant. Dogs only look at you because they just want you to give them some food. So, they look at your eyes like they're going to be your friend. And if you give them something to eat, like a dog bone or something, they stop looking at you and just bite the bone all up. Like you aren't even there! Because that's all that dogs ever want in the first place. They don't want to be your friend. They never want to be your friend. Dogs just want you to give them some food. They look at you with their eyes like you're a friend, like they want to be your friend. And then after you give them a bone and they eat it or hide it or bury it, the next thing they do is just start barking at you and clapping their teeth at you and even biting you on the ankle if they can.

Some people say dogs are smart. But it's not dogs that are smart. It's people who feed them all the time that are not so smart. Which only makes the dogs seem smart.

Anyways, horses don't bite people unless you make them afraid of you. Which is what Daddy says. If you don't make horses afraid of you, they just stand around, moving their heads up and down, looking at you, paying attention, being observant. And they are very calm.

The only one time that I know when I ever rode on a horse was when I was only a little boy the way my little sister is a little girl now. I think I was barely even talking. And I don't remember much about that only one time that I know when I ever rode on a horse. But in the room where Daddy and my Mother and now my baby brother sleep, they have a picture of me on the horse. So, even if I don't remember much, I can see on that picture that the horse that I rode on that only one time was a small horse. That horse was so small that if he got into races at the horse race track that Daddy and I go to, he will lose to every other horse in every race. Even the very slow ones. Because the horse that I rode on that only one time was not much bigger than me. And I was only a little boy the way my little sister is a little girl now. Maybe even more little than her.

In the picture that Daddy and my Mother have, that small horse is very calm. He even has his eyes closed. He looks like he was sleeping. Except he wasn't. I know he wasn't sleeping because the one thing I remember is he made a big mess right there by my Aunt Gwendolyn's house. Which is where my Mother and I lived when Daddy was in Korea.

My Mother says a man came by one day with this little horse and asked her if she wanted a picture of me on it. My Mother has a lot of pictures of me and of my little sister and now of my baby brother. My Mother likes pictures of everybody. She likes pictures of everybody but especially pictures of me and my little sister and my baby brother. Who doesn't even know you're taking a picture of him because his eyes don't see that good. My baby brother can't even see good enough to pick something out of the shop window at Picou's Bakery.

So, when the man came by one day with this little horse, right away my Mother wanted a picture of me on it. Because my Mother also probably knew that it was going to be the only one time that I was going to ever ride on a horse. Which is because one day I am going to be too big to be a jockey. Which is what Daddy says.

In the picture of me riding the horse that is in the room where Daddy and my Mother and now my baby brother sleep, besides the very calm little horse, there is me riding on top of him. Where I am dressed up just like a cowboy. Which is with a cowboy hat and this handkerchief the man tied around my neck and a cowboy jacket and some covers to wear on top of my dungarees. Which are called chaps. Which some of the people wear on some of the horses at the horse race track. In the picture, I look like I'm very happy. I have a big smile on my face. Which I don't understand because I remember thinking that the little horse might wake up and then run down the street with me riding on top of it the way sometimes the horses do on TV programs. Where guys chase each other around on horses that run very fast for no reason. They are not even in a race like the horses at the horse race track. The horses on TV programs don't even run in a circle. They just run and run for no reason.

But the little horse in the picture didn't wake up. He didn't wake up because he wasn't even sleeping. He was just a very calm little horse. And he wasn't going to run anywheres. Because he was not the kind of horse that even runs.

After the man took the picture and took back all of the cowboy clothes, the very calm little horse made a big mess right there in the yard by my Aunt Gwendolyn's house. Right on the green grass by the house! It smelled bad right away. When the very calm little horse made a big mess, everybody started laughing. Except for me. The man laughed. So did my Aunt Gwendolyn. And even my Mother laughed.

"That's quite a big mess to come out of such a little horse," my Aunt Gwendolyn said. And everybody laughed again. Except for me again.

"He may be little," the man said back. "But he's got quite an appetite." All I can remember is that it smelled bad right away. Which made me want to go inside. Which I did while my Mother talked to the man and gave him some money for the picture.

But even if that was the only one time that I know I ever rode on a horse, I like horses a lot anyways. And I especially like the horses at the Fair Grounds. Which is the name of the horse race track that Daddy and I go to sometimes after he comes home from work. Except not on Monday. Because the horse race track is closed on Monday. Because it is open on Saturday. And the people who work there need two days to rest. The horses too!

The horses at the Fair Grounds are very big. Which is much bigger than the very calm little horse that I only ever rode on that one time. They are bigger even than Daddy is. Some of those horses, their eyes are higher up than even the top of Daddy's head. Which is much higher than the top of my head. Even if I am sitting on top of the rail, the horses' eyes are higher up than the top of my head. But even if they are bigger, the horses at the horse race track are still very calm. Just like the little horse that I rode on in the picture. They don't make noise. Which means they don't bark at you like dogs do. And they don't clap their teeth at you. Which means they don't clap their teeth like dogs do. And they don't try to bite the rail around the horse race track to get out. Which means they don't try to bite the fence like dogs do. Horses are just very calm. They just move their heads up and down. And they always look at you to see what you're doing. Horses are always paying attention. No matter what! They are observant.

Like I already told, I like horses a lot. And I like going to the horse race track with Daddy a lot too!

At first, when Daddy came home from work on Wednesday, I just thought he forgot about everything. Because when Daddy came home from work on Wednesday and walked into the kitchen where I was sitting at the table with my Mother and my little sister, he just said, "Hi, Vonny, my boy. What do you say we go to the Fair Grounds for a few races?"

I thought he just forgot about everything.

For instance, I just thought Daddy forgot about how I didn't come home until late on Monday night after Henry and me were chased by John Smith and Pocahontas. Which made my Mother angry. Me coming home late. Not me being chased. Which she doesn't even know.

And I just thought Daddy forgot about Lenny Mahoney's mother coming over last night, Tuesday night, with Lenny and with the visible woman with her breasts, and about the whole story about me telling lies about buying two visible people. Which made my Mother more angry.

And I just thought that Daddy forgot that my Mother was even more and more angry about everything after Daddy said that pretending to buy only one visible person instead of really buying two was not the same as telling a lie about it. After all, Daddy said, I never said I didn't buy two visible people. I just pretended I bought only the visible woman, and then I just pretended I returned the visible woman to Burdine's, and then I just pretended I traded her for the visible man at Burdine's, and then I just came home with the visible man. I never said I just bought one visible person. I never said I didn't buy two visible people. I never said I returned the visible woman to Burdine's. I never said I didn't trade the visible woman for the visible man with Lenny.

Which made my Mother even more and more angry! Which was so angry that she said last night right in front of Lenny Mahoney's mother and Lenny too that I wasn't allowed to go outside after school all week and that maybe even on Friday night when Charly is suppose to come over to take me to the Bell to see that movie about these little kids who sing all the time about some old man who plays different kinds of games on his knee.

But then I remembered what Daddy said about pretending is not the same thing as telling a lie. And too, Daddy said after I just started crying, standing right there in the middle of the parlor on Monday night, that my Mother upset me. And too, Daddy always calls me his boy.

So maybe Daddy didn't just forget everything.

"I think he learned his lesson," Daddy just said to my Mother when he came home from work on Wednesday. He wanted me to go to the Fair Grounds with him. "Besides, he's still punished," Daddy said again. "He still can't play with his little friends." Who are not little because they are in the second grade like me.

But my Mother is very smart. She's too smart for me. I think sometimes she may even be too smart for Daddy too. My Mother looked at me with her blue eyes almost on fire. "Did you ask your Daddy to take you to the horse race track today, Mister?" I just shook my head. Because I didn't. I didn't even pretend to ask him. "After everything you did this week! Coming home late on Monday. And hiding from me that you bought the invisible man and the invisible woman. Don't think I didn't know you were up to something. You and your two dimes in your back pocket." Which I don't know why my Mother said that. Because she didn't even know everything about the visible people. She didn't know about me going cow with John Smith. Even if Daddy did.

I just kept shaking my head. I didn't say anything. But the whole time I was thinking "No! No! No!" And when my Mother said don't think she didn't know I was up to something, I felt my eyes get a little wet. Because I want my Mother to trust me. I don't want her to always think I am up to something. Especially when I am not. But even if I am too.

My little sister was hopping around the kitchen, waving her little arms in the air, as usual, and shaking her little head just like me. Except she was saying out loud, "No! No! No!"

"Stop it, Sharon," my Mother said out loud. "Stop it now!" That's when I knew my Mother was very, very angry. "And you still didn't tell me how you got the money to buy those two invisible people!" my Mother said again out loud. And then she pointed at me. She pointed at me like I did something wrong.

I started to say something to my Mother about going cow with John Smith. Which Daddy already knew about. I started to say something because I want my Mother to trust me. But then my little sister started crying because my Mother said "Stop it!" out loud to her. And when she did, my Mother took my little sister by her little arm and made her sit in the chair next to me.

"Listen," Daddy said. "Vonny knows he did wrong, don't you, Vonny, my boy?" This time I nodded my head. My little sister can't help herself. So, sitting in the chair next to me, she started nodding her little head too. "And he's sorry for what he did, aren't you, Vonny, my boy?" I just kept nodding my head. Which my little sister kept nodding her little head too. But now instead of crying, she was laughing like a little goofball. "And we won't be long," Daddy said again.

"Which is what Vonny said Monday night too before he came home almost at eight o'clock!" my Mother said back. And then she folded her arms. Which my little sister folded her little arms too. She can't help herself. Daddy and my Mother stood in the kitchen just looking at each other while I sat like a dope still nodding my head. And my little sister sat on the chair next to me like a little goofball still nodding her little head, just like me, and with her arms folded, just like my Mother. It was very quiet. The only sound I heard was the clock in the kitchen ticking out loud and water dripping from the faucet into a pot in the sink. Tick, tick, tick. Plink, plink, plink. Then, my Mother looked at me again and pointed at me again and said again, "You'll have your supper the minute you come back with Daddy and then it's off to bed with you for the night."

I wanted to say to my Mother that Jimmy Broom was coming home from the Hotel Dieu. And I wanted to go over and see how he is doing after supper because he was gone for a week and has broken bones. But I didn't say anything. Even if I wanted to ask Jimmy about the black Pontiac and did he see the driver. I just kept nodding my head. Which my little sister just kept doing too. And I rubbed the back of my hand under both of my eyes to make any water there go away. Which my little sister didn't do. Because she wasn't still crying. She was laughing. And then she stopped.

It was very quiet again. Tick, tick, tick. Plink, plink, plink.

And so, without anybody saying anything else, Daddy just said, "Let's go, Vonny, my boy." Daddy and I just left to go to the horse race track. And even when we were walking on Columbus Street in front of his house, I still thought I was going to be able to see Jimmy Broom after supper after we came back from the Fair Grounds.

That was what was suppose to happen. But here's what happened instead.

After we left our house, while Daddy and I were walking to the horse race track, walking down Columbus past the St. Rose de Lima Bean School to Broad Street by Mister Lee's laundry, which had a fancy sign outside that said "Mr. Lee's Laundry", and then across the wide street to the other side of Bayou Road, around the bend in the road, and then in front of the Bell across the street from Stallings Playground, I started thinking about how Monday night Henry and I had to walk back from the Trinity Zion African Methodist Episcopal Congregation Church after John Smith and Pocahontas chased us there. Which was not anywheres near my house. Or Henry's. And after they drove away with Henry's bicycle in the back of their black Pontiac.

While we were walking Monday night, Henry didn't say anything at first and I didn't say anything at first too. We just walked. And then after a while, we got to Columbus Street. "I better go this way," Henry finally said, pointing up Dorgenois to Harp Street when we got back to the alley behind Bruno's. Which is where we got chased from before. "They may be looking for us."

Henry was right. It was late. The sky was black. Daddy and my Mother went looking for me on Saturday night after I went to bed without telling anybody. If they were outside looking for me on the street again, I didn't want them to see me with Henry. Who doesn't live on our street. And they always tell me not to talk to strangers. Even if Henry's family seems nice to my Mother.

On the corner at Bruno's, I saw there was a light on behind the heavy door. There were probably a few old crocodiles in there drinking beer from their glasses. Henry started walking away. But I called him and he turned around. "Why don't you have a confession box in your church, Henry?"

He stopped and walked back to me. "What's a confession box, California?" he said back. "What's that?"

"It's a place where you tell the priest what you did wrong," I said back. "If you did bad things or said mean words or thought impure thoughts."

"What's an impure thought?" Henry said back.

I just moved my shoulders up and down. "I don't know," I said back again. "Nobody can tell me!"

Henry just said back, "We just don't do that, California. So, we don't need a confession box."

"You don't do anything wrong or you just don't have to tell anybody about it if you do?" I said back.

Henry moved his shoulders up and down. "I guess both, California," he said back.

"Are you going to tell your daddy about what happened?" I said to Henry in a low voice. "About us meeting tonight? And us getting chased? And us hiding in the church? And about your bicycle?"

Henry shook his head. "I can't tell him I was with you. And I can't tell him I wasn't with you. Those guys can show up at my house anytime. They can show up there tonight. I can't say anything. And you can't too!" he said again.

"I think we need to tell somebody," I said back.

"You want your daddy to know you were with me tonight?" Henry said back. "At the Trinity Zion African Methodist Episcopal Congregation Church on St. Ann Street?" Henry scratched the short hair on his head. "If you did, and if my daddy was your daddy, you are going to have to find another daddy because your daddy is going to lock you up and then he is going to be locked up himself," Henry said again. "You can't say anything about this!"

"What if they come to my house?" I said back.

"That's what your daddy is for," Henry said back. "But you and me, we need to be quiet for now. We need to meet up again. What are you doing Friday night, California?"

"We can't wait until Friday," I said back.

"After tonight, I'm going to be punished all week," Henry said back. Which I was going to be punished too. At least from playing with my friends. And from meeting Henry.

"I'm suppose to go to the Bell with my cousin Charly to see a movie about some kids."

"Charly?" Henry said back.

"It's my cousin's name," I said back. "She's a girl. Even if it's a boy's name."

"Well, maybe we can meet somewheres at the Bell on Friday," Henry said again.

I thought about it. "Sure. I can say tell Charly I have to go to the bathroom," I said back. "I'll just tell her during the movies. Then I can go out by myself."

"That's good," Henry said. "We'll meet again Friday. You come upstairs to the balcony at the Bell to get me."

Negro people get to go upstairs in the balcony at the Bell. And at the Rivoli too. It made me worry when Henry told me to meet him in the balcony. I remembered what Henry's daddy said about people being afraid of white people. "Do you think everybody upstairs will be afraid of me?" I said back. "You know?" I touched my arm. "Because I'm not brown?"

Henry just shook his head. "I don't think so, California. Besides, nobody is going to see us in the dark. You find out what your daddy knows about the man at the barber shop. I'll find out what my daddy knows too. You got it?" I nodded my head. I got it. "See you then," Henry said again. And then he just walked away on Dorgenois Street, on the sidewalk, to where his street is just behind Columbus Street. And I went home too. To trouble.

So, two days later, on Wednesday after school, when Daddy and I were walking in front of the Bell across the street from Stallings Playground, I thought about meeting Henry Friday night when I go to the movies with Charly.

When Daddy and I reached the sidewalk on the other side of the street, Daddy waved at a negro man who was standing in front of the gate where you walk into the Fair Grounds by a sign that said "White Only Entrance" in black letters on a white board. The negro man came over to us. He was holding some newspapers. Daddy gave him a dime and the man gave Daddy one of the newspapers. "Thanks," Daddy said.

"You got it, boss," is all the man said back. That's the way he talked. You got it, boss. We walked over to the rail on the horse race track and some horses were running in both directions a little at a time the way they always do before the race starts.

"What race are we on, Mister Chester?" Daddy said to the dark brown man with the crocodile skin. Who was walking by on the other side of the rail taking money from some people who were on our side of the rail. "Is it the eighth?" Daddy said again. The man nodded. "How long until post time?" Daddy said again.

"What's post time, Daddy?" I said.

"It's the time when the race is suppose to start," Daddy said back. The man looked at his watch and held up two hands showing ten dark brown fingers. Daddy said again to the man, "And how much time do I have to bet?" This time the man held up just one hand showing just two dark brown fingers.

"Two minutes, Vonny, my boy," Daddy said. "We have to be quick." He rubbed me on the head. Then he asked a man standing near us by the rail, "Who's the speed in this one?"

"The eight," the man said back.

Daddy was looking at the newspapers that he got on the street from the negro man by the "White Only Entrance" sign. "He looks cheap in the form," Daddy said back again.

"Sure, he does," the man near us by the rail said back. "But the race will be over before any of the other horses find out how cheap he is. And by then it will be too late." The man laughed a little.

Daddy laughed a little too. "You want to go cow with me, Vonny, my boy?" he said. He didn't even look at me. Daddy was still looking at the writing in the newspapers in his hand.

"Go cow?" I said back. "Me?"

"Who else?" Daddy said back. He turned to the man standing near us by the rail. "This boy's got all the luck," he said. I looked around but Daddy was pointing at me. "He won twelve fifty Saturday." Then Daddy picked me up and gave me a boost up on the rail. "Went cow with a guy playing a pinball machine at the Triangle over on Bayou Road."

"No joke," the man said back. He smiled at me.

"Can you believe that?" Daddy said again. "Went cow with a total stranger and came home with twelve fifty!"

"Who you got in this race, kid?" the man said. Which is the way the man talked. And then Daddy and the man laughed.

I just moved my shoulders up and down. I didn't like Daddy talking about me going cow with John Smith. And also, a lot was happening that I didn't expect to happen. First, Daddy talked my Mother into letting me go to the horse race track. Which she did even if I was very late to come home Monday and then she found out that I was pretending about the two visible people on Tuesday. And then, while we were at the horse race track, Daddy wanted to go cow with me. Which is betting. Which is why I had to buy the two visible people in the first place. To get rid of the money that I won when I went cow with John Smith. And now, Daddy was telling everybody about it!

"So, what do you say, Vonny, my boy?" Daddy said. "You bring any money?" Which I didn't. Because I didn't think my Mother was going to let me go to the Fair Grounds with Daddy. And because even if she did, which she did, Daddy never let me bet before, which now he did too.

I just shook my head. "I didn't bring any, Daddy," I said back.

"That's okay, Vonny, my boy," he said back. "How much do you have at home?"

I had to think. I still had the two visible people because Lenny threw away the Burdine's bag with the receipt. Except my Mother put the visible woman somewhere I don't know. "Only three dollars, I think," I said back. Which was what I had before I went cow with John Smith. And before I bought the two visible people. "But it's not here."

"I know. I know," Daddy said back. "That's okay. I'll front you the three dollars. What do you say we take the eight horse for two dollars across the board?" I just nodded. I didn't even know then what that means. Which now I do because I found out since. "That's three dollars to you and three dollars to me. You for that, Vonny, my boy?" I just kept nodding. Yesterday was a mess. But today I was with Daddy back at the horse race track. And we were going cow together for the first time. "Great!" Daddy said. He called over to the dark brown man with crocodile skin. "Mister Chester! Mister Chester!" Which the dark brown man walked over to us. "Get this in for us, Mister Chester, will you?" Daddy said again. "Two across on the eight for me and my partner here. Two dollars each, to win, to place, and to show. Got it?" Daddy put his arm around my shoulders. The dark brown man nodded and then wrote some numbers on a little piece of paper. Then he wrote the same numbers on another piece of paper and handed it to Daddy. And then Daddy gave Mister Chester a five dollar bill and a one dollar bill. "Cheap but fast, Vonny, my boy," Daddy said when the dark brown man walked away. Then Daddy said again, "That's true about a lot of good things in life, isn't it?" Daddy laughed and handed me the little piece of paper that Mister Chester gave him. Who is the dark brown man with crocodile skin. Which I put in my pocket.

Like he always does, Daddy brought his special glasses that let you see far away. So, I tried to find the horse with number eight on him. "How much money do we get if he wins, Daddy?" I said.

"Don't know," Daddy said back. "You know the odds on the eight horse?" he said again to the man near us by the rail.

Who had too some special glasses that he looked through back at the big building where everybody was. "Looks like eight to one," he said back. "That's it. Eight to one," he said again.

"That's great, Vonny, my boy. Your mother's going to be so proud of you when we win."

"Daddy!" I said back. "You can't tell Mama we went cow. She's very angry at me now. Very, very angry," I said again.

"She's not angry at you," Daddy said. He was standing right behind me and now he was looking through his special glasses with his arms almost just over my head. Almost around me. "You see that eight coming along there, Vonny, my boy. Right there on the turn, coming right at us." Which I did. It was a big red horse. Not red like a fire truck. And not red like crimson red. Not like the lady's dress in my Grandpa's book. It was more red like auburn red. Like somebody's hair. And the horse had a big white spot right in the middle of his head. He looked smart. And when he came by us, he was very calm. He was very big and very, very calm. His head moving up and down. Always looking at us. Always paying attention. Observant. "Your mother's just afraid because you're growing up now, Vonny, my boy." The whole time, Daddy was looking through his special glasses at number eight. Even if he was right in front of us. Big, calm, auburn, number eight. "What a beauty," Daddy said. "Eight to one on number eight in the eighth race. And he's red!"

Which the horse wasn't. A fire truck is red. Number eight was auburn. But I didn't contradict Daddy.

Then just after the big auburn horse walked by us, he lifted his tail and made a big mess right on the horse race track! Just like the very calm little horse made a big mess right there in the yard by my Aunt Gwendolyn's house that only one time that I know when I ever rode on a horse. And the big mess at the horse race track was not that far away from us. "That's disgusting!" I said. "Did you see that, Daddy?"

He was still looking through his special glasses. Daddy started laughing. And so did the man near us at the rail started laughing. "That's just good luck for us, Vonny, my boy. We can't lose now. Don't you know that means he's going to win?" Which I didn't know it means that number eight is going to win.

And then Daddy told me and the man near us at the rail a story about how his uncle use to take Daddy to the horse race track when he was a boy like I am a boy now and how they use to go cow all the time, Daddy and his uncle, and how his uncle said it was good luck when a horse made a big mess on the horse race track right before a race because it means the horse is going to win. No matter what!

"What's his name, Daddy?" I said.

"Uncle Nunzio," Daddy said back.

"No, Daddy! I mean number eight," I said back. "What's number eight's name?"

Daddy looked in his newspapers. And then the man near us by the rail said something. Except I didn't know what he was saying.

"How do you spell that?" Daddy said back.

"Look here," the man said back and he showed Daddy a little book. "See here." And then the man spelled something. Like a word in a spelling bee at school. Except a word I never heard before. "S-A-T-N-O-H-A-C-O-P," the man said again. "I don't know how you say that. Sat, no, hay, cop maybe?"

"Sat, no, hay, cop?" Daddy said back. Except he said it like it was four different words.

"That's it," the man said again. "Sat like sit, no like the opposite of yes, hay like what horses eat, and cop like a policeman." Except my Mother says it's rude to call policemen cops. "Sat, no, hay, cop," the man said again.

"God bless you!" Daddy said back. Like the man sneezed. And then Daddy laughed. "Is that the owner's name?" Daddy said again.

"No," the man said back again. "The owner's name is Fontenot."

Daddy laughed again. "Well," Daddy said back, "that's a long name for a cheap horse to carry. But he's our cheap horse, Vonny, my boy. Eight to one on number eight in the eighth race. You like that name?" I was looking at the little book that had all the names of the horses in it that the man near us on the rail was holding in front of Daddy. Which the man was holding for me to see too. "You mind if I see your program for a minute?" Daddy said to the man. Who then handed the little book to Daddy. "Look here, Vonny," Daddy said. "This is all the horses in the race."

In the little book Daddy showed me, there was a big black eight on the top of the page. And then there were all the numbers of the horses in the race. From one to eight. And next to each number in black block letters there were all the names of the horses in the race. I guessed it was the names of the horses in the race because next to the number eight at the bottom of the page was written SATNOHACOP. Just like the way I just wrote it. In black block letters. And in the boxes where they had the names of the horses in the race, there was a lot of other things you can read too. "What is all this suppose to mean?" I said to Daddy. And I pointed at the words that were above and below and next to the names of the horses in the race.

"Right here is the race number," Daddy said back, pointing to the big black eight on the top of the page. "And these are the numbers and the names of the horses. See? Here's number eight. Our horse. S-A-T-N-O-H-A-C-O-P," he spelled it out. "Sat, no, hay, cop." Then Daddy started pointing at all the other things that were written in the box where Satnohacop's name was. "See here? That's the name of the jockey. Jay Broussard. He's a good one. And here's the owner. Mister Fontenot. Don't know him."

"What's these names, Daddy?" I said back. And I pointed at very little letters that were right above Satnohacop's name.

"That's his daddy and his mother," Daddy said back. "See Smitty's Revenge. That's his daddy. And Native Princess is his mother. And this is his mother's daddy. Captain John R. That's his grandpa on his mother's side." My Grandpa on my Mother's side is dead.

"Why do they put his grandpa's name in there?" I said back.

"Because speed is in the blood, Vonny, my boy."

"What does that mean, Daddy?" I said back.

"It means if his daddy was fast and if his mother was fast and if his mother's daddy was fast, then our horse will be fast too. It's in the blood. It's why you have wavy hair like me." Which I do. Daddy rubbed my head. And now I know that my wavy hair is in my blood too.

"Who are these people?" I said again, pointing to some other names.

"That's the trainer and the breeder," Daddy said back again.

The man near us at the rail said, "He asks a lot of questions, doesn't he?"

Daddy laughed and said back, "We're just getting started."

"What's a breeder?" I said. I know what a trainer does because I saw one time some dogs on a TV program with a dog trainer. "What does a breeder do, Daddy?"

"A breeder breeds the horse," Daddy said back.

"What does that mean, Daddy?" I said back.

Daddy looked at the man near us on the rail. Who just lifted his shoulders up and down. "Don't look at me," the man said to Daddy. "You're the one doing all the explaining."

Daddy just lifted his shoulders up and down too. "Well, you know how your mother had your baby brother in her belly?" I nodded my head. "And then he was born a few weeks ago?" I nodded my head again. "It's the same way for horses. They live in their mothers' bellies before they are born."

"They do!" I said back. Which I didn't ever know.

"And then the breeder helps them be born," Daddy said again.

The man near us on the rail was laughing a little. "Close enough," he said. But he wasn't looking at us.

"And these numbers are the odds," Daddy said again. "The lower the odds, the better the chances the horse is suppose to win the race. See here? Number four is the favorite. He's two to one."

"Number eight is a twenty," I said back, reading the odds where Daddy told me for Satnohacop.

"Not anymore," Daddy said back. "He's eight to one now. I guess people think he's going to do better than he's suppose to."

"We think so, right, Daddy?" I said back. Because Daddy and I were going cow on number eight. Two across!

Daddy laughed. "We know so, Vonny, my boy. And this number here is how much weight each horse is carrying," Daddy said again. "Which is the jockey. See here. One hundred fifteen pounds for our guy." And he pointed to the numbers 1 and 1 and 5 next to Satnohacop's name. Just like the way I just wrote it.

Right when Daddy said that I closed my eyes to see if I was able to spell the horse's name on the little invisible blackboard in my head with invisible chalk. Which is the way Sister Marianna never lets me do for spelling bees. I closed my eyes and wrote out S-A-T-N-O-H-A-C-O-P on the little invisible blackboard in my head. Then I opened my eyes and looked at the name in the little book Daddy got from the man near us at the rail. It was the same! And then I closed my eyes again to look at what I wrote on the little invisible blackboard in my head. Which is when I saw a surprise I didn't see before. "Daddy!" I said. "It spells Pocahontas backwards, Daddy."

"What's that?" Daddy said back. He was still looking at the little book.

"Sat, no, hay, cop," I said back. "It's how you spell Pocahontas backwards."

"Pocahontas?" the man near us on the rail said and leaned over to look at the little book that Daddy was holding. And then he laughed. "The kid's right," he said.

"Look at that," Daddy said. "You're right, Vonny, my boy. We got a horse named for a indian running for us!"

Which was not true. "It's Pocahontas backwards, Daddy," I said back. I didn't want to contradict him. It wasn't Pocahontas. Who was a indian. It was Satnohacop. Who was not a indian. Who was nobody I ever heard of.

Daddy rubbed my head. "Close enough, Vonny, my boy. Close enough," is all Daddy said back.

When I saw that Satnohacop was Pocahontas spelled backwards, a thought popped into my head. Was it an accident or an incident? Did it just happen or did it happen on purpose?

But I didn't have time to think about it because all of the horses were right in front of us now. They were all stopped running and were just walking to where the start of the race was. Which was on the other side of the horse race track from the building where all the other people were.

By the stables. Which was what Daddy told me. But not too far away from us.

I knew it was going to be a short race where we won't even be able to see the horses running except right at the beginning and then only after it's already over. Which use to get me mixed up sometimes. Because in the short races the horses are slowing down by the time they get back to us. And the horse that gets back to us first after the race is already over is not always the one who is the winner. Even if it looks like the winner because it's ahead of all of the other horses when it gets back to us. And I knew it was going to be a short race because the short races always start not too far away from us on the other side of the horse race track from the building where all the other people were.

Anyways, just like the horses, I was paying attention. I was observant. I was watching all of the horses walking over to where the race was going to start. Except not all of the horses walking over to where the race was going to start are in the race. Some of them are just there to walk with the horses in the race. I can tell the difference because the horses in the race have a cloth on their backs with their number. And also, the riders on the horses in the race wear shiny colors on their shirts. Which are the jockeys. The other horses are just there to make sure that the horses in the race don't run away before the race starts. Which is what Daddy told me. For every horse that is in the race with a cloth on its back with its number and with a jockey wearing shiny colors on their shirts, there is another horse with only a big saddle on its back and no number and with a person riding it who looks almost like a cowboy. Which means they are wearing a cowboy jacket. And even chaps too. Like I did that only one time that I know when I ever rode on a horse.

I saw Satnohacop with a black cloth with the white number eight on it and with Mister Broussard the jockey on top of him wearing a shiny purple shirt with a big white letter F on it at the end of the line of all of the horses in the race while they were walking to the place where the short races start. Which looks a little like a train car where all of the horses go into little boxes and stand behind little fences while they wait for the race to start. I know it's going to be a short race whenever I can see where the horses start from because then I only see them again when the race is already over. When it's a long race, I see the horses two times because they run in front of us one time while it's the middle of the race and the horses are running very fast. And then they come by us one more time after the race is over and the horse that gets back to us first after the race is already over is not always the one who is the winner. When it's a long race, we don't even see where the horses start from. They just come flying by the first time we see them.

"Do you think we're going to win, Daddy?" I said while I was looking at all of the horses and especially at Satnohacop.

Daddy was looking through his special glasses. "He looks good, Vonny, my boy. He looks very good," Daddy said back. "But if looks won the race, even I might win," he said again. And then he laughed. "You want to see?"

I took again the special glasses from Daddy and tried to look at number eight just as he was walking into the little box behind the little fence. He was the last horse to go into the little box. Then I heard a bell ring out loud, and all of the horses ran out of the little train car and started running away from us to where I wasn't able to see them anymore. "I can't see them, Daddy," I said back. My stomach felt like it does when Daddy goes fast over the bump in City Park. Like I was dizzy.

Daddy quick took the special glasses back from me and held them up to his face. "He got out okay, Vonny, my boy. Broke on top."

"What does that mean?"

"He was first out of the gate, Vonny, my boy. Too bad they have to keep running."

There were only a few men standing by the rail like we were. Sometimes one of them said a number out loud. For instance, "Let's go three." Or "Move that five. Move him!" Like maybe the horses were able to hear them so far away. But Daddy was just very quiet at first. He just held the special glasses up to his face with one hand and put the other one on my shoulder. We were very calm, very quiet, very observant. Just like the horses. Daddy was just looking though the special glasses trying to find our horse, and I was just looking at Daddy.

Then, all of a sudden, Daddy said out loud, "Come with that eight! Come with him!"

"Are we winning, Daddy?" I said back. "Is he winning?"

"Dropped back into second place, Vonny, my boy. But I can see a purple shirt starting to move inside on the rail." Then he said out loud again, "Move him, Broussard! Go! Go!"

Over where the building is where all of the other people watch the races, there were a lot of people yelling. It was like people at the football game I went to with Daddy and my cousin Earl when we were outside. I heard all the people making noise inside Sugar Bowl stadium. But I wasn't able to see why they were making noise. "Did he go, Daddy?" I said back. "Did he?"

Daddy still had the special glasses up to his face. "Go!" he said out loud. "Go! Go!" And then Daddy took off his hand from my shoulder and made a fist and hit the rail right next to me. "Damn!" he said. Which I hope my Mother doesn't see I just wrote it. "He just missed, Vonny, my boy."

"Did we lose, Daddy?" I said back.

"It looks like he's second," Daddy said again. "Just missed!"

While Daddy was talking, the number eight horse, Satnohacop came running right in front of us ahead of all of the other horses. Which was our horse. Except he was slowing down because the race was over. But I know better now that the winner is not always the horse that gets back to us first after the race is already over. Because sometimes the horse that wins just lets other horses pass him up when the race is over and it doesn't matter anymore. Then number four ran by us. And then all of the other horses did too one at a time until they were all past us again and almost back to where the race started just a little while ago. Some of the other men on the rail were calling over to the jockeys, "Who won? Who won?" The horses that got to us last turned around first and started to walk back to the building where all of the other people were. "Who won? Who won?" the other men kept saying.

One of the jockeys on a horse that was already turned around waved the whip in his hand and said back, "How do I know? I was too far back to tell."

Then some other horses came back and one of the jockeys said, "Four." That's all he said. "Four."

And Daddy hit his fist against the rail again. "The favorite got us, Vonny, my boy. We'll still get place and show money though."

"Did we win, Daddy?" I said back.

"We bet him across the board, Vonny, my boy. So we'll get some money back anyways. But it won't be a lot."

"How can we get money back if he lost," I said back.

"He lost the race but it looks like he came in second," Daddy said back. "It was him and the four at the finish. So we'll get some money back because we bet on him to come in second too."

"We get money back even if he lost?" I said back again.

"That's right," Daddy said back again. Just then the horse with the number four was walking by us back to the building where all of the other people were. "But we won't get back as much as if the eight won." Right in front of us, big auburn Satnohacop came running up behind number four and then stopped right near him.

The jockey on Satnohacop pointed his finger at the one on number four. "You're coming down," he said out loud. "You're out. You're coming down!"

The two horses were right in front of us. "What happened, Jay?" Daddy said.

"This dope cut me off," the jockey on Satnohacop said back. "Bumped me into the rail." Mister Jay the jockey turned again to the other jockey on number four. "And still we just missed. By a nose!" Mister Jay's face was red. Not auburn. But red.

The other jockey on number four just lifted his shoulders up and down. "You didn't have the horse today, Broussard," he said back. "You can't win them all." Which is what Daddy says sometimes. It's not fair to the other people. And then the other jockey on number four made a little noise and made his horse run away.

"Well, maybe I can't win them all," Mister Jay the jockey said back. And then he said out loud, "But this one I can. And I did. You better have a good story for the judges." Then Mister Jay the jockey looked back at all of us on the other side of the rail. "Don't throw away your tickets just yet." And then he tapped his whip just a little on the side of Satnoha-cop. Who went running past the number four horse that everybody said won the race. Who was still just running too. Except slower.

"Well, Vonny, my boy," Daddy said. "Sometimes you just can't trust your eyes. We may get all the money yet."

Which Daddy was right. Because that's what happened.

While we were waiting for a long time, Daddy told me that some-times if one of the horses does something bad or one of the jockeys does something bad then some people who are sitting in the building where all the other people are will change the horses around and move the second horse to first or the third horse to second or the first horse anywheres else. For instance, Daddy said, it's okay to get in the way of a horse that's behind you but not one that's next to you. And Mister Jay the jockey said he was blocked while he was next to number four.

So, when the dark brown man with crocodile skin came back and handed Daddy three ten dollar bills and two dollar bills, Daddy thought number four got moved from first to second and Satnohacop got moved from second to first. "They take down the four?" Daddy said to Mister Chester. "He blocked the eight, right? Like Broussard said?" Except Mister Chester wasn't around when Mister Jay the jockey said that. "Is that right?" Daddy said again.

Mister Chester just shook his head. He didn't say anything back. He just shook his head and walked down by the rail handing out money to other people. Then, when he was walking back past us again, Mister Chester just said, "Photo." And then he rubbed me on the head and said, "You got them good, boss," and kept walking the other way. Like when the man with the newspapers called Daddy boss too.

Daddy said back, "Photo?" But Mister Chester didn't even turn around. Daddy looked at the man near us on the rail and just lifted his shoulders up and down. "What do you think that means?"

"I guess it means the eight won," the man said back. "Even Broussard didn't know he got him."

Daddy didn't say anything at first. He just looked at me. And then he made a funny face and started laughing. "Unbelievable!" Daddy finally said back. "Vonny, my boy. We can't lose! Even if we lost, we were going to win. And the jockey didn't even know he won. You are a lucky charm, Vonny, my boy. Just like Buck said."

"Buck the barber?" I said back. I remembered about Daddy being at the barber shop yesterday before we went to the disgusting meat shop. Which is the baby cows' head shop.

Without looking at us, the man near us on the rail said, "They say Buck cuts hair there once in a while." And then he smiled at Daddy. "It is a barber shop after all."

"Was it Buck that told you about me going cow with John Smith?" I said out loud to Daddy. I was thinking maybe John Smith told Buck on Sunday when we were walking down Bayou Road to Picou's Bakery after Mass. Like we always do. And then Buck maybe told Daddy when

Daddy went to get a haircut yesterday before we went to the baby cows'
head shop.

"Vonny, my boy, you need to calm down," Daddy said back. "Do
know how much you won?"

"Sixteen," I said back out loud. "Half of thirty two." I was mad that
John Smith told Buck and that Buck told Daddy and that Daddy told
the man near us at the rail about me going cow with John Smith last
Saturday at the Triangle.

"Not quite," Daddy said back. "You owe me three for your share of
the cow."

"So, I get thirteen," I said back out loud right away.

"Not quite," Daddy said back. "We have to give Mister Chester a little
something. What do you say we give him a dollar?" Daddy said again.
"It's only fair. Fifty cents each."

I just moved my shoulders up and down. "Okay," is all I said back. I
was calming down a little.

"So," Daddy said. "You did it again, Vonny, my boy." Daddy handed
me one of the ten dollar bills and then two dollar bills from the ones
Mister Chester just gave him. "You get twelve fifty again. I'll give you the
four bits when we get home. I don't have any change on me now."

The man near us on the rail said, "Why are you going to school, kid?
You can just play pinball and come to the horse race track. Twelve fifty a
day is decent money for a six year old." He was laughing.

"I'm seven," I said back. I wasn't laughing.

Daddy and the man laughed again. "Even for a seven year old," the
man said again.

I put the money in my pocket where I still had the little piece of paper
that Mister Chester gave Daddy. Who rubbed me on the head. "Let's get
out of here, Vonny, my boy," Daddy said. "We used up all our luck for
one day. We thought we lost, then we thought we won for one reason,
and then we finally won for another reason. We're not going to do better
than that." Daddy put his hands under my arms and lifted me off the rail
and helped me get down to the ground. "Not today, we won't," he said
again. He waved at the man near us at the rail. "Get them good," is all
he said.

So then, Daddy and I just walked home. Which was why Wednesday was not a happy day for me. Even if I went cow with Daddy for the first time at the Fair Grounds and won twelve fifty again.

While we were walking home, first across from Stallings Playground and then past the Bell and then around the bend in the road, I said again, "So, Daddy, was it Buck the barber who told you about me going cow at the Triangle with John Smith?"

"John Smith?" Daddy said back.

I said back right away, "The man who ran over Jimmy Broom with his black Pontiac."

We were at the corner of Bayou Road and Broad Street when Daddy said back, "Did what? Who?"

"At the corner of Columbus Street and Dorgenois," I said again while we were crossing over Broad. Which is a wide street. I didn't want to tell Daddy about what happened to Jimmy Broom. Because I didn't want Daddy to know that I was investigating who ran over him. Like the police are. Because I didn't want Daddy to know about how Henry and me were chased to the Trinity Zion African Episcopal Methodist Congregation Church. Because I didn't want Daddy to know about how Henry and I are friends. "John Smith ran over Jimmy Broom with the black Pontiac," I told Daddy. "With Pocahontas in the car with him." I was afraid of John Smith. Especially if he was telling people like Buck about me. So, I said again, "Was it Buck the barber who told you about me going cow at the Triangle with John Smith?"

When we got to the other side of Broad, Daddy was laughing. "What are you talking about, Vonny, my boy?" he said back. "The police got the guy who ran over your little friend." Which Jimmy is not little. He's in the second grade like me. "He was drunk. They already have him."

We crossed over Bayou Road in front of Burdine's. "Daddy," I said back. "Did you see that man who was talking to Buck in front of the barber shop on Sunday when we were walking to Picou's Bakery after Mass?" I said again.

"Like we always do," Daddy said back. And then he didn't say anything for a little, like he was thinking while we turned by Mister Lee's laundry onto Columbus Street and were walking between St. Rose de Lima Bean Church on our side of the street and St. Rose de Lima Bean School on the other side. Then, finally Daddy said, "That guy?" He started laughing again. "So you think that guy ran over your friend Jimmy?"

"He did, Daddy!" I said out loud. "And he's the man I went cow with at the Triangle last Saturday. Then he tried to trap me and Lenny Saturday when I was coming back from Burdine's when I bought the two visible people. Him and his friend. They tried to kill Jimmy!"

Without telling him why, I made Daddy cross Columbus Street before we even got to second base in front of the snowball stand because I didn't want to walk in front of the black and brown dog at third base. Even if Daddy says he's just a big puppy dog who is as scared of me as I am of him. Which is not true. I know I'm more scared! "Well," Daddy said back, "that guy's name is not John Smith." He started laughing again. "And, believe me, Vonny, my boy, he did not run over Jimmy Broom."

"Do you know John Smith, Daddy?" I said back. We were walking in front of Bruno's where in the street I wasn't even able to see any dirt over Jimmy's blood. It was all clean.

"Not in a black Pontiac or any other car," Daddy said again.

"How do you know that, Daddy?" I said back. "He's a bad man. He did it! Yesterday when we were walking home from getting the veal liver I saw him on Bayou Road punching Buck the barber in the stomach for no good reason. Right in front of the church!"

We were in front of Jimmy Broom's house. Which is the same as my Uncle Roger's house. "He did?" Daddy said back. "You think he punched Buck?"

"He did, Daddy! I saw it! Right there on Bayou Road!"

We reached the brick sidewalk in front of our house and then walked up the stairs onto the porch. "Well, Vonny, my boy," Daddy said back, "sometimes you see things and are not sure about what you saw. And even if you are sure about what you saw, it's not always clear what the meaning is of what you saw." Which is exactly what Uncle Martin told me too.

Daddy opened the door into the parlor.

"Is that you, Albert? Vonny?" my Mother said out loud from the back of the house when we walked in the front door. My little sister ran up the hallway and wrapped her arms around one of Daddy's legs.

"Hello, precious," Daddy said.

"Daddy," I said, "if it's not always clear what the meaning is of what you saw, how do you ever know if something is true?"

"Vonny, my boy, I don't know how you come up with these questions," Daddy said back.

"Vonny? Are you coming back here?" my Mother said out loud again from the back of the house, from the kitchen.

"We're coming. We're coming," Daddy said back. He had to walk slowly because he was dragging my little sister on his leg. He laughed.

When we got to the room where my little sister and I sleep, I saw in the kitchen the back of a man's head. But I didn't see who it was. It didn't look like my Uncle Martin or my Uncle Roger or any of my other uncles who didn't live on Columbus Street. Like my parain or Uncle Charles. It was a man with almost no hair. And then when I got to the door to the kitchen, I stopped right away. Because I saw another man standing in the corner of the kitchen all the way the other side. Who was Pocahontas!

I turned around and said in a low voice, "Daddy, it's them! The men who ran over Jimmy Broom!"

My Mother was standing in another corner. She was pouring milk into a cup of coffee. "Do you take sugar too?" she said to the man who was sitting down. Who I saw when I was in the middle of the kitchen was John Smith!

My Mother walked over to the kitchen table and put the coffee cup in front of him. And then Daddy came into the kitchen.

"Hello!" Daddy said after he finally walked back to the kitchen. "Oh, it's you guys. What can we do for you?" Daddy knew them! But nobody said anything back. "What's the matter?" Daddy said again. "Somebody die?" And then he laughed.

Which was not funny. "It's them, Daddy!" I said out loud. "It's the men who ran over Jimmy Broom with their black Pontiac. It's them!" I ran over to my Mother.

"Calm down, Vonny," my Mother said. "Do you know these gentlemen?"

I nodded my head. "Yes, Ma'am. I do. They ran over Jimmy Broom with their car."

"Now, why would they do such a thing, Vonny?" my Mother said back. When she said this, I saw John Smith smile. His face was crooked when he did. "But, tell me something, Vonny," she said again. "Where did you meet these two gentlemen?"

"At the Triangle, Mama. Last Saturday. When I went to get the roast beef poor boy for us."

John Smith smiled again and said in his froggy voice, "The best roast beef poor boys in the whole wide world! Right, kid?"

"Their sandwhiches are good, aren't they?" my Mother said back. She looked at me again with her blue eyes almost on fire. "And then what happened when you were there, Vonny?" My Mother was angry. She wasn't biting her finger like she does sometimes when she is angry. But she said in a mean voice, "Tell me how you got the money to buy the invisible people, Vonny."

"Those invisible people are expensive," Pocahontas said in his squeaky voice.

"Is that what you spent your money on, kid?" John Smith said. "I thought you were smarter than that."

"Okay, fellows, are you here to put him away for playing pinball?" Daddy said.

"Don't let them take me, Daddy!" I said back.

"Albert!" my Mother said. "I want Vonny to tell me how he got the money to buy those invisible people last week."

I started crying. I didn't want to. I just did. I was hardly able to talk to my Mother. "He wanted me to go cow with him," I said back while I was crying. "And so I gave him two dimes. And then he won. And then I got twelve fifty."

"So, not only were you talking to a total stranger," my Mother said back, "but you were betting with him too? Is that right?"

I just nodded my head. "He's a very lucky kid," John Smith said. "A real good luck charm."

"Well, young man," my Mother said again, "you're just lucky that the stranger you decided to talk to was a policeman."

"What?" I said out loud.

"Policeman! Policeman! Policeman!" my little sister said while she was hopping around the kitchen waving her little arms in the air.

"That's right, kid," John Smith said. He reached into his coat pocket and pulled out a little wallet like the one I bought Daddy at Richard's

Five and Dime last year for Father's Day. John Smith opened it and showed everybody his badge.

"You see," Daddy said, "Vonny, my boy. Sometimes you see things and are not sure about what you saw."

"Now, Vonny," my Mother said, "why don't you tell these policemen everything you know about that little boy being run over by that car?"

Eleven, or
Richard's Five and Dime

Yesterday was suppose to be a happy day for me. Which was Wednesday. Because it was a very good day in school for me. Because there was an arithmetic game. Which I always win because I am the only kid who can add up triple numbers in my head without having to write them down and carry them over on a piece of paper. I close my eyes and it's like I see a little invisible blackboard in my head where I write the triple numbers on it with invisible chalk and then just add them up. I try to do the same thing in the spelling bees on Fridays. But Sister Marianna always says, "Open your eyes, Vonny! Wake up!" Which makes everybody laugh. And which makes Louie Canale cackle. Except Sister Marianna lets me close my eyes for the arithmetic game. Sometimes I think she knows I have a little invisible blackboard and invisible chalk in my head and she just lets me use them anyways because it's hard to add up triple numbers. Even on a visible blackboard with visible chalk. And even harder on invisible ones in your head!

Yesterday was suppose to be a happy day for me. Which was Wednesday. Even if my Mother was still angry about me being out after dark on Monday night. Which is when I was with Henry and when John Smith and Pocahontas were chasing us to the Trinity Zion African Episcopal Methodist Congregation Church. Even if my Mother was still very angry with me about the two visible people I bought at Burdine's and then didn't tell her about both of them. Which she found out Tuesday night because Kenny Mahoney's mother found the visible woman under his bed and didn't leave well enough alone.

Still, yesterday was suppose to be a happy day for me. Which was Wednesday. Because Daddy and I went to the Fair Grounds. Where he let me bet with him for the first time by going cow for the race that Satnohacop won. And I got as much money going cow with Daddy on the horse race as I got when I went cow with John Smith. I got enough money with Daddy to buy two more visible people if I wanted to. Which I didn't want to. I got enough money with Daddy to buy my Mother something very nice at the Richard's Five and Dime when it is going to be Mother's Day. Which is in May.

But then yesterday, which was Wednesday, after I got all that money at the Fair Grounds from going cow with Daddy, he and I left the horse race track and walked back to our house. Where John Smith and Pocahontas were sitting in the kitchen drinking coffee with my Mother and going over the whys and the wherefores of how I went cow with John Smith at the Triangle. And then my Mother was very, very angry. Because my Mother put two and two together. Because she is smarter than me. She knew that I got the money to buy the two visible people from going cow with John Smith and that I even lied about where I got the money for the two visible people even after Lenny's mother came over with Lenny and my Mother found out that I was lying about how many visible people I bought.

So then, after my Mother found out everything, she made me give back twelve dollars and fifty cents of the money I got with Daddy at the horse race track. Which was all of it! To John Smith. Who is a policeman! Even if he talks mean and rude to everyone. Even if I can't even write the way John Smith talks because he's so mean and rude to everyone. Even if he calls Henry and Henry's daddy mean names. Even if he calls other people rude names. Including Pocahontas. Who is named Mack and is suppose to be John Smith's friend. Except John Smith is even mean and rude to him. Who is also a policeman!

So instead, yesterday was not a happy day for me. Which was Wednesday. Even if it was suppose to be!

After John Smith and Pocahontas left last night, my Mother sent me to bed without supper. Which I was very hungry for. I asked for something to drink too. Because I was very thirsty when we were talking to them. But my Mother said I had to go straight to bed. I didn't even get to take a bath. After the policemen left last night, my Mother just looked at Daddy and then she just looked at me. She bit her finger when she looked at me like she does when I forget to say "Ma'am" and like she does when she is very, very angry. Which she was last night. She was even mean to my little sister. Which my Mother almost never is. And she even said things out loud to Daddy too.

But the worst thing about yesterday, which was Wednesday, after Daddy and my Mother now knew all about my lying, Daddy and my Mother didn't think anything was a mystery anymore. All they knew was that I am a liar. A liar who didn't even know how to tell the truth anymore. A liar who lies to anybody anywheres anytime. And my first confession was only a week away.

"After I tell Sister Marianna about everything you did," my Mother said last night just before she turned off the light in the room where my little sister and I sleep, "it won't surprise me if she doesn't even let you make your First Communion." Which I will be the biggest dope in the class if that happens!

I knew, while I was in my bed wondering if Sister Marianna was going to let me make my First Communion, that after all that, Daddy and my Mother still didn't even know anything about me talking to Henry on Monday morning and then on Monday night or about me and Henry even getting chased after dark by John Smith and Pocahontas to the Trinity Zion African Methodist Episcopal Congregation Church after I lied after supper about me having to go out and run an errand. John Smith and Pocahontas didn't even say anything about any of that last night. Because they probably didn't want Daddy and my Mother to know that they are the kind of guys who chase second graders around the neighborhood for no reason. Even if they were policemen!

So, yesterday was not a happy day for me. Which was Wednesday. Because the worst thing was, Daddy and my Mother still didn't know all of the things I already did.

After all that, last night, it took me a long time to fall asleep. I had a thousand thoughts popping into my head. I was mad that Daddy and my Mother thought I was a liar and that they thought I didn't even know how to tell the truth anymore. But I am one! I am a liar. And I don't even know how to tell the truth anymore. So, I am just mad at myself too. I am just mad at myself because of what I am. I am just mad at myself because of what I did. I am just mad at myself because of what happened.

But I can't change it. I can't change what I am. I can't change what I did. I can't change what happened. I can't change that Jimmy Broom got run over. I can't change that John Smith and Pocahontas are policeman and so they can't be the people who ran over him. I can't change that I went cow with John Smith at the Triangle. Or now that I went cow with Daddy too. I can't change that I bought the two visible people. I can't change that I lied about it.

My Mother said last night if I told her I wanted to go cow with John Smith, and asked to, it was better than doing it anyways and then lying about it. But she wasn't going to let me go cow with John Smith! I am suppose to be old enough to be a responsible citizen in the kingdom of the Lord. Which is what Monseigneur Deutsch says. But I can't even do anything I want to! I have to tell my Mother everything I want to do. And then she says if I can do it or I can't do it. Which my Mother always says I can't do it. And even if I don't tell her, then I can't do anything anyways!

So, last night, it took me a long time to fall asleep. Without any supper. Without anything to drink. And without a bath. I even cried in my bed before I fell asleep. I don't like to cry. I hate to cry! I don't even like to whine. But I do sometimes. I whine sometimes when my Mother is just too smart for me. When she has an answer for everything. When she knows all the whys and the wherefores. When she doesn't leave well enough alone. But I hate to cry! Even if I sometimes do. Not because of my Mother. Or because of Daddy. When I cry, it's because of me. It's because of who I am. Which is a dope sometimes. Or because of something I did. Which is act like a goofball sometimes. Even if my Mother says it's rude to call somebody a dope or a goofball.

I'm not perfect! Even if I want to be. I never make a perfect score when I play golf in the back yard. I never make no mistakes when I use my cousin Marly's writing machine to try to write twenty times now is the time for all good men to come to the aid of their party. I never tell the truth anymore. And so I cried in my bed last night because now Daddy and my Mother think that I am just a liar. Daddy and my Mother think that I am somebody they can't trust!

While I was crying in my bed and trying to fall asleep, the thousand thoughts that were popping into my head were about John Smith, who is really named Jake, and Pocahontas, who is really named Mack. I never saw them before like I did in the kitchen last night. When they were sitting right next to me where I was able to see them right in their eyes. Before that, they were always standing up like at the Triangle or talking out loud at me from their car like on Saturday when Lenny and I were coming back from Burdine's or running after me like on Monday when they chased me and Henry to the church. Which means I was never able to see their eyes.

But sitting in the kitchen last night, I was able to see John Smith and Pocahontas and their eyes and I was able to hear them talk in a normal way because they weren't standing or talking out loud at me or running after me. They were just telling Daddy and my Mother about what they knew I did. Which was about me going cow with John Smith and all the rest.

Except they didn't say anything about Henry. It's a mystery why they didn't. John Smith and Pocahontas just never talked about Henry last night. Or about how they went to his house to talk to his daddy last Sunday night. Or about how they chased Henry and me to the Trinity Zion African Methodist Episcopal Congregation Church last Monday night. They didn't say one word about him. Not a peep!

While I was sitting in the kitchen last night listening to everybody talk about me, I saw that John Smith's head isn't round. His head looks like a piece of clay that we have at school for art projects. Except John Smith's head looks like somebody made a ball out of a piece of clay and then just dropped it on the floor where it made a flat spot right about where his forehead is. But just on one side. I never saw a head like that before. With a flat spot on one side of his forehead. And I never saw that John Smith's head is like that before. Maybe because the light at the Triangle is not so good. Even if it's better than at Bruno's. Or maybe because I don't look too good at people when they are talking out loud to me. Or maybe because I don't have eyes in the back of my head to see people who are chasing me when I am running away.

And John Smith's nose looks like it has a flat spot on it too. Except on the other side from the bigger flat spot on his forehead. Where he almost has no hair on his head. Just a few black hairs that are combed on the top of his head so it doesn't shine so much.

And John Smith has black eyes. Like Daddy's eyes. Except Daddy's eyes sparkle. Because Daddy is friendly. John Smith's eyes aren't friendly.

His eyes don't sparkle. They're just flat black. Which is a color paint that I buy in little bottles at Burdine's to put on my model airplanes or boats. Flat black means that the light goes into John Smith's eyes but it never comes out. Light just stays in John Smith's eyes.

But John Smith's skin is the opposite. No light at all goes into John Smith's skin. All of it comes out. Because his skin is very white. Almost like the chalk we have at school. And John Smith's skin even makes powder when he scratches it. Like the chalk does too.

Pocahontas doesn't look right either. Except instead of having flat spots in some places like John Smith's head and nose, Pocahontas is just long and skinny. And his face is long and skinny too. Even his nose is long and skinny. He has blue eyes that are so close on both sides of his nose that if you don't focus good when you look at Pocahontas it seems like he only has one big blue eye. Which is right above his long and skinny nose.

And Pocahontas has a lot of hair on his head. A lot more than John Smith. But he never even combs it. Or if he does, he doesn't do it very good. He doesn't put any grease in his hair the way Daddy and I do. Which is so that it's easy to comb and is shiny. The hair on Pocahontas's head just sticks out everywhere. Just like the hair on his arms. Which there is a lot of. It's like his hair is made out of hay or straw. Like that guy in the wizard movie. Except that the guy in the wizard movie wants to get a brain at the end from the wizard. But Pocahontas isn't too smart. Not if you listen to the way John Smith talks to him. Which is not very friendly. Which is like Pocahontas is a dope. It's the way some kids talk to Louie Canale at school.

So, when I was lying in bed last night, crying, trying to fall asleep, thinking about John Smith and Pocahontas and the way they looked in the funny way they do and the way they talked in the funny way they do, one froggy voice and one squeaky, and the way they acted in the not very funny way they do, I finally did fall asleep. I finally forgot I was hungry and forgot I was thirsty and forgot I was dirty and forgot I was a liar and forgot that Daddy and my Mother can't trust me anymore and I just fell asleep anyways.

And the way I know I just fell asleep anyways is because, in the middle of the night, I woke up in my bed. Which was very wet! But not because I wet my bed. Which is something I never do. Which is something my little sister did two times after my baby brother came out of my Mother's belly and came home from the Hotel Dieu. But which is something I never do.

My bed was wet for the same reason that my pajamas were wet when I woke up. My bed was wet and my pajamas were wet because I was sweating a lot. Which I was sweating a lot because I had a bad dream. Which sometimes I do. Even if I don't ever wet the bed.

And the bad dream I had last night, I never had before. It was not a bad dream about Jimmy Broom getting run over by the black Pontiac. Like my Mother thinks I had when I sleepwalked to my Uncle Roger's house in the middle of the night. Even if I don't remember it. And it was not a bad dream about John Smith trying to smother me with his hand. Like the one I had in the front room at my Grandma's house who is alive. Which I do remember it because it was just last Sunday. And it wasn't a bad dream about dead people coming to get me. Like the one I had after I saw a TV program one time and then Daddy told me, "Vonny, my boy, don't you ever worry about dead people. It's the live people you have to look out for. If you're going to be afraid of anybody, be afraid of live people." Which I also do remember even if it was a long time ago.

The bad dream I had last night was not like any of those bad dreams or any other bad dream I ever had. The bad dream I had last night was a bad dream about my Mother. And it was a very bad dream too. Not only because it was about my Mother. But also because it was mostly about something that already happened, something that I knew already happened.

Which was this.

Richard's Five and Dime is a store on Bayou Road next to the St. Rose de Lima Bean Church where they can sell you anything you ever want. It's called Richard's Five and Dime because the people who use to work there were named Richard. Except the people named Richard don't work there anymore. But they did when my Mother was a little girl like my little sister is a little girl now. And also, almost everything you can buy there is suppose to cost either a nickel or a dime. Which is five or ten cents. Except everything you can buy there now only use to cost either a nickel or a dime. Because a lot of things cost a lot more than five or ten cents now. Even if everything use to cost a nickel or a dime when my Mother was a little girl like my little sister is a little girl now.

Of all the places that my Mother sends me on errands to get things, except for Burdine's where usually I am getting something just for me, like a model airplane or boat or little bottles of paint to put on the models, Richard's Five and Dime is my favorite store. Because they have everything there!

And the everything they have at Richard's Five and Dime is really everything! Which means all kinds of toys. All kinds! Balls and bats and gloves for baseball. Which is my favorite game because I get to run around on grass. And crayons and colored pencils and brushes and paints and papers for drawing and painting. Which I one time took lessons because my Mother wanted me to. Except there were only girls in the class. And comic books and joke books and venture books and war books and sports books. Which I like to read when it's raining outside or if we are driving somewheres a long time in Daddy's car. And games like the one where you buy and sell streets and houses and hotels and the one where you go up and down depending on what number you throw and the one where it's like checkers where you jump over little round marbles except the board looks like a big star and the one where you answer a lot of questions like in school and you get to be the best student in the world. Which I like to play all of them. Except the one where you just go up or down depending on what number you throw. Because anybody can win that game no matter if they are paying attention or not. And yo-yos and tops and marbles and pick up sticks and other games that you can play with inside if it's raining or outside if it's not. Which I use to have every one of them! Except it's hard to play them on the brick sidewalk in front of our house. And little metal cars and little metal guns and little metal other things. Which I like to collect. Except my little sister likes little things too. So, she puts them in her mouth and almost swallows them and then my Mother doesn't want me to get anymore little metal cars or little metal guns or little metal other things.

And also at Richard's Five and Dime they have everything I need to give Daddy or my Mother for Father's Day or for Mother's Day or for Christmas or for their birthdays. Which I do! I got one time for Daddy a wallet to put his money in. Which he liked a lot because he doesn't like to just have money in his pockets because he can lose it. And I got my Mother one time some ashtrays. Which she liked a lot because she smokes cigarettes that I buy for her at Bruno's when she says it's too hot to put on a dress, even a summer one, just to go down for cigarettes, and it takes too long to put one on anyways. I even one time got my little sister a present for her birthday. Which was last month. Which she liked too because my little sister likes to try to play jacks. Which is a game just for girls and which she is too small to do now but which she will get bigger and be able to do after she is in kindergarden.

Like I already told, at Richard's Five and Dime, they have everything there.

And also, I already told about how my Mother has lots of brothers and sisters. Who a lot of them live near us. Except one of my Mother's sisters lives in Alabama. Which is not in our neighborhood. You have to get in Daddy's car and drive a long time to get to Alabama. Which sometimes we do so we can visit my Mother's sister who lives there. Who is my cousin Queenie's mother. And my cousin Dub's mother too.

Sometimes my Mother's sister who lives in Alabama drives a long time to get here to our neighborhood. So she can visit with her sister. Who is my Mother. Which she did last summer after I got out of first grade and before I was in second grade but after I was seven on my birthday. And when my Mother's sister from Alabama, who is my aunt, came last summer to visit her sister, who is my Mother, she came by herself. She didn't bring any of my cousins with her. She didn't bring my cousins Queenie and Dub. Who are big like I am big. And she didn't bring my cousins Buddy and Dean. Who are bigger and older like my Uncle Roger is bigger and older. My aunt from Alabama just came by herself.

Anyways, one day last summer I was playing my golf game in the back yard by myself. Which was just hitting my plastic golf ball that Uncle Martin gave me last summer for my birthday from the back door in the kitchen all the way to the fence at the back of the back yard. And then back again. Trying to get a perfect score. Which is two. Because there are only two holes. My little sister was at my Aunt Audra's playing with my cousin Suzette. Who is little like my little sister is little. So, she didn't want to play golf with me or try to get hit by the plastic golf ball. And my baby brother was still in my Mother's belly. Which means I wasn't able to hear him crying if he ever did cry when he was in there. So, it was quiet in the back yard while I was playing my golf game. And also I didn't have to watch my baby brother if my Mother went over to see my Aunt Audra too. Because my baby brother just went wherever my Mother went before he came out of her belly.

But my Mother was home while I was playing my golf game. When I was getting ready to hit my golf ball with one of my plastic golf clubs, I heard her calling. "Vonny!" my Mother said out loud through the kitchen door when I was all the way at the fence at the back of the back yard. "Vonny! Come and kiss your Aunt Lily! She drove all the way from Alabama just to see you." Which at first I pretended I didn't hear. "Vonny!" my Mother said again. Only more out loud than before. "Come inside, Vonny!" I looked up to see if she saw me in the back of the back yard. And when I looked up, I saw that my Mother did see me and I also saw her. She saw my eyes and I saw her eyes. I wasn't able to say I didn't see her. My Mother waved at me. I had to go and talk to her.

My Aunt Lily is a very nice lady. Except she is as old as my Grandma who is alive is old. Which is older than anybody I know. And she is not skinny like my Mother is skinny. But my Aunt Lily is a very nice lady. A very nice and big lady. Who talks different than the way my Mother talks. Who talks different than the way Daddy talks. Who talks different than the way I talk. Who talks different than the way anybody else talks!

When my Aunt Lily talks, she sounds like she's singing. It almost sounds like she's singing the way birds sing songs in City Park when I go there to caddy for my Uncle Martin sometimes in the morning or when I go there with Daddy and my Mother and my little sister and my baby brother for a picnic on Bayou St. John sometimes in the afternoon. When my Aunt Lily talks, she sounds like a very nice and big bird that is singing a song in the park. Except that birds that sing songs in the park can't smile. Because they don't have lips! But my Aunt Lily does have lips. And so my Aunt Lily is always smiling when she talks like a very nice and big bird that is singing a song in the park. She always has something nice to say to me. Which is like Charly too.

So, after my Mother saw my eyes and I saw her eyes and I had to go and talk to her even if I was playing my golf game in the back yard last summer, after I went through the back door into the kitchen and then walked through the room where my little sister and I sleep and then the hallway by the bathroom and then through the room where Daddy and my Mother and now my baby brother sleep and then into the parlor, Aunt Lily smiled at me and held her arms apart like I was suppose to walk over and get a hug and then she sang a song that went, "Oh, Vonny! You're getting to be so handsome. Just like your daddy." Which made me smile too. "Come over here and give your Aunt Lily some sugar." Which means come over here and give your Aunt Lily a kiss. Which I did. "You're such a strong, handsome young man," she sang again. "And I hear you're doing well in school too. Is that right?" I nodded my head. I didn't want to tell Aunt Lily about how I only come in second place every week in the spelling bee. "Has the cat got your tongue, Vonny? Can't you say anything? Open your mouth for me now, so I can look to see if the cat got your tongue."

We don't even have a cat! "I can talk," I said. And I smiled. My Aunt Lily makes me smile. It's the way she smiles all the time. And the way she sings very nice and big bird songs when she talks. And also the nice things she says to me all the time. She reached and tickled me under my arm. Which made me laugh.

"Sit here now, Vonny," my Aunt Lily sang. "I have a favor to ask."

"You need to go to Richard's," my Mother said, "to run an errand for your aunt." My Mother never says Richard's Five and Dime. She just says Richard's. My Mother was going there when she was little like my little sister is little. It's just Richard's to her. "Your Aunt Lily forgot some things at her house in Alabama and needs you to run an errand for her."

"Sure!" I said back. "What do you need?" I like to run errands.

Aunt Lily put her hand over her mouth, laughed, and then reached into her purse. "I wrote out a list on this little piece of paper, Vonny," she sang back. Like a very nice and big bird singing a song. She handed me a little piece of white paper. Which she folded in half. "I'm sure a sales clerk will be able to help you find everything," she sang again. "Just give this to the clerk at the store and you'll be able to get everything I need. You're such a strong and handsome young man."

"Oh, okay," I said back. I took the paper and put it in my pocket. Which was still folded.

"Oh, okay, what?" my Mother said.

"Oh, okay, Ma'am," I said again.

"Here's a twenty dollar bill," Aunt Lily sang.

"You be careful to get the right change, Vonny," my Mother said.

"Sure, Mama," I said back. "I'll be careful." Which I always am.

"And come right home, Vonny."

"Yes, Ma'am," I said back to my Mother. "I will."

And then I went out the front door onto the porch and down the stairs and out onto the brick sidewalk in front of the house on Columbus Street. I turned to walk down to where Bruno's is. It was before I ever saw the calendar with the ladies with hammers and no shirts. So, I didn't even think about them. Which I sometimes do now when I walk by Bruno's.

But before I got to the corner and before I crossed Dorgenois to where first base is, I took the little piece of white paper out of my pocket and unfolded it and tried to read it. Which was written in very fancy script. Not the kind of script that we are learning at St. Rose de Lima Bean School. But a very fancy one. And this is what I read. My aunt wrote bobby pins on the top line. Then below that hair spray. Which makes sense. My aunt needs to fix her hair. Then she wrote toothpaste below that. And after that, at the end of the list, was a word I wasn't able to read. Because of the very fancy script. Except I saw that the first letter was a P. And next to the word, whatever was written, was the number sixteen. Except it was written with numbers. Like 1 next to 6. Just like the way I just wrote it.

Because my Aunt Lily said the sales clerk will be able to help me, even if I wasn't able to read the last word, I just folded up the little white piece of paper and put it back in my pocket. Which is where it stayed until I crossed Dorgenois to first base and then Columbus to second base in front of the snowball shop, across the street from the black and brown dog who was probably sleeping because I didn't hear any barking, and then walked down to the corner where Picou's Bakery is and then turned up Bayou Road past the Buster Brown shoe store and then got to Richard's Five and Dime. Where I went in one side of the big double glass door and walked up to a lady who was standing behind a counter where there was a gizmo on it like the one at Burdine's. Which adds up how much things cost.

"Excuse me, Ma'am," I said to her.

The lady was tall the way Daddy is tall and skinny the way my Mother is skinny. She had auburn hair. Not red hair like a circus clown. But auburn hair like the lady in my Grandpa's book that I read in the front room at my Grandma's house who is alive. Who had bright green eyes and was too tall for the tight crimson dress she was wearing when she met Sam the policeman. The lady in the book had bright green eyes. Not my Grandma who is alive. "What can I do for you today, young man?" the tall, skinny lady behind the counter at Richard's said to me when she saw me.

"Well," I said. I was trying to get the little piece of white paper that was folded up in my pocket out. But it was stuck there. So, I just said, "I need to buy some things that my aunt forgot at her house in Alabama."

"Oh, I love Alabama!" the lady said back. "It's so beautiful and peaceful there. The bay. The trees. The lovely homes."

I was still trying to get out from my pocket the little piece of white paper. Which I remembered some of the things. "I need some bobby pins and some hair spray."

"For your aunt?"

"Yes, Ma'am," I said back. "Not for me. For my aunt." And then like a dope, I said, "I put grease in my hair like my daddy. Not hair spray."

The tall, skinny lady smiled. "Of course, you do. But, do you know what kind of bobby pins your aunt needs? What kind of hair spray?"

I finally got out the little piece of white paper from my pocket and unfolded it. I held it up to the lady. "Here!" I said out loud. "This is where my aunt wrote the things that she forgot at her house in Alabama. She said you'll be able to help me find everything so I can get everything I need."

The lady behind the counter took the little piece of white paper from me and put it on the counter in front of her. She tried to make it flat by running her hands over the top of it on the glass top of the counter. But she was so tall that she didn't see everything that was written on it. So, to be able to see everything, she bended over so far that her nose was almost touching the paper. "All right," she said after she looked at the paper and was coming from behind the counter. "Just follow me, my little friend." Which I am not little. Because I am in the second grade. And I am not her friend. Because she didn't even know my name. "Just follow me," she said again. And when we were walking, me behind her, she said, "So, what's your name, young man?"

"It's Vonny, Ma'am," I said back. "Vonny Foster."

"What a charming name," the lady said back. Whatever that means. "How wonderfully charming. Just follow me, Vonny." Which I did. And then she turned around and said while we were walking. "And unusual."

At first, we went all the way to one side of Richard's, me behind her, where there are a lot of things just for ladies. Like lipstick and perfume and things that boys don't need. Without saying another word, the tall, skinny lady with auburn hair just handed me down a little white package of black bobby pins and then we walked a little more and she gave me a bigger can that was gold colored with a black plastic top. Which I looked at and it said HAIR SPRAY on it. Just like the way I just wrote it. Except in script and not in block letters.

Then we walked all the way to the other side of Richard's, me behind her, where there are a lot of things for everybody. Like hand cream and soap and things that everybody needs. Like toothpaste too! And the lady still didn't say anything else to me. Except she said, "Do you know what kind of toothpaste your aunt uses, Vonny?"

I just lifted my shoulders up and down. "I don't know," I said back. Which I didn't.

"Well," the lady said. "Let's just say it's this one." And then she smiled at me with her very white teeth. "Because this is the one I use." She handed me down a little box that was long and had a picture on it of a man smiling. Who had very white teeth too.

"Thank you, Ma'am," I said.

And then the tall, skinny lady held the little piece of white paper up to her eyes so close to her nose that it was almost touching it. "Do you know what this says, Vonny?" she said back. I just lifted my shoulders up and down again. I wasn't able to read the fancy script that my aunt wrote with because it's not at all like the script that we learn at St. Rose de Lima Bean School. Which I know how to read. "You do know how to read, don't you, Vonny?" the lady said again.

"Of course, I do!" I said back out loud. "Watch!" And then I read all the names on the things in front of us. "Dial soap. Ivory soap. Colgate toothpaste."

"Okay," the lady said while she was laughing a little. "Okay! But can you read this?" she said again and held the little piece of white paper in front of me while she was pointing at the word that I wasn't able to read in front of Bruno's.

"My aunt said if I give you this paper I'll be able to get everything I need," I said out loud again.

"All right, Vonny," the lady said back. "Just stay calm. That's probably true. Let's just try to figure this out. I'm going to need my glasses though. Follow me." Which I did again. When we were walking, me behind her, I saw that the tall, skinny lady with auburn hair was pretty the way my Mother is pretty. Her skin was very white. Also, she had very blue eyes. Which I didn't see while we were walking. And her auburn hair was very long and wavy. When we got back to the counter where I first saw her, the lady went behind it again and bended over again and then got back up again and when she did she had some little black glasses on her nose. "Do you wear glasses, Vonny?" she said. I shook my head. "I didn't when I was little either," she said again. Which I am not little! The tall, skinny lady put the little piece of white paper on the counter again between her and me where both of us were able to see it at the same time. "So," she said, "what does that letter look like to you?"

Which was easy. "That's the letter P!" I said back. Which I saw in front of Bruno's.

"That's what I thought too," the lady said. "And then these next two look like A and R. But I can't tell what this one is. Is that a L or a T?" she said again. It was like when my Mother showed me how to read. Which was when I was little the way my little sister is little.

I looked close. There was a little cross that was almost invisible. "I think it's a T," I said back. "See?" And I pointed to the little cross.

"Oh," the lady said back. "You're right! There's a little cross there. You're right, Vonny." She looked over the top of her glasses at me and smiled. "So, we have P and A and R and T. Then, this looks to me like an I," the lady said again. "You see there, Vonny? Doesn't that look like a tittle over the I?"

"A what?" I said back.

"That little dot there over the I is called a tittle," the lady said back. "It must be an I."

"A little tittle?" I said back again. I had to look up how to write it when I got back home. And it sounded funny too.

"That's right," the lady said back while she was laughing a little again. "Exactly right, Vonny. A little tittle."

"Why isn't it just called a dot?" I said again.

"Because it's not," the lady said back again. "I don't make up the rules, Vonny. I just follow them." Just like what the man behind the counter at

Burdine's said. Then she scratched her nose. Which was very small. "It's not a dot. So, we have a P and A and R and T and I." She scratched her nose again. "And these are E and S!" she said out loud. P-A-R-T-I-E-S."

"Parties!" I said out loud too.

"Parties!" she said again. "That's it, Vonny. Parties. That wasn't so difficult."

"So," I said back, "do you have any parties here?" Like a dope. "For my aunt?"

"Parties," she said back again. "Parties? That's a good question, Vonny. Do we have any parties?" The tall, skinny, pretty lady took her black glasses off and looked up at the ceiling with her very blue eyes. And then she twisted her mouth the way sometimes my Mother twists her mouth when she is thinking about the whys and the wherefores. "Parties?" she said again. "That doesn't make any sense, does it, Vonny?" She put her black glasses back on her nose in front of her very blue eyes and looked at the little piece of white paper again. "What's this?" she said.

"I think it says sixteen," I said back. "You know, a one and a six."

"You're right again." And then she just said, "Parties. Sixteen. Parties? Sixteen? Whatever does that mean? Parties. Sixteen." The tall, skinny, pretty lady said that again and again and again. And I tried to think what it means too. Which I didn't know. And then, the tall, skinny lady behind the counter started smiling at me. With a bigger and bigger smile with her very white teeth. And then, she started laughing. At first a little and then a little more and then a lot and then a lot more. She was laughing so hard that she bended over and put her hand on her skinny stomach. "Oh, my, Vonny. That's so funny!" she said while she was standing back up. She bended over again and this time she took off her black glasses while she was bended over and put them back in her purse. Which I was able to see behind the counter. She was laughing and laughing so hard that she wasn't even able to say anything. After a while, she was laughing a lot but not as much and she was able to say, "Oh, my! Your aunt must be a very large lady." She was still laughing. "Am I right, Vonny? Is your aunt a very large lady?"

I just lifted my shoulders up and down. "She's bigger than my Mother," I said back. Which my aunt is. "Who is skinny like you!" I said again. Which my Mother is.

"Oh, Vonny," the lady behind the counter said. "You are a funny little boy." Which I am not little and I am not a boy. I am in second grade and I am a young man! "Follow me one more time," she said again. Which I did. Me behind her. Her still holding the little piece of white paper. Except this time, we went to a part of Richard's where all they had all over the place was underwear for women. "You see this, Vonny?" the tall skinny lady said to me. It's not a R in the middle of this word down here. It's a N!"

"It is?" I said back.

"It's not P-A-R, but P-A-N. It's a N, not R. See? N! It's P-A-N-T-I-E-S."

"Panties!" I said out loud. Like a dope! And then I put my hand over my mouth. Like a goofball!

"Size sixteen panties. That's what your aunt forgot at her house in Alabama," the tall, skinny, pretty lady said. I didn't look at her again. I was just looking around Richard's to make sure no one I knew was there. My Mother sent me on an errand to Richard's to buy underwear for my aunt from Alabama! Who the tall, skinny, pretty lady says is a very large lady. My aunt. Not my Mother. "You think these will fit her?" the lady said while she was holding up some ladies' underwear in front of me right out in the open at Richard's.

I held my hands over my eyes. Like I do at the baby cows' head shop! And I held the bobby pins and the hair spray and the toothpaste over them too! "I don't know!" I said out loud. "Can you just put them in a bag for me?"

While we were walking back to the counter, me behind her, the tall, skinny, pretty lady laughed. "Oh, poor Vonny. You didn't know that your aunt sent you to buy her panties, did you?"

Of course I didn't! It was like my cousin Dottie's red girl's shoes. Which my Mother thought would be a good idea for me to wear to school. Red shoes! Girl's shoes! That was when I was in first grade. Last year. When I was a new kid at St. Rose de Lima Bean School. A little, new kid! Except I was able to see the red girl's shoes before my Mother thought it would be a good idea for me to wear them to school. Which I wasn't able to see the word panties written on the little piece of white paper that my aunt gave me before my Mother thought it would be a good idea for me to buy them at Richard's Five and Dime. Because of the fancy script. "No, Ma'am," I said back. "I didn't know."

"Well, your aunt must have quite a sense of humor," the lady said back. Whatever that means. "Quite a sense of humor," she said again while she was putting everything in a bag.

"It's my Mother that has quite a sense of humor," I said back. And I didn't even know what it means.

"Well, that's seven dollars and fifty cents," the lady said back again. "Including tax." She just kept smiling at me. I tried to smile back while I was giving her the twenty dollar bill my aunt gave me. But I was only thinking about my Mother sending me on an errand to buy underwear for my aunt. And thinking about how my Mother is smarter than me. "Here's twelve dollars and fifty cents change, Vonny. Your receipt is in the bag."

"Thank you," I said. "Ma'am."

I started to walk away from the counter. I wanted to get out of Richard's as fast as I can. "No," the tall, skinny, pretty lady with the auburn hair and very white teeth and very blue eyes and very white skin said. "Thank you, Vonny! Thank you." I got to the door and was about to walk out of Richard's onto Bayou Road when I heard the lady say again, "Oh, Vonny." She was calling me back. "Listen, Vonny. I need to tell you something else."

I turned around to look at her. "What?" I said back.

"What what?" the lady said back. Which is what my Mother always says.

So, I knew what to say back. "Oh," I said back again, "I meant, what, Ma'am?"

And then the tall, skinny, pretty lady said back, "Vonny, dear. I'm so sorry that your mother died."

My Mother died? I dropped the bag with all of the things that my aunt forgot at her house in Alabama. When? Which included her very large lady underwear. How? I started shaking and sweating. My Mother died! My Mother died?

Which was when I woke up from my bad dream. And which was when my bed was wet for the same reason that my pajamas were wet when I woke up. My bed was wet and my pajamas were wet because I was sweating a lot. Which I was sweating a lot because I had a bad dream.

Which was my Mother died! The bad dream I had last night was not like any other bad dream I ever had. And it was a very bad dream too. Not only because it was about my Mother. But because it was about something that already happened to me. Which was my Mother sending me on an errand to Richard's Five and Dime to buy underwear for my very large aunt.

I quick tried to jump out of my bed when I woke up, even in the dark, because I wanted to run into the room where Daddy and my Mother and now my baby brother sleep. Because my Mother is always sleeping on the same side of the bed. So, I wanted to quick run over to her side of the bed and put my hand in front of her nose. Which sometimes I do in the middle of the night. Because then I can feel if she is breathing. I can feel if my Mother is alive.

But my foot was tied to the bed! Like the doctor said to do. Because I sleepwalked. So, I wasn't able to jump out of bed. I wasn't able to run into the room where Daddy and my Mother and now my baby brother sleep. I wasn't able to run over to her side of the bed and put my hand in front of her nose. I wasn't able to feel if she is breathing, if my Mother is alive.

I tried to get the rope off of my foot. I turned. I twisted. But it was tied tight. It burned. It hurt. So, I called out loud. "Mama!" I said out loud. "Mama!" I said even more out loud. And then I said even more and more and more out loud, "Mama! Mama! Mama!"

My little sister woke up and started crying. She started saying out loud too, "Mama! Mama! Mama!"

And then I heard my baby brother start crying in the room where Daddy and my Mother sleep. I heard somebody moving in there. "Mama!" I said out loud again. "Mama!"

"What's the matter, Vonny?" I heard my Mother say from the other room. "Why aren't you sleeping?"

It was just a bad dream! When I heard my Mother, it was like I was feeling the air come out of her nose. I knew she was breathing. I knew she was alive. My Mother is alive!

My bad dream about Richard's Five and Dime wasn't true. Except the part about my Mother sending me on an errand there last summer to buy underwear for my aunt. Which she did. And which was true. Except the lady who helped me last summer was a large lady. She was not tall or skinny or pretty. And she didn't have auburn hair or white teeth or blue eyes or white skin either. Instead, she was a large lady. Not a very large lady like my aunt from Alabama is a very large lady. But large anyways. And she was old like my Grandma who is alive is old. And except that all the things I got for my aunt from Alabama didn't cost seven dollars and fifty cents. They cost six dollars and thirty two cents instead. Including tax.

After my bad dream, it took my Mother a long time to calm down my little sister and my baby brother. And after my bad dream it took me a long time to fall asleep again too. Even if my bad dream wasn't true, it still took me a very long time to fall asleep again. But I did. I fell asleep anyways. And the way I know I fell asleep anyways is because, in the morning, my Mother woke me up.

"Time for school, Vonny. Time to get up," my Mother said.

Right away I said back, "I don't feel good, Mama." Which I didn't. "I feel sick." Which I did.

"The work of the world today is being done by people who feel a lot worse than you, Vonny," my Mother said back. Whatever that means. "Now, get out of bed and get ready for school. I already untied your foot." Which she did.

But I didn't want to go to school on Thursday. And I didn't go to school on Thursday. Yesterday was suppose to be a happy day for me. Which was Wednesday. But instead, I didn't get to eat anything before I went to bed. And I didn't get to drink anything before I went to bed. And I didn't get to take a bath before I went to bed. Then it took me a long time to fall asleep. And after I did fall asleep, I had a bad dream. So then my bed and my pajamas were wet. And I woke up everybody in the house. And after everybody was calmed down, it took me another long time to fall asleep again.

So, I was sick when my Mother woke me up on Thursday morning. I didn't feel good. I didn't care if the work of the world today was being done by people who felt a lot worse than me. I wanted to sleep more. And then take a bath. And then drink something. And then eat something!

Which is what I did after my Mother let me stay home when she knew how I didn't feel good and how I was sick. At first, because I was crying so much the night before while I was trying to fall asleep, my Mother thought I had rabbity pink eyes like Sharon the Roach when she saw them in the morning. But then, she finally just said after she knew how bad I felt, "You're still upset about that little boy being run over by the car, aren't you, Vonny?" But I didn't feel bad about Jimmy Broom anymore. He was at his house now, the one next to my Uncle Roger. I felt bad about everything that happened since then. And about how Daddy and my Mother think I am a liar and that they can't trust me. And I felt bad because I still didn't tell them about Henry and being chased by John Smith and Pocahontas and about how I am still suppose to meet Henry on Friday to figure out why the black Pontiac ran over Jimmy Broom.

So, I just stayed in bed all morning. My Mother took my little sister to my Aunt Audra's house so I was able to sleep. Which I did. And then at lunch time, my Mother woke me up and asked me did I feel better. Which I did too. Because I was able to sleep. Without any bad dreams. Without sweating. And then, at the same time that my Mother woke me up, she told me that while I was sleeping she went to the Triangle and got for us a roast beef poor boy, dressed, with mayonnaise and creole mustard. And barbeque chips and two root beers! And did I want to share it with her? Which I did!

My little sister and baby brother were taking a nap while my Mother and I were eating. And I was waiting for my Mother to ask me questions about everything that happened. About John Smith. About the visible people. About everything else. That was what was suppose to happen, I thought. That was why my Mother let me stay home from school. So she was able to ask me a lot of questions about everything. Because I'm not the only one in my family who likes to ask questions.

But what happened instead, while my Mother and I were eating the roast beef poor boy together, was that I was thinking about what my Grandpa who is dead told my Mother about paradise that she said last Sunday while we were driving in City Park to my Grandma's house who is alive. Which is that paradise is whatever you want it to be. My Mother said last Sunday while we were driving in the car after I saw Sportsman's Paradise written on a license plate, "Every person makes his own paradise is what my daddy use to say." Which means her daddy. Who is my Grandpa who is dead. Who is now in his paradise probably. Which is the paradise he made, the one Daddy says is probably in a barroom.

So, while my Mother and I were eating the roast beef poor boy together on Thursday, I just said, "Mama, if it's true what your daddy said about paradise is whatever you want it to be, what is it you want paradise to be?" My Mother twisted her mouth a little and then smiled and put down on the table her half of the roast beef poor boy that she was eating. "What do you want paradise to be, Mama?"

My Mother wiped her mouth with a paper napkin. "Vonny, Vonny, Vonny!" she said back. "Where do you come up with these questions of yours?"

I just lifted my shoulders up and down. "I don't know, Mama," I said back. "They just pop into my head." Which they do. "It's an accident."

"You want to know what I want paradise to be?" my Mother said back again. "Well," she said, "I guess I think being in paradise is going to be a lot like being right here. Just the way it is here. Right now." She wiped her hands on the napkin and then rubbed me on the head. "Eating a roast beef poor boy with you." And then she took another bite of her sandwhich. "And with your little sister and baby brother too. And Daddy, of course."

"Your daddy or my daddy?" I said back.

"Both of them!" my Mother said back out loud. "Paradise is being with the people you love and being with the people who love you. That is what I want when I am in paradise. Just having the people I love around me. I want you to be with me. And Daddy. And your little sister and baby brother. And my daddy and my mother. Your aunts and uncles. Your cousins. The whole family. Everyone I love."

"But you have that now, Mama!" I said back. "That's what Daddy said. He said we already live in paradise. If paradise is what you have now, why do you have to die to go to paradise?" Which is what Sister Marianna says.

My Mother said back, "Well, I don't have everyone with me all the time here, Vonny. I have you now. And Daddy will be home later. But my daddy is not here. My mother is not here. In paradise I will be with all of you all the time."

"But what if we're not dead too, Mama?" I said back. Which is true. "How can we be with you if you're in paradise and we're here?" Which is true too. I was thinking about my bad dream.

My Mother started laughing. "Oh, Vonny!" she said back. "Don't tell me that thought just popped into your head. Now I know why you can't sleep at night. You're too young to think about all of that."

"But I do, Mama," I said back. "I do think about it. When Jimmy was hit by the car last week, I was thinking about if he died where he will be living, where he will be."

"But he didn't die, Vonny," my Mother said back. "He's safe at home now with his parents. He's going to be fine now."

"But what if he wasn't, Mama? What if Jimmy died and didn't have time to figure out what his paradise is suppose to be like?"

My Mother put her sandwhich down and just looked at me. She twisted her mouth again. She was trying to figure out something. Just like I was trying to figure out what happens if you don't live long enough to figure out what your paradise is suppose to be like. "Put your sandwhich down a minute and come over here," my Mother said back. Which I did. I put my sandwhich down, stood up, and walked over to my Mother at the table in the kitchen. "Now sit here on my lap," she said again. Like I already told, I'm too big to sit on my Mother's lap now. I'm a skinny kid. But my Mother is skinny too. So, I just leaned back on her knee, halfway standing and halfway sitting, and she put her arms around me and held my hands in hers in front of me. I felt her chin on top of my head. "Now, listen, Vonny," my Mother said. "I know you were worried about your little friend. Who is going to be fine now. And I know you did some things and said some things that you are not proud of. Which is going to pass too. You are going to feel better now that Daddy and I know about those things." Which they don't know even all of them! "But, you worry me sometimes with these thoughts you have. You're just a little boy." Which I am not! "You're suppose to be having fun now. Playing with your friends. Enjoying yourself." Which I do. At least sometimes I do. "You don't need to think about what happens when people die." Which I do sometimes do too.

"I just do, Mama," I said back. "I don't want to think about it. It just pops into my head."

"It's good to be curious, Vonny," my Mother said again. And she squeezed me tight when she said it. "But I just don't understand where these thoughts come from."

"I don't too, Mama!" I said back. Which I don't. "I don't know where any thoughts come from. They just happen to me. They're like accidents!"

My Mother started laughing. "Is that what you think, Vonny? Do you think thoughts just happen to you?"

"To me they do, Mama!" I said back. "I don't try." Which is true. My Mother was still laughing. "I don't!" I said again out loud. "I don't want to think about why the black Pontiac ran over Jimmy Broom, Mama, or if he is going to die or if he is going to paradise after he dies or what paradise is like if he goes there. It just happens to me. It does! I promise."

"Well, you don't have to worry about any of that now, Vonny. Your little friend is fine. He's home now."

My Mother kissed the top of my head. She squeezed again my hands in hers. Then another thought popped into my head. I was thinking about my visible man and all the bones and all the organs and about when I was trying to put them together Tuesday before Daddy came home from work and then we went to the baby cows' head shop to buy veal liver. Which is where I met Buck from the barber shop on Bayou Road before I saw John Smith punch him in the stomach for no good reason. "Mama," I said, even if I knew my Mother maybe was going to laugh at me, "I was reading my visible man book about all my organs. And I know my heart makes my blood go around my body and my liver makes me be able to eat food and my lungs get air in my body so I can breathe and my brain makes them all work together."

My Mother laughed out loud. "Oh, Vonny!" she said. "You're so funny!" Which I am not. I am curious.

"But what organ makes thoughts pop into my head?" I said back. "Do you know, Mama? Is it some invisible organ? Where do thoughts come from? I wasn't able to find it in my visible man book. I looked it up," I said again. "Is it just another mystery, Mama? Like you say things are sometimes."

My Mother was laughing and laughing. She squeezed me even tighter than before. And then she kissed the top of my head again.

"Vonny," my Mother said back, "I only went to high school. So, I'm not sure where thoughts come from or what organ they come from either." She kissed the top of my head even again. "But I know that the best thoughts come from here." I felt my Mother squeeze her hands over mine, one of her hands on top of both of mine and her other hand on top of her first hand, all of them together over the middle of my chest. "They come from right here."

Which is where my heart is.

Twelve, or Mr. Lee's Laundry

We go to my Aunt Gwendolyn's house a lot. Especially during the summer when it's too hot to stay at our house. At my Aunt Gwendolyn's house, even in the summer, it's very cool. Because they have a machine in their house that makes the air cold. Which is not a fan. Which we already have at our house and which just blows hot air all around us. The machine at my Aunt Gwendolyn's house is like the machine at the hamburger shop on Broad Street. Where I went last summer to get a birch beer with my cousin Floyd. Who sometimes lives by us when my Uncle Charles is back from the army. Or sometimes they just come to visit in the summer. Which is what happened last summer. Which is why my cousin Floyd and I went to the hamburger shop on Broad Street to get a birch beer. Which I thought I wasn't able to drink because Daddy doesn't let me drink more than a sip of beer. Except I found out from Floyd that birch beer is not beer.

Anyways, we go to my Aunt Gwendolyn's house a lot in the summer because they have the same machine that makes the air cold like they have at the hamburger shop on Broad Street. So, we are cool there when it's too hot outside. Which it always is in the summer!

My Aunt Gwendolyn's house is where my cousins Charly and Marly live. Who are twins. Which means they look the same. Except Charly and Marly are never at home when we visit in the summer. Because they are in high school and go wherever they want to go whenever they want to go there. Even with their boyfriends. And even their brother is never there too. Who is my cousin Ned and who is in high school too. The only kids who are there when we visit are my two little boy cousins who are little like my little sister is little. So, there is nobody for me to play with while my Mother and my Aunt Gwendolyn sit around in the kitchen all day playing cards and talking and smoking cigarettes and drinking soft drinks. Which is what they do.

So, what I do at my Aunt Gwendolyn's house is go into the room where Charly and Marly sleep. And then I play with the writing machine that Marly has for her school. In high school they don't write in block letters or even script. They have a machine to write for them! Just like they have a machine to make the air cold in their house during the summer. At our house the only machine we have is the frigidaire. Which makes our food cold. We don't have a machine to make the air cold. We don't have a machine to write with either.

Anyways, my cousin Marly one time showed me how to use the writing machine. She showed me where all the letters are and how to put your fingers on the letters and how to push the letters and then words are spelled out on a piece of paper that you put in. Except at the end of every line of words you have to push this little shiny piece of metal all the way to the left and then a bell rings. Ding! Like that. And then you can write on the next line. Marly also showed me how to put the paper in the machine. Which sometimes is not so easy. And she also showed me how to practice writing words with the machine. Which is to write over and over and over again now is the time for all good men to come to the aid of their party. Whatever that means. The only party I ever go to is a birthday party. So, I don't know what that means. And there are no men at the parties that I go to. Just kids. But Marly told me that if I write over and over and over again now is the time for all good men to come to the aid of their party, I will learn how to use the writing machine. And when I go to my Aunt Gwendolyn's house, that's what I do. I practice almost the whole time.

Now is the time for all good men to come to the aid of their party. Ding! Now is the time for all good men to come to the aid of their party. Ding! Now is the time for all good men to come to the aid of their party. Ding! Now is the time for all good men to come to the aid of their party. Ding! Over and over and over and over again. Ding! Ding! Ding! Ding! Until I do it right ten times. Marly says practice makes perfect. Which is what her teacher told her. Which is what Daddy says to me when we play baseball at Stallings Playground. So I write and write and write with the machine until I can write perfect now is the time for all good men to come to the aid of their party ten times in a row without a mistake. If I make a mistake, even just one, I change the paper and start over again until I get it perfect. And then after I get it perfect ten times, then I try to get it perfect twenty times. Which I never do! The most times I wrote it perfect was sixteen times.

So, when I go to my Aunt Gwendolyn's house, that's what I do while my little sister plays with my little boy cousins in the other room. And while my Mother and my Aunt Gwendolyn sit around in the kitchen all day playing cards and talking and smoking cigarettes and drinking soft drinks. Because that's what Marly showed me. And that's how I learned how to use the writing machine. At least on the one at my Aunt Gwendolyn's house. Which writes in little black letters. Which I am not doing now. Because we don't have a writing machine at my house. And we don't even have a writing machine at my school too. Which is St. Rose de Lima Bean School. Where I have to write everything out long hand. Mainly in block letters but sometimes in script. Which is what I am doing now. Because I like writing in script.

Anyways, after spending all day yesterday at home, which was Thursday, because I was sick in bed and didn't feel good, this morning, which is Friday, even before I went to school, my Mother made me go to Mister Lee's laundry to get some clean clothes for Daddy. And some clean clothes for me too. Which was my First Communion suit.

Like I already told, I don't like to go to Mister Lee's laundry. Which is on Broad Street too. Like Burdine's. Which is where I bought the two visible people and where John Smith bought a red top for Jimmy Broom. And like the hamburger shop. Which is where they have a machine that makes the air cold too and where my cousin Floyd bought me a birch beer. Which I like to go to by myself now too. And even if I still don't like to go to the baby cows' head shop more than I don't like going to Mister Lee's laundry, I still don't like to go to Mister Lee's laundry anyways. Even if it's better than going to the baby cows' head shop. Because at Mister Lee's laundry on Broad Street, I have to look at Mister Lee. And especially I have to look at his hook. Because when I go to Mister Lee's laundry, I either have to give him a little piece of paper with all the clean clothes he wrote on it so I can pick them up or I have to take back from Mister Lee a little piece of paper with all the dirty clothes he wrote on it so I can drop them off. And sometimes I have to do both! I have to give him a little piece of paper and then take one back.

I'm not sure if it's an impure thought about not wanting to give Mister Lee the little piece of paper or get one back from him. I don't know if I have to put that on my confession list too. But I don't like to do it. And I can't close my eyes the way I do at the baby cows' head shop. I can't close my eyes because I don't want something bad to happen. Because on one of Mister Lee's arms, instead of having a hand, he has a hook! Which is a metal hook that shines like silver and that curves around and makes a point that you are able to stab somebody in the chest with. Like an ice pick! And when you give Mister Lee a little piece of paper, he holds out his hook in front of you and reaches at your hand to take it with his hook. Which he then opens up into two little hooks and then he closes the two little hooks around the little piece of paper and takes it from your hand just like he had a hand instead of a hook. Which is scary! And when you take back from Mister Lee a little piece of paper, he holds it out in his hook in front of you and reaches at your hand with his hook and then when you touch the paper the hook opens up so you can take it. Which is scary too!

One time my Mother asked me why I don't like to go to Mister Lee's laundry. Which I told her is for three things.

First, Mister Lee's hook is very sharp. It has a point on it like an ice pick. Like I already told. If he doesn't pay attention, the hook might go into my finger or my hand or my eye or even my chest! You have to always pay attention. You have to always be observant when you are at Mister Lee's laundry. Which most of the time I am. Or else you might get stabbed by his hook. Or else! Which is what John Smith says. And Lenny too.

And second, when I am at Mister Lee's laundry, a thought always pops into my head to know where is Mister Lee's missing hand. Which is the one that he has a hook instead of. Where did it go? Where is Mister Lee's missing hand? One time I asked my Mother if a crocodile ate Mister Lee's hand where the hook is now. Not one of the old crocodiles at Bruno's who drink their beer in glasses. But a real one. A real crocodile! Because I saw on a TV program about Peter Pan this man who a crocodile ate his hand that got cut off too. Which the man put a hook where his hand was. Like Mister Lee. And then the crocodile ate a clock too. So the man always knew when the crocodile was close and trying to eat the rest of him because he could hear the clock ticking inside of the crocodile's belly. Which is where his hand was too. Which is disgusting the way the baby cows' head shop is disgusting. Somebody's hand in a crocodile's belly!

My Mother just laughed at me and said a crocodile didn't eat Mister Lee's hand.

So, then I remembered Mister Lee looks like all the people who were in the world war against us. Like against Lenny Mahoney's cousin Red's pop. Which is what Red calls his daddy. Who killed two thousand Germans with a dagger. Except Mister Lee looks like what Lenny calls Japs. And maybe Mister Lee was in the world war too. And maybe that's how his hand got turned into a hook. Maybe it blew up somewheres. Maybe Red's pop blew up Mister Lee's hand in the war when he wasn't stabbing Germans with his dagger.

And last, I don't like to go to Mister Lee's laundry because I can't even always write the way Mister Lee talks. Because sometimes I don't even know what he is saying. He doesn't talk the way I do. Or the way Daddy or my Mother talk. Or the way anybody else talks. Mister Lee doesn't talk Australian like my Aunt Audra. And he doesn't even talk like my Aunt Anna. Who is my Uncle Roger's wife and who is from some other place too. Like my Aunt Audra. I can write how my Aunt Audra talks. Because I know how to write Australian. And I can even write how my Aunt Anna talks. But I can't always write how Mister Lee talks. It's too hard. He just says little words. Which sometimes don't even go together. Which don't even make sense to me all the time.

So that's the three things why I don't like to go to Mister Lee's laundry.

"Mama," I said this morning, "can't I go to the laundry with Daddy after school today?" It's like the baby cows' head shop. I can go to Mister Lee's laundry. But I don't like to go there by myself.

"You won't have time, Vonny, if you want to go to the movies with Charly after supper." Which was true. Now that I told my Mother almost everything, she said I can go to the movies at the Bell with Charly. Which she said Wednesday when she was very, very angry I can't go.

My Mother is smarter than me. And I was still tired on Friday morning. So, because my Mother is smarter than me and because it was early in the morning, I didn't even try to talk her out of it. "Okay, Mama," I just said back. "But I need the little laundry paper."

Which my Mother gave me two of. "There's one for your Daddy's uniform and one for your First Communion suit," my Mother said back. The little laundry papers are colored green. Light green. And they have on the top MR. LEE'S LAUNDRY in red block letters. Just like I just wrote it. My Mother kissed me on the forehead. "Here's a dollar bill. And be sure to get the change." Which I always do anyways. "Now, you be careful, Vonny. Your First Communion is only a week away."

Which means my first confession is less than a week away. Next Thursday. Which used to be scary but isn't anymore. Not after everything that I had to tell Daddy and my Mother this week about the things I did that I wasn't supposed to do and about the lies that I made up that I wasn't supposed to make up. Instead of being something scary now, my first confession is just going to be me telling Monseigneur Deutsch everything I already told Daddy and my Mother. And it was a lot harder telling Daddy and my Mother that I did things I wasn't supposed to do and made up lies that I wasn't supposed to make up than it will be to tell Monseigneur Deutsch. Who sometimes doesn't even hear too good anyways!

After my Mother gave me the two laundry papers and the dollar bill in the kitchen, I went through the hallway to the front of our house and then out the front door onto the porch and then down the stairs onto the brick sidewalk and then along Columbus Street across Dorgenois to Broad Street. There were already some kids walking to school because even if it was early in the morning it was time for school to start soon. So, I quick walked as fast as I can to Mister Lee's laundry, the whole time hoping that instead of Mister Lee there would be this other woman who works with him. Who looks like Mister Lee but who is smaller than him and who doesn't even talk at all and just takes the little piece of paper from you with her hand or just gives a little piece of paper to you with her hand and just smiles and nods her head when you say hello or goodbye. Because she doesn't even talk as bad as Mister Lee does. She doesn't even talk at all. But she's not as scary as him. Because she has two hands.

Except, when I turned the corner and walked into Mister Lee's laundry, it wasn't the woman who doesn't talk behind the counter. It was Mister Lee. And instead of wearing his hook like he always does on his arm where his missing hand used to be, Mister Lee wasn't wearing his hook at all. He was holding his shiny metal hook in his other hand. In his only hand! Which when I saw it, I said out loud, "Oh!" Because it was scary!

"Hello, boy," Mister Lee said. He saw me looking at the hook. Which was in his other hand. His only hand. "Oh," he said again. "You want touch?" He held out the hook to me. It wasn't even on his arm. "You want feel?" Only it was like he said fee. "You want fee?"

"No!" I said back. Which was rude. "No, Sir," I said back again. "No, thank you, Sir."

Mister Lee started laughing. "No hurt," he said back. "No hurt little boy." Only it was like he said lil lil boy. Which I am not lil lil! I'm in the second grade. "See?" Mister Lee put the hook on the counter in front of me, right in front of my eyes. "No hurt lil lil boy." And then he stepped back, away from the counter. "Put ticket here," Mister Lee said again, pointing to the counter. Only it was like he said tickle he. "Put tickle he. I get clothes." Only it was like he said close. "Put tickle he. I get close."

Which I did. I put the little laundry papers on the counter and then Mister Lee took them with his only hand and then he walked behind a curtain into the back of the laundry. He didn't even take his hook! Which was right on the counter in front of my eyes.

I didn't want to touch the hook. But then a thought popped into my head. Without me even wanting it to. Which always happens. Which was that Mister Lee's hook was just a little shiny piece of metal. That's all it was. Like the one on the writing machine at Aunt Gwendolyn's house that you push all the way to the left to start a new line and then a bell rings. Ding! Both Mister Lee's hook and the little shiny piece of metal on the writing machine at Aunt Gwendolyn's house are long. Ding! And skinny. Ding! And both are made out of metal. Ding! Shiny metal. Ding! While I was waiting for Mister Lee, I was thinking that his hook was just the same as the little shiny piece of metal on the writing machine. And I am not afraid of that one.

So, after a while, while I was still waiting for Mister Lee, I picked up his hook from the counter with both of my hands and just looked at it. Mister Lee's hook had a point on it. Which the one on the writing machine did not. But it still was almost the same. It was long and skinny. And it still looked the same. It was made out of shiny metal.

And when I was holding Mister Lee's hook in my left hand, I pretend pushed it to the left with my right hand like it was the little shiny piece of metal on the writing machine. Like I was moving the writing machine to the next line. And then I said in a low voice, "Ding!"

After I did that a couple of times, I saw on the counter the little shiny metal bell that is there so you can ring it to let Mister Lee or the other woman know you are there in case they are behind the curtain in the back of the laundry and can't see you. You just tap the top of the little bell and then it rings. Ding! Like the bell on the writing machine at my Aunt Gwendolyn's house. So then Mister Lee or the other woman knows you are there.

And then I pretended that Mister Lee's hook in my left hand was the little shiny piece of metal on the writing machine and I pretend pushed it to the left like it was on the writing machine and then I tapped the top of Mister Lee's little bell on the counter. Ding! And then I did it again. Pretend push. Ding! And again. Pretend push. Ding! And again and again and again. Push. Ding! Push. Ding! Push. Ding!

Mister Lee came back into the front of the laundry. Who was carrying Daddy's uniform and my First Communion suit. "Oh," he said again. "You like ring bell?" He saw the hook in my hand. "See? No hurt. No hurt." He laughed. "You like now?"

I put Mister Lee's hook back on the counter. "Sure," I said back. Even if I didn't like the hook. But I wasn't lying. I was just pretending. Like Daddy says. But the hook wasn't scary anymore. "It's okay," I said again.

"Look," Mister Lee said back. "Look. Look." He reached under the counter with his hand that was there and with his hand that was missing. Mister Lee was reaching for something. When I saw his hands again, the one that was there and the one that was missing, there was like a tube on his arm where there was the missing hand. "Look," Mister Lee said again. "Look." And then he picked up the hook, put the other end of it, the end that was not the hook, on the little tube, and then turned and turned the hook so that it stayed in the little tube. "See? See? No hurt," he said. "No hurt lil lil boy." And then Mister Lee quick reached over the counter, the pieces of the hook opened up, and he quick put it over my nose. Like he was play pinching my nose. Which is what Daddy always does. But Mister Lee did it so quick, I didn't even move. "See? Boy nose no hurt. No hurt." And then Mister Lee rang his little bell on the counter. Ding! Which made me jump back so my nose wasn't between the hook anymore. And then he rang it again. Ding! Ding! "Ding, dong!" Mister Lee said. "Ninety cents for clothes." Only it was like he said nineteen cent for close. "Nineteen cent for close." I handed Mister Lee the dollar bill my Mother gave me and he gave me back ten cents from the gizmo on the counter. With his hand, not with his hook. "Here, boy. Here dime." Only it was like he said he die. "He die," Mister Lee said. "And he close too." Then he handed me Daddy's uniform and my First Communion suit over the counter. Which were on hangers and underneath a big paper bag. Mister Lee rang his little bell. Ding. Then he said again, "Ding, dong!"

"Thank you, Sir," I said back and turned for the door.

"Goodbye, boy," Mister Lee said. "Ding, dong!" And he rang his little bell again. Ding! Ding! "Ding, dong!" he said again. Ding! Ding! Ding!

When I was back outside on Broad Street, I saw Henry riding a bicycle on the other side of Columbus. Which he was too big for. "Hi, Henry!" I said out loud. The bicycle was too small for him. His knees were hitting the handlebars. So he had to ride it standing up.

"California!" Henry said back out loud.

"Stay there," I said, and then I crossed over to his side, the side of Columbus Street where the school is.

He saw me looking at the small bicycle. "It's my sister's," Henry said back. "Those guys still have mine. Listen, I'm late for school," he said again. "Can't talk long."

"Me too," I said back. "I have to take these clothes home first too. You know Mister Lee there?" I said again. I waved across the street at the laundry.

Henry pointed to his arm. "My daddy says he doesn't want our business," Henry said back. "Are you going to the movies at the Bell tonight still?" he said again. I nodded. "You find out anything since Monday?"

"They're policemen," I said back.

"Who?"

"John Smith and Pocahontas. Who you call Jake and Mack."

Henry made a face. "At the church Monday, you said they weren't policemen, California. You remember that?"

"I know," I said back again. "But it's not true. They came to my house. They talked to my Mother and then to Daddy and me. So now, everybody knows everything. And they are policemen."

"Jake and Mack know we were in the church Monday?" Henry said back.

"They didn't say anything about it," I said back.

"They know we got in the church?" Henry said back again. "Or how?"

I shook my head. "I don't think so," I said back. "I didn't say anything about it too. Daddy and my Mother don't know."

"That's good, California." Which is on my confession list too. Sin of omission. "They know I heard them talking to my daddy about the barber shop?" Henry said back again. I shook my head again. "Then they don't know everything. And they don't know we're meeting up at the Bell tonight?" I shook my head again. "What time is the movie?"

"My Mother will only let me go at six o'clock," I said back. "She said the eight o'clock show is too late."

"Okay," Henry said, while he was jumping up on one of the bicycle pedals. "I'll see you at the Bell later. You come up the balcony stairs about fifteen minutes after the movie starts. Okay?" I nodded. Henry started to ride the bicycle away. But then he stopped and turned around. "Not the cartoons," he said again. "Fifteen minutes after the movie starts. Okay?" I nodded again. "Okay, see you."

"See you," I said back. And then Henry was gone again. For a kid in the second grade, Henry acts like he's a lot older.

Anyways, I took the clean clothes home, quick ate breakfast, which was just toast, and went to school. Which was the day when I learned the most at school than I ever learned before.

At first, in the morning, we didn't do much in class. And then just before lunch, we had an arithmetic game. Which I won and got another chocolate milk ticket. Daddy says soon I'm going to be able to open up a dairy farm. And then after that, Sister Marianna said we have to study our vocabulary because we have a big reading test after Easter and we have to practice and learn a lot of new words and what they mean and how to spell them. Which is why I don't spell vocabulary like vocabulerry anymore because I learned that Friday afternoon while we were spelling all these new words.

"New rules for this week's spelling bee," Sister Marianna said. Which made me sit up at my desk because Sharon the Roach always wins with the old rules. "If someone gets a word wrong, instead of the next person having a chance to spell that word, we'll just go to another word. Everyone understand?"

Everybody said out loud, "Yes, Sister."

And Sister Marianna said again, "That's a little harder. But that way, we can do more words." I raised my hand. "No questions, Vonny," Sister said. "Just listen, please." I put my hand down. "Also, if you spell a word, you will also have to tell me what it means. Understand?"

Everybody said out loud again, "Yes, Sister."

"Good," Sister Marianna said again. I raised my hand again. It was almost like when I had to spell furlong and then use it in a sentence at the end of the year in first grade. "Now, Vonny, because you are so eager to speak, you get the first word." But I still had a question! "Stand up, please, Vonny." Which I did. But I raised my hand too. "Put your hand down, Vonny. No more questions." I didn't even get to ask one question! Then Sister said, "The first word is shrug."

I just stood there. "Sister?" I said. I wanted to ask my question. Which was can we just use the word in a sentence instead of saying what it means.

"Please spell the word first, Vonny."

I just stood there still. I just lifted my shoulders up and down. I didn't know what shrug means. "Can I use it in a sentence instead of telling what it means?" I said back.

"Please just spell it first, Vonny!" Sister said back in a loud voice.

So, I just sounded it out. Which is how my Mother told me how to read. I was able to hear rug was in there. R-U-G. I knew that much. And then the beginning sounded like show. Like S-H-O-W. Like shhhh! Like when you hush someone. S-H. I closed my eyes and tried to write it out on the invisible blackboard with the invisible chalk in my head. S-H-R.

"Open your eyes, Vonny!" Sister said out loud. "Wake up!" Which made everybody laugh. And which made Louie Canale cackle.

Like she always does, Sister made me open my eyes. And I wasn't able to write it out on the invisible blackboard in my head with the invisible chalk. So, I just quick said back, "S-H-R-U-G, shrug."

"That's correct," Sister said back.

"Now, tell us all what shrug means, Vonny."

I just lifted my shoulders up and down again. "Can I use it in a sentence instead of telling what it means?" I said back again.

"Perhaps you can, Vonny," Sister said back. "But you may not." Whatever that means. "The rule is you must tell us what it means. Can you tell us what shrug means, Vonny?"

I just lifted my shoulders up and down still. I didn't know what it means. So, I guessed. I said, "Sister, a shrug is a bush that you plant around your house in your garden."

Sister Marianna put her hand over her mouth. It looked like she was almost laughing. Then she coughed. And I knew I was wrong when she did that. So, I just sat down. I turned around and saw that Sharon the Roach was smiling like she was just named the best student ever. "Will you please stand back up, Vonny," Sister said. "A bush that you plant in your garden is called a shrub. S-H-R-U-B. It ends with B."

"Oh," I just said back. Like a dope.

"That was a good guess, Vonny. But I'm afraid you're the first one out of the spelling bee this week. Like I said, this week is a lot harder," Sister said. "And, so you know, shrug is what this is," Sister said again. And then, she just lifted her shoulders up and down. Like I do all the time when I don't know something! Just like I was doing when I didn't know what shrug means! That's what it means to shrug! Just when you lift your shoulders up and down when you don't know something. That's a shrug! "You may sit now, Vonny." Which I did. Like a dope. And to make it as bad as possible, Sharon the Roach then raised her hand. Sister Marianna just nodded at her. So Sharon the Roach stood up, waited for everybody in the class to look at her, and then said, "Sister, I have a question."

"Yes, Sharon?"

The no questions rule was not for Sharon the Roach! "Is shrug also a verb?"

"Very good question, Sharon," Sister said back. "I'm glad you remembered our lesson about action words. Class, what do you think?" Of all people, Louie Canale raised his hand. "Yes, Louis," Sister said again.

Louie stood up, waited for everybody in the class to look at him, and then he lifted his shoulders up and down. "See!" he said back. "It's an action word. So, it's a verb!"

"You're correct, Louis. You may be seated. Very good question, Sharon." Of course it was a very good question! It was Sharon the Roach's question. Who started to sit back down. But then Sister Marianna said, "Because you're already standing, Sharon, the next word is for you." She stood back up next to her desk. "Your word is kindergarten."

Sharon the Roach smiled. And then she looked right at me and said, "Sister, I think everybody knows what kindergarten means." Sister smiled.

And after Sharon the Roach said this, she looked over at me again, smiled again, and just shrugged. A few of the small girls put their hands over their mouths like maybe their teeth might fall out or something if they laughed. Which they didn't.

"Well, why don't you tell us anyways?" Sister Marianna said back. The spell it first rule was not for Sharon the Roach too!

"Kindergarten is the grade before first grade, Sister. It's the grade you start school in."

"Very good, Sharon," Sister said back again. Very good? The grade before first grade? Even a dope knows what kindergarten is! "Now, please spell it for us."

"That's easy too," Sharon the Roach said back. And then she looked at me again. And smiled again. And shrugged again. And then she said out loud, "K-I-N-D-E-R-G-A-R-D-E-N, kindergarten."

Sister Marianna did not put her hand over her mouth. It did not look like she was almost laughing. And she did not cough too. But right away, I knew that Sharon the Roach was wrong when Sister didn't say anything. Even if that's the same way I used to know how to spell kindergarten. Instead, Sister just said, "Please try that one more time, Sharon. I'm not sure I heard you."

"K-I-N-D-E-R-G-A-R-D-E-N, kindergarten," Sharon the Roach said back again out loud. She was still smiling. Poor Sharon the Roach didn't even know yet. She just thought Sister Marianna wasn't sure she heard her. Which Sister did hear her. I wanted to be happy that Sharon the Roach was going to be out of the spelling bee. Because I already was out. But I wasn't happy. It was like looking at Jimmy Broom's blood in the street in front of Bruno's. I wasn't happy about that too. And I didn't want to look. But I had to do it anyways. Even when Jimmy's blood was covered over with dirt. I had to look! And so I turned around in my desk and looked over at Sharon the Roach. Who was standing there. Still smiling right up until when she saw me turn around and look at her. And then, when she saw me looking at her, poor Sharon the Roach finally knew what I knew. Which was not yet how to spell kindergarten. But which was that I knew and she then knew that, whatever it was, it was not K-I-N-D-E-R-G-A-R-D-E-N.

"I'm afraid," Sister started to stay.

"No!" Sharon the Roach said out loud. "No! No!" She made fists with both of her hands.

"Excuse me, Sharon," Sister said back.

Poor Sharon the Roach started to cry. "I'm sorry, Sister," she said and then she sat down, hitting her desk with her hand.

"Can anyone help Sharon?" Sister Marianna said. Can anyone help Sharon? Sister looked at me. I just shrugged. Not me. I can't help her. Because I spell it the same way she does. The wrong way!

But Louie Canale raised his hand again. "Yes, Louis. You're quite busy this morning."

Poor Sharon the Roach was still crying at her desk, covering her face with her hands, saying in a very low voice, "No! No! No!"

Louie stood up and said, "Sister, it's K-I-N-D-E-R-G-A-R-T-E-N, kindergarten."

Garten? What's a garten? Everybody knows what a garden is. A garden is where you plant shrubs. But what's a garten?

"Good, Louis. You are correct. You may sit down."

Louie smiled like he just won a thousand dollars. "It's German, Sister. My mom's family is German," Louie said again. I was thinking about Red's pop and if he killed anybody in Louie's mother's family with his dagger.

"You're correct, Louis," Sister said. "It is a German word." And then she smiled. "Well, class. We're going to have a new winner this week." Poor Sharon the Roach didn't stop crying even by the end of class. The two of us sat there at our desks all afternoon listening to other kids doing what we were supposed to be doing. Which was getting the answers right, spelling the words right, saying what the words mean right. Except Sharon the Roach and I were both already out. Me first, for once. Her second, for once.

And sitting there listening to everybody is how I finally learned that dramatick is really spelled dramatic. Which my Mother is a lot and which I am sometimes too. And vocabulerry is spelled vocabulary. Like I already told. Which is what different words are. And etiket is really spelled etiquette. Which is how Uncle Martin says I am supposed to act on the golf course. And instead of suppose to or use to, it's really supposed to and used to. For instance, I used to think that supposed to is spelled suppose to. Which it isn't. And I was supposed to write I used to instead of

I use to. Which I didn't. And now, I don't even have time to go back and change everything I already wrote down to what it's supposed to be.

Anyways, after Sharon the Roach was out, because Louie kept raising his hand, Sister Marianna then called on him. "Genuflect," she said. Which is a hard word!

But Louie got it right away. He quick said the letters very fast. And then when he was supposed to say what it means, he just did it. He just got down on one knee and hopped right back up again. Like he was across the street at the church. And when he finished, Louie smiled and said, "It's a verb!" And then he sat down.

A few boys in class laughed. Which made Sister raise one of her hands up. Which is Sister's way of saying, "Be quiet." Except she doesn't even have to say anything. Sister just raises one of her hands up. And then everybody knows what that means.

Around the class Sister went, asking a lot of hard words that a lot of kids didn't know. And each time they didn't know how to spell it, then Sister would spell it out. Or ask somebody to. Which we were supposed to remember. Or if they didn't know what the word meant, then Sister would say what it meant. Which we were supposed to remember too.

But while all the other kids were standing up and spelling words and saying what they mean, because I wasn't going to be able to win, even if Sharon the Roach was already out of the spelling bee even if she was in class and not missing school because of her rabbity pink eyes, I just kept thinking about John Smith and Pocahontas. Thoughts about John Smith and Pocahontas just popped into my head all afternoon. I kept trying to figure out what kind of policemen they are. Because they don't even act like policemen or talk like policemen. Not like any policemen I ever knew! Even if the only policemen I ever knew, except on TV programs, are the ones who ride on horses in parades around Mardi Gras time. But John Smith and Pocahontas, or Jake and Mack like Henry calls them and like they call themselves, don't even act like policemen are supposed to act. And they don't talk like policemen are supposed to talk.

First, they don't wear a uniform and they don't even tell people that they are policemen. They just ask people questions. For instance, when I saw John Smith and Pocahontas the first time at the Triangle while I was getting my Mother a roast beef poor boy with barbeque chips and root beers, they were just sitting at a table in the middle of the room drinking beers out of glasses like the crocodiles do at Bruno's. While they were supposed to be working! And when they didn't look like policemen because they weren't wearing uniforms. And when John Smith walked over to talk to me while I was waiting for the poor boy and asked me to go cow with him, he didn't even say he was a policeman. Pocahontas didn't say anything too when he came back. Both of them just acted like they weren't policemen. And John Smith was even betting on the pinball machine! And getting money from Larry the cook. Who was also the man who made the sandwiches. Who John Smith and Pocahontas didn't even tell him that they were policemen too. John Smith only said to Larry, "We were just passing through." Which they weren't. They were investigating an incident. Which is how Jimmy Broom got run over by a black Pontiac. Which I thought they did it! And then I found out they are policemen.

And, John Smith and Pocahontas don't even know how to talk like policemen. For instance, when I saw John Smith and Pocahontas the first time at the Triangle where John Smith was playing the pinball machine after we went cow, he said a bad word I can't write here without getting into trouble. And when I saw John Smith and Pocahontas on the corner of Columbus Street and Dorgenois when they tried to trap me and Lenny when we were coming back from Burdine's with the visible people, when Henry rode his bicycle up to us to say hello, John Smith called him a name I hope my Mother doesn't even find out I had to write that word. Which is punk. Except they didn't say punk. They said something worse. And also, John Smith and Pocahontas never even say sir or ma'am to anybody. Even to Daddy and to my Mother! Which policemen on the TV programs do all the time.

And, John Smith and Pocahontas are rude. Which policemen on the TV programs are not. For instance, whenever John Smith talks to Pocahontas, he always tells him to shut up. Or says other rude things to him. Which is not friendly. And when I heard them at Burdine's where they were asking questions, John Smith talked to the man behind the counter and said to him that buying Jimmy Broom the red top was none of the man's business. Which it was. Because the man works at Burdine's. And when I saw John Smith with Buck the barber on Bayou Road in front of his shop across the street from St. Rose de Lima Bean Church while Daddy and I were walking home from the baby cows' head shop, John

Smith just punched Buck in the stomach for no good reason. Like the big kids at school think about doing to me unless my cousin William is around. And like Red does sometimes to me and Lenny. Which is rude too!

And, John Smith and Pocahontas don't even like kids. Which policemen on the TV programs all do. And even the policemen on horses in the parades do too. Because they drop down beads to kids during the parades. For instance, when I saw John Smith and Pocahontas at the corner of Columbus Street and Dorgenois two times, once with Lenny when we were coming back from Burdine's with the visible people and once with Henry when we were talking in the alley behind Bruno's, they tried to trap us and catch us. They even chased me and Henry all the way to the Trinity Zion African Episcopal Methodist Congregation Church in that other neighborhood. And then they even took away Henry's bicycle.

Thoughts kept popping into my head about John Smith and Pocahontas because I was supposed to meet Henry later Friday night at the Bell when I went to the movies with Charly. And Henry only found out that John Smith and Pocahontas are policemen when I told him this morning on my way back home from Mister Lee's laundry.

"Louis, it's your turn again," Sister Marianna said. "Please stand." Which Louie did. "Your next word is library." Which I just learned how to spell right on Monday night from Henry! Because Henry's mother works at a library.

"Library," Louie said back. But when he said it, he said it just like I say it. It was like Louie said liberry. He said it just like I used to spell it. Like strawberry. Which was what made Henry laugh at me. "Library," Louie said again. Except it sounded like liberry again. I looked at the only other kid in the class who was still in the spelling bee. Who was one of the small girls who hold their hands over their mouths when they laugh like they think their teeth might fall out or something.

Everybody thinks Louie is a goofball. Still, I wanted him to win! But I also kept hearing him repeat the word. "Library. Library. Library." Which Louie kept saying, "Liberry. Liberry. Liberry." And I knew he was going to spell it that way too. I knew Louie was going to lose!

Then I remembered Henry again. So, I tried to talk to Louie in a very, very low voice. Who was standing right near by me. "A library is not a berry, Louie." But I said it the only way I know how. Which sounds like liberry. "A liberry is not a berry, Louie," I said. "Not a berry," I said again.

Sister Marianna right away said, "Please stand up, Vonny. Do you have something you want to share with the class?"

"No, Sister," I said back while I was getting up from my desk. "Nothing to share, Sister."

"Were you whispering something to Louis, Vonny? Please tell us what you said to Louis just now."

"Well, Sister," I said back again, "I only said that a library is not a berry." Except I said liberry. A few kids laughed. Louie cackled. Right in the middle of his turn! "A liberry is not a berry is all I said, Sister."

"Very disappointing, Vonny. Trying to distract Louis. Sit down now, please," Sister said back. "And I don't want to hear a peep out of you for the rest of the day unless you want to be sent to the office after school." Which I didn't. "Not a peep!"

"Okay, Sister," I said while I was sitting back down.

"Library," Louie said again. Except he said liberry again!

And then Sister Marianna saved Louie. She just said, "It's not fair that Vonny talked during your turn, Louis. Because of that, we're going to skip you for now. You have him to thank for that." Sister pointed at me. "You may sit down, Louis." And then she pointed at the little girl who was the only other person not already out of the spelling bee. "Patricia," Sister said. "Please stand." Which the little girl did. "Patricia, you can take Louis's word, the word Vonny was so helpful with. Library."

Poor little Patricia. She spelled it just like I used to. She sits in the back of class and didn't hear me whisper to Louie that it wasn't a berry. So, Patricia just said "Library." Just the way I say it. "Liberry." And then she spelled it. Just the way I used to. "L-I-B-E-R-R-Y," she said. "Library."

Sister looked at me. She wasn't smiling. "Please stand, Vonny." Which I did. I didn't make a peep. So, I didn't know what Sister was making me stand again for. "Please spell the word library for the class, Vonny."

I stood back up. "L-I-B-R-A-R-Y," I said back. "Library." Which I still said like liberry even if I knew better.

"Definition, please, Vonny," Sister said back.

"It's the place where they have books you can get to read. My friend Henry's mother works at one."

"Your friend Henry?" Sister said back.

"Yes, Sister," I said back. "Henry lives in the neighborhood." I pointed to the back of the school room. "On a street over that way." Which is where Henry lived.

"Does your friend Henry go to school here?" Sister said again. "Is he in our school?"

"No, Sister," I said back. "He doesn't. He isn't."

"So, your friend Henry goes to the public school?" Sister said again.

I said back, "He can't go there either, Sister. He's not a publican."

Sister Marianna smiled. And then she closed the book she was holding that had all of the spelling words in it. "He can't go to public school?" she said again.

"No, Sister," I said back. "And he can't come to school here either."

"And why is that, Vonny?" Sister said back. "Is your friend Henry too little to go to school yet? Too little even for kindergarten?"

"Oh, no, Sister," I said back again. "Henry's old enough for school. He's the same as me. He's seven. In the second grade. He's almost exactly just like me!"

Sister said back, "How is your friend Henry almost exactly like you, Vonny?"

"Well, Sister," I said back, "he wears dungarees and polo shirts like I do."

"He does?"

"Yes, Sister. And he goes to church on Sunday with his daddy and his mother and his little sister just like I do."

"So, your friend Henry goes to our church?"

"No, Sister. He goes to another church?"

"Your friend goes to another church? Isn't he Catholic, Vonny?"

"No, Sister," I said back. "He goes to another church where they don't have a confession box. And where there's a hole in the floor that you can sneak into when the doors and windows are all locked up." What I dope I was to say that!

Sister Marianna folded her arms and stared at me. Then she made a face. "Are you telling us the truth about your friend Henry whose mother works in a library, Vonny? What kind of church has a hole in the floor?"

"It's called Trinity Zion African," I said back. "Or something like that."

"Oh, my!" Sister said back. "Well, that explains why your friend Henry doesn't come to our church. But why can't he go to public school?" Sister said back.

"I think it's because Henry is a negro, Sister." It's why Henry always points to his arm to show me his brown skin.

Sister Marianna unfolded her arms and then quick walked down the aisle between the desks shaking her finger at me. "Vonny Foster! Do not ever use that word in this classroom again," she said. "Never! I never want anyone in this class to say that word."

"But, Sister," I tried to say back. "Henry has brown skin."

"Not ever!" Sister said again. "Do you understand me, Vonny?"

"Yes, Sister," I said back. "I understand."

Sister waved her finger and hand over the whole room. "Class?"

"Yes, Sister," everybody said back.

"Good!" she said. "Now, please take your seat again, Vonny." Sister walked back to the front of the class. Where she picked up the book again with all of the spelling words in it. I don't know why she wanted to talk about Henry anyways. All I did was spell library right. Even if I said it wrong. "Louis," Sister said. "Please stand for us again. Your word is sandwich."

Which right up until then I used to think was spelled sandwhich. Because I love them! Especially the roast beef poor boys at the Triangle. The best in the whole wide world! And it was the easiest word to spell. Just like the words sand and which. I thought I knew it. But the only kid in the class who knew better than me was Louie.

"S-A-N-D-W-I-C-H," he said right away. "Sandwich! You make it out of two pieces of bread and some kind of meat and you eat it," Louie said again. "Like a poor boy!" And then he quick sat down, smiling at everyone in the class. Like a goofball. Because like when I spelled furlong at the end of last year, Louie knew he was right. Louie knew he won. Even if I thought he forgot the other H, Louie knew he was the spelling bee winner. For the first time ever!

Sister Marianna closed her book with all of the spelling words in it. And then she put it down on her desk in front of the room. Sister looked over at Sharon the Roach. Who had her head down on her desk and was still hiding her eyes. Which were probably red now instead of pink because she was crying all afternoon.

And poor little Patricia looked like she wanted to cry too. But her eyes were too small even to have any tears in them. So, little Patricia just looked very sad. It was as close as she ever was to winning the spelling bee. And now she was only going to be the last person to lose. "Patricia," Sister Marianna said, "please come to the front of the classroom for your award for second place." My chocolate milk ticket! Patricia got out of her desk. Poor little Patricia was only a little bigger than my little sister was little. She didn't look like she was in second grade. She looked like maybe she was in kindergarten. Or maybe not even that. After Sister called her, Patricia walked up the aisle very slowly. Being in second place in the spelling bee is not so bad. I know because I do it almost every week! Except when little Patricia finally got to the front of the classroom, instead of a chocolate milk ticket, Sister Marianna handed her a bag. Which was almost bigger than little Patricia. "One of our parents gave this very nice gift to the school for a special student," Sister said again. "Let's everyone clap for Patricia." Which we all did. When Sister handed her the bag, Patricia looked down into it and at first made a funny face. And then she started smiling a lot. She stopped looking sad once she saw what was in the bag.

"What's in the bag?" a boy in the back said out loud.

"Quiet, children," Sister Marianna said. "I'm sure Patricia will be happy to show you her prize after the school bell rings in a few minutes."

When Patricia was walking back to her desk at the back of the room, carrying the bag that was almost as big as she was, she started skipping in the aisle. That's how happy she was! She was skipping in the classroom. When she skipped past Sharon the Roach's desk, Sharon put her head up and looked over into the bag. And then she just put her head back down on her desk and started crying again.

"Louis," Sister said again. "Please come to the front of the room for your award now." Louie stood up and held his arms over his head and was shaking them with his hands together like he was heavyweight champion of the world. All of the boys in class started clapping for him. When he got to the front of the room, right in front of Sister, Louie turned around to face everybody and then he bowed. Like he was a movie star. Like a goofball! "Now, Louis, let's be serious," Sister Marianna said. "This is quite an honor that you earned. I think this is your first time winning the spelling bee, isn't it?"

Louie nodded his head. "Sister," he said back, "it's my first time winning anything!"

"Well, you did win, Louis," Sister said again. "Fair and square. So, here's a nice book for you about a girl who becomes a novice." Which is on the way to being a nun! And about what her life is like, and where she lives, and what she does during the day, and how she gets dressed in the morning, and what she wears, and what she eats, and how she prays, and how she gets ready for bed at night. It was the same book that Sharon the Roach got last year for being in second place when I won the special spelling bee by getting furlong right. When for winning last week I only got one more ticket for chocolate milk after Mass on First Friday. Which is the same prize I always get every week for being in second place.

Louie got my book!

He took the book and said, "Thank you, Sister." And then Louie walked back to his desk holding his arms over his head again and shaking them again with his hands together holding the book like he was still heavyweight champion of the world. Except now he had a book about a girl who becomes a novice.

While Louie was doing that, I was thinking about how everybody at school always thinks that Louie Canale is a dope and a goofball because of the way sometimes in school he does dopey things and sometimes he says goofball things. For instance, holding his arms over his head and shaking them with his hands together like he was heavyweight champion of the world. When instead, Louie is the best speller in the whole class! At least this week. Even better than Sharon the Roach. And especially when the words are very hard. Maybe the words being hard is what makes Louie pay attention. Maybe when we're in the third grade, Louie will win the spelling bee every Friday because the words will be hard and he'll pay attention. And Sharon the Roach and I will have to find out each week who gets the ticket for chocolate milk after Mass on First Friday. Maybe everything will be different in third grade.

And right when I was thinking that, the school bell sounded. So, everybody in the classroom, every boy and every girl, stood up right away to leave. "Take your time, children," Sister Marianna said. "Pack your things and be sure to take home what you need for your homework this weekend. Don't forget anything. Remember, this is the last weekend before your first confession. Which is next Thursday. Be sure to finish your confession lists."

I forgot all about my confession list! And I just wanted to quick get home and change into my dungarees and polo shirt. Because I had to quick eat right away so I can go to the movies at the Bell with Charly. Where I was going to meet Henry to talk about what his daddy knows about the man at the barber shop. Who is Buck. And I was going to tell Henry what Daddy knows about the man at the barber shop. Who is still Buck. And how I saw John Smith punching Buck in the stomach for no good reason. Even if he is a policeman. John Smith. Not Buck.

A lot of kids were in the back of the room around little Patricia. Who was holding open the bag she got her prize in so everybody was able to see what it was. I was in a hurry. And I didn't want to be back there with all of the other kids. Who were mostly girls anyways. Including Sharon the Roach. Who finally stopped crying. So, because I wanted to know what Patricia's prize was, while I was packing up my books, I just asked a kid who was behind me what it was. "I don't know," he said back. "I can't see back there."

"Well, ask them," I said back. "Just ask somebody who is back there."

"Hey, you!" the kid said to another little girl who was between him and the circle of other kids standing around little Patricia. "What's in the bag?"

"What's in the bag?" the other little girl said to one of the girls in the circle. Who was standing next to Louie. Who was also back there.

While I was tying my strap around my books, Sister Marianna walked up behind me and tapped me on the shoulder. When I turned around, I said, "Oh! Hi, Sister."

"Please take this note home to your parents for me, Vonny," Sister said. And then she handed me an envelope.

I nodded. I was thinking about what my Mother said about if after she tells Sister Marianna about everything I did it won't surprise my Mother if Sister Marianna doesn't even let me make my First Communion. "Sure, Sister," is all I said back. And I just put the envelope in one of my books.

I looked in the back of the room and saw little Patricia holding the bag up over her head. Like she didn't want anybody else looking in it anymore. "I have to leave now," I heard her say. "My mother is picking me up now. I have to go! I have to go! I have to go!" She had a little voice too.

One of the girls in the circle standing around little Patricia turned to another little girl and leaned over and said something into her ear in a low voice. And then the other little girl turned to the kid behind me and leaned over and said something into his ear in a low voice. And then the kid behind me leaned over and acted like he was going to say something into my ear in a low voice.

But instead, just as I was noticing what kind of bag it was that little Patricia was holding up over her head, the kid behind me turned his face up to the classroom ceiling and said out loud, "Hey, everybody. It's an invisible woman."

Little Patricia got my visible woman!

Louie cackled. "She even has breasts!"

Thirteen, or Bell

My heart is what my Mother says makes thoughts pop into my head. At least the best ones.

But then there's the smaller book that came inside the box with the visible man. The one with two pictures of a skeleton, one facing the front and the other facing the back, that had a lot of little arrows pointing to all of the bones in the visible man with their names on the other end of the arrows. Which were not normal names. The book with pictures of all of the organs and what they do. The one that says it's the brain that makes the organs all work together. So, maybe it is my brain that makes thoughts pop into my head. And not my heart.

Which can't be true! How can my brain be the organ that makes thoughts pop into my head? Which is where my brain already is! It can't be my brain that makes thoughts pop into my head. Because then the thoughts are already in my head before they even pop into it.

For me, what organ makes thoughts pop into my head is what my Mother calls a mystery. Except for my Mother, it's not.

Anyways, after school on Friday, after I learned all the things I learned while we were spelling all those new words and Louie Canale was finally winning a spelling bee and getting the book I wanted, which is why I don't spell vocabulary like vocabulerry anymore, after I quick ran home and then changed into my dungarees and polo shirt, I asked my Mother if I can go over next door by my Uncle Roger's house and see if Jimmy Broom's mother will let me go inside his house and talk to him now that he's back from the Hotel Dieu or not.

Which they both did. My Mother let me go over next door to see Jimmy Broom. And Jimmy Broom's mother let me go inside his house and talk to him.

Jimmy's house is a lot like our house. Which has every room behind another room all the way from the front porch to the back yard. Except in Jimmy's house you have to walk up a bunch more stairs from the brick sidewalk on Columbus Street to get up to the porch in the front and walk down a bunch more stairs to get down to his back yard. So, there is an underneath to Jimmy's house. We don't have an underneath to our house like Jimmy's house does. Except our house has a space under it like at the Trinity Zion African Episcopal Methodist Congregation Church where to get underneath it you have to get on your knees and duck your head down and crawl in the dirt. Where there are a lot of worms.

Jimmy Broom's house has an underneath that you can walk into. Even if you are big like Daddy is big. Which is where Jimmy's daddy keeps his red truck that he uses to fix tires whenever he is not fixing tires. Which is the red truck that is always on the street when Jimmy's daddy is fixing tires. It's like a garage except it's not outside Jimmy's house like the garage at my Aunt Tallulah's house. Because Jimmy's house is up a bunch more stairs than our house, so there's room for an underneath. Which is where the garage is.

I never went into Jimmy's house a lot before he got run over by the black Pontiac. Like I already told, my Mother doesn't like me going into other kid's houses. For instance, the one in California where I went into it the first time I lied to my Mother. Where a kid Pepe and I were playing baseball with wanted to show us a snake. And my Mother especially doesn't like me to go into Jimmy Broom's house because she thinks his parents don't give him enough attention. But even if my Mother thinks Jimmy's mother may not be the best mother, she knows she cares about her boy. She knows Jimmy's mother worries to death about him. Which is what she said last Saturday night when everybody was playing cards in our kitchen and I was pretending to be asleep.

So, when I walked into Jimmy's house after I said, "Thank you, Ma'am," to Jimmy's mother after she said I was able to see him and to talk to him now that he was home, it was a little scary because everything was dark inside and I thought maybe Jimmy might have a mask on like sometimes sick people do on TV programs or even Jimmy might be in one of those machines where they put kids in who get sick and can't walk except with the metal things on their legs. But after I walked through the front room and then the room where somebody sleeps and then the hallway next to the bathroom, just like our house, and then into the room where Jimmy sleeps, I saw Jimmy was just sitting on the side of his bed without any mask on or being in any machine. He was just wearing dungarees and a polo shirt. Just like me. Except one of the legs of his dungarees was cut short. And on that leg was a white cast. Where some people wrote their names already. Which I didn't want to. Because I wanted to ask Jimmy questions instead.

"Hey, Jimmy," I said when I saw him.

"Vonny!" he said back. "How are you, pal?" Jimmy calls everybody pal. He calls me pal too! "You miss me in school?"

Which I didn't. Jimmy is not in Sister Marianna's class. He's in another one. I think Jimmy is in the one with Lenny where the teacher is not a Sister. "How is your leg?" I said again.

"Well, you see, pal," Jimmy said back. "It's broke." I know it's not right. But that's the way Jimmy talks. Like John Smith.

Jimmy is a little kid, even more little than me. But he's like Henry because he acts a lot older, a lot bigger. "Does it hurt?" I said back.

"Not anymore," he said. "But I can't walk on it or nothing, pal." I know that's not right too. But it's the way Jimmy talks. "It'll hurt if I walk on it." He smiled and shrugged. "So, I don't."

"Everybody said you were going to die," I said back. Which I don't know why I said that. I didn't want to make Jimmy feel bad again about him maybe being dead.

But Jimmy just laughed out loud. "Who said that?" he said back.

It was the crocodiles at Bruno's who said Jimmy was going to die. Because of the blood in the street. And because he was supposed to have a broomstick in his arm. I just shrugged. "I don't know," I said back. I didn't want to tell Jimmy about what the crocodiles at Bruno's said about him. He doesn't even know any of them. His mother doesn't smoke. "I think maybe because you got a broomstick in your arm," I said back again.

Jimmy laughed more out loud. "What a joke! I never got a broomstick in my arm, pal. I don't even know if I had it with me while I was running around the bases. But even if I did, I threw it down before I ran into the car. I was trying to make it home safe, pal. Trying to score!"

I saw that both of Jimmy's arms were out in the open. No bandage. No cast. Not even a scratch. "So, you didn't get a broomstick in your arm?" I said back. He shook his head. "Then, where did all the blood in the street come from?" I don't know why I said that too. I didn't want to make Jimmy feel bad again about him having his blood all over the street.

But Jimmy only laughed even more out loud. "My leg, pal. My leg. I got a cut from my ankle all the way up to my knee." He pointed to his cast. "It's underneath there. And there was blood everywhere."

"Jimmy," I said again, "did it hurt when the car hit you?" I don't know why I said that too. I didn't want to make Jimmy feel bad again about him having a car run over him.

But Jimmy only laughed the most out loud he did since I got there. "What do you think, pal?" he said back.

"I guess it did," I said back.

"You guess it did?" Jimmy said back again. "Let me tell you, pal. It did! It hurt a lot when I ran into that car. But then the ambulance came and they gave me some medicine and then I fell asleep and then it didn't hurt anymore."

"So, you didn't almost die at the hospital?" I said again. I didn't want to keep asking Jimmy about almost dying and bleeding all over the street and getting hit by a car. But thoughts just kept popping into my head. Because I wanted to know. And words kept popping out of my mouth. Because I really wanted to know!

"Do I look like I almost died, pal?" Jimmy said.

I shrugged. I never saw anybody who almost died. So, I didn't know. "Why were you in the hospital so long?" I said back.

"You ever run into a car, pal?" Jimmy said again. "They had to fix my leg. They had to make sure my head was okay."

"Is it?"

"Is what?" Jimmy said back.

"Is your head okay?" I said back.

"Well, pal," he said, "my old lady says my head is too hard to do any damage to it. Even with a car!" Jimmy laughed again. When Jimmy says old lady, he means his mother. Which I can't even think about calling my

Mother. Unless I want to live in some other house. Anyways, my Mother isn't even old.

Jimmy's mother called from the kitchen in the back. "James! I thought I told you not to call me your old lady," she said out loud.

"Sure, sure," Jimmy said to me in a low voice. "Okay, Mom," he said to her out loud. "Anyways," he said again back to me, "my head's okay. And my arm's okay." He slapped his thigh on the leg where his dungarees were cut short. "It's just this now. I didn't almost die. I was barely sick. I just broke my leg. That's all!"

"Then what did you do in the hospital all week, Jimmy?"

"Mainly ate ice cream and read comic books, pal. They got a million of them!" I know it's not the best way to talk, the way Jimmy does. "Watched TV programs and had all these people telling me how I was a good kid and a brave boy." He talks like John Smith.

Which reminded me. "So, did John Smith go to the hospital to see you?"

"Who?" Jimmy said back.

"John Smith!" I said back. Then I remembered and said, "Maybe you call him Jake. A policeman. Who is always with another policeman named Mack. Who are both going around asking questions about you and about your daddy and about the barber over on Bayou Road."

"I don't know no policeman called John Smith. Or Jake or Mack or whatever you call them," Jimmy said back.

"I saw them at Burdine's last week," I said back. "They went there to buy you a present. A top. Did they bring it to you at the hospital?" Jimmy shrugged. "A top that cost less than a dollar?" I said again. Jimmy shrugged again. "A red one?"

"Nobody gave me a red top," Jimmy said back. "Oh, wait! Except my old man." That's what Jimmy calls his daddy.

Jimmy's mother called from the kitchen in the back again. "James! I thought I told you not to call your pop your old man," she said out loud.

"Sure, sure," Jimmy said to me in a low voice. "Okay, Mom," he said to her out loud. "So," he said again back to me in a low voice, "before I came back from the hospital two days ago, two guys tried to come in my hospital room. But my old man didn't let them. The door started to open and my old man saw these two guys and then he just pushed them back into the hall and said he didn't want them in my hospital room. So, I didn't see them, pal. I just heard them talking in the hall."

"What did they say?" I said back. I wanted to be able to tell Henry what I found out from Jimmy Broom about John Smith and about Pocahontas and about them both going around asking questions about Jimmy and about his daddy and about the barber over on Bayou Road. Who is Buck. And about Henry's daddy too!

"Didn't hear them, pal," Jimmy said back while he was shrugging. "The door to my room was closed. All I know is, when my old man came back into the room, he gave me a box with this top in it." Jimmy pulled it from under the pillow on his bed. "The old man said his friends dropped it off for me." Jimmy handed me the top. "Except my old man didn't act like they were his friends." The top was red.

"That's the top that John Smith and Pocahontas got at Burdine's last Saturday," I said. "A dollar and two cents. With tax. They said they were buying it for you."

"Maybe," Jimmy said back. "But I don't know who you're talking about, pal. I don't know no John Smith or Pocahontas." Which is the way Jimmy talks. He rubbed the top of his head, and then he laughed. "Hey, pal. Are you pulling my leg or something? Are your pulling my broken leg? Isn't John Smith that guy from Thanksgiving? The guy who came to America in a boat after Christopher Columbus? And Pocahontas too? Except she was already here. Next thing you're going to tell me is Santa Claus was at Burdine's buying me a comic book."

Which he wasn't. And which wasn't the next thing I was going to tell Jimmy. If I wanted to tell Jimmy everything I knew about John Smith and Pocahontas and where I met them and what I was doing there and what I did instead and how they are always in the neighborhood since he got hit by the black Pontiac and asking people questions and punching people in the stomach for no good reason and trapping me and Lenny and chasing me and Henry all over, I wasn't going to have time to find out what I wanted to find out. Because I had to quick go back home and eat supper because Charly was coming over to take me to the Bell where we were going to see the movie about the old man who always plays games on his knee like the song my Mother and my little sister are always singing now. Except I was going to meet up with Henry again too. But I still wanted to know one other thing. Just one. So, I said, "Jimmy?"

"You got another question for me, pal?" he said back.

"I do," I said back. Just like I didn't want to ask Jimmy about him almost dying and him bleeding all over the street and him getting hit by a car, I didn't want to ask him about the car that ran over him too. But like those other things I didn't want to ask Jimmy, I just did. So, I said again, "Jimmy, did you see the car that ran over you?"

"How was I going to miss it, pal? I didn't hit the ball that far. The kid had it in his hand when I was rounding second and I was looking at him to see if he was going to be able to get it home in time. You know? To get me out. I was looking down the street down where Picou's is on the corner of Bayou Road. And the car was behind me on Dorgenois where I didn't see it. Because I don't have eyes in the back of my head. And I didn't see that it was going to turn onto Columbus Street when I came around third base trying to make it home. I didn't even see it before I ran into it. And now I wish I held at third instead."

"So, you didn't see it?"

"What did I say, pal? I saw it after I came around third. But it was too late!" Jimmy made a fist with one hand and punched it into his other one. "Smack! All I saw after I came around third was the little yellow indian and then I was out."

"You got tagged out?" I said back. Like a dope!

"No, pal. Knocked out! Knocked out cold. Like I got hit by Floyd Patterson or something. I don't remember what happened after that."

"Did you see what color was the car?" I said back.

"I know it was black," Jimmy said back. "Because my old man told me it was black. All I saw was the little yellow indian on the car just when I ran into it."

"It ran over you or you ran into it?" I said back again.

"Does it matter?" Jimmy said back. "My leg is broke either way!" Then he shrugged and said, "I guess both, pal. Because I was running too."

"Did you see the license plate on the car?"

Jimmy shook his head. "Out, pal," he said back.

"Did you see who was in it?"

"Out, pal" is all he said back again. "Knocked out!"

"Did you see what kind of car it was?"

"I already told you, pal, all I saw was the little yellow indian. So, it had to be a Pontiac. But that's all I know. Now I wish I held at third instead."

Jimmy shrugged. "But I almost made it home." And then he laughed again. "It took running into a car to get me out, pal. A car!"

I wanted to ask Jimmy if he thought the Pontiac ran over him on purpose. Whether it was an incident or an accident. But he didn't know anything else. Jimmy didn't even know the car was behind him when he was rounding second or coming around third. He just was looking at the kid with the ball and trying to figure out if he was able to make it home. Which he was. If the black Pontiac didn't hit him first. Which it did. Or if he didn't run into it first. Which he did too.

"So, Vonny. What's going on with you?" Jimmy said. "You staying out of trouble?"

It was my turn to laugh. "Mostly," I said back and I shrugged too. "Are you going to be able to make your First Communion next week, Jimmy?"

He nodded. "Monseigneur came to the Hotel Dieu."

"He did?" I said back. "What for?"

"Not to give me a red top!" Jimmy said back. "But he said if I can walk on crutches next week, then I can make my First Communion with everybody else." And then Jimmy reached behind him on his bed, picked up two wooden crutches, and then got right up on them by his bed. "Watch this, pal." He was practically running around the room hopping on them. "See! I think I'll be able to go. What do you think?"

Jimmy's mother said out loud from the kitchen, "James! James! Put those crutches down right now and get back in your bed. You want to wind up back in the hospital?"

Jimmy made a face. He moved his lips like he was yelling at his mother. Except he didn't say anything. "Some old lady I got, right?" he said to me in a low voice instead. "Okay, Mom," he said out loud.

While Jimmy was talking about his mother, I thought about what Jimmy's confession list looks like. If he even has one. Did he say mean things to his mother? Which calling her an old lady is mean. Did he lie to his old man? Did he talk to strangers? Did he bet on pinball games? Did he bet on horses? Did he stay out late after dark getting chased by policemen? "Well, Jimmy," I said back. "I have to go now. I'm going to the Bell to see a movie with my cousin."

"A war movie?" Jimmy said back.

"I don't think so."

"A monster movie?" Jimmy said again.

"I don't think it's that either."

"An outer space movie?" Jimmy said even again.

I shook my head. "No," I said back. "It's just about this old man who always plays games on his knee, I think. But everybody says it's supposed to be a good movie for kids. That's what my Mother says."

"You mean your old lady?" Jimmy said back.

I didn't nod. I just said back, "Daddy and my Mother."

"Right," Jimmy said back. "Well, I'm stuck here for another week, pal. So, stop by, will you?"

I nodded my head. I put my hands in my pockets. I didn't want to talk to Jimmy about the black Pontiac anymore. But I did want to know something else. Just one more thing.

"Jimmy?" I said again.

"What, pal?" he said back. He was sitting on the bed again with his chin leaned on his crutches.

"Do you know Buck?"

"You mean the barber?" Jimmy said back.

I nodded again. "Right! The one over on Bayou Road," I said again.

"Sure," Jimmy said back again. "He gives me a haircut every week." Then he looked down at the cast on his leg and at his crutches. "Well, not this week, pal. But every other one. And my old man, he's good friends with Buck. Very good friends. They talk all the time."

I wanted to tell Jimmy about how Buck asked Daddy when he was at the barber shop for a haircut Tuesday afternoon to tell Jimmy's daddy that it would be good if Jimmy's daddy stopped over at the barber shop sometime soon and that Buck knows about Jimmy but he said he needs to talk to Jimmy's daddy about something. But then I didn't. Because if I do then I will want to tell Jimmy about how I saw John Smith punch Buck in the stomach for no good reason while Daddy and I were walking back from the baby cows' head shop. Which is also the disgusting meat shop. And then I will have to tell Jimmy everything about John Smith and Pocahontas. And maybe even about Henry. Who is a negro boy. And about how I was investigating the incident.

But Jimmy didn't need to know everything. So, instead, I just waved at him and said, "Well, Jimmy, I'll see you around."

"See you later, pal," Jimmy said back. And then I just turned and left and quick went home to have supper.

After everything that happened this week, after me and Henry being chased, and Lenny Mahoney's mother finding the visible woman, and John Smith and Pocahontas coming to my house, and me having a bad dream, and me being sick, and me being the first person out of the spelling bee, by the time I finished my supper, I was ready to go out to the movies at the Bell.

Charly knocked on the back door in the kitchen just about when I finished my eggs. I eat eggs a lot on Friday night. Which is when we don't eat meat. Which sometimes I don't eat meat anyways even if it's not Friday. For instance, if it's veal liver Daddy cooks, I don't eat it. I eat eggs instead. But nobody eats meat on Friday. Because you're not supposed to. I'm not really sure why we're not supposed to eat meat on Friday. But we don't. Even when it's not Lent. Which happens right before Easter. Which it is now. Because some people even give up meat for Lent too. Which my Mother does sometimes. And if my Mother gives up meat for Lent, then I give up meat for Lent too. And my little sister does too and my baby brother does too! Even if they don't eat meat anyways. And even if it's Lent and my Mother doesn't give up meat for Lent or if it's not even Lent, we still don't eat meat if it's Friday. We just don't eat meat on Friday. Ever! Which means Daddy and my Mother eat fish. But I don't eat fish. Ever! Because when Daddy brings fish back home after going fishing they have eyes in them that look at me no matter where I go just like the picture of Jesus on the wall in the room where Daddy and my Mother and now my baby brother sleep and just like the eyes in the baby cows' heads that I don't like to look at. So, I just don't eat fish. I just almost always eat eggs on Friday night. Or soup. Or a peanut butter and jelly sandwich.

When Charly knocked on the door, she was singing "This old man, he played one, he played." Then she sang something I didn't understand, and then, "On my thumb," and then some other words I didn't know either. Then she said, "Hi, Nanny."

"Charly! Charly! Charly!" my little sister said out loud and started hopping around and waving her little arms in the air.

Charly singing and my little sister hopping around made me think about when we were driving here from California when I was in first grade. When all we did all day while we were driving here from California was sit around in Daddy's car while he was driving and my Mother and my little sister were singing songs all the time. My baby brother wasn't born yet. He didn't have to listen to all the singing. He was lucky!

When we left California to come here, I didn't want to. Daddy and my Mother made me leave California. But I liked being there for all the things I already told. My friend Pepe lived there. All my girl cousins and my cousin Willy lived there. And I liked California and all the people I knew there. But my Mother was a little girl like my little sister is a little girl in the same neighborhood where we live now. Right by Columbus Street. And my Mother wanted to come back here. So, we had to leave California. Even if I didn't want to. And when we left, my Mother said "Vonny, you're going to like your new school and your new friends and your new neighborhood when we get home." Which I did. Even if home for me was in California. "And you'll be able to see all your cousins too," my Mother said again. Which I did. Even if all my girl cousins and my cousin Willy are in California still and I don't get to see them anymore.

Anyways, all we did all day while we were driving here from California was sit around in Daddy's car while he was driving and my Mother and my little sister were singing songs all the time. I tried to read the newspapers every day while we were driving. Because there was always a different kind of newspapers every morning. Because every morning we were always in a different place. Usually a place where we all slept in one little room. And where sometimes there was a swimming pool. Which was never as big as the one at Stallings Playground. But a big enough swimming pool for me.

Except I was never able to read the newspapers for most of the time we were driving here from California. Because all day long my Mother was teaching my little sister, who was my baby sister then, all these little girl songs that my Mother used to sing when she was little the way my little sister is little now. I didn't like any of those songs.

For instance, there was a song about animals that eat oats. Which my Mother says is like cereal. Which I don't even like to eat! And at first you didn't even hear that they were eating oats. Because all the words sounded like one very long word that didn't make any sense. Like Satnohacop! And there was a song too about little fish and their mother swimming around somewheres. Which is what fish do. Unless Daddy catches them first and eats them! And there was a song too about how it was sad that a big boat sank and went down to the bottom of the sea. Which is where maybe the little fish and their mother were swimming too. And there was a song too about some guy who has the whole world in his hands. Which is not possible. Because the world is too big!

Like I already told, I didn't like any of those songs. And none of them was as good as Johnny Horton singing about the battle of New Orleans!

But all day long, while we were driving here from California, my Mother and my little sister, who was my baby sister then, were singing all these little girl songs that my Mother used to sing when she was little the way my little sister is little now. While I was trying to read the newspapers.

"Mama," I said one time in the middle of the day when it was hot in the car because Daddy was driving it across a desert, "why don't you teach her how to read?"

"Oh, it was sad," my Mother sang back. "It was sad." And then my baby sister started singing with her. "It was sad when the great ship went down. To the bottom of the."

"Mama!" I said out loud before they could finish.

My Mother turned around from where she was sitting in the front seat next to Daddy. She looked at me and my baby sister. And then she smiled. "I think we're bothering Vonny, little monkey. Maybe we need to be quiet so he can read."

"Thank you, Mama," I said back.

And then my Mother looked just at my baby sister and said, "I don't think so!" And she started singing again. "Oh, it was sad. It was sad." And then my baby sister started singing with her again. "It was sad when the great ship went down. To the bottom of the sea."

That's the way every day was when we were driving here from California. Which was four days. All day long! And I didn't even want to leave California.

So, when Charly knocked on the back door in the kitchen and was singing "This old man, he played three, he played," something I didn't understand on his knee and the rest of that song, I thought my Mother and my little sister were going to sing too. Which they started to do! All of them, my Mother and Charly and my little sister were all singing about this old man.

Because I was finished my eggs, I said, "Mama, can I please go outside and play with Lenny before we go to the movies?" It was polite the way I said it. Because I said please.

"I want to go! I want to go! I want to go!" She was hopping around the kitchen waving her little arms in the air.

"Perhaps you can, Vonny," my Mother said back. "But you may not." Just like Sister Marianna said in class! Which I still don't know what it means.

"Does that mean that I can?" I said back.

"It's almost six o'clock, Vonny. Go and wash your face and hands. You and Charly have to leave."

"I want to go! I want to go! I want to go!" my little sister was laughing and then was crying and then was laughing again. With my little sister, she's either laughing all the time or she's crying all the time, one or the other. Or both! My Mother then said something to my little sister in French that she always said when that happened. Something that her mother, who is my Grandma that is dead, told her that means if you laugh too much you're going to cry.

I quick left the kitchen and walked through the room where my little sister and I sleep and then into the hallway by the bathroom and then into the bathroom. Where I washed my face and hands like my Mother said. When I walked back through the room where my little sister and I sleep, I saw my school books sitting on my bed. Which were tied up in my book strap. And then I saw the envelope that Sister Marianna gave me at the end of class while everybody was still around little Patricia trying to see what she won in the spelling bee. Which was my visible woman.

"Please take this note home to your parents for me, Vonny," Sister said while I was tying my strap around my books in the classroom. The envelope had written on it in black ink "Parents of Vonny Foster" in the script that Sister Marianna always writes with. Which is very fancy like the script that my very large aunt from Alabama writes with. Maybe they went to the same school. When Sister Marianna gave me the envelope, I was thinking maybe she wanted to tell Daddy and my Mother about how for the first time I was the first one out of the spelling bee. Which never happens!

And then I remembered what my Mother told me two nights after John Smith and Pocahontas were at our house. And I thought maybe my Mother told Sister Marianna about all the bad things I did that week since Jimmy Broom was run over by the black Pontiac. And that Sister wasn't going to let me make my First Communion. Which I will be the biggest dope in the class if that happens! And maybe that's what Sister was writing to the parents of Vonny Foster. Who is me! And who are Daddy and my Mother!

So, after I washed my face and hands when I was walking through the room where my little sister and I sleep, even if I saw the envelope that Sister Marianna gave me while I was leaving the classroom that had written on it "Parents of Vonny Foster" in script, I didn't give it to my Mother. Because I wanted to go to the movies with Charly.

Quick after I came back into the kitchen, Charly and I left through the back door in the kitchen. My little sister was crying. My Mother was holding her on her lap, the way she held me on her lap the day before. She was holding my little sister's hands over her heart the way she held my hands over my heart the day before. But my little sister was crying too much to have any thoughts pop into her head. Even ones from her heart.

I like going to the movies with Charly. We used to go to the movies all the time. Which was with Marly. Who is her twin sister and my cousin too. And then Charly and Marly got boyfriends. Because my Aunt Gwendolyn said they were old enough to have boyfriends now. Which they weren't before, my Aunt Gwendolyn used to say. I don't know why. And Marly was with her boyfriend that Friday night.

Anyways, when I was between being a baby the way my little brother is a baby and being little the way my little sister is little, Charly and Marly used to take me to the movies all the time. Because they didn't have boyfriends yet. But I was so little when I went to the movies with them that I didn't even know that a movie isn't real. I didn't know that movies are just pretend stories about people who are just pretend people. Not real people. Like the boy and the girl in Henry's comic book who like each other but their parents don't like the boy and the girl to talk to each other because everybody is different and because they are from two different families who don't like the other family and then the boy makes a mistake by accident and kills the girl's brother but not on purpose. Instead, when I went to the movies with Charly and Marly all the time, I was so little that I used to think that what was happening up on the movies was happening right there at the Bell. Or at the Rivoli.

For instance, when in the wizard movie I saw a lot of monkeys dressed up in fancy clothes flying around, I was thinking that the monkeys were in the Rivoli and were going to fly inside of it. So, when in the same movie I saw the flying monkeys jumping on the scarecrow and pulling him apart so that his legs were in one place and his body was in another place, I was waiting for them to fly around the Rivoli and maybe jump on us and maybe even pull us apart too. Which was why when that started happening I got under the seat that I was sitting on so the monkeys weren't able to see me. I was hiding from the flying monkeys. Like a goofball!

And also for instance, when in the movie about this guy who sings all the time no matter where he is, even after he goes to jail, where he keeps singing anyways, he gets beat up by some bad guys, I was thinking that the men were fighting inside the Bell and that they were going to start fighting with us. And maybe even punch us in the stomach for no good reason. So, when that started happening I got under the seat that I was sitting on so that the bad guys weren't able to see me. I was hiding from the bad guys. Like a dope!

When I was under the seat, Charly and Marly just laughed and laughed. Which I didn't know why then. Because I was thinking they were going to be pulled apart by flying monkeys or beat up by bad guys.

I didn't know that movies are just pretend stories about people who are just pretend people. Not real people. I don't think that anymore. I know what's pretend and what's not pretend now. Because I pay attention. I'm observant.

Anyways, while Charly and I were walking down Columbus Street to the movies at the Bell, she asked me what happened at school and I told her I didn't win the spelling bee. I didn't tell her I was the first one out for the first time ever. I just said I didn't win. Which was true. Also, I didn't tell her that little Patricia won my visible woman for being in second place after Louie. Because then I was going to have to tell Charly about everything.

When we reached St. Rose de Lima Bean School, up ahead of us I saw Henry on the other side of Broad Street on his little sister's bicycle again. He was going to the movies at the Bell too. Because we were going to meet up in the balcony to talk about what we found out about who ran over Jimmy Broom. Even if Jimmy wasn't going to die.

Then a thought just popped into my head. So, while Charly and I were walking to the movies at the Bell, I said, "Charly, who is your favorite?"

"My favorite what?" Charly said back.

So, I said back, "Who is your favorite of God, his son Jesus, and the Holy Spirit?"

Charly started laughing. We were walking across Broad Street and she made me hold her hand the same way Daddy makes me hold his hand. Even if I'm not little anymore. "My favorite?" she said back.

"Right," I said back. "Like Mickey Mantle is my favorite baseball player. And like that guy Rock is your favorite movie star. So, who is your favorite in the holy trinity, Charly?"

She laughed. "Well," Charly said back. She looked at me and crinkled her eyes. Which she does a lot. "I never really thought about it. I don't know. I think I just like them all the same."

"But you have to have a favorite, Charly!" I said back. "Don't you like one of them more than the other two?"

Charly laughed again while we were walking around the bend in the road. "Well, who's your favorite?" she said back.

"That's easy!" I said back. "The Holy Spirit."

Charly laughed out loud. I was able to see Stallings Playground across the street because we already walked all the way around the bend in the road. "Why the Holy Spirit?"

"God the father is just a father," I said back. "And I know all about fathers. Because I know Daddy. And I know fathers are important. And I know God the father is the most important father. But I just know all about them. Because I know Daddy too!"

Charly laughed more out loud. "Well, what about Jesus?" she said back. We were almost at the Bell.

"It's the same," I said back. "Jesus is just a son. And I know all about sons. Because I'm a son. And my friend Lenny is a son. And my friend Jimmy is a son. And my new friend Henry is a son too. And I know sons are important. And I know Jesus is the most important son. But I just know all about them. Because I'm a son too!"

Charly laughed even more out loud. "So, I guess that leaves just the Holy Spirit," she said back.

"Not only that, Charly," I said back. "I like mysteries." Which I do. "And Sister Marianna said the Holy Spirit is a mystery." Which she did.

Charly laughed even more and more out loud. And she was still laughing even more and more out loud when we turned the corner and saw three people standing in the line for the movies in front of the lady in the flowery dress in the little room at the front of the Bell where she sold tickets. There was a negro man at the front of the line. Who bought his ticket from the lady and then walked over to the door on the other side of the Bell. Where the stairs to the balcony are. And then there was a girl and a boy. Who looked like they were as big as Charly and her boyfriend are. Who the boy bought two tickets and then the girl and the boy walked in the glass doors right behind the lady in the flowery dress.

The Bell is only a little like the Rivoli. For instance, the Bell is across from Stallings Playground, which is far from my house on Columbus Street, and the Rivoli is across from the Triangle, which is close to my house. And which too is right next to the house where my Mother lived when she was a little girl like my little sister is a little girl now. So, my Mother used to go to the movies at the Rivoli all the time too. But not the Bell. And the people at the Rivoli just let my Mother go to the movies by herself, because they knew her because she lived right next door, without even having to pay a penny or whatever it cost to go to the movies then. And they even gave her free candy too! The people at the Bell didn't even know my Mother. I don't even think they know her now because I always only go there with Charly and Marly.

Also for instance, the Rivoli is a very old building and sometimes doesn't smell so good. And it's always dark inside. Always! I don't even think they have any lights in the whole place. But the Bell has these red and yellow and blue and green and white lights on behind the counter in the lobby where I buy candy and drinks before the movies. Popcorn too! And sometimes even while the movies are still playing if I have some change left over and I'm still hungry. All the lights behind the counter spell out different kinds of food and drinks. One says popcorn in fancy script that is yellow and all lighted up. Another one says hot dog in red block letters. Which is lighted up too. Whenever I buy a pickle at the Rivoli and ask "How much?" the man just looks at me and says, "Same as last week, kid." Which is always a nickel. And there is a funny sign on the jar on the counter that says "NICKEL PICKLE" in black block letters.

Just like the way I just wrote it. At the Bell, they don't even have pickles. But when I buy food at the Bell and ask "How much?" the man just tells me how much. A nickel or a dime or a quarter. He just says what it is. He doesn't talk to me like I'm a dope. The lady and the man at the Rivoli are never nice to us. Sometimes they are even very rude. And because there are lights at the Bell, I can see. So, I never dropped my popcorn by accident in the lobby like I did at the Rivoli. Where the floor sticks to the bottom of my sneakers from people dropping candy and drinks. Because it's so dark! Which is not what happens at the Bell. Because also at the Bell there is a negro man who is always cleaning up if somebody drops something even if there is enough light to see.

And also for instance, at the Rivoli the seats squeak. Even when you sit still and don't move around a lot. Which we don't! At the Bell, there are these tiny lights on the floor right by the end of each row. So you can find your way without bumping into anybody. And sitting in the seats at the Bell is like sitting on a big pile of towels. Big, soft towels. And at the Bell the seats don't squeak. Even if you don't sit still and move around a lot. Which we don't anyways!

And finally for instance, at the Rivoli I mainly go with Lenny on Saturday afternoons and they mainly show scary movies there. Like the Tingler. Which Charly and Marly went to see there with their boyfriends last Saturday because they really love horror movies. Which is what my Mother said. Except she called it trash. But most kids don't like to go to scary movies. Except for me and Lenny. Because we both know better. Lenny and I both know that the scary things in the scary movies are not for real. Because of what Daddy said about don't ever worry about dead people. So, we both know better. And the other kind of movie they always show at the Rivoli that we like are about guys going into outer space on rocket ships. Which is where I want to go if I ever get enough money to buy a rocket ship. Which I might when I get bigger. But at the Bell I mainly go on Friday nights with Charly and Marly. Which I already told. And the movies at the Bell are not scary or about rocket ships. They are about a lot of things. Like one time there was the movie about Old Yeller. Who was a dog. And who Travis finished off in that movie where I cried almost all night after it even if I didn't want to. Even if I hate to cry! And in this other movie this other time there was a group of big kids. Eighth graders. Or maybe even in high school. Where some of them were nice.

And some of them weren't nice. And the ones who weren't nice always wanted to fight with the nice ones. Except the nice ones didn't want to fight. And so the ones who weren't nice hanged a dead chicken by the neck on the door of one of the nice kids. Because they said he was chicken. And then somebody drove a car over the edge of a cliff. I didn't cry after that movie. I was just thinking about whether when I get bigger if any kid I know will be a kid who is not nice.

Anyways, that's the kind of movie that we see at the Bell on Friday nights. Different kinds of movies. About people doing things. Pretend people doing pretend things. Like Henry said.

After Charly got our tickets from the lady in the flowery dress and then we got some popcorn and then we found some seats and then the lights went out, I closed my eyes sitting on my soft seat at the Bell that didn't squeak. I like being in the dark waiting for the movies to start. And if I want it to be even darker, I just close my eyes. It's as dark as can be. And in the darkest dark, sitting next to Charly, I was thinking about if I was going to know when it was about fifteen minutes after the movie starts. Because that's when I was supposed to go and meet Henry in the balcony.

Just then, I heard some music in the dark. Which I knew right away it was cartoon music. For instance, Bugs Bunny this time. Who I like a lot! And then, after Bugs Bunny ran away about a thousand times from the man who always tries to get him about a thousand times, the movie started.

Which was very slow at the beginning. Because it was not about some old man who played games on his knee. It was about a lady who wanted to go to China! Except everybody told her not to. Everybody told her it was not a good place for her. And also they told her she wasn't good enough to go there. When the pretend people in the movie talked, everybody talked like they were from Australia. Which my Aunt Audra is from too. Except the lady who wanted to go to China. Who talked a little like my Aunt Anna. Who I don't know where she is from.

And, after a while, even if everybody told the lady not to go to China and that she wasn't good enough to go there, the lady went there anyways! This happens a lot in the movies at the Bell. It's always some pretend person who wants to do something. For instance, play baseball for the New York Yankees. Like I do! And everybody tells the person not to do the thing they want to. Which is play baseball for the New York Yankees. Because the person isn't good enough to. But the person who wants to play baseball for the New York Yankees does it anyways. Which makes the pretend person feel good in the movies. And which makes us feel good too in the Bell. Just like the brothers who wanted to fly the first airplane. Or just like the man who wanted to go into outer space in a rocket ship. Or just like Peter Pan who wanted to stay a boy forever. Or just like Pinocchio who wanted to become a real boy one day. Everybody told them not to do it. Not to try to play baseball or fly an airplane or go into outer space or stay a boy forever or become a real boy one day. Everybody told them they weren't good enough to do any of that. But they just do it anyways!

Just like the lady who wanted to go to China. She worked hard for a man and got some money and then bought a ticket to go to China. Which was when the movie was slow at the beginning. Because the lady bought a ticket for a train. Not an airplane. So, it took her a very long time to get there. And when she finally did get there, in this place in China, all the people there looked like Mister Lee. And all the people in the movie who looked like Mister Lee looked different from me. And all the people in the movie who looked like Mister Lee looked different from Henry too. Who looks almost exactly like me! The people in the movie all had black hair and they all had eyes that looked like they were closed. Even when they were open! It was in their blood. The way my wavy hair was in my blood, their eyes looking like they were closed was in their blood. Which is what Daddy said. About my hair. Not about their eyes.

I whispered to Charly, "Why do all of those people have black hair, Charly? Why do their eyes look different?"

"They're from China," Charly said back in a very low voice.

"Where's that, Charly?" I said back in a very low voice too.

"You remember when your daddy was in Korea?" Charly said back again. I nodded. "It's by there."

Right then in the movie a man lifted up a big knife to chop off another man's head. So, even if I knew it was pretend, I closed my eyes anyways. I only heard a lady scream. In the movies. Not at the Bell.

Then, after I opened my eyes again, while I was watching the movies with Charly at the Bell, looking at all the people in China who looked different from me, I was thinking about how at school last year at the end of first grade for spring festival my Mother had to wear some black hair on her head, which her hair is not black, and she had to put yellow paint on her face, which her face is not yellow, and she had to put black paint on her eyes to make her eyes look like Mister Lee, which her eyes do not look like Mister Lee. Because my Mother and some other ladies at the school were singing a song about China and pretending that they were from China too. Like all the people in the movies are from China. Except my Mother and the other ladies were just pretending.

And then when in the movies a man told the lady that all of the people in China were afraid of her because she was white, I was thinking too about how Henry said his daddy thinks white people are dangerous. And I was thinking too about how, at the same time as my Mother and the other ladies pretended to be from China at school last year at the end of first grade for spring festival, some men put black paint on their faces, which their faces were not black, and white paint on their lips, which their lips were not white, and put black hair on their heads too, which their hair was not black, because the men were singing a song about ne-gro people and pretending that they were negro people. Like Henry is a negro.

And while I was watching the movie, I was thinking that if at school for spring festival somebody wanted somebody from China to sing a song about China, all they had to do was ask Mister Lee and the lady who works sometimes in his laundry to do it. And then no ladies like my Mother would have to put on black hair or yellow paint on their faces or black on their eyes.

And I was thinking too if at school for spring festival somebody wanted somebody who was a negro to sing a song about negro people, all they had to do was ask Henry's father and mother to do it. Even Henry too! And then no men would have to put black paint on their faces or white paint on their lips or black hair.

Right in our neighborhood we have people from China and negro people, so we don't have to pretend like they do in the movies.

Then in the movie a soldier started talking to the lady and I remem-bered I had to quick go and see Henry in the balcony. "Charly, I have to go," I said.

Charly put her hand up to my mouth. "Talk lower," she said back. "Go where?"

"The bathroom," I said back. I wasn't lying. I was just pretending. Like Daddy says. Like my Mother does when she puts on black hair and yellow paint on her face and black on her eyes. My Mother isn't from China. She just pretends. I didn't have to go to the bathroom. I was just pretending.

"Okay," Charly said back. "Hurry back! You don't want to miss the movie." Which I didn't want to. Even if I did miss it.

I waited until it was lighter in the movie so I was able to see how to get back up the aisle to the door and into the lobby. Which I did. Then I had to go upstairs to the balcony from there. I wasn't able to stay in the lobby without buying some drinks or food. The man behind the counter was going to tell me to either go home or go back into the movies if I didn't. And Henry wasn't even allowed to be in the lobby! So, I waited until the man's back was turned and then I ran over to the side of the Bell where the stairs go up to the balcony. There is a door by the stairs that goes outside. So that the people who go up into the balcony have a separate door they come in. Who are the negro people. They don't have to come in the glass door I have to use that's in front of the Bell. They have a special door just for them. And it's right by the stairs to the balcony. Which is their special place to sit. Just for them. And I can't even go there because, like Henry's daddy said, I'm white and so everybody will think I'm dangerous. Even if I'm not! But I don't want to scare anybody in the balcony. So, when I got to the top of the stairs, I just sat down on the floor with my back to the side wall of the Bell so nobody can see me there.

Where I was sitting, I was too low to see over the top of the balcony rail. So, I wasn't able to watch the movies. But I was able to watch all of the negro people in the balcony while they were watching the movies. It was funny to see everybody laugh all at the same time or sometimes cover their eyes all at the same time or sometimes make a noise all at the same time. If something was funny or scary or surprising. I was able to hear the lady talk the way my Aunt Anna talks and to hear the people from China talk the way Mister Lee talks, which I can't even write how Mister Lee talks, and to hear everybody else in the movie talk Australian. But I wasn't able to see anything except the faces of all of the negro people in the balcony watching the movies. Which sometimes their faces were lighted up by the movies and sometimes their faces were very hard to see in the dark. Even if I had my eyes open as far as I was able to open them.

I looked at all the faces in the balcony at the Bell and was trying to find Henry. Who is small like I am small. So, I wasn't able to see him anywheres without standing up and just facing away from the movie and looking at all of the faces. Which is what I did.

"Hey, son!" a man in the balcony said. "You can't be up here! You have to go back downstairs."

And a lady sitting by him said, "Shhhh! What's that boy doing up here? Tell him to go downstairs with his kind."

It was true what Henry's daddy said. People were thinking I was dangerous. Which I am not! "Son," the man who talked first said again. "You can't stay here. You just can't, son."

But then I looked up into the balcony rows right when the movie lighted up the whole Bell, and I saw a boy stand up and start walking by other people. "Excuse me, sir. Excuse me. Excuse me, ma'am," he said in a low voice. It was Henry!

"I'm just waiting for my friend," I said back to the man who said I can't stay there. I pointed up the balcony. "He's coming now."

I heard the lady sitting next to the man say in a low voice, "His friend? He ain't got no friends up here. Tell him to go back where he belongs." I know that's not the way to talk. But that's what she said.

Henry came over to me and said, "What took you so long, California?"

"You boys go on now!" the man said again.

"Nothing but trouble," the lady sitting next to him said again.

"Let's go down the stairs a little," Henry said.

While we were walking down a few steps on the stairs, I said back, "I think they all think I'm dangerous, Henry. Like your daddy said."

"They just don't know you, California," he said back. We were about half the way down the stairs when Henry said, "Let's just sit here." Which we did. On one of the steps. "The man in the lobby won't let us talk down there," he said again. "What did you find out?"

"I talked to Jimmy Broom," I said back.

"The boy who got run over?" Henry said back.

"Right," I said back. "The policemen went to his hospital to give him a red top."

"Jake and Mack?" Henry said back. I nodded. "What for?"

"Maybe to talk to Jimmy to find out if he knows anything about the car that hit him," I said back again. "But his daddy didn't let him talk to them at the hospital. He just took the top."

"Did he see the car that hit him?" Henry said back. I shook my head. "Or the people in the car?" I shook my head again.

"He was out," I said back. "He didn't see anything after he ran into the car."

"So, what about Buck the barber?" Henry said back again.

"I think people give him money to bet on horses," I said back. "I know Daddy does. Daddy gives Buck money to bet on horses when he goes to his barber shop for haircuts."

"How do you know that, California?" Henry said back.

"Because on Tuesday I saw Buck the barber give Daddy some money at the baby cows' head shop."

"The what?" Henry said back.

"The disgusting meat shop," I said back.

"The what?" Henry said back.

"Where they sell liver!" I said back again.

"I love liver!" Henry said back again.

I made a face. "The meat shop on Bayou Road across from the Tri-angle."

"We can't go in there," Henry said again. He pointed at his arm. "Any-ways, he comes to my house too."

"My daddy?" I said back.

"No!" Henry said. "Buck the barber. Buck the barber comes to our house, California."

"Buck goes to your house?" I said back. "Do all the people on your street think he's dangerous too? Like me?"

"Buck came to see my daddy last night," Henry said back.

"He did?"

"People on my street come to our house and talk to my daddy," Henry said. "And then my daddy talks to Buck the barber."

All the people on Henry's street are negro people. "They do?" I said back.

Henry nodded and said, "And I think people give my daddy money that my daddy gives to Buck the barber to bet on horses."

"They do?" I said back. "I mean, he does?"

"Because the people on my street can't go to the barber shop," Henry said again. And then he pointed at his arm again.

"Maybe that's what Jimmy Broom's daddy is doing too. Maybe that's why the light is on at their house all night and they don't ever sleep," I said back. "Like my Uncle Roger says."

Then, Henry said back again, "Buck the barber told my daddy last night to meet him tomorrow morning at the playground."

"Stallings Playground?" I said back.

Henry just said back, "I don't know what it's called. The one across from where the horses race. Where they have baseball fields and a big swimming pool." Henry pointed across the street. "The one over there."

"That's Stallings," I said back. "I took swimming lessons there last summer."

"I heard Buck tell my daddy to meet him there tomorrow morning," Henry said again. "My daddy kept asking Buck about his friend over on Columbus Street."

"What friend over on Columbus Street?" I said back.

Henry just shrugged. "I don't know, California. I just heard my daddy say that. But Buck just kept saying it's none of my daddy's business."

The whole time we were talking I was able to hear people talking in the movies. But I wasn't paying attention to them. And then I quick heard a noise that wasn't from the movies. "You two! You! What are you two doing up there?" I looked down and saw the man from behind the candy counter standing at the bottom of the stairs. He pointed at me. "You can't go up there, son!" Henry and I quick stood up and started walking down the stairs from the balcony. Then the man pointed at Henry. "And you can't come down here!" he said again. "What are you two doing up there?"

Henry and I just kept walking down anyways and were almost on the bottom step when I heard a man with a froggy voice say out loud, "Move over, buddy!" And then I saw a hand push the man from behind the candy counter out of the way. "Out of my way, buddy. Police business," John Smith said again. He quick grabbed my polo shirt with one of his hands and pulled me down to the lobby. And at the same time he quick grabbed Henry's polo shirt with the other one and pulled Henry down to the lobby. "We've been looking for these two wise guys all night!"

Fourteen, or Stallings Playground

The way I know about Stallings Playground is for four things.

First, it is right across the street from the Fair Grounds. Which is the horse race track where I always go with Daddy after he comes back home from work and before we eat supper. And when Daddy and I are walking to the Fair Grounds, I can always see from across the street the baseball fields with kids running around the bases and throwing balls around the field. And I can see basketball courts with bigger kids running and bouncing the ball up and down and throwing it in the air at the basket. And I can see the big swimming pool where in the summer everybody is usually standing in line getting ready to go into the locker rooms, one for boys and one for girls, where they can change their clothes and then get into their swim trunks and then take a shower before they go into the pool and then jump into the water from the sides and even from the high dive. Which is at the deep end! And from across the street when Daddy and I are walking to the Fair Grounds, I can always hear all the kids making a lot of noise when they're doing all that.

And when I see and hear all the kids at Stallings Playground, I think maybe they wish they were going to the horse race track with their daddy instead of playing ball or swimming. But then sometimes I think maybe I wish I was playing ball or swimming instead of going to the horse race track with Daddy. Even if I like going to the horse race track with Daddy a lot!

Second, Stallings Playground is where Daddy took me last summer after first grade to learn how to play baseball. Which I already knew how to do. But, Daddy says I can do better if I practice. Daddy always says practice makes perfect. And I want to be perfect if I can be. I want to be perfect in golf in my back yard by getting the ball to go into the hole in just one shot. I want to be perfect using Marly's writing machine at Aunt Gwendolyn's house by writing as many times as I can without any mistakes now is the time for all good men to come to the aid of their party. And I want to be perfect in baseball at Stallings Playground by catching every ball that Daddy throws or hits to me and hitting every ball that Daddy pitches to me.

So, last summer when the horse race track was closed, instead of going to the Fair Grounds, Daddy and I walked over to Stallings Playground across the street to practice baseball. I always had a baseball. Ever since I was a baby like my baby brother is a baby. And I always had a glove and a bat. Ever since I was little like my little sister is little. I even always had a uniform with the number seven on it. Like Mickey Mantle. Who is the best baseball player ever!

Third, all my older cousins talk about Stallings Playground all the time. Like I already told, my Mother has a lot of brothers and sisters. Who all had a lot of kids like my Mother had kids. Except my Mother's brothers and sisters, almost all of them, had a lot more kids than my Mother had. Which is just me and my little sister and my baby brother. So, like I already told, I have a lot of cousins. And a lot of my cousins are a lot older than me. Like my Uncle Roger. Who is not my uncle but is really my cousin and who is older than my Mother.

And because my Grandpa who is dead and my Grandma who is dead lived in the same neighborhood where we live now when they were not dead, all of their kids, who are my Mother and my aunts and my uncles, lived too in the same neighborhood when they were little. And because all of my aunts and my uncles lived too in the same neighborhood after they got bigger and had kids too, all of my cousins lived too in the same neighborhood when they were little. So, when my cousins who are a lot older than me like my Uncle Roger were little, they all used to go to Stallings Playground too. So now, whenever all my older cousins are together, they always tell stories about things that happened at Stallings Playground when they were little. Which was when they went there all the time.

For instance, one time my Uncle Dingle, who like my Uncle Roger is not my uncle but is really my cousin, said his brother Earl, who is also my cousin that knew a guy at Sugar Bowl stadium when we went with

Daddy to a football game, fell off of the high dive at the deep end of the pool at Stallings Playground and missed the water and fell on the ground and cracked his head instead. Which Daddy says is true. And also for instance, one time my Uncle Roger when he was talking to Daddy and me said he was able to hold his breath under the water in the pool at Stallings Playground for ten minutes when he was little. My Uncle Roger did. Which was why my Uncle Roger said he was able to swim across the Mississippi River. Which Daddy says is not true.

And the fourth way I know Stallings Playground is because it's where my Mother took me last summer after first grade to learn how to swim before I was even seven years old. Because of Pepe's sister being missing when we all went swimming at the beach.

When we lived in California, we used to go swimming at the beach. Which was usually with Daddy and my Mother and my little sister who was my baby sister then and with my friend Pepe and his family. Who used to live next door to us the way Lenny Mahoney lives next door to us now. Except Pepe's house was the same house as our house the way my Uncle Roger's house is the same as Jimmy Broom's house. Where there is just a wall between the houses, with separate doors. There was just a wall between our house and Pepe's house, with separate doors. Pepe was almost exactly like me. The way Henry is almost exactly like me. Which is also because all three of us have little sisters. Who hop around and wave their little arms in the air all the time. Me, Pepe, and Henry.

So, this one time in California, we were all at the beach swimming. Which means me and Daddy and my Mother and my baby sister and Pepe and his family. Which was his daddy and mother and little sister. This was when the way I used to swim was just me standing in the water and holding onto Daddy's hand and trying not to get knocked down by the waves that were rushing on the beach. Which were two times bigger than me! I didn't put my face in the water when I was swimming then. Except by accident. Because sometimes the waves were so big they knocked me down and then Daddy let go of my hand because it was wet and then I went under the water for a little while and the water got in my nose and made my eyes itch. Which I didn't like. But that's the only way I knew how to swim when we were in California. Which I know now is not even swimming at all!

And because my little sister was so small, Daddy and my Mother didn't even let her go anywheres near the water. Because she was not even my little sister then. She was still my baby sister! And my Mother said if my baby sister fell in the water like I sometimes did when I was swimming with Daddy she was going to wash out into the sea and get lost forever. My little sister. Not my Mother. And even maybe die! So, my Mother didn't let my baby sister get anywheres near the water because my Mother was afraid she might get lost forever. It wasn't my Mother being dramatic. It was something that happens!

I know it was something that happens because one day while we were all swimming at the beach in California, before anyone even knew it, Pepe's baby sister was missing. Because nobody was paying attention. Because no one was observant. And then Pepe's baby sister was gone. And no one was able to find her. It was an accident.

The sun at the beach was falling down into the water. And everybody was running up and down in the sand on the beach looking all over the place for Pepe's baby sister. Who was missing. I ran up and down in the sand on the beach too and was looking all over the place for Pepe's baby sister too. Because I wanted to be the one who was able to find her. I wanted to be the one who helped. But we looked and looked and looked and the sun was falling down and down and down. Which was into the water. Just like Pepe's baby sister.

Except the sun was going to come back the next morning even if it was gone at night. And Pepe's baby sister was lost forever.

After a while, Pepe's mother was being very, very dramatic. She was screaming and crying and shaking while we were all running up and down in the sand on the beach looking all over the place for her baby girl. Who was Pepe's baby sister. And who was only able to walk the way my baby sister was able to walk then. Which was not very good. Which was falling down a lot.

While I was running up and down in the sand on the beach, I was thinking if Pepe's baby sister fell into the water the way I fall into the water sometimes when the waves are so big that they knock me down and then Daddy lets go of my hand because it is wet and then I go under the water for a little while and the water gets in my nose and makes my eyes itch, then she was going to stay in the water. Pepe's baby sister was not going to be able to get out. If she fell in the water, she was going to wash out into the sea and get lost forever. Like my Mother said.

Then the sun fell all the way into the water at the beach in California. The waves were making a lot of noise when they rushed up on the beach. Everyone was getting tired. After running around for a long time, my Mother just sat down on a blanket in the sand holding my baby sister very tight in a blanket that she wrapped around her and cried a lot. I didn't know why my Mother was crying. She just kept holding my baby sister and saying, "My baby. My baby girl. My precious baby girl." Over and over and over again she said that. "My baby. My baby girl. My precious baby girl." While me and Pepe and Daddy and Pepe's daddy were still running up and down in the sand on the beach looking for Pepe's baby sister. And Pepe's mother too. Who was still screaming and crying and shaking. Pepe's mother was making even more noise than the waves did when they rushed up on the beach.

While I was running up and down in the sand on the beach in California, I saw the blue sky near where the sun fell all the way into the water was turning to be orange and pink colors. And too I saw a few clouds over the water near where the sun fell all the way into the water were turning to be blue and purple colors. It was the most beautiful sky I ever saw! I can close my eyes even now and still see how beautiful it was. And I said to Daddy while we were running up and down in the sand on the beach, "Look, Daddy! Look at the sky!"

Daddy only said back, "It's just a sunset, Vonny." Which it wasn't. It was the most beautiful sky I ever saw! Even if Pepe's baby sister was lost forever. And Daddy just kept running up and down in the sand on the beach and running in the waves that were rushing on the beach. He didn't even look at the sky.

"Look, Mama!" I said. "Look at the sky!" I said again to my Mother while she just kept holding my baby sister very tight in a blanket that she wrapped around her. "Look at the sky, Mama!" But my Mother didn't say anything too. She just kept crying. She didn't even look at the sky too. Just like Daddy.

It was getting dark on the beach in California. And I was getting tired from running up and down in the sand on the beach looking for Pepe's baby sister. I wanted to find her. But she was lost. Pepe's baby sister was lost forever.

So, because I was so tired from running up and down in the sand on the beach, I finally just sat down and looked at the sky near where the sun fell all the way into the water. I looked at the orange and pink and blue and purple sky. Which was getting less orange and pink and more blue and purple. I never saw a sky more beautiful than that one. Which was far away over the water. Where Pepe's baby sister was lost forever.

Sitting on the beach in the dark, I listened to the noise of the waves rushing on the beach. Which are so big that sometimes they knock me down and then Daddy lets go of my hand because it is wet and then I go under the water for a little while and the water gets in my nose and makes my eyes itch. And I was very sad while I was sitting on the beach and looking at the sky and listening to the waves. Because my Mother was crying. And because Pepe's mother was screaming and crying and shaking. And because Daddy and Pepe's daddy and even Pepe were still running up and down in the sand on the beach. I was very sad while I was just sitting down and looking at the most beautiful sky I ever saw, which was more and more purple and black, and listening to the noisy waves and to Pepe's mother screaming.

And while I was just sitting down in California because I was tired from running up and down in the sand on the beach, I felt somebody start rubbing the hair on top of my head. I thought it was Daddy. Because he does that all the time. Daddy likes to mess my hair up so that he can put grease in it and then comb it again so it looks like his hair used to look when he was a boy. It's what my little sister does to her baby doll. She messes up its hair so that she can put curlers in it and then comb it again so it looks like her hair.

But it wasn't Daddy. Because I heard a voice. It was a baby voice like the baby voice my little sister had when she was my baby sister. Which was when we were in California. And the baby voice that I heard while I was sitting down in the sand on the beach just looking at the most beautiful sky I ever saw and listening to the waves said only, "Pepe! Pepe! Pepe!" Which was all she was able to say. Because she was a baby!

I quick turned around. And when I saw her, I quick stood up too, the now dark black sky behind me, the waves rushing on the beach behind me. "Daddy!" I screamed. "Daddy! Daddy!" It was Pepe's baby sister! Who she thought I was Pepe. Which was why she was rubbing the hair on the top of my head. Because we look almost exactly alike. Like me and Henry do. So, Pepe's baby sister thought I was Pepe. She wasn't lost forever! I quick took her little hand in my hand. "Mama! Mama!" I was screaming. But nobody was able to hear me because of the noise the waves made when they were rushing on the beach. And nobody was able to see me too. Because it was dark now. "Daddy!" I said out loud again. "Mama!" Pepe's baby sister kept falling in the sand. Because she didn't walk so good. Which was the way my little sister used to walk when she was my baby sister.

When finally Pepe's baby sister and I got back to where my Mother was sitting in the sand on the beach holding my baby sister very tight in a blanket that she wrapped around her and crying, my Mother saw me and then saw Pepe's baby sister and then started crying even more. Which made my baby sister start crying. And which made me start crying too.

And then Pepe's daddy came over with Pepe. And they saw Pepe's baby sister and saw us all crying and they started crying too. And then Pepe's mother finally came over, still screaming and crying and shaking. And she saw Pepe's baby sister and saw us all crying too and she cried more than anybody and held her precious baby girl the way my Mother was still holding her precious baby girl. Who is my little sister.

And then Daddy came over last. And he saw us all. Which was Pepe's baby sister too! And I saw Daddy rub his eyes with the back of his hand. The way I do when I don't want my Mother to know I am crying.

Everybody was crying. Everybody was crying except Pepe's baby sister. Who was not lost forever!

Anyways, because of Pepe's baby sister being missing when we all went swimming at the beach in California, after we moved to Columbus Street near where my Mother and her brothers and sisters lived when she was a little girl, my Mother said I had to take swimming lessons at Stallings Playground. So if we ever go back to the beach in California again, I won't get lost forever. Which at first I wanted to take swimming lessons at Stallings Playground. But then I didn't want to. Which was after my Uncle Dingle told about how my cousin Earl fell off of the high dive at the deep end of the pool at Stallings Playground and missed the water and fell on the ground and cracked his head instead. Because some kid in school told me that part of the swimming lessons at Stallings Playground is at the end you have to jump off of the high dive at the deep end of the pool!

"Maybe I can just learn how to swim with you and Daddy," I said to my Mother the morning last summer after first grade that I was supposed to go start my swimming lessons at Stallings Playground.

"We can do that too, if you want," my Mother said back. "We can go to Pontchartrain Beach with Daddy. But this way, Vonny, you'll get a swimming badge too." My Mother likes badges. She like badges more than I do even. "I can sew it on your swim trunks. And besides," my Mother said again, "Marly and Charly are swimming teachers at Stallings Playground." Which they are. They teach kids how to swim. "So, you'll be able to learn how to swim with your big cousins."

Which was true. That was why at first I wanted to do it, why at first I wanted to take swimming lessons at Stallings Playground. Because Marly and Charly teach kids how to swim there. And then when I heard my Uncle Dingle tell the story about his brother Earl, who is my cousin that knew a guy at the Sugar Bowl stadium, falling off the high dive and missing the water and falling on the ground and cracking his head instead and when I heard the kid at school talk about the high dive at the deep end of the pool, I didn't want to take swimming lessons at Stallings Playground. Even if I might get lost forever if we ever go back to the beach in California again!

But because my Mother is smarter than I am and because sometimes she doesn't leave well enough alone, even if I didn't want to take swimming lessons at Stallings Playground, I did. And I did have to jump off of the high dive at the deep end of the pool like my cousin Earl. But I didn't fall off the high dive or miss the water or fall on the ground or crack my head instead. While Marly and Charly were watching, I just climbed up the ladder and then walked out on the platform and then jumped off and then landed in the water at the deep end and then got a lot of it in my nose which made my eyes itch.

So, that's the four ways I know about Stallings Playground. Because of going to the horse race track across the street with Daddy, because of baseball practice last summer with Daddy, because of my older cousins always talking about it, and because of swimming lessons last summer with Marly and Charly.

And knowing about Stallings Playground is how I can tell about what happened after John Smith and Pocahontas found me and Henry Friday night in the movies at the Bell.

When John Smith saw us on the stairs to the balcony at the Bell, he grabbed my polo shirt with one of his hands and pulled me down to the lobby. And at the same time he grabbed Henry's polo shirt with the other one and pulled Henry down to the lobby. "We've been looking for these two wise guys all night!" he said in his mean, froggy voice. "Let's go you two. I had enough of the both of you!" That's the way John Smith talks.

Pocahontas was with him too. And they made us quick walk through the lobby and then past the candy and popcorn counter and then out the door and past the lady in the flowery dress in the little room at the front of the Bell where she sold tickets. "Police business, Ma'am," John Smith said to her. "Show her your badge, Mack." Which Pocahontas did while he was walking in front of her. It was still a little light outside. But it was getting darker. The black Pontiac was parked on the street right in front of the Bell. With its little yellow indian head on front and its Sportsman's Paradise license plate with its pelican bird and the numbers 3 and 6 and 7 and 4 and 7 and 4 on it. Just like the way I just wrote it.

"How did you know we were at the Bell?" I said while Pocahontas was opening the back door of the black Pontiac.

"There's not much we don't know, kid," John Smith said. And then he pushed me into the car. "And what little we don't know I can find out easy enough." And then he pushed Henry into the back seat of the car too. "I have a way of making people talk even when they don't want to. And that's what I plan on doing tonight. Which is find out what you know that I don't know!"

While John Smith was pushing me and Henry into the back seat of the black Pontiac, Pocahontas walked around to the other side of the car and got in behind the wheel where the driver sits. "But who told you we were here?" I said back again out loud.

John Smith leaned through the back door into the car, reached under his coat, and then held it open. "Look here, kid," he said. I saw a little black and blue gun in a holster under his coat. "Take a good look at it," he said again. "You and your punk friend there!" Only he didn't say punk. "Don't even think about jumping out of the car or trying to run away again." I looked at the gun and then at John Smith and then at Henry. Who did the same. Except he looked at me. "You may be able to run faster than us. But you won't run faster than this!" Which was the gun.

John Smith made me mad. I knew I was supposed to leave well enough alone. Especially with John Smith having a gun. But I said back anyways, "What kind of policeman will shoot a kid?"

Pocahontas said, "We better get moving, Jake. We can't stay here in front of the movies. It's still light out. She's staring at us." Which was the lady in the flowery dress. Who was looking at the black Pontiac.

"I'll tell you what kind of policeman will shoot a kid?" John Smith said. "Me! I am the kind of policeman who will shoot a kid. So, don't make me have to use it." And then he closed his coat, closed the back door of the black Pontiac, and then turned and waved at the lady in the flowery dress in the little room at the front of the Bell where she sold tickets. "Kids!" is all he said to her. "We have to bring them back home." Which was not true! Because Henry and I can walk. But then, after he opened the front door and got in the front seat of the black Pontiac, John Smith turned around, looked at me and Henry, and said, "Your little friend you call Jimmy Broom told me you were here tonight, kid." Which Jimmy is not little! He's in the second grade like me. "We just had a nice visit with him and his pop." Just like Red calls his daddy.

"You mean Jimmy's daddy?" I said back.

"I don't mean his mother, kid," John Smith said back. He turned back around and said to Pocahontas, "That old lady is giving us the evil eye, Mack. Let's get out of here." Which she was. And which Pocahontas did. But instead of making a right turn onto the street that goes to Broad Street, Pocahontas drove straight across and went on the street next to the part of Stallings Playground where there were a few big kids playing basketball. Just a few. Because it was getting dark. "So," John Smith said again. "We're just going to drive around a little and you're going to tell me everything you know about who ran over your little friend you call Jimmy Broom."

While I was trying to figure out what to do next, I was looking at Henry. It was scary. "Are you really a policeman?" I said back.

"You saw our badges, kid," John Smith said back. "You saw my gun too, didn't you? You don't think this is a police car? It's black, ain't it?" I hope my Mother doesn't read this part. But that's the way John Smith talks.

"Then why did you punch Buck the barber in the stomach for no good reason?" I said back. "And why did you chase us all the way to the Trinity Congregation Church? And why do you always call Henry a punk?" Except I said punk and not the worse word that John Smith uses instead.

John Smith turned back around and looked at us. "Because Buck deserved it. Because you deserved it. And because your friend Henry here is a punk!" he said back out loud. Except he said the worse word that he uses and not punk instead. Then John Smith turned back around and faced the front of the car. "Any more questions, kid?"

Pocahontas turned the black Pontiac again onto a street that was on the other side of Stallings Playground from the street where the horse race track is. "Sure," I said back. "Why did you want me to go cow with you last week at the Triangle?" I said back again. "You weren't even looking for me then. You just saw me getting a roast beef poor boy."

"The best roast beef poor boys in the whole wide world! Right, kid?" John Smith said back. "I heard you talking about living on Columbus Street," he said again while he was turning around. "Where you get cigarettes for your maw at Bruno's. And I just wanted to know what you know about who ran over your little friend you call Jimmy Broom. Because I'm a policeman, remember?"

"So, why didn't you just ask me questions?" I said back. "Instead of making me go cow!" I was mad.

"Hey, kid!" John Smith said back. "I didn't make you do anything. I asked you if you wanted to go cow with me. Because I wanted to show you I'm a good guy," he said again. "Because I am a good guy."

"But you're not!" I said back. "You're not a good guy!" When I said that, Henry held a finger up to his lips and shook his head. Like he wanted me to be quiet. "He's not going to hurt us, Henry!" I said back. "What kind of policeman shoots a kid?"

John Smith turned around again and looked at me and then Henry. "Listen, Mister know it all! Vonny Foster." He stopped for a second and turned to Pocahontas. "What kind of name is Vonny anyways? It sounds like a girl's name to me." Then he turned back to me. "Your punk friend here probably knows people that were shot by policemen, don't you, punk?" Except he didn't say punk again. Henry just nodded his head. "I figured as much. So, don't think you know everything, Vonny."

"It's a boy's name," I said back out loud. Henry started laughing.

"Doesn't Vonny sound like a girl's name to you, Mack?" John Smith said again. And he started laughing too. John Smith and Pocahontas and Henry were all laughing at my name.

"That's why I call him California," Henry said, while he was laughing.

Then John Smith said in his mean, froggy voice, "Who asked you to talk, punk?"

"I don't think you're a policeman!" I said out loud. "I think you're just pretending. I think you and Pocahontas are bad men. Like on the TV programs."

"Are you a bad man, Mack?" John Smith said. "I mean, Pocahontas?" Who just shook his head. "Are you just pretending to be a policeman?" Pocahontas just shook his head again. "Or are you just a policeman investigating an incident where a seven year old boy was run over by a black Pontiac ten days ago, Pocahontas?" Who just nodded his head. "There you have it, Mister know it all!" John Smith said again. "We're just two policemen investigating an incident. Now it's my turn to ask the questions."

While John Smith was saying this, I was thinking about Sam the policeman in my Grandpa's book and about him trying to find the guy who ran over his wife when she was running for the bus. Except Sam the policeman and his wife and their little children and even the lady with the cigarette in her hand and one long leg crossed over the other beneath a smart red dress and long auburn hair and bright green eyes were all pretend people. Like the ones in the stories Henry likes to read. Made up stories. Not stories about the war or about sports. But pretend stories about people who are just pretend people. Not real people. But instead pretend stories about pretend people doing pretend things.

And I was thinking how, instead, John Smith was not a pretend person. I know what's pretend and what's not pretend now. Because I pay attention. I'm observant. And John Smith was not pretend. He was sitting in the front seat of the black Pontiac talking to me and to Henry and to Pocahontas. Who too was not pretend. And the black Pontiac was not pretend. And John Smith had a little black and blue gun in a holster under his coat. Which was not pretend too. Everything about John Smith was not pretend. So, why did I think he was a pretend policeman or that he was only pretending to want to know everything I know about who ran over my little friend I call Jimmy Broom?

"Okay," I said back to John Smith. "Ask me some questions and I'll tell you all the whys and the wherefores."

When I said that, Pocahontas started laughing while he was driving on the street behind Stallings Playground. "Shut up, Mack!" John Smith said out loud. "There's nothing funny about this kid. Him and his whys and his wherefores. He ran out on us twice already. He thinks he's a wise guy." Which I don't even know what that means. "He thinks he's smarter than we are." Which I know what that means. Except I don't.

"Can we go home now?" I said.

"Not until you tell me what I want to know," John Smith said back.

"So," I said back, "what do you want to know?"

Pocahontas was driving the car very slow on the streets behind Stallings Playground, on the other side from the Fair Grounds. It was almost dark. John Smith said, "Do you know what your little friend Jimmy Broom's paw does for a living?"

"I don't know what that means," I said back. Which I didn't.

"It means do you know where he works?"

I said back, "I think he fixes tires. Right in front of his house. In a red truck that is parked there a lot. On Columbus Street." Which is true.

"Do you ever see people coming to his house?"

"My Uncle Roger said he does," I said back. "Who lives next door."

"What does your Uncle Roger say?" John Smith said back.

"He's not really my uncle," I said back. "He's my cousin."

"Then why do you call him uncle?" Pocahontas said back.

"Because he's older than my Mother," I said back. "My Mother has a lot of brothers and sisters. And."

John Smith didn't let me finish. "I don't care about your maw's brothers and sisters!" he said out loud. "Why do I even care about what your Uncle Roger says?"

"He's not really his uncle," Pocahontas said back.

"Shut up, will you, Mack?"

"Well, he's not," I said back. "But my Uncle Roger even lives exactly next door to Jimmy Broom and his daddy."

"Okay, kid," John Smith said. "So, what does your Uncle Roger, who is really your cousin, say?"

I said back again, "He says the light is always on all night at that place, at Jimmy Broom's house, people coming and going all night, even before the incident."

"You mean when this kid you call Jimmy Broom was run over?" John Smith said back.

"Right," I said. "I even sleepwalked there one time. But I don't remember if the light was on or not. It was the night after Jimmy Broom got run over."

"Do you know why the light is always on all night?" John Smith said. "Why people are coming all night?"

I just shrugged. "My Uncle Roger didn't say why," I said back. "I just know what he said."

"I think they were betting," Henry said.

"Who asked you, punk?" John Smith said back right away. But then he said again, "Wait! What did you say, punk?"

Henry said again, "I think they were betting."

"What do you mean betting, punk?" John Smith said back.

Henry shrugged. "You don't know what betting is?" he said back.

"Of course, I know what betting is, punk," John Smith said back. Except all those times he was not saying punk. John Smith was saying something worse. "Betting on what, punk?"

"I think horses racing," Henry said back.

"What makes you think that, punk?" John Smith said back again.

Henry didn't say anything at first. He just looked at me and shrugged again. And then Henry just said back again, "Because people come to my house all night too."

"How do you know that, punk?" John Smith said back.

"Because I see them," Henry said. "Because I hear them." Because Henry pays attention. Because he's observant. Because he's like me!

"So, punk," John Smith said, "do you think your paw is doing the same thing as Jimmy Broom's paw? Taking bets from people, I mean?"

"I don't know what Jimmy Broom's daddy does," Henry said back. "I just know what my daddy does."

"And you think he's taking bets from people?" John Smith said back. Henry just shrugged and nodded.

"Buck the barber takes bets from people too!" I said again.

John Smith turned around. "How do you know that?"

I didn't want to tell him about how Daddy's thing happened last Tuesday and how Buck the barber saw him from down the block when we were walking to the baby cows' head shop. Which is the same as the disgusting meat shop. Or how Buck the barber pulled two white envelopes from his pocket and handed one to Daddy and the other white envelope to the man behind the white case at the baby cows' head shop. Or that there was money in the white envelope. So, I just said back to John Smith, "Why were you punching Buck the barber in the stomach for no good reason last Tuesday?"

Then John Smith said something out loud that I can't even write. It's worse than anything he ever said. He was saying a lot of bad words. And he made a fist with his right hand and hit the inside of the black Pontiac in front of him very hard. Very, very hard! So hard that Pocahontas stopped the car. "Keep this car moving!" John Smith said out loud. "You want them to run again, you dope!"

Pocahontas just was driving the car slow after John Smith said that and even didn't stop when he came to stop signs. And then nobody said anything after I asked John Smith why he was punching Buck the barber in the stomach for no good reason last Tuesday. John Smith didn't say anything. Or Pocahontas. Or even me or Henry. We were just all driving around and around and around in the black Pontiac on the same four streets in a square behind Stallings Playground while the sky was getting darker and darker and darker. Lights were coming on in the houses and people were sitting outside on their porches and some kids were even playing stickball in the street at one of the corners. Even if it was dark. I even saw Bobby Robby playing pitcher.

And that's all we did for a long time. Just drive around in a circle. Which was really a square. We did that for so long that we were driving through the corner where the kids were playing stickball five or six times. Which was not the same corner by Bruno's. This one was closer to Stallings Playground.

After a while, after we were driving around and around and around for a long time with nobody talking, John Smith said something in a very low voice I wasn't able to hear. Pocahontas said back, "You say something, Jake?" And then John Smith said it again. But nobody heard what he said again. Or nobody knew what it was. Because what John Smith said was just a sound. He didn't say a sentence or even words or even letters. Or even one word or one letter. John Smith just said a sound. And it was a sound that made me think about the black and brown dog at third base on Columbus Street across from Bruno's. And then John Smith said it again. It was more like he was barking. And then he did it again. And then he did it out loud. And then he did it out loud again. And again. And then more out loud. And then more out loud again! And more and more and more! "Jake!" Pocahontas said out loud. "Jake! Calm down!"

John Smith said out loud, "Calm down?" He made a fist with his right hand again and hit the inside of the black Pontiac in front of him very hard again. "What I said, dope, is that these kids know too much!" Except when he said that, he said each word more and more out loud than the one before. "These! Kids! Know! Too! Much!" John Smith was very, very angry.

Just then, the black Pontiac was passing very slow through the corner again where Bobby Robby and some other kids were playing stickball. I was sitting on the side of the car where third base and home were. Henry was on the side where first and second base were. And when Pocahontas got to the corner he wanted to make a left turn like he did a lot of times before while we were driving around and around and around on the same four streets in a square behind Stallings Playground. Pocahontas wanted to turn between third base and home.

Except Pocahontas was looking where he was turning and in the dark he didn't see what Henry saw. Which was a kid who was quick heading to second base and looking like he was going to try to make it home instead of holding at third.

"Watch out!" Henry said out loud while Pocahontas was starting to turn left. "Somebody's in the street!" Which was true.

Pocahontas quick stepped on the brake after he turned. John Smith quick took the Lord's name in vain out loud. And the kid didn't hold at third and just quick ran home right in front of the black Pontiac. Where he scored!

"Shut up, punk!" John Smith said more out loud.

I heard Bobby Robby say out loud, "Watch where you're going, old man!"

"Who are you calling old man?" John Smith said back even more out loud. The car windows were open. And then John Smith opened his door to get out. Some other kids who were playing with Bobby Robby ran up to the car too and started calling John Smith an old man too.

Pocahontas said, "Where are you going, Jake? We better get moving. We can't stay here."

When all of this was happening a thought just popped into my head. Like an accident! Which was about what my Mother said when she was going to make me wear my cousin Dottie's red girl's Buster Brown shoes. To St. Rose de Lima Bean School! Which was, "Don't wait until you grow up to become who you are, Vonny. Be who you are now."

That's when I quick decided to be who I am now. And I quick opened the back door of the black Pontiac on my side and grabbed Henry by the arm. "Come on, Henry!" I said. We both got out of the car and started running. "Follow me, Henry!" I said again. We ran behind the black Pontiac onto the sidewalk and down the street the opposite way the car was pointed. John Smith didn't even see us because his back was turned when he was talking out loud to Bobby Robby and the other kids. Pocahontas heard us get out of the car. But he didn't even try to stop us. We were too fast. "Quick, Henry!" I said out loud. "I know where we can hide."

Which wasn't the Trinity Zion African Episcopal Methodist Congregation Church with a hole in the floor. It was Stallings Playground with a hole in the fence in the back by the place where kids play basketball. Even if Stallings was closed now and the fences were locked because it was dark. This time it was me leading Henry. Because I know Stallings Playground. Like I already told. Because of going to the horse race track across the street with Daddy, because of baseball practice last summer with Daddy, because of my older cousins always talking about it, and because of swimming lessons last summer with Marly and Charly.

I heard John Smith behind us saying out loud to Pocahontas, "Why did you let them out of the car, you dope? Let's go. Back up and go the other way." I heard the car door slam shut.

"This way, Henry." I turned right at the next street. We were only a block away from the back fence at Stallings, the one where there is a hole so you can get in even if it's after dark and the fence is supposed to be locked. We were running as fast as we can. But I knew John Smith and Pocahontas were going to catch up to us with the black Pontiac before we got there. "Let's go over here, Henry," I said. And we quick ran into an alley between two houses on the street. There was nobody on the porches. In the alley, where it was even darker than on the street, I said to Henry in a very low voice, "We can wait here until after they pass by in the car. Then, after they turn on the street up by the fence, we'll run for it." Henry just nodded.

That was what was supposed to happen. But here's what happened instead.

"What are you two boys doing out there?" a lady's voice said. "Get out of my alley. Get out of my alley before I call the police!"

I looked up at one of the houses the alley was between. There was a lady standing with her face in the window right above us. Who was older even than my Grandma who is living. Who was very skinny too. I didn't want to tell a lie. But I had to pretend. Or John Smith and Pocahontas were going to get us! So, I just put my finger up on my lips. "Please, Ma'am," I said back. "We're just playing hide and seek." Which was almost true. Except we were playing with adults. "We don't want to get caught, Ma'am." Which was true. Because the adults had guns!

The lady said back, "Is that boy a negro?" She pressed her face against the screen in the window to look at Henry. "Is that a negro in my alley?"

I pretended again. "Oh, him?" I said back. "He's just brown. He's my cousin Henry. My cousin from California." Henry started laughing. I have a lot of cousins I don't even know. So, he might be. Henry might be my cousin. I said again to the lady, "He's not a negro, Ma'am." Which was not pretending. "You're not a negro, are you, Henry?" He was still laughing.

"Police! Police! Police!" the lady started saying out loud. And then more and more out loud. "Police! Police! Police!"

"Let's go, Henry!" I said. "We can't stay here."

"Help! Help! Help!"

But when we ran out of the alley and back to the sidewalk, the black Pontiac was right out front. John Smith saw us and said out loud, "Stop, Mack! Stop!"

"This way, Henry!" I said again. I headed back the same way we just came from. So the black Pontiac was pointing in the wrong direction again. And when we got to the corner again, we turned left and ran back on the same sidewalk to the next corner where Bobby Robby was still playing stickball. "We have to go down one more street, Henry," I said. "They'll just come right back here looking for us."

When we ran by Bobby Robby, he said to me, "You want to play?" Which made us stop. Then he looked at Henry. "You know that kid?" he said to me. "What's he doing here?"

"He's my cousin," I said back again. I was out of breath. "They're trying to kill us!"

"Who?" Bobby Robby said back.

"The same guys who ran over Jimmy Broom!"

"No kidding!" Bobby Robby said back again. "Run that way." He pointed to the next corner where I told Henry we had to go. "We'll tell them you went back where you just came from."

"Thanks," I called back. Because we were already running when he said it.

Then I heard Bobby Robby say again out loud, "You know that kid?"

When we got to the next corner, I turned left and headed to the back fence at Stallings, the one where there is a hole so you can get in even if it's after dark and the fence is supposed to be locked. We were only a block away again. "I don't think I can keep running," Henry said.

"We have to, Henry," I said back. "We have to get through hole in the fence before they come back around." Which we did.

Like I already told, Stalling Playground has a very big swimming pool and two big baseball fields and about ten basketball courts. During the day and even at night in the summer there are always kids swimming or playing baseball or basketball. Stallings even has lights so you can do everything at night too.

But only in the summer. When it's not summer, at night a man puts a big chain and lock on the gate where everybody has to go in. Which is on the street across from the horse race track. Which is the Fair Grounds. So nobody can go in at night. And besides, even if you can get in at night when it's not summer, you can't swim because there is no water in the pool and you can't play any games because they don't turn on the lights. Except two little yellow lights that are by the locker rooms for the swimming pool. One at the door for the boys' locker room and one at the door for the girls' locker room.

Except on the street all the way on the other side of Stallings, the side that is not across the street from the horse race track, there is a hole in the fence that almost every kid knows about. Because some kids sometimes just want to go and play around at Stallings even if it's closed and there's no water in the pool and there are no lights. I never did it. But I heard some kids at St. Rose de Lima Bean School talk about it. Big kids. Eighth graders! About where the hole in the fence is. And about how you can get in there. "Where are we going?" Henry said when we got to the fence.

"Right here," I said back. "It's like the hole in the floor at your church." I held the fence back for Henry so he was able to crawl in. Down the block I saw the lights on a car coming at us. "Quick, Henry," I said again. "Hold this for me so I can get in." Which he did and which I did.

"What are we going to do in here?" Henry said back.

"What we did at your church, Henry," I said back. "We're going to hide until they just go away."

That was what was supposed to happen. But here's what happened instead.

Even if there wasn't any light at Stallings Playground, except for the two little yellow lights that are by the locker rooms for the swimming pool, when the black Pontiac reached the hole in the fence, Pocahontas backed up the car and pointed its lights at the baseball field where we were sitting down low. "They're going to see us," Henry said.

"Not so loud, Henry," I said in a very, very low voice. "Get down."

Then John Smith got out of the car and walked over to the hole in the fence. "Mack!" he said out loud. "There's something here. In the fence. See if you can cover the field with your headlights." Which Pocahontas did. He backed up the car so the lights were pointed inside Stallings Playground right where we were. "Maybe we can spot them in there."

Which they did! "Let's go, Henry! Follow me!"

"There they are!" John Smith said out loud in his froggy voice. "Stop!" he said more out loud. "Stop or I'll shoot!"

I was scared! But we didn't stop. And John Smith didn't shoot too.

Last summer, after I finished taking my swimming lessons, sometimes on Friday nights when I didn't go to the Bell or the Rivoli with Marly or Charly and when Daddy and my Mother didn't get dressed up and go to some movie with a bunch of other people, like my aunts and uncles and some cousins who are a lot older than me, and my little sister was at my Aunt Audra's house playing with my cousin Suzette who is little like my little sister is little, and we didn't have my baby brother yet, Daddy and my Mother and I used to go to Stallings Playground to go in the swimming pool. Sometimes we went just the three of us. And sometimes we went with some of my aunts and uncles and some cousins who are a lot older than me. After I jumped off of the high dive, I liked the Stallings Playground swimming pool a lot. It was a lot of fun to go there on Friday nights last summer with Daddy and my Mother.

But the thing I didn't like about the Stallings Playground swimming pool was the boys' locker room. And I didn't like it for three things. First, the floor was always slippery because everybody was always going into the pool and coming out of it and getting water all over the floor. Which was very shiny! And very slippery! And very hard! People were always falling and hurting themselves. Daddy even fell one time. And I fell one time and hurt my back. I didn't want to but I cried. I cried a lot. And I hate to cry! And also, in the boys' locker room is where you had to put on your swim trunks. Which means you have to take off your dungarees and polo shirt and underwear and socks and sneakers and everything else you're wearing. Right in front of a thousand other people in the locker room! Which I don't like. And last, after you change right in front of everybody and before you go into the Stallings Playground swimming pool, you have to take a shower in your swim trunks. Which Daddy says is so the water in the pool doesn't get dirty. But the shower in the boys' locker room at the Stallings Playground swimming pool is the coldest water anywheres. The water is so cold it makes your head hurt! Like when you put too much snowball in your mouth at one time. After you take a shower at the Stallings Playground, you're like the black and brown dog at third base across from Bruno's. Because your teeth are just clapping in your mouth!

Anyways, the one thing I liked about the boys' locker room at the swimming pool at Stallings Playground is there is a man in a little room who stands behind a counter and who, if you go up to him and ask, will give you a clean towel. So you can dry off by the swimming pool if you get too cold. Or when you want to dry off before you put all your clothes back on right in front of everybody again. He's a nice man. Who smiles at everybody. And the towels are nice too. They are clean and soft and white.

One time Daddy boosted me up so I was able to ask the man for a towel by myself. Which is when I saw the room where he works behind the counter. Which is big! Because there are a lot of towels. And there are big washing machines in there too. And there are big laundry baskets too. Which are almost as tall as me. And hold about a thousand towels each! And where in two of them the man takes out clean towels to give to people who are just going swimming and in the other two he puts back the dirty towels when people give them to him before they go home.

After John Smith didn't shoot, I ran over by the swimming pool. It was very dark. "Don't fall in, Henry!" I said.

"I know," he said back. "I don't know how to swim."

"Don't worry about that, Henry," I said back while we were running. "There's no water in there. You'll just crack your head if you fall in!" I turned around and saw that the black Pontiac was driving around the fence over by the basketball courts. John Smith and Pocahontas were too big to fit through the hole in the fence. Just like the hole in Henry's church! When the black Pontiac was pointed the other way, I said to Henry, "Quick! In here!" It looked like they were driving around to the gate on the street in the front of Stallings. Across from the Fair Grounds. Which was locked.

But the door to the boys' locker room was not locked. So, Henry and I quick went in. It was very dark. And we didn't want to turn on any lights because then John Smith and Pocahontas will know we are in there. Even if the gate in the front of Stallings Playground is locked. "What do we do now, California?" Henry said.

"We wait until we can see something," I said back. Which if you wait long enough in the dark you can see everything. Which is what Daddy told me one time when the lights didn't work at our house.

"You see anything yet?" Henry said back.

"Just wait," I said back again. "Besides, I know where everything is in here. Just wait."

It was very quiet in the boys' locker room. There was nobody there except me and Henry. So when the car pulled up to the gate out in front, Henry and I heard it.

"It's them," Henry said. "What do we do?"

"We wait," I said back.

"For what?" Henry said again.

"Okay," I said back. "I can see now. Can you see me?"

"Sure," Henry said back again.

We walked across the locker room to a window by the street where the car just pulled up. I heard somebody pushing the gate out in front of Stallings Playground. "We know you're in there!" John Smith said out loud. "Don't make us come in to get you!"

"It's got a chain and lock on it," Pocahontas said in his squeaky voice.

"So?" John Smith said back. "Stand back." And then I heard a very loud bang. Bang! Like a gun. "That does it!" he said back again.

"They're coming in!" Henry said.

"Follow me, Henry. Let's go in here." I went over to the door to the big room where the man works behind the counter who gives out and takes back towels. Where they have washing machines. And laundry baskets. And lots of towels. "Get in here," I said again.

"Where?" Henry said back. It was even darker in the big room.

"Here!" I said back again. I grabbed Henry's hand and put it on the top of the laundry basket. "You see here? Can you feel that? Climb into this basket. It's full of clean towels. Get under them and try not to mess them up." Which Henry did. But I didn't see if he didn't mess the towels up. "Put the towels on top of you, Henry. And be very quiet," I said in a very low voice. "Very, very quiet."

I did the same thing. I climbed into the other basket that was full of clean towels. And I got under them. And I tried not to mess them up. Which I didn't. Just before I put the last clean towels over the top of my head, I heard a click and saw the lights go on in the boys' locker room.

"Here's the switch," John Smith said in his froggy voice. I heard his shoes making noise on the shiny, hard floor in the boys' locker room. It wasn't slippery because it wasn't wet. Then I heard somebody else's shoes making noise too.

"You think they're in here?" Pocahontas said in his squeaky voice.

"Where else are they going to be, dope?" John Smith said back.

"I don't know, Jake," Pocahontas said. "This is starting to get out of hand. People in the neighborhood are going to call in a gun shot."

"What's getting out of hand is those kids," John Smith said back. I heard him walking back where the showers were. "They know too much now," he said again. "The kid saw me working Buck over right on Bayou Road. And they know he's taking bets from the neighborhood. From that Jimmy kid's pop. Even from the punks up the street." Except he didn't say punks. "What's this over here?"

I heard John Smith knocking on the piece of wood that sometimes covers the counter when the man who gives out and takes back towels is not there. Which he was not there then. Because it was not summer. "Some kind of counter, it looks like," Pocahontas said. "Probably another room in the back. There's a door over there."

I heard somebody open it. Which was the door Henry and I used. "Well, look at this!" John Smith said back. "I guess everybody gets a towel at this place. No wonder the city don't have enough money for extra pay for honest cops." Which John Smith is not a honest cop. And I hope my Mother doesn't see that I wrote that. I heard his shoes walking around the room where the washing machines are. And walking around the laundry baskets. Which were in the middle of the room. He even touched the bottom of the laundry basket I was in with the bottom of his shoe. "There's a lot of towels in here, Mack. You think anybody will miss them if I take home a half dozen to the little lady?"

There was a siren outside. "You hear that, Jake?" Pocahontas said. "Everybody in the neighborhood heard you shoot the lock off."

"Because I don't have a key, you dope," John Smith said back. "What are you worried about? We chased some bad guys in here."

Which Henry and I are not bad guys. We're just kids!

"They're coming our way," Pocahontas said.

"Let them come," John Smith said back. I heard another car pull up to the gate out in front of Stallings Playground. "Listen," he said. "This place will be perfect for our meet. Do Buck and the others know?" John Smith said again.

But Pocahontas didn't say anything back. Instead, somebody else ran into the boys' locker room. "Hi, Dudley," Pocahontas said in his squeaky voice.

"How's tricks, Dudley?" John Smith said in his froggy voice. Whatever that means. "You can put that back in your holster," he said again. "There's no one in here except us good guys." Which is not true!

"A woman at the Bell thought she heard a gun shot," another man said. "A couple other calls came in too. They sent me over to check it out."

"We spotted a couple of punks on Broad Street," John Smith said. Except he didn't say punks. "Looked like they were up to no good." Which is how he talks. "So, we followed them, they saw us, and then they took off."

"Somebody busted the lock," the other man said.

"More like the punks shot it off," John Smith said back. Which was not true! "That's probably the gun shot that got called in, Dudley." Which was true! "We saw the busted lock. So, we came in and took a look around. But there's nothing here but a bunch of towels." Which was not true too!

"We need to get going, Jake," Pocahontas said.

"Sure, Mack," John Smith said back. "Can you close this up here for us, Dudley? Turn off the lights, will you? Chain the fence." John Smith laughed. "And shoot the first punk you see?"

"Well, okay," the other man said back. "You guys go ahead. I'll close it down."

I heard their shoes on the shiny, hard floor, first walking out of the room where Henry and I were, and then to the door of the boys' locker room at Stallings Playground.

"I wonder if they let punks swim here," John Smith said while he was walking out of the boys' locker room. "What do you think, Mack? First, they make you go to school with them. Then, they make you swim with them." And then I heard John Smith take the Lord's name in vain.

Fifteen, or Mid-City

It was my Mother who was always teaching me about how to read when we were in Florida and then mostly in California after that. Like I already told. Because my Mother reads all the time! Which are always stories about mysteries. Like for instance about Sam, the policeman who used to be married to a pretty lady that died because she was run over by a car and killed in an accident because she was in a hurry to catch the bus and to get to her house to cook supper. Just like Jimmy Broom! Except Jimmy was just trying to make it home instead of holding at third.

And it was Daddy who was always telling stories. Like I already told. Because Daddy tells stories all the time! Which are always stories about when Daddy was a boy the way I am a boy now. Like for instance about his uncle, the one who said that if a horse messes on the race track right before a race you have to bet on him because he's going to win. The horse. Not Daddy's uncle. Just like Satnohacop! Except Daddy already bet on Satnohacop before he messed on the race track right before the race.

And Daddy always tells stories that make you laugh. Like for instance also, he told about the guy at his work who went fishing and got another guy's fishhook caught in his nose. And how they just kept fishing anyways. That was funny! It always makes everybody laugh.

Except when Daddy tells stories, even if it's the same story he already told, he always changes it a little. He tells the same story. But it's not exactly the same story! Every time Daddy tells a story, he tells about it in a way that is not exactly like the way he told about it before. It's the same story. Except it's different. And then sometimes when Daddy tells a story, he tells about it in a way that is not at all like the way he told about it before. It's the same story. Except it's almost all different. Which means it's not the same story.

So, one time I said to Daddy after he told about the man who got the other man's fishhook in his nose, "But, Daddy, the last time you told that story you said that the two men were fishing on a boat. And this time you told the story you said that they were fishing from a bridge over Bayou St. John. Were they on a boat or a bridge, Daddy?"

Daddy just said back, "Vonny, my boy, who cares where they were fishing? Who cares if they were on a boat or a bridge? It's the fishhook in the guy's nose that matters. And that they kept fishing anyways."

"But, Daddy," I said back, "where were they really when the man got the other man's fishhook in his nose? Were they fishing on a boat? Or on a bridge? Or maybe even somewheres else? Like at City Park maybe." Which is where Daddy takes me sometimes for the fishing rodeo.

Daddy just shrugged. "How do I know, Vonny, my boy? It's just a story about two guys fishing."

"But, Daddy," I said back, "if you know the story about the two men fishing, don't you know where they were? Don't you know what really happened? Don't you know whether the two men were fishing on a boat or from a bridge over Bayou St. John? Or somewheres else? Don't you know the truth, Daddy? The truth about what happened?"

Daddy just said back, "Who knows what the truth is, Vonny, my boy?" He rubbed the top of my head the way he always does. Then he said to me in a low voice, "Let me tell you a little secret, Vonny, my boy. Sometimes, it's only by telling the story, it's only when you tell the story, that you figure out what the truth is. Who did what to who and where." He rubbed my head again. "And how and why they did it."

"The whys and the wherefores?" I said back.

Daddy laughed. "That's right, Vonny, my boy," he said back. "The whys and the wherefores."

"You mean it's like pretending?" I said back again.

Daddy shook his head. "It's not pretending, Vonny, my boy," Daddy said back. "It's just letting the story tell itself." Then Daddy laughed again. "It's getting out of the way and just letting the story tell itself."

Whatever that means!

Anyways, on Saturday afternoon, the day after Henry and I were hiding all Friday night under piles of clean towels in laundry baskets in the boys' locker room at Stallings Playground, I sat down after lunch to finish my confession list. Which Sister Marianna said we had to do by Monday because we have to do our first confession this coming Thursday.

In class one time, Sister said a good way to figure out if you did any bad actions or said any mean words or thought any impure thoughts was to write down the ten commandments and then read each of them over and over and over again and then think about if you did. Which is what I did Saturday afternoon after I came back home with Daddy from getting some roast beef poor boys at the Triangle for him and my Mother and me, and from getting a haircut for my First Communion at the barber shop on Bayou Road. Which Daddy and I did all on the walk back from Stallings Playground. Where I was hiding all Friday night under a pile of clean towels in a laundry basket in the boys' locker room.

Like Sister said in class that one time, after all that and after Daddy, my Mother and I ate the roast beef poor boys for lunch, on Saturday afternoon I wrote down the ten commandments and looked at each of them over and over and over again. And I thought about whether I did any bad actions or said any mean words or thought any impure thoughts.

1. I am the Lord thy God, who brought thee out of the land of Egypt, out of the house of bondage. Thou shalt not have strange gods before Me. I wrote this down exactly the way it looks. Except it's colored red in my catechism and I don't have a red pencil. Thy and thee and thou mean the same thing as you. Which is what Sister said. And shalt means shall. Which means the same thing as will. Which is what Sister said too. It's the way people used to write those words before they learned how to write. Like the way I used to write etiquette like etiket before the spelling bee on Friday when Louie won. Anyways, this commandment is easy. Even if I never went to Egypt. Because I believe in the only one God. Which means I don't believe in any other ones. Even if they are strange or not. Sister Marianna said that a long time ago people used to believe in lots of different ones. Gods that were able to fly real fast. Gods that looked like animals. Gods that lived in the forest or in the sky. Gods that lived everywhere except at the St. Rose de Lima Bean Church. But, I only believe in the only one God. Who lives at the St. Rose de Lima Bean Church. Which is close to our house. Which is where the only one God really lives. Except maybe sometimes the only one God visits the Trinity

Zion African Episcopal Methodist Congregation Church too. Like I did with Henry!

2. Thou shalt not take the name of the Lord thy God in vain. This is what people do whenever they say God's name in some way that is not praying. Which I just did. Except it's when you say God's name in some way that is not praying and when you are angry or mad. Which I did not just do. But which John Smith did all the time! It's like when people say "Jesus!" except they are not praying to Jesus when they say it and they are angry or mad. I never say God's name unless I am praying or unless I am telling about not using the name of the Lord in vain. Which is what I just did!

3. Remember thou keep holy the Sabbath Day. Sister Marianna said Sunday is the same as the Sabbath Day. Which is why we go to Mass on Sunday too. For instance, it doesn't count if you go to Mass on every day of the week except Sunday. It doesn't count if you go to Mass on Monday or Tuesday or any of the other days. Even if you do. Like we do on First Friday. You have to go to Mass on Sunday or it goes on your confession list. And keeping holy the Sabbath Day also means you can't work on Sunday. Which I don't ever do anyways. Because I don't ever go to work on any day. Because I'm not old enough to go to work! Even if I am in the second grade. Except sometimes my Mother makes me do my homework on Sunday. Which one time when I asked if doing homework on Sunday wasn't the same thing as working on Sunday, my Mother just said back that doing homework is another way to keep holy the Sabbath Day. Like I already told, my Mother is smarter than me!

4. Honor thy father and thy mother. Sister Marianna said this means I am supposed to be nice to Daddy and to my Mother. Which I am. All the time! I run errands for them almost every day. For instance, when I run errands to get cigarettes for my Mother at Bruno's. Or when I run errands to the Triangle to buy a roast beef poor boy for Daddy or my Mother. Or when I go to the horse race track with Daddy. Because he doesn't like to go alone. Or, also for instance, when I play games with my little sister or when I hold my baby brother while my Mother is talking to one of my aunts in the kitchen and drinking coffee and smoking cigarettes. I honor my whole family!

5. Thou shalt not kill. On the TV programs, this is the commandment that people always do not listen to. On the TV programs, people

kill people all the time. On the TV programs, indians kill cowboys. And then cowboys kill indians back. Soldiers kill other soldiers. And then some more soldiers kill the other ones back. Policemen kill bad guys. And then bad guys kill policemen back. No one on TV programs listens to this commandment. Someone is always killing someone else! Or killing them back! But I tried to think if I know anybody who killed somebody or who even just got killed. And I don't know anybody who killed somebody. Or anybody who even just got killed. Except Jimmy Broom almost got killed because of John Smith. Which if Jimmy Broom was killed because of John Smith, this is the commandment John Smith will have to put on his confession list. Thou shalt not kill Jimmy Broom!

6. Thou shalt not commit adultery. Sister Marianna said this commandment is a mystery. So, we don't have to learn about it in second grade. Which makes me think that we will probably learn about adultery in third grade maybe. I think it means when a kid tries to act like an adult. For instance, if you are in the second grade and you try to smoke cigarettes like my Mother does. Which Red one time tried to do in the alley by our house. Who is Lenny Mahoney's cousin from Florida. Except he choked himself! Or also for instance, if you are in the second grade and you try to drink beer from glasses like the crocodiles do at Bruno's. Which Mister Bruno will never let me! Or also for instance, if you are in the second grade and you try to bet on horse races at the barber shop like Daddy does and like Henry's daddy does and like Jimmy Broom's daddy too. Which I only do at the Fair Grounds when I go cow with Daddy. So, even if it's a mystery, I don't think I ever committed adultery. I'll find out for sure probably next year in third grade maybe.

7. Thou shalt not steal. Sister said this means you can't take something from somebody without paying for it. Or at least telling them you took it. For instance, if I take a visible person from Burdine's without paying five dollars and ninety five cents for it. Plus tax! Which I did pay for it. I paid for two of them. Which is one of the ways how I got into trouble last week. But if I just took the visible people instead of paying for them or if I just took one visible person instead of paying for it, then I will have to put this commandment on my confession list. Which I don't have to. Because I paid for the visible man. And the visible woman too. Which I already told.

8. Thou shalt not bear false witness against thy neighbor. Sister Marianna said this is the same thing as telling a lie. And even if it says neighbor in the commandment, it's not just telling a lie about your neighbor. So, even if I didn't tell any lies about Lenny Mahoney, who is my neighbor on one side, or about my Uncle Roger, who is my neighbor on the other side, I still have to put this commandment on my list. A lot of times! Because of all the lies I made up. For instance, I already told about all the lies I had to tell starting with when John Smith asked me to go cow with him. And I already told about all the lies I had to tell after that. Which were not just pretending like Daddy says some lies are. The lies I told were not just pretending. They were just not true! While I was thinking about this commandment over and over and over again on Saturday afternoon after lunch, I practiced my confession the way Monseigneur Deutsch told us. "Bless me, Father, for I have sinned. I was bearing false witness about a thousand times!"

9. Thou shalt not covet thy neighbor's wife. One of our neighbor's wifes is my Aunt Anna who lives with my Uncle Roger and has two little girls. And the other one is Lenny Mahoney's mother who lives with Lenny and his daddy and his big sister and his little sister and his baby brother. Who was just born at almost the same time as my baby brother. Sister Marianna said that this commandment is something we will maybe talk about again when we are in seventh grade in time for confirmation. But I'm pretty sure it won't be a problem even then. When I will be very big. Too big to be a jockey. Because I am always nice to my Aunt Anna. And to Lenny's mother too!

10. Thou shalt not covet thy neighbor's goods. Which Sister says is not always just taking from your neighbor things that don't belong to you. For instance, it's not just me taking something from Lenny or from my Uncle Roger or from Jimmy Broom. Who lives next door to my Uncle Roger. This is the same thing as taking something from anybody when it's not yours. It's the same as commandment number seven. Except it's different. It's like when Daddy tells a story. It's the same story. Except it's different. When I asked in class one time what the difference is between this one and number seven about not stealing, Sister Marianna said this one is not just about stealing. Because this one is also about not thinking about stealing. Which is harder not to do. Because thoughts just pop into your head. You can't stop them! If I just think about taking a visible

person from Burdine's without paying for it, I have to put this commandment on my confession list. Even for just thinking about it! Which is an accident. Except I never even just think about stealing. Because I already have everything I want.

So, after reading the commandments over and over and over again on Saturday afternoon after lunch, my confession list was not very long after all. It was just this. "Bless me, Father, for I have sinned. I told a lot of lies!"

After I finished my confession list Saturday afternoon, I was tired. I was very tired. I wanted to take a nap. But I wasn't able to sleep because I kept thinking about how it's true what my Uncle Martin said, and Daddy too, about even if you are sure about what you saw, it's not always clear what the meaning is of what you saw.

Which was exactly what happened at Stallings Playground on Saturday morning after Henry and I spent the night there in the boys' locker room.

After John Smith and Pocahontas, and Officer Dudley too, went away on Friday night, I was too afraid to come out from under the pile of clean towels in the laundry basket. Just seeing John Smith's gun in the car made me too afraid to want to come out. And Henry was afraid too. That's what he told me Saturday morning after everybody finally found us. So, we didn't move even a little all Friday night. We just wanted to stay there, hoping somebody else will find us.

Before I fell asleep in the dark while I was hiding all Friday night under a pile of clean towels in a laundry basket in the boys' locker room at Stallings Playground, I was thinking about what Charly was thinking when the movie at the Bell was over and I wasn't back. After the movie was over, Charly probably looked for me all around the Bell. Under the seats where sometimes I used to hide when I was little. In the bathroom where I told her I was going. Maybe even in the balcony. And then, she probably thought I just got tired and went back home.

Then I was thinking too about what my Mother was thinking after Charly came back from the movies looking for me at home and then nobody found me there too. My Mother can be very dramatic sometimes. Which I can be too. I was thinking about what she told Daddy, "I told you we can't trust him! I told you all he does is lie now. We don't know what he got himself mixed up in." And then I was thinking about what my Mother told me about what kind of mother isn't going to be worried about their son who is out in the street after dark. Because my Mother is the kind of mother who is going to be worried about their son who is out in the street after dark. Which was me hiding all Friday night under a pile of clean towels in a laundry basket in the boys' locker room at Stallings Playground.

After it was all over on Saturday morning, Daddy said to me, "Well, since we're already out here, we might as well stop by the barber shop on Bayou Road and get your hair cut for your First Communion next week before we go home. We'll ask your Uncle Martin to let your mother know we found you."

"But, Daddy," I said back, "what about Buck?" Who was not going to be at his barber shop. Because Buck was in an ambulance on the way to the Hotel Dieu. Just like Jimmy Broom was last week. Except Buck was not run over by a black Pontiac.

"Somebody else will be there cutting hair," Daddy said back. "There's always another guy who works on Saturday. Because it's busy." I was thinking about Buck and what happened to him in the boys' locker room. Then Daddy said again, "And after your haircut we can stop by the Triangle and pick up a couple of roast beef poor boys for us and your mother."

I was very hungry. It was a scary morning! And I am almost always very hungry after I am scared. So, I said back, "Okay, Daddy." I wasn't tired then. I was excited about what happened.

"We can go cow on the pinball machine while we're waiting," Daddy said again. And then he just laughed and messed up even more the hair on my head. Which was already messed up from sleeping under the pile of clean towels in a laundry basket.

When Daddy and I were walking out of the boys' locker room at Stallings Playground on Saturday morning, even in the very bright light of the sun that was almost making me blind, I saw John Smith in the back seat of a police car on the street. A red light on top of it was blinking under the sun. And I also saw Pocahontas standing outside on the sidewalk by a big tree talking in his squeaky voice to another policeman. Who I saw he was a policeman because he was wearing a uniform. With a badge on it. And I also saw next to that policeman who was talking to Pocahontas my Uncle Martin. Who was also talking to another policeman. Who was the one who came into the boys' locker room at Stallings Playground with Uncle Martin. Who was the only one policeman that was really investigating what happened to Jimmy Broom. Who was Officer Dudley. Who was the only one policeman that Uncle Martin told about everything it was he saw when he was driving home from work on the day the black Pontiac ran over Jimmy Broom while he was trying to make it home instead of holding at third.

Also, when Daddy and I were walking out of the boys' locker room at Stallings Playground on Saturday morning, Henry and his daddy were standing behind the big fence that separates the baseball fields from the rest of the playground. They were standing like they were looking at an invisible baseball game. Except Henry was sitting on his bicycle. So, I figured somebody got it out of the back of John Smith's black Pontiac. When we walked by them, Henry and his daddy had their backs to us. Daddy said, "Well, I guess these boys did okay after all, didn't they?" Daddy laughed. But it wasn't funny. It was scary! Because John Smith had a gun.

Henry's daddy laughed a little too and then turned around. "Not without scaring us half to death first though," he said back.

Henry turned around and said, "I was scared, daddy." He saw me. "Hi, California!" Then Henry said again, "That's why we hid under the towels." Which was true. "It's a good thing Vonny was here before."

"I was scared too," I said. "Very scared! Especially when I saw John Smith's gun!"

Daddy got down on one knee. Like he was genuflecting at church. "Listen, Vonny, my boy," he said. "You're okay now. You and Henry are both fine. You boys don't have to worry about that guy anymore." And he waved at the police car where John Smith was sitting in the back seat. "He's going to a place where he can't hurt you. You two are the good guys." Daddy rubbed my head when he said that. And then he rubbed Henry's head too. "You play baseball too, buddy?"

"My name is Henry," he said back. "I like to play baseball," Henry said again. "I'm good at it too. But it's too far to ride my bicycle to where I can play. And my mother won't let me play in the street."

Daddy looked at Henry's daddy and said. "Are you going to sign him up here at Stallings for little league this summer?"

Henry's daddy just made a face. "Somewheres," is all he said back. Henry's daddy shrugged. "He'll play somewheres. Hope to see you around sometime," he said again. And then Henry's daddy turned around to look at the invisible baseball game again. But Henry's daddy said, "Hope to see you around sometime," like he was never going to see Daddy around ever again. Or see me around ever again too. It was sad the way Henry's daddy said he was going to see us around sometime. Like he was never going to.

Daddy and I started to walk away. "See you, California," Henry said. Except Henry said it like he was going to see me again.

"See you, Henry," I said back, looking over my shoulder. I thought about what my Mother was going to say when she finds out about Henry.

While we were walking toward the street between Stallings Playground and the Fair Grounds, I said to Daddy, "How did you know Henry and I were here, Daddy? Did Henry's daddy know? Did Henry's daddy come looking for him at our house last night? Or this morning?"

But Daddy didn't say anything back.

After everything was over Saturday morning, while Daddy and I were walking from Stallings Playground to the barber shop on Bayou Road, we first crossed the street near where the entrance to the Fair Grounds is. Where the "White Entrance Only" sign in black letters on a white board is. And then we walked under the big trees past the Bell at the corner and then around the bend in the road to Broad Street. Where at the corner on the left across the street I saw on one side Mister Lee's laundry and at the corner on the other side on the right I saw the hamburger shop where they have birch beer and at the corner in the middle I saw Burdine's right on Bayou Road. After we crossed over the wide street, we walked down the side where just across Bayou Road from the St. Rose de Lima Bean Church there is the barber shop where Buck used to work before he had to go to the Hotel Dieu in an ambulance.

While Daddy and I were walking from Stallings Playground to the barber shop on Bayou Road on Saturday morning, a thought popped into my head without me even trying. Which was again how my Uncle Martin said, and Daddy too, about even if you are sure about what you saw, it's not always clear what the meaning is of what you saw. And the thought that popped into my head was that it's also true about what you think too. Not just what you see. Even if you are sure about what you think, it's not always clear what the meaning is of what you think.

For instance, like I already told, I thought my first confession was going to be very hard to do because of everything Monseigneur Deutsch and Sister Marianna said about it and because of how long my list was going to be now that I did a lot of things I wasn't supposed to. When instead, confession is going to be easy next Thursday. Because I already told my Mother last Thursday almost everything about what I did that I wasn't supposed to. And now Daddy even knows everything about Henry and about John Smith chasing us all the time and everything I did to find out who ran over Jimmy Broom and why. And also, my confession list is not so long. I obeyed nine out of ten commandments! Which I already told about.

And also for instance, everybody at school thought that Louie Canale was a dope and a goofball because of the way sometimes in school he does dopey things and sometimes he says goofball things. Even I thought so. When instead, Louie is the best speller in the whole class! Better than me. Who used to always come in second. And better even than Sharon the Roach. Who used to always win. And especially when the words are very hard. Because that's the only one thing that makes Louie pay attention.

And also for instance, everybody thought that Jimmy Broom got a broomstick through his arm because of all the blood in the street. When instead, only his tibia was broken because he threw the broomstick down before he ran or while he was running and then tried to make it home instead of holding at third and then ran into the black Pontiac. Because he didn't see it. He ran into the black Pontiac himself! It didn't run over him. Which is why he didn't get killed and why John Smith didn't break the fifth commandment. It was an accident! It wasn't an incident.

And also for instance, everybody thought that Jimmy Broom was going to die at the Hotel Dieu because an ambulance took him there after he ran into the black Pontiac. When instead, Jimmy only just laid around in a hospital bed all week mainly eating ice cream and reading comic books and watching TV programs and having people tell him he was a good kid and a brave boy.

And also for instance, Daddy and Henry's daddy thought that me and Henry were very different because Henry lives on a different street where all of the other negro people live and I live on a different street where none of the negro people live. When instead, Henry and I are almost exactly the same because we are both skinny and not very tall and have brown hair and brown eyes and big, white new front teeth, and we both wear dungarees and polo shirts most of the time and wear bow ties and jackets on Sunday, and we both have little sisters who hop around all the time! Even if we don't go to the same school, Henry and I are almost exactly the same.

And also for instance, I thought John Smith was called John Smith because that's what he told me at the Triangle last Saturday. When instead, his real name is Jacob Mackenzie and everybody calls him Jake. And also, I thought John Smith was a bad guy because he was always asking questions about Jimmy Broom last Saturday and Sunday and chasing me and Henry around last Monday and punching Buck the barber in the stomach for no good reason last Tuesday, and then I thought he was a policemen because he told Daddy and my Mother and me that he was and then he showed us his badge last Wednesday. And then I thought John Smith was a bad policeman because he chased me and Henry out of the Bell and all over Stallings Playground last night. Which was Friday. And then I thought John Smith wasn't even a policemen at all when he pulled a gun out this morning in the boys' locker room at Stallings Playground and acted like he was going to shoot Daddy and Henry's daddy and Jimmy Broom's daddy too. And then when he really did shoot Buck this morning!

When instead, John Smith was just a very bad policeman. A very, very bad policeman! Who was betting all the time. Which I found out at Stallings Playground this morning with Henry and where everybody else's daddy was there too. And with Uncle Martin and the policeman he told about what he saw. And the other policemen too.

And also for instance, I thought Pocahontas was called Pocahontas because that's what John Smith called him at the Triangle last Saturday. When instead, his real name is Mackenzie Jacobs and everybody calls him Mack. And, just like John Smith, I thought Pocahontas was a bad man and then a policeman and then a bad policeman and then not a policeman at all.

When instead, Pocahontas wasn't anything I ever thought he was. Pocahontas was an agent. From the FBI! Who was investigating John Smith because he was a very, very bad policeman.

And finally for instance, everybody thought my Uncle Martin didn't tell the police about everything it was he saw when he was driving home from work on the day Jimmy Broom ran into the black Pontiac while he was trying to make it home instead of holding at third. Because my Uncle Martin didn't talk about it at all. Which is what I was thinking the whole time. I thought my Uncle Martin didn't want to have to talk about the whys and the wherefores. I thought he just wanted to leave well enough alone.

When instead, my Uncle Martin told the police everything he saw right away. All the whys and the wherefores. He didn't just want to leave well enough alone. But he didn't want anybody to know he didn't! Which was how all the good policemen came to Stallings Playground just in time on Saturday morning with my Uncle Martin. Who was supposed to be golfing at City Park again.

So, even if you are sure about what you think, it's not always clear what the meaning is of what you think.

When we got to the barber shop on Bayou Road, I asked Daddy again, "So, how did you know I was with Henry, Daddy? Who told you? Did Buck the barber tell you that too?"

Daddy just pushed the door in and all he said back was, "Sister Marianna. Now, get on in there!" Which I did. But I was thinking about how did Sister Marianna tell Daddy anything this morning.

And it was at the barber shop on Bayou Road that I got my first ever haircut from somebody that was not my Mother. Which was for my First Communion next week. Buck was in the ambulance on the way to the Hotel Dieu with a bullet in his leg. Which was probably his tibia. Which I know because of the visible man. And because of Jimmy's broken one. So, the man who cut my hair was not Buck. He was another man. Who I didn't know his name.

When we walked into the barber shop, Daddy said to the man, "You hear about Buck?"

The man nodded. He was very short. Not as short as I am short but as short as the jockeys who ride horses at the Fair Grounds are short. "A cop came by a little while ago," the man said back. "Flesh wound is what the cop said," he said again. Like I already told, a cop is what some people call policemen. I hope my Mother doesn't read this part.

"Daddy, what's a flesh wound?" I said.

"It means Buck is going to be okay," Daddy said back. "No broken bones like your friend Jimmy. Just a scrape."

"Except from a bullet," I said back.

"It's all the same," the man at the barber shop said. "But that kid's old man is a handful."

"You mean Jimmy Broom?" I said back.

"Hop up here," the man said to me. "I take it you're here for you, young man, since your old man just got a cut four days ago." Then he said again to Daddy, "The kid's old man don't pay his bills, if you know what I mean." Which I know isn't right. But it's how the man talked.

Daddy looked at the man, pointed at me, and then put a finger up to his mouth. "First Communion next week," Daddy said back.

The man whistled. "We'll give you the special then," he said again. But this time talking to me.

"What's the special?" I said back.

"Does he ever stop asking questions?" the man said to Daddy.

Daddy shook his head. "Not yet," he said back.

And then the short man gave me a boost up into the seat of the big chair where you sit to get a haircut. Once I was up there, he took a little white piece of paper and tucked it into the back of the collar on my polo shirt right by my neck. And then he took a big white cloth that looked like a sheet and wrapped it around my front and tied it in the back of my neck too. There was a mirror in front of me where I saw myself. Daddy was standing behind the man who was standing behind me. So, I saw Daddy too. "Anyways," the man said, "that Jimmy kid's old man is why Buck got behind. The guy owed him close to five hundred. How do you want this?" the man said again. He was looking at me in the mirror.

I just shrugged. My Mother always cut my hair before. But she never asked me how I wanted it cut. She just cut it. So, I just kept shrugging. Then Daddy finally said, "Just thin it out. He combs it back in a wave up front with a part on the left." Which I don't. But which Daddy does. Then Daddy said again, "Razor sharp on the edges though."

The man picked up some clippers like my Mother has and then looked at me in the mirror. "That's the special," he said. "Razor sharp!" Then he turned on the clippers so they made a buzzing noise the way my Mother's clippers do, and then he started to cut my hair just like my Mother does. Then the man said, "So, this Jake. He's a bad guy. A very bad guy."

"We know," Daddy said back. "Don't we, Vonny, my boy?"

"Supposed to be a cop," the man said again. "Some cop, right? Shaking down barber shops and such. And not a nice man. Not a nice man at all."

"I saw him last Tuesday punch Buck in the stomach for no good reason," I said. Like the man was talking to me.

"Don't move," the man said. He put his hand on my head. "Now, say that again, kid. But don't move when you do. Except your lips."

"I said I saw John Smith punch Buck in the stomach for no good reason last Tuesday," I said back.

The man turned the clippers off and looked at me in the mirror again. "Who's John Smith?" he said again.

"That's what he calls the dirty cop," Daddy said back. I hope my Mother doesn't see how Daddy talks sometimes. "He calls him John Smith."

"You don't say," the man said back while he was brushing hairs off of my neck and face with a little brush. "John Smith?"

"He calls the other one Pocahontas," Daddy said again. And he laughed.

"Really?" the man said back again. "John Smith and Pocahontas?" He took some scissors from the counter and a comb. "That's pretty funny. You're funny, kid. Even if you do ask too many questions." The man kept opening up and closing the scissors real fast. Like he was going to cut my hair. Except he didn't. Instead, he turned around to Daddy and said, "Say, Al. Did you catch that Satnohacop in the eighth the other day?"

"Did we catch him?" Daddy said. And he pointed at me when he did. "This guy went cow with me. We got him at eight to one. Only bet of the day! Two across paid thirty two bucks."

"Is that right?" the man said back. He looked at me in the mirror. "So, you play the horses too, Junior?" Which is what my Grandma who is alive calls Daddy.

"My name is Vonny," I said back.

"What grade are you in, Vonny? Third? Fourth? You look kind of small for fourth."

"Second grade," I said back.

"Oh, that's right," the man said back. "You're making your First Communion next week." He started snipping some hair with the scissors. "I forgot about that." Then he stopped again and said, "What a country! You catch an eight to one shot one week and make your First Communion the next. All I have to say is God bless America, Vonny. God bless America!"

Which I don't know if that's taking the Lord's name in vain or not. Because it's also the name of a song we sing sometimes at St. Rose de Lima Bean School. "Did you know that Satnohacop is Pocahontas spelled backwards?" Daddy said. Which turned out to be just an accident. In the mirror I saw Daddy pointing at me. "He figured that out all by himself."

"Why do you think I brought it up?" the man said back. He stopped cutting my hair again. And then he walked around in front of me. "But why do you call those guys John Smith and Pocahontas?" he said to me.

I shrugged. "That's what they told me their names were," I said back. Which was true. "At the Triangle last week. Where I met them."

"So," the man said, while he was pointing the scissors at me in the mirror, "if I tell you my name is Margaret, are you going to call me Peggy?"

Daddy started laughing. And I started laughing too. Then I said, "I'll call you Peggy if you want me to!" And I kept laughing. "Okay, Peggy?" I was laughing more and more.

The man looked at Daddy and said, "Don't you know we have too many wise guys in here already?" Which is what John Smith called me last night. And then the man messed up my hair. "Just for that, we're going to start over." Which he did. The short man was whistling while he was cutting my hair again. I saw Daddy sitting behind me in a chair looking at the newspapers. After a while, the man said, "So, what's your name again, kid? You got one, don't you?" I know it's not the way to talk. But it's the way the man talked anyways.

"Vonny," I said back.

"Did you say Donnie?"

"No!" I said back. "Vonny! Vonny Foster."

The man looked at Daddy in the mirror. Who was still sitting behind him. And then he made a funny face. "Sounds like a girl's name to me," he said back.

"Like Peggy?" I said back.

"Just what I need," the man said again. "Another wise guy!" Then he took a little brush out of a drawer and rubbed it on the back of my neck to get the hairs off. Which tickled! And then the man rubbed the same brush on my face and then started to take the white sheet off of me. "That's eight bits to you, Vonny," he said. "Six bits for the special and two bits for calling me Peggy."

Daddy stepped up to him. Who was the short man who cut my hair. "I'll take care of that," Daddy said. And he reached into his pocket to pay him.

Which is exactly what Daddy said this morning after he and Henry's daddy walked into the boys' locker room at Stallings Playground. Where there was already John Smith and Pocahontas and Jimmy's daddy and Buck the barber. Daddy said, "I'll take care of that," after John Smith said Jimmy's daddy owed Buck the barber five hundred dollars and Buck the barber owed John Smith one hundred dollars. Which is a lot of dollars!

"What's that punk doing here?" is what John Smith first said after Daddy and Henry's daddy walked into the boys' locker room at Stallings Playground looking for us. Except John Smith didn't say punk. He called Henry's daddy something worse. Like what he always called Henry.

"He's with me," Daddy said back.

"And what are you doing here?" John Smith said.

Daddy said back again, "Our sons went missing across the street at the Bell last night. One of the people who lives across the way said this morning that they saw a white boy and a negro boy run this way yesterday just after dark."

"You mean a white boy and a punk, right?" John Smith said again. Except he didn't say punk again. "So you being a punk lover decided to come over here with your punk friend to see if you can find your boy and this punk's punk kid?"

Henry and I were still under the piles of clean towels in two different laundry baskets in the boys' locker room at Stallings Playground. Where nobody was able to see us. And where we weren't able to see anybody too. Nobody even knew we were there. Then Henry's daddy said, "There's no reason to talk that way, Detective."

"You see this, punk?" John Smith said out loud in his froggy voice. "You think I can't shoot a punk like you just for fun? I got something right here says I can shoot punks like you whenever I want to." Which I know isn't right. But it's how John Smith talks. And then he said again, "I got it right here in my coat pocket. All I need is this and my badge."

Then Pocahontas said in his squeaky voice, "Jake, maybe this isn't the time. We know where to find Buck here. And this other one. All these guys want to do is find their boys. Maybe this isn't the time."

"Shut up, Mack!" John Smith said back out loud. "Either I get my hundred dollars from Buck here or Buck here leaves bleeding. And this guy with him." Who was Jimmy's daddy. Because then John Smith said, "And maybe even this punk lover here and his punk friend." Which was Daddy and Henry's daddy. Then John Smith said again, "You guys just walked into the wrong place at the wrong time looking for your boys."

That was when I jumped up out from under the pile of clean towels in the laundry basket I was hiding in all Friday night. "No, they didn't!" I said out loud. "We're here! We're right here!"

John Smith quick turned around to me. He was holding his gun. Which was pointed right at me. "Hey, buddy!" Daddy said out loud. "Put that thing away, will you?"

Then Henry jumped up out from under the pile of clean towels in the laundry basket he was hiding in all Friday night. "Daddy!" is all he said. Which meant his daddy. Not Daddy.

And all Henry's daddy said back was, "Henry!"

Whenever somebody said something, John Smith turned and looked at them and then pointed his gun at them. "Come on, buddy!" Daddy said out loud again. "Put that thing away, will you?" Which was now pointed at Daddy.

Henry and I were still standing in the middle of the laundry baskets where we were hiding all Friday night, where we spent the night after being pulled out of the Bell by John Smith and Pocahontas and chased by them around Stallings Playground. Buck the barber and Jimmy's daddy were standing right by us. Right by the laundry baskets. Where we were only able to see their backs. And they were standing right in front of John Smith and Pocahontas. Where we were only able to see their fronts. And Daddy and Henry's daddy were over to the side by the door to the boys' locker room at Stallings Playground. Where we were only able to see their sides.

"Let me tell you the whys and the wherefores," John Smith said in his froggy voice. He pointed the gun at Jimmy's daddy. "This stiff here owes Buck here five hundred dollars." Then he pointed the gun at Buck the barber. "And Buck here owes me one hundred dollars. And like I said, either I get my hundred dollars from Buck here or Buck here leaves bleeding. And this guy with him." Who was Jimmy's daddy.

Daddy stepped up to John Smith. "I'll take care of that," Daddy said. Just like he said to Peggy the barber later in the morning at Buck's shop. And then Daddy reached into his pocket. Just like he did later too.

Except John Smith pointed the gun at Daddy. Which Peggy the barber did not. "Get your hands up over your head where I can see them!" John Smith said out loud in his froggy voice. Which Daddy did.

"All I'm saying," Daddy said back, "is I'll take care of it." With his hands up over his head. "I have two hundred in my pocket here." Daddy looked down at his pocket. "Just take it. Take all of it. We're just here for our boys. You take the money and settle up with Buck and this guy later. After we're gone."

Later Saturday morning, after Daddy paid Peggy the barber and we left Buck's shop, Daddy and I walked down Bayou Road again on the same side past the dead chicken store across from Richard's Five and Dime, and then past the disgusting meat shop, which is the baby cows' head shop, across from the Buster Brown shoe store, and then across the street from Picou's Bakery on the corner. And then, after Daddy looked both ways and made me give him my hand, we walked catty corner across where Dorgenois and Bayou Road cross each other to the Triangle. Where they make the best roast beef poor boys in the whole wide world! Which is just across the K street from the Rivoli. Which is next door to the house my Mother used to live in with my Grandpa and Grandma who are dead now. And all her sisters and brothers. Who are my aunts and uncles.

When we were outside of the Triangle, I said again to Daddy, "Who told about me and Henry, Daddy?"

Daddy looked at me. "You have to talk to your mother, Vonny, my boy. One minute she finds the note from Sister Marianna in your book on your bed and the next minute I'm on the street in my pajamas knocking on doors in a negro neighborhood at three o'clock in the morning." Then Daddy just pushed in the door to the Triangle. "Let's get us some poor boys." Which we did.

The more very large lady who was there last week when I met John Smith and Pocahontas was not there anymore. Nobody was there. Except Larry the cook. Who when he saw me said, "Aren't you the kid who was in here buying cigarettes last week?"

"Are you smoking now too?" Daddy said.

I just shook my head. "For Mama, Daddy. They were for Mama."

"Oh," Larry the cook said. "You're the best roast beef poor boys in the whole wide world kid. I remember you. You won a few bucks off the pinball machine, didn't you?"

I just nodded. "He probably wishes he didn't," Daddy said back. "But you learned a lot in a week, didn't you, Vonny, my boy?"

Which is exactly what Daddy said this morning after my Uncle Martin and a policeman who was the only one policeman that was really investigating what happened to Jimmy Broom walked into the boys' locker room at Stallings Playground. Which was when Daddy was trying to give John Smith two hundred dollars that were in his pocket.

When he saw Uncle Martin and the policeman come into the boys' locker room, John Smith said, "What are you doing back here again, Dudley?"

The policeman was wearing a uniform with a badge on it. He was standing next to my Uncle Martin. Who was standing next to Daddy. Who still had his hands up over his head because John Smith was still pointing his gun at him. Then the policeman said to Pocahontas, "You want to do it, Mack, or do you want me to?"

John Smith looked at Pocahontas. Who looked at John Smith. Who now put his gun down so it wasn't pointing at Daddy. "You do it, Dudley," Pocahontas said in his squeaky voice.

"Detective Mackenzie," Officer Dudley said, "you're under arrest."

John Smith laughed out loud. "Under arrest?" he said back. "For what? For shaking down a barber and a bum!" He pointed his gun at Buck the barber and then at Jimmy's daddy. "Where's the harm in that, Mack?" He looked at Pocahontas.

"Attempted murder," Officer Dudley said back.

John Smith laughed out loud again. "I didn't shoot anybody," he said again. "At least not yet!"

"Attempted murder by motor vehicle of one James A. Brown, age seven, resident of Columbus Street," Officer Dudley said again.

"My Jimmy?" Jimmy's daddy said back. "It was you who run over Jimmy?" he said again. And then Jimmy's daddy ran at John Smith with his hands over his head like he was going to hit him. And then John Smith pointed his gun at him.

"Get down, Vonny, my boy!" Daddy said out loud.

Which I did. And which Henry did too. So, we didn't see anything else except I heard a lot of pushing. And then I heard a lot of talking out loud. And then I heard two gun shots. Which one hit the tile in the ceiling and broke it all up into little pieces that flew everywhere in the boys' locker room. And which the other one hit Buck the barber in his leg so that there was blood on the tile floor in the boys' locker room when finally Daddy came over and lifted me out of the laundry basket where I was hiding again.

"Are you okay, Vonny, my boy?" Daddy said.

"I think so, Daddy," I said back.

Uncle Martin walked over. I saw Pocahontas and Officer Dudley holding John Smith by the arms and pushing him out the door of the boys' locker room. I saw Buck the barber on the floor holding his leg while Jimmy's daddy was kneeling down by him and trying to help him stand up. I saw Henry and his daddy in a corner of the boys' locker room. Where Henry's daddy was hugging Henry tight and rubbing the top of his head and talking to him in a low voice. "You okay, my boy?" my Uncle Martin said. I nodded. "I guess you weren't able to leave well enough alone after all, were you?" he said again. I shook my head. "Well, you probably learned a lesson or two."

"He probably wishes he didn't," Daddy said back. Which is what Daddy said later at the Triangle. "But you learned a lot in a week, didn't you, Vonny, my boy?" Which is what he said later at the Triangle too.

Which I did learn a lot. Except I didn't learn everything. "So, Daddy," I said. "Did John Smith try to run over Jimmy Broom for no good reason?"

"Who's John Smith?" my Uncle Martin said. "The father of the kid who got run over?"

"That's what he calls the dirty cop," Daddy said back. "He calls the other one Pocahontas."

"Very funny," my Uncle Martin said.

"So, did he?" I said again. "Did John Smith try to run over Jimmy Broom for no good reason?"

"Some other man was driving the car," my Uncle Martin said back. "But the police think your John Smith paid him to try to scare the kid.

As a way to try to scare the kid's father. Who owed money to the barber. Who owed money to John Smith."

"So, John Smith did try to run him over!"

My Uncle Martin said, "It's not clear, my boy. The guy driving the car was drunk. At least that's what Officer Dudley told me. He says the guy said he was driving by just trying to scare the kid when the kid surprised him by heading for home instead of holding at third."

"What?" I said back.

"And so the kid just ran into the car," my Uncle Martin said again.

"What?" I said back again.

"That's what the guy says," my Uncle Martin said back again. "He told Officer Dudley that he thought the kid was going to hold at third when instead he headed for home and ran right into the car."

"Into the black Pontiac?"

"Into the black Pontiac," my Uncle Martin said back.

"He thought Jimmy was going to hold at third?" I said back.

"That's what the guy says."

So, that's why I think it's true what my Uncle Martin said, and Daddy too, about even if you are sure about what you saw, it's not always clear what the meaning is of what you saw. It makes me think I need to be more like the horses at the horse race track. It makes me think that I need to always pay more attention. No matter what! I need to be more observant.

After all that, after everything that happened, it was the black Pontiac that was hit by Jimmy Broom in front of Bruno's last Tuesday afternoon! And not the other way around. It made me think about what was in the newspapers last week. Which was not true. I was thinking what the newspapers were supposed to say.

New Orleans – March 6, 1959 – A vehicle was struck by a moving boy on the afternoon of Tuesday, March 3rd, at the corner of North Dorgenois and Columbus Streets in Mid-City.

The black 1956 Pontiac, operated by an unidentified male driver, was struck by James A. Brown, 7, a resident of Columbus Street. The boy is a student at St. Rose de Lima School.

The driver was questioned by police at the scene following the accident. Police are investigating.

Anyways, that's the whole story of what happened since then, since Jimmy Broom ran into the black Pontiac. And almost all of what I told about is true. Maybe not true the way my Mother and Monseigneur Deutsch think things are supposed to be exactly true. But none of what I told about that isn't exactly true has to go on my confession list. If I told about anything that isn't exactly true, it's just me pretending. Which Daddy says is not lying. It's like the kind of stories that Henry likes. Made up stories. Like the story about the boy and the girl where their families didn't want them to see each other. Not stories about the war or about sports. But pretend stories about people who are just pretend people. Not real people. But instead pretend stories about pretend people doing pretend things. Except almost all of what I told about is true. Except the part that is just me pretending.

And what part of what I told is true and what part of what I told is just me pretending is what my Mother and sometimes Sister Marianna calls a mystery. Like the Holy Spirit is a mystery. And like the sixth commandment is a mystery. Which is what Sister said when I asked her one day in class what is adultery.

Besides, I'm not always sure about what I saw. And even if I was sure about what I saw, like Uncle Martin said, and Daddy too, it's not always clear what the meaning is of what I saw. I'm big now and in second grade. But I don't see everything or even understand everything I see.

And if I don't see everything or even understand everything I see, that goes double for everything I think. Because thoughts just pop into my head. I can't help it. They just happen. Thoughts are like accidents, not incidents. And all I can do is write them down. Somebody else can tell me what they all mean. I just know what happened since Jimmy Broom ran into the black Pontiac in front of Bruno's.

Anyways, after I finished my confession list Saturday afternoon after lunch, my Mother asked me to watch my baby brother while she went to Bruno's to buy some cigarettes. She was wearing a summer dress because it wasn't too hot to put on a dress and it didn't take too long to put one on anyways.

So, I sat on the sofa in the parlor holding my baby brother while my Mother went to Bruno's. Instead of me. And while I was sitting with him and thinking again about everything, my baby brother started moving his head around, with his eyes for the first time always looking at my eyes. For the first time, my baby brother followed my eyes around with his eyes. The way the picture of Jesus does in the room where Daddy and my Mother and now my baby brother sleep. The way the horses at the Fair Grounds do when they are moving their heads up and down. For the first time, my baby brother was being observant!

I smiled at him while I was on the sofa in the parlor holding him. Then I kissed my baby brother on the forehead like my Mother does to me. He was like a little visible man. Except he had skin on. And some hair. But the rest of him was the same. With one of my hands I felt his little skull in his head. With the other one I felt his little tibias in his legs and then his little ribs. It tickled him when I touched his ribs because he smiled at me again. Then I felt his little chest and his little heart beating beneath his little shirt. Which was making blood go around his little body. And I knew his little liver made him able to eat food. Even if I didn't see it. Because my baby brother can eat! And I knew his little lungs were getting air in his body so he can breathe. Because I felt his little chest moving up and down when his lungs were getting air in his body. I knew about his heart and his liver and his lungs because I read about them in the little book that came with the visible man.

I kissed my baby brother on the forehead again. I was thinking about what kinds of thoughts were popping into his little head. Was he thinking about the difference between an accident and an incident? Was he thinking about what paradise he wanted to go to when he is old and after he dies the way my Grandpa who is dead did? Was he thinking about what was his favorite out of God, his son Jesus, and the Holy Spirit?

And while I was looking at my baby brother's eyes, I was thinking too about where did his thoughts come from. Were they coming from his brain? Which was inside his little head right behind where I just kissed him. Or were they coming from his heart? Which was beating inside his little chest under my hand.

My baby brother looked up at me. I smiled at him. And then he smiled back at me. I saw for the first time that he was seeing me. His eyes were finally starting to work. He saw me smile, and he smiled back. And it was then that I knew for sure he was able to see me for the first time. It was then that I knew that my baby brother was able to see. Because he smiled back at me again. I wondered whether he was going to be a boy who asked a lot of questions. Or whether he was going to be a boy who hopped all over the place and waved his little arms in the air.

And right away, another thought popped into my head. Which was, now that my baby brother was able to see, what kind of doughnut is he going to pick out of the shop window at Picou's Bakery after Mass on Sundays?

Just then, my little sister came inside from the porch. Who was at my Aunt Audra's house playing with my cousin Suzette. Who is a little girl too like my little sister is little. Except she doesn't cry as much. "Vonny! Vonny! Vonny!" my little sister said out loud. Hopping as usual. Waving her arms as usual. Except also she bended over and picked up a piece of paper that was on the floor in the parlor. My little sister walked over and kissed my baby brother on the forehead. "He's so cute!" she said. Which he is. And which my little sister is too. She hopped up and sat next to me on the sofa and starting rubbing my baby brother's little chin with her little finger. "Cute! Cute! Cute!" is all she said.

"What's that?" I said to my little sister. Which was the piece of paper she was holding.

"You read! You read! You read!" she said back. And then my little sister gave it to me. Which I took with my hand that I didn't have under my baby brother's head. The piece of paper that my little sister picked up from the floor was the note from Sister Marianna. The one she gave me at the end of class Friday while everybody was still around little Patricia trying to see what she won in the spelling bee. Which was my invisible woman! It was the note Daddy said outside of the Triangle that my Mother found in my book on my bed. "You read! You read! You read!" my little sister said again. Which I did.

"Okay. Okay," I said back. I looked at the piece of paper and then said, "Dear Mr. and Mrs. Foster." The note wasn't about whether I was able to make my First Communion. I said again, "I thought you would want to know that Vonny told the class today about his new friend Henry." It was written in script. Which I can read.

"Vonny! Vonny! Vonny!" my little sister said.

"Sincerely yours, Sister Marianna."

"Let me see! Let me see! Let me see!" I gave the note back to my little sister and she pretended to read it. "Dear Mr. and Mrs. Foster," she said. "Vonny has a friend Henry. Sister Marianna." My little sister started laughing. "I can read! I can read! I can read!"

Which was not true. Because what I read to my little sister was not true. I was just pretending. Because what Sister Marianna's note really said was, "Dear Mr. and Mrs. Foster, I thought you would want to know that Vonny told the class today about his new friend Henry, who is a negro boy who lives in your neighborhood. Henry is not a Catholic. Sincerely, Sister Marianna." And then under her name Sister wrote too, "P.S. Thank you so much for the gift of the invisible woman, which a deserving student won today." Which was little Patricia.

My little sister pretended to read the note and said again, "Dear Mr. and Mrs. Foster, Vonny has a friend Henry. Sister Marianna." And then she stood up and started hopping around the parlor and waving her little arms in the air, all the while pretending to read the note over and over and over again. Sister Marianna's note made my little sister think now she can read. And it made me think now I know all of the whys and the wherefores about how Daddy knew about me and Henry.

Sitting on the sofa in the parlor, holding my baby brother with one of my hands under his little head because he's not strong enough to hold it up himself and my other one over his little heart, I was thinking again about how we have everything in our neighborhood. Which is what Daddy calls Mid-City. Our school, church, laundry, hamburger shop, five and dime, music store, shoe store, cookie, doughnut, and cake bakery, grocery, egg, and dead chicken store, regular meat shop, disgusting meat shop, which is the baby cows' head shop, the best roast beef sandwich shop in the world, movies, and a snowball stand. And a place to buy cigarettes for my Mother. Which is Bruno's. All in our neighborhood. All right where I can walk to them from our house on Columbus Street without even having to get into a car or take a bus or ride my bicycle or anything.

Those families on the TV programs have a lot of grass all around their house. And trees too. But I don't know where they even buy their groceries. Or anything else. They never buy anything on TV programs. They just already have everything. But we don't have anything unless we go and buy it somewhere. And in my family, I'm usually the one who has to go on errands and get it.

The End

Ronald Fisher was born and educated in New Orleans, Louisiana. He currently works from homes located in Bryn Mawr, Pennsylvania and on the Eastern Shore of Maryland.

CPSIA information can be obtained at www.ICGtesting.com
Printed in the USA
BVOW07s1318250515

401650BV00006B/318/P